WITHDRAWN

SUSAN MALLERY

With more than 25 million books sold worldwide, *New York Times*
bestselling author Susan Mallery is known for creating characters
who feel as real as the folks next door, and for putting them into
emotional, often funny situations readers recognize from their
own lives. Susan's books have made Booklist's Top 10 Romance
list in four out of five consecutive years. *RT Book Reviews* says
"When it comes to heartfelt contemporary romance, Mallery
is in a class by herself." With her popular ongoing Fool's Gold
series, Susan has reached new heights on the bestseller lists and
has won the hearts of countless new fans.

Susan grew up in Southern California, moved so many times
that her friends stopped writing her address in pen, and
now has settled in Seattle with her husband and the most de-
lightfully spoiled little dog who ever lived. Visit Susan online a
www.susanmallery.com.

SARAH MAYBERRY

lives by the sea near Melbourne, Australia, with her husband
and a small black cavoodle called Max. She is currently enjoying her recently renovated house—complete with gorgeous new
kitchen!—and feeling guilty about her overgrown garden. When
she's not writing, she can be found reading, cooking, gardening,
shoe shopping, and enjoying a laugh with friends and family.
Oh, and sleeping. She is inordinately fond of a "nana nap."

New York Times Bestselling Author

SUSAN MALLERY

Prodigal Son

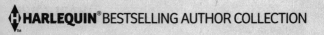

Recycling programs for this product may not exist in your area.

ISBN-13: 978-0-373-18080-6

PRODIGAL SON
Copyright © 2014 by Harlequin Books S.A.

The publisher acknowledges the copyright holders of the individual works as follows:

PRODIGAL SON
Copyright © 2006 by Harlequin Books S.A.

THE BEST LAID PLANS
Copyright © 2010 by Small Cow Productions Pty Ltd.

Printed in U.S.A.

www.Harlequin.com

CONTENTS

Dear Reader,

There's something very sexy about a confident man. Whether he's in business or running a ranch or playing football—as long as he has a bit of swagger in his soul (along with a sense of humor and a serious appreciation of all things chocolate) I'm there. It's not so much about *what* he does, as *how* he does it.

One of the advantages of writing romance novels is I get to hang out with sexy, confident men. A lot! Jack is one of my favorites—mostly because he's trapped in a situation he doesn't want because of circumstances he can't control. Yes, Jack is both confident and responsible. He's the kind of man who will do the right thing and then knock your socks off in bed. Assuming you were wearing socks at that moment in time!

Enter Samantha—a woman from his past and pretty much his opposite. She's creative and impulsive. On the surface, so different. But at her core, she's as honorable as he is and that's what makes their journey so fun.

I hope you'll enjoy *Prodigal Son*. And, as a special treat, there's a wonderful bonus book included.

Happy reading,

Susan Mallery

PRODIGAL SON
Susan Mallery

Chapter One

Samantha Edwards had never minded the interview process, even when she was the one looking for a job. But having seen her prospective boss naked made things just a little tricky.

The good news was Jack Hanson was unlikely to bring up that single night they'd shared. Not only wasn't it relevant to her employment application, it had been nearly ten years ago. She doubted he remembered anything about the event.

Well, not just the one event. Her recollection was completely clear. There had been three "events" that night, each of them more spectacular than the one before.

"Ms. Edwards? Mr. Hanson will see you now."

Samantha looked up at the sixty-something assistant behind the modern metal-and-glass desk in the foyer in front of Jack's office.

"Thank you," Samantha said as she rose and moved toward the closed door.

She paused to tug on her suit jacket. Her clothing choices had been deliberately conservative—for her, at least. Black slacks, a cream-and-black checked jacket over a cream silk shirt. It killed her to avoid color, but ten years ago Jack Hanson had been the poster boy for straitlaced conservative types. She was willing to guess that hadn't changed.

Except he hadn't been the least bit conservative in bed.

The wayward thought popped into her head just as she pushed open the door to his office. She did her best to ignore it as she drew in a deep breath, reminded herself how much she wanted this job and walked confidently toward the man standing behind his desk.

"Hello, Jack," she said, shaking hands with him. "It's been a long time."

"Samantha. Good to see you."

He studied her with a thoroughness that made her breath catch. How much of his steady perusal was about sizing up the candidate and how much was about their past?

She decided two could play at that game and did a little looking of her own.

He was taller than she'd remembered and he still seemed to exude power and confidence. She wanted to say that was a natural attribute for someone born to money, but she had a feeling Jack would have been a winner regardless of his upbringing. He was simply that kind of man.

Time had been kind, but then time had always preferred men to women, she thought humorously. Jack's face showed character in addition to chiseled features.

She wondered if life ever got boring for the physically perfect. While he had to deal with things like broad shoulders and a smile that would have most of the female population lining up to be seduced, she had unruly red hair that defied taming, a stick-straight body, small breasts and a butt that could only be described as bony. Was that fair?

"Please," he said, motioning to one of the chairs. "Have a seat."

"Thanks."

He did the same, claiming his side of the desk. He looked good there—in charge and powerful. But she happened to know he was new to the job.

"I read about your father's death a couple of months ago," she said. "I'm sorry."

"Thanks." He motioned to the office. "That's why I'm working here. The board asked me to step in and take care of the company for a while."

"I'd wondered," she admitted. "Last I'd heard, you were practicing law."

"It would be my preference," he told her.

"But you did so well at business school." She would know—they'd been competing for the top spot, often by working together. He'd been the detail-intensive, organized half and she'd been the creative member of the team.

"Hated every minute of it," he said. "I realized I preferred the law."

Jack thought about the day he'd told his father he wasn't entering the family business. George Hanson hadn't been able to comprehend that his oldest son wasn't interested in learning how to run a multimillion-dollar company. The older man had been disappointed and furious. It had been the only time Jack hadn't done what was expected of him.

Ironically, today he was exactly where his father had wanted him to be.

But not for long, he reminded himself.

"I guess your father's death changed your plans," Samantha said.

He nodded. "I'm on a three-month leave of absence from my law firm. Until then Hanson Media Group gets my full attention."

"Are you sure you want the CEO act to be temporary?"

"I'm not the tycoon type."

She smiled. "I would say you have potential. Word on the street is you're bringing in a lot of new people."

"That's true. My father hated to hand over control of anything. He was still the head of at least three departments. With a company this big, no one has the time or energy to run them and the rest of the business. I'm looking for the best people possible to join the team."

"I'm flattered."

"It's the truth. You're only here because you're good. I need creative types. It's not my strong suit."

She smiled. "A man who can admit his weaknesses. How unusual."

"Samantha, the only reason I passed marketing was because I was on your team. You carried me through the whole class."

"You tutored me through cost accounting. We're even."

She shifted slightly as she spoke, causing her slacks to briefly hug her slender thighs. The other candidates had been highly skilled with incredible résumés, but unlike Samantha, they'd come in dressed in business suits, looking equally comfortable in a boardroom or law office.

Not Samantha. Despite the conservative colors, she was anything but ordinary. Maybe it was the bright green parrot pin on her lapel or the dangling earrings that hung nearly to her shoulders. Or maybe it was that her long, fiery red hair seemed to have a will and a life of its own.

She was not a conservative businessperson. She was avant-garde and wildly creative. There was an independence about her he admired.

"You left New York," he said. "Why?"

"I wanted to make a change. I'd been working there since graduation."

He studied her as she spoke, looking for nuances. There were plenty, but none of them worried him. Per his research, she was coming off a divorce. Her previous employer had done his best to keep her from leaving.

"You have to know this is a dream job," she said. "You're offering complete creative control of Internet development, with more than a million-dollar budget. How could anyone resist that? It's my idea of heaven."

"Good. It's my idea of hell."

She smiled. Her full mouth curved and he felt himself responding. Subtle tension filled his body.

"You always did hate a blank page," she said, her smile widening to a grin.

"You always did hate rules," he told her.

"Me?" She raised her eyebrows. "You were happy enough to break them when it suited your purpose."

He shrugged. "Whatever it takes to get what I want. What I want now is a great staff and the company running smoothly. Let's get down to specifics."

He passed her information on several current Internet campaigns. After she'd flipped through the material, they discussed possible directions for growth.

Samantha became more animated as the conversation progressed. "Children," she told him. "There's so much we could do for kids. After-school programs on the Web. Not just the usual help with homework, but interactive programs linking kids all over the country."

As she spoke, she leaned toward him, gesturing with her hands to make her point. "We can also cosponsor events with popular movies or TV shows."

"Cross-advertising," he said.

"Yes. Your competition is already doing it, and the potential for you is huge. And that's just younger kids. I have even more ideas for teens."

"They're the ones with the disposable income and the time to spend it," he said. When she raised her eyebrows in surprise, he added, "I've been doing my research."

"Apparently. It's true. With more single-parent families and more families with both parents working, teens are often a real source of information on what items to purchase. They actually influence adults' decisions on everything from breakfast cereal to cars. Plus they've grown up on computers, which means they're comfortable in a digital environment. To them, the Internet is as much a part of their lives as phones were for us."

"So you're interested in the job," he said.

"I distinctly recall the word *heaven* coming up in the conversation. I wasn't kidding. I'd love the chance to grow this part of the company."

Her excitement was tangible energy in the office. He liked that. She'd always thrown herself into whatever it was she was doing and he doubted that had changed.

He'd been surprised to see her name on the short list of candidates, but pleasantly so. He and Samantha had worked well together at grad school. They'd been a good team. Just as important, she was someone he could trust.

"The job is yours, if you want it," he told her. "The formal offer would come from my human-resources person in the morning."

Her green eyes widened. "Seriously?"

"Why are you shocked? You're talented, qualified and someone I'm comfortable working with."

"You make me sound like a rescue dog."

He grinned. "If I could find one that could work a computer…"

She laughed. "Okay, yes. I'm interested. But I have to warn you, I'm very much the creative type. I'll want control of my staff."

"Agreed."

"We're not going to be wearing three-piece suits."

"I don't care if you wear frog costumes, as long as you do the job."

She didn't look convinced. "This isn't like the law, Jack. You can't always find an answer in a book."

"Can I get disapproving and difficult before you give me the lecture?" he asked, mildly amused by her concern. "I get it—creative people are different. Not a problem."

"Okay. Point taken."

She rose. He stood as well. In heels she was only a couple of inches shorter than him. He walked around the table and held out his hand.

"Leave your number with Mrs. Wycliff. You'll be hearing from my HR office first thing in the morning."

She placed her palm against his. As he had when

they'd touched a few minutes ago, he felt a slight sizzle, followed by a definite sensation of warmth somewhere south of his belt.

Ten years after the fact and Samantha Edwards still had the ability to drop him to his knees. Sexually speaking. Not that he would act on the information or let her know how she got to him. They were going to work together, nothing more.

He released her hand and walked her to the door. "How soon can you start?" he asked.

"The first part of next week," she said.

"Good. I hold a staff meeting every Tuesday morning. I look forward to seeing you there."

She hesitated before opening the door. "I'm excited about this opportunity, Jack. I want to make a difference."

"I'm sure you will."

She looked into his eyes. "I wasn't sure you'd consider me. Because of our past."

He pretended not to know what she was talking about. He wanted to make her say it. "Why would knowing you in business school make a difference?"

"Not that."

He waited.

Color flared on her cheeks, but she continued to hold his gaze. "Because of what happened that night. When we…" She cleared her throat. "You know. Were intimate."

"Water under the bridge," he said easily, mostly because it was true. He'd never been one to dwell on the past. Not even on a night that had made him believe in miracles. Probably because in the bright light of day, he'd learned that dreams were for fools and miracles didn't really happen.

* * *

Promptly at four in the afternoon, Mrs. Wycliff knocked on Jack's office door.

"Come in," he said as he saved the work on his computer, then looked up at his father's former assistant.

"Here are the daily reports," she said, placing several folders on his desk.

"Thank you."

He frowned as he looked at the thick stack that would make up his evening reading. In theory, he knew plenty about running a company. He had the MBA to prove it. But theory and reality often had little in common and this was one of those times. If one of the employees was accused of homicide—that he could handle. Right now, a charge of first-degree murder seemed simple when compared with the day-to-day ups and downs of a publicly traded corporation.

"How is the staff holding up?" he asked the older woman. Although he was confident Mrs. Wycliff hadn't been born into her position, he couldn't remember a time when she hadn't worked for his father.

She clutched the back of the chair and shook her head in refusal when he invited her to take a seat.

"They miss him, of course. Your father was well liked in the company. Of course he would be. He was a good man."

Jack was careful to keep his expression neutral. George Hanson had been a man of business. He had lived and breathed his company, while his children had grown up on the fringes of his life. That wasn't Jack's definition of *good*.

"Several people have stopped by to tell me how much they miss him," Jack told her. It happened at least once a day and he never knew what to say in return.

She smiled. "We all appreciate you stepping in to run things. Hanson Media Group has been home to a lot of us for a long time. We'd hate to see anything happen to the company."

"Happen?" He'd only been on board a couple of weeks. From what he'd been able to find out, the only problems seemed to be his father's need to micromanage departments. Once Jack got the right people in place, he figured the firm would run smoothly.

Mrs. Wycliff smoothed her already perfect gray hair and absently fingered the bun at the back of her neck. "Your father was very proud of you. Did you know that?"

Jack wasn't fooled by the obvious change in subject, but he figured he would do a little digging on his own before he grilled his assistant for information.

"Thank you for telling me," he said.

She smiled. "He often talked about how well you were doing at your law firm. Of course he'd wanted you to come to work for the family business, but if the law made you happy, he was happy, too."

Jack tried to reconcile that description with the angry conversations he'd frequently shared with his father. George Hanson had tried everything from bribes to threatening to cut Jack out of the will if he didn't come work for the company.

He'd long suspected his father had shown one side of his personality to the world and kept the other side more private.

"We had a deal," he said. "After law school, I got my MBA. Then I decided which I liked better." He shrugged. "It wasn't much of a choice."

"You followed your heart and your talents," Mrs. Wycliff told him. "That's what your father always said." She smiled. "He brought in champagne the day you made partner."

"Junior partner," Jack corrected absently. Champagne? When he couldn't get hold of his father, he'd left a message with Helen, his stepmother, telling her about the promotion. She'd sent a card and a stylish new briefcase as a gift. Ever polite, Helen had signed both their names, but Jack had known it was all really from her. His father had never bothered to call him back.

"He was a good man," Mrs. Wycliff said. "Whatever happens, you have to remember that."

"That's the second time you've been cryptic," he told her. "Want to tell me why?"

She had dark blue eyes and the kind of bone structure that spoke of great beauty in her youth. If she had been a different kind of woman, he would have suspected something between her and his father. But while George might have been interested, Jack was confident Mrs. Wycliff herself would not have approved.

"I can't," she said, her voice low.

"Can't or won't?"

She clutched the back of the chair more firmly and met his direct gaze. "I don't know anything. If I did, I would tell you. You have my complete loyalty."

"But there's something?"

She hesitated. "A feeling. I'm sorry. I can't be more specific. There's nothing more to say."

He'd known the woman all of two weeks, yet he would have bet she wasn't lying. She didn't know. Or she was a damn fine actress.

Feelings. As a rule, he didn't trust emotion, but gut responses were different. He'd changed his line of questioning during a trial more than once based on a feeling and each time he'd been right.

"If you learn anything," he began.

"I'll tell you. I've been talking to people. Listening."
She swallowed. "I lost my husband a few years ago.
We never had children and a lot of our friends have
retired and moved south. This company is all I have.
I'll do anything to protect it."

"Thank you."

She nodded and left.

Mysteries he didn't want or need. As for Mrs.
Wycliff, while he appreciated her concern and her
willingness to provide him with information, who was
to say if they had similar goals? She wanted Hanson
Media Group to go on forever, he wanted out. If those
two objectives came into conflict, he had a feeling
his once-loyal secretary would become a bitter enemy.

With employment came paperwork, Samantha
thought two days later as she sat in an empty office
and filled out her formal job application, along with
pages for insurance, a security pass, a parking space
and emergency contact information.

She worked quickly, still unable to believe she'd
landed her dream job with little or no effort on her
part. She'd been so excited to get going, she'd come in
before her start date to do the paperwork.

"Thank you, Helen," she murmured, knowing her
friend had somehow managed to get her name on the
short list of candidates. She'd wanted to mention that
to Jack during their interview, but on Helen's advice
had kept quiet. For reasons that made no sense to Samantha, Jack, along with his siblings, thought Helen
was little more than a trophy wife.

Hope I'm around when they all discover that there's

a very functioning brain behind those big eyes, Samantha thought.

She signed the application and moved on to the next piece of paper.

"Morning."

She looked up and saw Jack in the doorway to the small office. He looked tall, sexy and just-out-of-the-shower tempting. What was it about a freshly shaved man that got her body to pay attention?

"Hi," she said.

"I heard you were here taking care of details." He leaned against the door frame. "Thanks for accepting the job."

"I'm the grateful one," she said with a laugh. "I can't wait to get started. But first there's all this to work through." She patted the papers. "I've been promised that if I do everything correctly, I get my own ID badge at the end of the day. And the key to my office."

"I heard that rumor, too. My intrepid assistant informed me we already have a meeting scheduled."

"Monday afternoon," she said. "I'll be working all weekend, bringing myself up to speed. I'll want to discuss parameters with you before I set my team on the task."

"You're not expected to work 24-7," he said.

"I know, but I'm excited and it's not as if I have a lot of things planned. I've just moved to Chicago. I'm still finding my way around."

"All the more reason to get out and explore."

She tilted her head. "Hmm, is my new boss *discouraging* me from working? That's a new one."

"I don't want you to burn out your first week. I need you around longer than that."

She knew they were just joking around, and she enjoyed that she and Jack seemed to have kept some remnant of their friendship intact. But why did she have to be so aware of him?

Even now, with him standing several feet away, she would swear she could hear him breathing. Heat seemed to radiate from his body, in a way designed to make her melt.

It had been like this before, she thought glumly. Back in grad school, she'd spent two years in a constant state of sexual arousal. She'd needed the friendship more than she'd wanted a lover, so she'd ignored the physical attraction between them. She'd been careful to always seem disinterested.

Until that one night when she'd been unable to stand it a second longer.

"I promise to explore often and well," she said. "But later. Right now I want to get to work."

He held up both hands. "Okay. I give up. Be a slave to your job. I'll stop complaining." He dropped his hands to his sides. "Are you already settled in your new place?"

"I have exactly two suitcases in my hotel room. It didn't take long to settle."

"Aren't you going to get an apartment?"

"Eventually. I'm too busy to look around right now." A partial truth. Apartment hunting would give her too much time to think. She wanted to avoid bursts of introspection whenever possible.

"My building has executive rentals," he said. "They come fully furnished and are rented by the month. That's how I found the place. I took a two-month lease, found I liked the building and bought something larger."

"Sounds interesting," she said cautiously.

He grinned. "Don't worry. It's a huge high-rise. We'd never run into each other."

Did he think she thought that was a problem? Okay, yeah, maybe it was. She had a feeling that running into Jack outside of work could be a complication, if not outright dangerous for her mental health. But hadn't she promised herself to face life head on? Wasn't she done with hiding from the truth?

"I appreciate the information," she said. "Do you have a phone number or person to contact?"

"I have a business card in my office. Let me go get it."

He walked down the hallway. Samantha turned her attention back to the paperwork in front of her, but instead of seeing it, she saw the empty apartment she'd left in New York only three weeks before.

She'd thought she would always live in New York. She'd thought she knew what to expect from her life. Funny how a lifetime of dreams could be packed up into a half-dozen boxes and the man she'd once trusted to love her forever had turned out to be nothing more than a lying thief.

Chapter Two

"We're working on the, ah, upgrades right now," Arnie said as he shifted in his seat. "The, ah, first set should be, ah, ready by the end of the month."

Jack had to consciously keep himself from squirming in sympathy. In his law practice his clients were usually so distracted by the charges brought against them that they didn't have the energy to be nervous and in court he didn't care if his cross-examination upset a hostile witness.

But Arnie wasn't a client or a hostile witness. He was a techno-geek from the IT department, and he was obviously uncomfortable meeting with his new boss.

Jack glanced down at the report in front of him, then back at Arnie. "Sounds like you're totally on schedule," he said, then smiled at the other man. "Good for you."

Arnie swallowed. "Thanks. We've been trying.

Roger, my, ah, boss, sort of said we had to. Oh, but not in a bad way."

"I appreciate your effort," Jack said, wishing Roger, Arnie's boss, had been available for the meeting. Jack couldn't take much more of the poor man's suffering.

"You're going to be working with Samantha Edwards," Jack said. "She started today. She's very creative and energetic. I'm sure you'll be impressed by her ideas."

And her, Jack thought, wondering what Arnie would think of Samantha's tall, slender beauty and infectious smile. Or maybe he didn't have to wonder. Harsh, but true, Arnie looked like the kind of guy who never got the girl. He was pale, with thinning brown hair, light brown eyes and glasses. He wore a plaid short-sleeved shirt and jeans, and his posture yelled, "Please don't hurt me."

Arnie's face contorted as if he were trying to decide if he should smile or not. "I heard there was going to be a lot of digital expansion. That's good for my department."

"It will be plenty of work," Jack told him.

"We can do it. I'm sure of it."

"I am, too," Jack said. "Once Samantha finalizes her plans, she'll get with you and your guys to work out the details. We may have some capacity issues. I don't know enough about the technicalities to know. I need you to stay on top of that. And help coordinate the launch date. We need to be aggressive, while being realistic."

Arnie nodded vigorously. "Okay. Sure. I can do all that. But, um, you know, George was never interested in the Internet. He always liked the magazine side of the business."

One of the reasons the company was in big trouble, Jack thought. Magazines were expensive propositions and no one could ignore the power of the Internet these days.

"I see Internet expansion as a way to build the business and expand our reach." He frowned. Shouldn't an IT guy know this?

"Oh, I agree," Arnie said quickly. "So do most of the guys in my department. But, you know, not everyone will agree."

Jack didn't like the sound of that. "Like who?"

Arnie instantly looked trapped. "Oh, it's—"

"We're a team here," Jack said. "We're only as strong as our weakest member." Hopefully that would be the hokiest thing he had to say this week, he thought grimly. But if it worked…

Arnie squirmed some more, ducked his head, sighed, then said, "Roger, my boss. He's not real big on change."

"Interesting," Jack said, wondering how someone like that rose to the level of running the IT department. Or maybe Jack's father had wanted it that way, considering his disinterest in all things high tech. "I appreciate you telling me that. I won't mention this conversation with Roger. You have my word."

Arnie sighed. "Thanks. I really like my job. I wouldn't want to get, you know, fired." He winced as he spoke, then shook his head. "Your dad was a great man."

"Thank you," Jack said.

"He was patient and kind and really interested in all

his employees. We all liked working for him and felt really bad when he died."

Jack nodded. He wasn't sure what to say when people talked about his father this way. They were describing someone he'd never met.

"Knock, knock."

He looked up and saw Samantha walking into his office. She looked from him to Arnie.

"Am I early or late?" she asked with a smile.

"Neither," he said. "Right on time. You're joining our meeting in progress."

Now that she had the job, she'd obviously decided there was no need to dress conservatively anymore—at least her definition of it. Gone were the black slacks and black-and-white jacket. In their place she wore a long skirt in a swirl of reds, greens and purples. A dark green sweater hung loosely on her hips. She had a scarf draped over one shoulder, a half-dozen bracelets on each wrist and earrings that tinkled and swayed as she walked.

"This is Arnie," Jack said, pointing to the man sitting across from him at the conference table. "He's from IT. He'll be working with you on the Internet expansion. You tell him what you want and he'll tell you if it's possible. Arnie, this is Samantha."

The other man rose and wiped his palms on his jeans, then held out his hand. His mouth opened, closed, then opened again.

"Ah, hi," Arnie said, his eyes wide, his cheeks bright with color.

"Good morning." Samantha beamed at him. "So you're going to be my new best friend, right? And you won't ever want to tell me no."

Arnie stammered, then sank back in his seat. Jack

did his best not to smile. Samantha had made another conquest.

He wasn't surprised. She walked into a room and men were instantly attracted to her. He was no exception. She was a weakness for which he'd found no antidote. Even now he found himself wanting to pull her close and run his hands through her curly hair. He wanted to stare into her eyes and feel her tremble in his embrace.

Not on this planet, he reminded himself. She hadn't been interested ten years ago and he doubted that had changed.

Okay, she'd been interested *once*. Apparently once was enough where he was concerned. She'd made it more than clear she didn't want a repeat performance.

"Don't let Samantha push you around," he told Arnie. "She has a tendency to do that."

Samantha looked at him and raised her eyebrows. "Me? Are you kidding? I'm the picture of complete cooperation."

"Uh-huh. Right until someone gets in your way. Then you're a steamroller."

Samantha sat next to Arnie and patted his hand. "Ignore him. Jack and I went to grad school together and he seems to remember things very differently. I've never steamrolled anyone." She paused, then smiled. "Well, at least not often. I can get tenacious about what I want, though. And I've read different reports from your department, Arnie. People have been pushing for this expansion for a while."

That surprised Jack. "I hadn't heard that."

Samantha looked at him. "His boss is the reason why. I also read memos from Roger explaining why it was all a bad idea. Apparently he had some backing on that."

She didn't specifically say by who, but Jack could guess. He doubted his father had been a fan of growing technology.

"That was the past," he said. "Let's focus on the future. You two need to get together and talk about specifics."

Samantha jotted down a note on her pad of paper. "I'll e-mail you, Arnie. You can let me know what works for you. I tend to put in long hours. I hope that's okay."

Arnie's pale eyes practically glowed. "It's fine. Sure. I'll be there." He stood and nodded. "Anytime. Just e-mail me."

"Thanks for your help," Jack said.

"Oh, yeah. No problem."

The other man left. Jack waited until the door closed, then turned to Samantha.

"You've made a friend."

"Arnie? He's very sweet, or so I've been told. I think we'll do fine together."

Jack told himself that she would never be interested in the other man and even if she was, it wasn't his business. He didn't care who Samantha wanted in her life as long as she did her job. He very nearly believed himself, too.

"What have you got?" he asked.

"Lots and lots of great ideas," she said with a smile. "I had an extremely productive weekend. I went over the existing website. It's pretty basic. There's so much room to improve and that's what I want. I want to start with kids twelve and under as our first target audience and I want to dazzle them."

She set a folder on the conference table and opened it. "We'll deal with the teens later, but first, let's get some buzz going. I want us to be the website the kids are dying to go to the second they get home from school. I want to do more than help them with their homework. I want us to be the coolest place on the web. I have a lot of ideas for developing all this. But our biggest concern is security. We're going to have to go state-of-the-art so the kids are totally safe on the site."

"I like it."

"Good."

Her smile widened and he felt it punch him right in the gut. Ever-present need growled to life.

"You don't need to run all this by me," he told her, doing his damnedest to ignore the blood rushing to his groin. "I trust you to run your department."

"I know, but this is big stuff. I'm talking about huge changes."

"That would be the reason I hired you."

She studied him. "You really trust me with all this?"

"Of course."

"Wow. Great. I guess I'll get my team to pull it all together and then we'll have a big presentation."

"I look forward to it." He leaned toward her. "That's how I run things, Samantha," he told her. "Until someone screws up, he or she has free rein."

"I would have thought you were more the control type."

"Because I wear a suit?"

"Sort of. You're a lawyer. That doesn't help with the image."

"What if I went into environmental law?"

She grinned. "Did you?"

"No. Criminal."

"So it's not just *suits*. It's designer suits."

"Mostly. But even at the law firm, I give my people room to grow and make mistakes. One screwup isn't fatal."

She tucked her hair behind her ear. "That sounds so balanced."

"I like to think of myself that way."

"You were less balanced in grad school. Much more…"

He looked at her. "Stick up the ass?"

Her mouth threatened a smile, but she held it back. "I would never have said that."

"But you were thinking it."

"Maybe a little. You had that study schedule."

"It kept me on track and freed up my weekends. I had plenty of time for fun."

"I remember," she said with a laugh. "Okay, I'll let it go. You weren't that rigid. I think you were just so much more together than any other guy I met. It scared me."

He wondered if that was true. Had he made her uneasy in ways he hadn't understood? Did it even matter now?

"You were the most unstructured successful person I'd met," he said.

"I was kind of crazy back then," she admitted. "I've calmed down some."

"I hope not. I liked you crazy. Remember the time we spent Christmas Eve in a stable because you wanted to know what it was like?" he asked.

She laughed. "Yes, and you kept telling me that I needed to pay attention to geography."

"I was right. We were in Pennsylvania in the middle of winter. Not exactly the Middle East."

Despite the cold, they'd had a great time huddled together. He'd wanted her with a desperation that had made him tremble more than the cold. The next morning, he'd driven her to the airport so she could fly home to spend Christmas Day with her mother.

Speaking of which… "How's your mom?" he asked.

Samantha's smile faded. "She passed away about three years ago."

"I'm sorry," he said. "I really liked her."

"Thanks. I miss her. It was hard to lose her. She'd been sick for a while, so it wasn't a big surprise. We were able to say our goodbyes, which made things better." She collected her papers. "Okay, I'm going to let you get back to work. I have to put my presentation together so that you're dazzled, too. You will be, you know."

"I don't doubt it."

He walked her to the door, then returned to his desk. Only a crazy man would continue to want what he couldn't have, he told himself. Which made him certifiable. It was the human condition, he thought.

And now she'd caught Arnie in her web. Jack could almost pity the guy. The difference was Arnie would probably fantasize about happily-ever-after while Jack only wanted Samantha in his bed. He'd learned a long time ago to concentrate on the physical and ignore the emotional. There was no point in engaging his heart— people who claimed to love quickly got over the feeling and then they left.

Samantha hadn't been sure what to expect when she'd signed up for "executive housing," but she was pleasantly surprised by all her condo had to offer. There was a spacious living room with a semi-view, a dining area and plenty of room in the kitchen, especially for someone who made it a point to dirty as few pots as possible.

Her bedroom held a king-size bed, a dresser and an armoire with a television. The closet was huge and she'd already soaked her troubles away in the massive whirlpool tub in her bathroom. There was even a workstation alcove with good lighting and a desk for her laptop.

The only downside to the space was the fact that it felt...impersonal. The neutral colors were so bland and the furniture so functional. There wasn't anything funky to be found.

Still, the condo worked for now and it was about double the size her New York apartment had been. As she stood in front of the slider leading out to her small balcony and considered take-out options for dinner, she felt a whisper of contentment steal over her.

Coming to Chicago had been a good idea, she thought. She'd needed to leave New York. Despite loving the city, there were too many Vance memories around, and she'd needed to get away from them and him. Here she could start over. Build new memories. There were—

Someone knocked on her door. She crossed the beige carpet and looked through the peephole.

"Jack?" she asked as she pulled open the door.

"I'm presuming," he said, holding up two brown bags. "I come bearing Chinese food. I have wine, too. Sort of a welcome-to-the-building thing. Interested?"

She was delighted, she thought, stepping back and motioning him to enter. Instead, a black-and-white border collie slipped by Jack and stepped into the apartment.

"This is Charlie," Jack said. "Do you like dogs?"

Samantha held out her fingers for Charlie to sniff, then petted him. "I love them." She crouched down in front of Charlie and rubbed his shoulders. "Who's a handsome guy?" she asked, then laughed as he tried to lick her face.

"He likes you," Jack said. "Smart dog."

She laughed. "Okay, now I *really* want to have dinner with you. Come on in."

She led the way to the kitchen, where Jack opened the wine and she collected plates for their dinner. As she opened the bags and began pulling out cartons of food, she noticed a bright red plastic bowl and a box with a big *C* on it.

"This is interesting," she said, holding up both.

Jack grinned sheepishly. "They're for Charlie. He loves Chinese, so the place I go mixes up a special rice dish for him. It's beef and chicken, rice, vegetables, light on the salt and spices. He loves it and the vet approves. It's kind of a special treat."

Samantha did her best to reconcile the straitlaced lawyer she knew Jack to be with a guy who would special order food for his dog.

"Now I know who's really in charge," she murmured.

"Yeah," Jack said easily. "He's the boss."

He helped her carry the cartons to the table. Charlie was served, but he waited until they sat down before digging in to his dinner.

Jack held out his glass of wine. "Welcome to the neighborhood. I hope you like it."

"Thank you." They touched glasses, then she took a sip of the red wine. "Very nice. All of this."

"No problem. I thought you might still be feeling out of place."

"Some. I like the apartment, but it's weird because nothing in here is mine. Like these plates." She held up the plain cream plate. "I would never have bought these."

"Too normal?"

"Too boring. Color is our friend."

"Agreed. But you'll get settled, then you can find a place of your own."

"I know. But for now, this is great. They make it very convenient."

Jack passed her the honey-glazed shrimp. "That's why I'm here. Dry cleaning right downstairs. The corner grocery store delivers. The dog walker lives across the street. There are over twenty restaurants in a five-block square around here and a great park close by where Charlie and I hang out on weekends."

She glanced at the dog, who had finished his dinner and was now sniffing the floor for rice grains he might have missed. "He's beautiful. But doesn't he need exercise and attention? You're a guy who works long hours."

"He's fine," Jack said. "Is it quiet enough here for you? That's the first thing I noticed when I moved in. How quiet it was. Good construction."

She started to agree, then realized he had not-so-subtly changed the subject. "It's great," she said. "What aren't you telling me?"

He looked at her and raised his eyebrows. "I don't know what you mean."

"About Charlie. You changed the subject."

"From what?"

"How he gets through the day without tearing up your place."

"He keeps busy."

Jack looked uncomfortable. She glanced from him to the dog. "What? He watches soaps and does a crossword puzzle?"

Jack sighed. "He goes to day care, okay? I know, I know. It's silly, but he has a lot of energy and border collies are herding dogs. I didn't want him alone and bored all the time so three days a week he goes to doggy day care. There he plays with the other dogs and herds them around. He comes home so tired that on Tuesdays and Thursdays he pretty much just sleeps. I have a dog walker who comes by twice a day to take him out."

The muscles in his jaw tensed slightly as he spoke. She could tell he hadn't wanted to share that part of his life with her.

She did her best not to smile or laugh—he would take that wrong—not realizing that women would find a big, tough, successful guy who cared that much about his dog pretty appealing.

"You're a responsible pet owner," she said. "Some people aren't."

He narrowed his gaze, as if waiting for a slam. She smiled innocently, then changed the subject.

After dinner they moved to the living room. Charlie made a bid for the wing chair in the corner. Jack ordered him out of it. The dog gave a sigh of long suffering, then stretched out on the carpet by Samantha.

Jack glanced around at the furniture, then studied the painting over the fireplace. "So not you," he said.

Samantha looked at the subtle blues and greens. "It's very restful."

"You hate it."

"I wouldn't have gone for something so…"

"Normal?" he asked.

She grinned. "Exactly. Too expected. Where's the interesting furniture, the splash of color?"

"I'm sure you'll do that with your next place."

"Absolutely. I miss fringe."

He winced. "I remember you had that horrible shawl over that table in your apartment when we were in grad school. It was the ugliest thing I'd ever seen."

"It was beautiful," she told him. "And it had an amazing color palate."

"It looked like something from a Dali nightmare."

"You have no taste," she said.

"I know when to be afraid."

He smiled as he spoke, making her own mouth curve up in return. It had always been like this, she thought. They rarely agreed and yet they got along just fine. She liked that almost as much as she liked looking at him.

He'd changed out of his workday suit into jeans and a long-sleeved shirt. The denim had seen better days. Dozens of washings had softened and faded the material, molding to his long legs and narrow hips.

A controlled sex appeal, she thought. Reined-in power that always made her wonder what would happen when he lost control. How big would the explosion be? She had an idea from their lone night together. He had claimed her with a need that had left her shaking and desperately wanting more.

Step *away* from the memory, she told herself. Talk about dangerous territory.

"Don't you have some furniture and decorations from your New York apartment?" he asked.

"I have a few things in storage," she said. A very few things. In an ongoing attempt to control her, Vance had fought her over every picture and dish. It had been easier and oddly freeing simply to walk away.

An emotion flickered in his dark eyes. "I know you're coming off of a divorce. How are you holding up?"

The news wasn't a secret, so she wasn't surprised that he knew. "Okay. It was tough at first. I went through the whole 'I've failed' bit, but I've moved on from that. Right now I'm feeling a lot of relief."

"It's a tough time," he said.

She nodded. "I had really planned to stay married to the same man for the rest of my life. I thought I'd picked the perfect guy." She paused. "Not perfect. Perfect for me. But I was wrong."

An understatement, she thought grimly. "We wanted different things in nearly everything. I could have lived with that, but he changed his mind about wanting children." She kept her voice light because if she gave in to her real feelings, the bitterness would well up inside of her. She didn't want to deal with that right now. Talk about a waste of energy.

"I'm sorry," Jack said. "I remember you used to talk about having kids all the time."

"I still plan to have them. I think I have a few good years left."

"More than a few."

She smiled as she spoke. Jack liked the way she curled up on the sofa, yet kept one leg lowered so she could rub Charlie with her bare foot.

She still painted her toenails, he thought, looking at the tiny flowers painted on each big toe. She even had a toe ring on each foot. None of the women he got involved with were the toe-ring type. Of course none of them wore jeans with flowers sewn onto the side seams or sweaters that looked more like a riot of colors than clothing.

"Enough about me," she said. "What have you been up to, romantically?"

"Nothing that interesting," he told her. "No wives, current or ex. I was engaged for a while."

"Oh. It didn't work out?"

"She died."

Samantha's eyes widened. "Jack, I'm sorry."

"Thanks. It was a few years ago, just before Christmas. Shelby's car spun out on an icy bridge and went into the water. She didn't make it."

"How horrible."

Samantha was the sympathetic type. She would want to say the right thing, only to realize there wasn't one. He'd heard all the platitudes possible and none of them had made a damn bit of difference. Not after he'd found Shelby's note. The one she'd written before she'd died.

"Was it very close to the wedding?" she asked.

"Just a little over a week. We were planning to get married New Year's Eve."

She bit her lower lip. "You must hate the holidays now."

"Not as much as I would have thought. I get angry, thinking about what was lost."

Not for him and Shelby—he'd done his best to let that go—but for her family. They were good people and he knew they'd yet to move on.

"Relationships are never easy," she said.

Charlie chose that moment to roll onto his back and

offer his stomach for rubbing. Samantha obliged him and he started to groan.

"That dog knows a good thing when he has one," Jack said.

She looked at him and grinned. "Oh, right. Because *you* don't spoil him."

"Me? Never." He sipped on his wine. "Are you overwhelmed by work yet?"

"Almost. Ask me again in two days and I'm sure the answer will be yes. There's so much to do, and that's what makes it all exciting. This is a great opportunity."

He was glad she thought so. He wanted energetic people solving company problems as quickly as possible. "Have you heard about the big advertiser party? It's in a few weeks. It's an annual function and very upscale. Formal attire required."

"Really? You mean I have an excuse to buy a new dress and look fabulous?"

The thought of her in something long and slinky suddenly made him look forward to the party in ways he hadn't before. "It's not just an excuse," he said. "It's an order."

"And you'll be in a tux?"

He grimaced. "Oh, yeah."

"I'm sure you'll look great. All the women will be fawning over you."

"Fawning gets old," he said, doing his best not to read anything into her comment. While he wanted to believe she was flirting, he'd been shot down enough in the past to know that wishful thinking got him exactly nowhere.

"Do you have a lot of it?" she asked, her green eyes sparkling with humor.

"Enough."

"And just how much is that?"

He sensed they were in dangerous territory, but he wasn't sure how to avoid getting in trouble.

"I date," he said cautiously.

"I would guess that you have women lining up to be with you," she said easily. "You're good-looking, successful, well-off and single. That's fairly irresistible."

Except for Samantha, that had always been his take on it, too. So why did he get the feeling that she didn't see the list as a good thing?

"Some women manage to resist," he said. "What about you? Ready to start dating?"

"I don't think so. Not for a while. Divorce has a way of sucking the confidence out of a person. Or at least it did me."

He couldn't believe that. She had always been confident. Smart, funny, gorgeous. "It doesn't show."

She smiled. "Thanks. I'm getting by on sheer determination."

"It's working."

He wanted to tell her she had nothing to worry about—that she was as desirable as ever and he was willing to prove it.

Not a good idea, he reminded himself. So instead of speaking, or acting, he stood. "It's late. Charlie and I need our beauty sleep." He whistled softly. "Come on, boy."

Charlie rose and stretched. He licked Samantha's hand, then joined Jack.

She got up and followed them to the front door. "Thanks for stopping by. Dinner was great. I appreciated the company, as well." She crouched down and rubbed Charlie's ears. "You're a very handsome boy. We'll have to get together again soon."

Charlie barked his agreement.

Figures, Jack thought with a grin. After all these years, she falls for the dog.

Chapter Three

Nearly a week later, Jack sat behind what had been his father's desk, cursing his agreement to take over the company, even temporarily. Every day brought a new crisis and, with it, bad news. At this point all he was asking for was twenty-four hours without something major going wrong.

He'd already had to deal with the IT people informing him that their webpages were nearly at capacity and, to support the expansion, they were going to have to negotiate with their server. The previous quarter's report showed magazine subscriptions falling for their three best publications. A train derailment had destroyed nearly a hundred thousand magazines heading to the West Coast markets and he'd just seen the layout for the launch of their new home-decorating magazine and even he could tell it sucked the big one.

There was too much to deal with, he thought. How

the hell had his father done all this *and* run several departments?

Jack leaned back in his chair and rubbed his temples. He already had the answer to that one—George Hanson hadn't done it well. Things had slipped and there'd been no time to fix them before the next crisis had appeared. Despite hiring department heads, Jack was still overwhelmed by the sheer volume of work.

As far as he could tell, there was only one way for Hanson Media Group to survive—he had to get more help.

He buzzed for his assistant. When Mrs. Wycliff entered his office, he motioned for her to take a seat.

"I need to get in touch with my brothers," he said. "Do you know where Evan and Andrew are these days?"

If the older woman was surprised that Jack didn't know where to find his brothers himself, she didn't show it.

"I'm sorry, I don't," she said. "Would you like me to try to find them?"

"Please. I suggest you follow the credit-card charges. That's generally the easiest way." Evan favored Europe and Andrew tended to follow the seasons—summering in exclusive beach resorts and wintering in places like Whistler and Gstaad.

Jack knew all the psychobabble about siblings. In every family each tried to get his parents' attention in a different way. For Jack, it had been about being the best at whatever he did. He'd learned early that he was expected to take over the family business and for a long time he'd worked toward that. But in the end, he'd walked away from Hanson Media Group, just like his brothers.

None of them had made the old man proud.

Did Evan and Andrew ever feel guilty? Jack had tried to make peace with his father more than once, but the old man had never seemed interested. All he'd talked about was how Jack should be at Hanson Media Group instead of practicing law.

Jack regretted losing touch with his brothers a lot more than he regretted disappointing his father.

"I'll get right on that," Mrs. Wycliff told him. "Have you spoken with your uncle?"

"Not about this," Jack told her. "But that's a great idea. Thank you."

She rose. "I'll let you know as soon as I locate them," she said, then left.

Jack buzzed David's office. "Hi. Are you available?"

"Absolutely."

The public relations department was the next floor down, on the main level of Hanson Media Group. Here the bright overhead lights contrasted with the rich blues and purples in the carpet and on the sofas and chairs.

Jack took the stairs and made his way to David's office. His uncle couldn't have been more different from Jack's father. Where George had lived and breathed business, David always had time for his nephews.

David's assistant waved him in. Jack pushed open the door and walked into David's large office.

The space had been designed to impress and put people at ease. It did both. David walked around his desk and shook hands with Jack, then pulled him close for a quick hug.

"How's it going?" David asked as he led the way to the sofas in the corner. "Still finding things wrong?"

"Every day. I'm hoping for some good news soon. I figure we're all due."

"Toward the end, George wasn't himself," David said. "I think the work became too much for him. I'm guessing. He didn't confide in me."

"Did he confide in anyone?" Jack asked.

"Probably not. You hanging in there?"

"Do I have a choice?"

Jack looked at his uncle. Like all the Hanson men, he was tall, with brown hair. His eyes were lighter and he was nearly twenty years younger than his brother. Maybe that was why David had always been closer to his nephews. Maybe that was why David had been able to be there for them, Jack thought. George had been more like a father than a brother to David.

"You always have a choice," David told him. "You could walk."

"I gave my word to the board. I'm here for three months to clear things up and then I'm gone. I'm trying to get ahold of Evan and Andrew."

David frowned. "Good luck with that."

"Mrs. Wycliff is going to follow the money. That always works." Jack shook his head. "They should be here. We should do this together."

"You've never been close. Why expect it now?"

"Good point." Jack didn't have an answer. "Who am I kidding? If I had the chance to bolt, I'd take it."

"No, you wouldn't," David said. "You could have told the board no and you didn't. You have a strong sense of responsibility."

"Great. Look where it got me—here."

"Is that so bad?"

"It's keeping me from my real job." Jack leaned forward. "Why don't you take over? You know more about Hanson Media Group than any of us. You could run the company."

"Not my thing," David said. "Even if it was, I would respect my brother's wishes. He wanted one of his sons to be in charge."

"We don't know that," Jack said. "And we won't until the will is read." He swore. "What was my father thinking? Why on earth would he want us to wait three months to read the will? It's crazy. Nothing can be settled until then. For all we know, he's giving his majority shares to the cat."

David grinned. "He didn't have a cat."

Someone knocked on the door. "Come in," David called.

His assistant walked in with a tray and set it on the coffee table. "Anything else?"

David smiled at her. "Thanks, Nina. You didn't have to do this."

"No problem. Oh, you had a call from the printers."

David groaned. "I don't want to know, do I?"

"Not really," Nina said cheerfully. "Don't worry. I've already fixed the problem."

With that she left.

Jack reached for one of the cups of coffee. "Tell me Andrew and Evan will at least come back for the reading of the will."

David looked at him. "Are you hoping to cut and run the second their plane touches down?"

"It crossed my mind. I have a law practice to get back to."

"Maybe you'll appreciate your career more if you have to suffer a little here," his uncle told him.

Jack narrowed his gaze. "If you start talking about Zen centering, I'm going to have to punch you."

David laughed. "You know what I mean. You shouldn't take things for granted."

"I don't. I'm not here to learn a life lesson. My father convinced the board that I was the only possible heir and now they're pressuring me to take over. It's all about self-interest. His, theirs, mine. My father didn't give a damn about what I wanted. He's doing his best to control me from the grave."

"George loved you," David said. "In his own way."

"That's like saying the black widow spider doesn't mean it personally when she kills her mate." He took another drink of coffee. "You've always defended him, even as you stepped in to take his place as our father."

David shrugged. "I wanted to help."

"You should have had a family of your own."

"So should you. Speaking of which, I put out a press release about the new people you've hired. One of the names was familiar."

"Samantha was the best person for the job," Jack said, refusing to get defensive.

"I don't doubt that. I'm simply saying it was interesting to see her name again. I remember her from your time in grad school. The one who got away."

"She was never that," Jack told him.

"You talked about her as if she were."

"That was a long time ago. Things are different now."

"Is she married?"

"No."

"Then maybe fate is giving you a second chance."

Jack looked at his uncle. "If you start drinking herbal tea next, we're going to have to have a talk."

David chuckled. "I'm just saying maybe you're getting a second chance."

"I don't believe in them."

David's humor faded and he gave Jack a serious look. "Not every woman is Shelby."

"I know that." He put down his coffee and stood. "Don't worry about me. I'm fine. As for Samantha, she's a co-worker, nothing more."

David grinned. "You're lying. But we'll play your game and pretend you're not."

"Gee, thanks. And if you hear anything on the whereabouts of my brothers, let me know."

"You'll be the first."

"Oh, my," Helen said as she looked around the condo. "It's very…"

"Plain? Beige? Boring?" Samantha asked with a grin.

"I was going to say very 'not you.' But those will work as well." She stepped forward and hugged Samantha again. "I'm so glad you're here."

"Me, too. Getting out of New York was number one on my to-do list. You made that happen."

Helen sank onto the sofa and dismissed Samantha with a flick of her wrist. "Oh, please. I got you an interview. I certainly didn't get you hired. It's not as if Jack would ever think to ask my opinion of anything. You got the job on your own."

Samantha settled next to her friend and touched her arm. "You look tired. How do you feel?"

"Exhausted. Shell-shocked. It's been two months. I guess I should be used to it by now, but I'm not." Tears filled her eyes, but Helen blinked them away. "Damn. I promised myself I was done with crying."

"There's no time limit on grief."

"I know." Helen squeezed her fingers. "You're sweet to worry about me. I'm fine."

"No, you're not."

"Okay. I'm pretending to be fine and that should count for something. Most of the time I do okay. I can now go for an hour or two without falling apart. In the beginning I was only able to survive minutes. So that's an improvement. It's just I miss him so much and I feel so alone."

Samantha didn't know what to say. Helen really *was* alone in all this. She didn't have any family of her own and George's sons hadn't exactly welcomed her with open arms.

"Have you tried talking to Jack?" she asked. "He's not unreasonable."

"I know," Helen said as she dug in her purse. She pulled out a tissue and wiped under her eyes. "He's very polite and concerned, but we're not close. I tried. I tried so hard, but no matter what I did, those boys resisted." She sniffed. "I suppose I shouldn't call them boys. They're all grown men. They were grown when I met them. It's just that's how George thought of them. As his boys."

Samantha angled toward her friend. "I don't get it, either. They should have adored you."

"Oh, I agree. I did everything I could think of. On my good days, I tell myself it wasn't me. George was a wonderful man, but he was never very close with his sons. I don't know why. Whatever problems they had existed long before he met me. Oh, but I loved him so much."

"I know you did."

Helen smiled. "All right. This is stupid. I didn't come here to cry. I want to talk about you. Tell me everything. Are you loving your job?"

Samantha accepted the change in subject. She didn't

know how to help her friend, so maybe distracting her would allow her a few minutes away from the pain.

"Every second," she said. "There's so much work, which is great. I like keeping busy. I have so many ideas for the new website that I've started keeping a pad of paper and a pen on the nightstand. I wake up two or three times a night with more details or directions or things we could do."

Helen wrinkled her nose. "I can see we're going to have to have the 'balance' conversation in a few weeks."

"Maybe," Samantha said with a laugh. "But for now, I'm really happy. I like the people I work with, I feel I'm contributing. It's great."

"Do you miss Vance?"

Samantha sighed. "No. And I really mean it. I thought I'd hurt more, but I think all the betrayal burned away the love. For the longest time I thought I'd never forgive him. Lately, I've come to see that I don't care enough to worry about forgiveness. He was horrible in so many ways. I have to think about myself and getting better. Not about him."

"Good for you. You've made a fresh start. You can get back on your feet. Look around. Maybe fall in love again."

Samantha held up her fingers in the sign of a cross. "Get back. There will be no talk of love or relationships in the context of my life, thank you very much." She lowered her hands to her lap. "I'm done with men."

"Forever?"

"For a while. I don't need the pain and suffering."

"It's not all like that," Helen said. "Vance wasn't the one for you. You figured that out and moved on. It was the right thing to do. But you don't want to turn your back on love. You don't want to miss the chance to have a great love. I believe there's one great love for everyone."

Samantha nodded. "And George was yours."

"He was everything," Helen said. "I was so lucky to find him. We shared so much. That's what I want to remember forever. How much we shared. How much we mattered to each other. I'll never find that again."

Samantha wondered if that was true. Helen was still a relatively young woman. And a beautiful one. Samantha had a feeling there was at least one other great love in her friend's life. As for herself, she wasn't interested in trying. Not when she'd been burned so badly.

"Speaking of men," Helen said. "What's it like working with Jack?"

"Good. He's very efficient and gives me all the room I need."

Helen raised her eyebrows. "And?"

Samantha shrugged. "And what?"

"Are there sparks? I remember there were sparks when you were in grad school with him. I remember long discussions about whether or not you should risk getting involved with him. I also remember saying you should, but you ignored me."

"He's not my type," she said, sidestepping the sparks question. Mostly because she didn't want to admit they were still there and starting fires every time she and Jack were in the same room.

"Type doesn't always enter into it," Helen said. "Some men simply turn us on."

"If you say so."

Her friend stared at her. "Jack isn't like Vance. He's honest and he's been hurt."

Samantha drew back. She was beginning to think

all men were like Vance. "Are you matchmaking? If so, stop right now. It's so not allowed."

"I'm not. I'm making a point. Jack's a great guy."

"For someone else."

"If you say so."

Jack's last meeting finished at four. He returned to his office and found several empty boxes by the wall. Mrs. Wycliff, efficient as ever, had delivered them while he'd been out. He planned to pack up a lot of his father's things and have them put in storage until his brothers showed up. Then the three of them could sit down with Helen and figure out who wanted what and what to do with anything left over.

He headed for the bookcase first. There were several out-of-date directories and registries. He dropped those into boxes without a second glance, then slowed when he came to the pictures of his father with various clients, city leaders and employees.

"No pictures of family," Jack murmured. No graduation shots, no informal photos taken on vacation or over holidays. Probably because they'd never much traveled as a family and, after his mother's death, holidays had been grim, dutiful affairs at best.

It should have been different, he thought. He knew guys with brothers and they were all tight. Why hadn't he, Evan and Andrew connected? Why weren't they close? They were all dealing with the death of their father. Wouldn't they do it better together?

"Did it matter? I don't even know where they are."

What did that say about the relationship? That he had no idea where to find either of his brothers? Nothing good.

He finished with the bookcase and started on the

credenza. He needed room to store reports, quarterly statements and the like. The credenza was perfect. He pulled out old files and glanced through them. Some of them were over a decade old. Was that what had gone wrong with the company? Had his father been unable to stay focused on the present?

Jack had a feeling he would never get those questions answered. He and his father had never been close and any opportunity for that had been lost years ago. What made the situation even worse was Jack could barely feel regret about the circumstances.

He filled more boxes with papers, files and bound reports. When the credenza was empty, he reached for the quarterly reports and started to slide them in place. But the shelf wasn't high enough.

"That doesn't make sense," he said as he looked at the credenza. "They should fit."

He reached inside and poked around, only to realize the base of the shelf was too thick by a couple of inches. What the hell?

After a little more prodding, he felt a narrow piece of metal, almost like a lever. When he pushed on it, the shelf popped up revealing a long, shallow recessed space and a set of leather books.

Jack's first thought was that his father had kept a diary. He was surprised to find himself anxious to read the older man's thoughts. But when he picked up the first book and flipped through it, there weren't any personal notes. Instead he stared at rows and rows of numbers.

His world was the law and it took him a second to realize he was looking at a detailed income statement. He glanced at the date and felt his stomach clench. This was for the previous year. He'd just spent the better part of the morning looking at the income statement for the past year. He was familiar with those numbers and they weren't anything like these.

Even though he already knew, he still found the first statement and compared it to the one his father had kept hidden. All the entry titles were the same but the amounts were different, and not for the better.

Anger filled him. Anger and a growing sense of betrayal. George Hanson had kept the truth from everyone. Jack didn't know how he'd done it, but the proof was here in the second set of books he'd hidden away.

Not only was the company close to bankruptcy, but his father's concealment had been criminal and premeditated. The company was totally screwed—and so was Jack.

Chapter Four

Jack carefully went through the books, hoping to find something to show that he'd been wrong—that his father *hadn't* defrauded employees, stockholders and his family. But with every column, every total, the truth became more impossible to avoid.

He stood and crossed to the window, where the night sky of Chicago stretched out before him. He could feel the walls closing in and fought against the sense of being trapped. With news like this, the board would pressure him to stay longer. They would insist that a three-month commitment to get things straightened out simply wasn't enough. In their position, he would do the same.

He heard someone knock on his office door, then push it open. He turned toward the sound.

"You're working late," Samantha said as she walked toward him. "I had a feeling you would still be here.

You executive types—always going the extra mile. Doesn't being so conscientious get—" She stopped in mid-stride and stared at him. "What's wrong?"

So much for a poker face, he thought grimly. There was no point in keeping the truth from her. He would be calling an emergency board meeting first thing in the morning. Time was critical. The financial information would have to be disclosed, first to the board, and then to the investors and the financial world. His father had insisted on taking the company public, which meant playing by the rules of the SEC.

"I found a second set of books," he said, nodding toward his desk. "I've checked them against the official financial statements and they don't add up. He was concealing massive expenditures and losses."

Samantha's eyes widened. "Fraud?"

"That's one word for it. I can think of fifty others. We're going to have to do a complete audit and find out the true financial situation. I doubt it's going to be good news. We're talking about a possible SEC investigation, plenty of bad press and downturn in the stock price." He returned his attention to the view. "At least the family owns a majority of the shares. We don't have to worry about a total sell-off. There will be a hit in our price, but it shouldn't be too bad. Not with a new management team in place and complete disclosure."

"I don't know what to say," she admitted.

"You and me both. Not exactly what you want to hear about your new employer. Ready to cut and run?"

"What? Of course not." She moved next to him. "Are you all right?"

"I'm not happy, if that's what you mean. Just once, I'd like to be surprised by good news."

"Jack, you're talking about your father. That he

concealed material financial information. That's a big deal."

"Good thing he's dead, then. Otherwise, he'd be going to jail."

He sounded so calm, Samantha thought. As if all this were happening to someone else. From what she knew, Jack and his father had never been tight, but this had to be hard for him. No one wanted to find out a parent had committed a crime.

"He wasn't a bad man," she said, not knowing if there was any way to make this easier for Jack. "Maybe he just got in over his head."

He looked at her. "You're trying to justify what he did?"

"Of course not. But from everything I've heard, he wasn't evil."

"He doesn't have to be evil to have broken the law. People do it all the time." He shook his head. "I'm almost not surprised. He ran several departments himself. He couldn't give up the control. Maybe this was just another way of holding on tight. The numbers weren't what he wanted them to be, so he modified them. No wonder he wasn't big on change—it would have made it tougher for him to hide the truth."

"But he did," she said.

"In spades. I wonder if David knows about this?"

"Are you going to ask him?"

"I'm going to ask everyone," Jack said. "The only way to ward off a crisis is to have a plan in place to solve the problem and to find anyone who may have helped him."

"You don't think he acted alone?"

"Unlikely. But I know it was his idea."

"You might want to talk to Helen," Samantha said

before she could stop herself. "She may know something."

Jack glanced at her. "You think she was involved?"

"What? No! Helen wouldn't do anything like this. But she might be able to tell you if George was acting stressed or if he suddenly seemed to change. She might have some suggestions."

His mouth twisted. "I don't need shopping advice."

Samantha stiffened at the insult to her friend. "Is that what you think of her? That she's a useless bimbo who only cares about clothes and jewelry?"

He shrugged. "I don't really know the woman."

"And why is that? She's been a part of this family for a while now. Why weren't you interested in even trying to get to know her?"

"I'm familiar with the type."

"Helen isn't a type. She's a person and she's not the person you imagine her to be. How interesting. You think your father got himself and the company in this position because he held on too tight to outdated ideas. It seems to me that you're a lot like that, too."

Samantha took notes as one of her team members wrapped up his presentation. "Great job, Phil," she said. "I really like how you're using colors to coordinate your section. It will make navigating the site really fun."

"Younger kids respond to colors. They're easier for them than instructions," he said with a grin. "I was thinking we could use the same format for the sections for older kids, but with the colors getting darker. Light blue flowing into dark blue into navy. So clicking on anything blue will automatically pop up math-related questions."

"Good idea," she told him, then looked at Arnie. "So, does that make your job harder or easier?"

Arnie rubbed his hand on his khakis. "Once we get it programmed, it's not a problem."

"Good." She found it helpful always to include the IT guys in on the planning stages of any Internet project. Better to get their cooperation and input while the work was still easily modified.

"It could be a series of questions," Arnie said. "Higher engagement. And then based on how they answer, they can go to another place on the site. Like if they get the answer right, they get a mini game. You know, for motivation."

Samantha glanced at her team, who all seemed pleased with the idea.

"Good thinking," she said. "You have a big thumbs-up on that one, Arnie. Thanks."

He shrugged and blushed. His gaze never left her face.

Samantha recognized the signs of a crush and wasn't exactly sure what to do about it. Not only wasn't she looking for love right now, Arnie wasn't her type. He was a nice enough guy, but nothing about him caused her to tingle.

Just then the conference-room door opened and Jack stepped inside. He didn't say anything and quietly took a seat in the back.

Instantly her body went on alert, just in case her brain hadn't noticed his arrival. She hated that even though she was still angry with him, she reacted physically. She found herself wanting to sit up straighter and push out her chest. Of course the complete lack of significant breast-type curves made that gesture futile, but still, the urge to flaunt was there.

Go figure, she thought. Arnie was available and pleasant and smart and probably completely uncomplicated. Nothing about him pushed any of her emotional buttons. Jack might be available and sexy, but he was also her worst-case scenario, man-wise, and totally unreasonable. He made her crazy with his assumptions about Helen.

Which they would deal with another time, she thought as she turned her attention back to the meeting in progress.

"The reward games should be related to the topic," Sandy said. "At least on some level. Like a blaster game based on times tables for the math color or something scientific for the science section."

"The difficulty of the games could increase with each grade level," Phil added.

"We're going to be spending a lot of time on content," Samantha said. "But it will be worth it. We'll need to take these ideas to research and get them going on questions and answers. We can do timed and non-timed quizzes. Maybe coordinate some of the questions with what's being studied in the textbooks. Are they standardized by region? Let's find that out. If we can emphasize what they're already studying, we'll reinforce the teachers' lessons."

The meeting continued. Ideas were offered and discussed. They had a limited amount of time to get the website up and running, so there would be a final of only the best. Still, she wanted as much to choose from as possible.

As people spoke and offered suggestions, Samantha was careful not to look at Jack. On the professional side, she knew it was important to put their argument behind them. As someone who cared about her friend, she was still really mad.

"That should take care of it for now," she said. "Good work, people. I'm impressed. We'll meet again on Friday."

Her staff stood and headed for the door. Arnie glanced at Jack, who remained seated at the table. The smaller man hesitated, looked at her, then left. Samantha had no choice but to acknowledge her boss.

"We're getting there," she said as she collected her notes.

"Yes, you are," he told her. "Your team works well together. I like where things are going."

"Good."

"You have an easy working style. You're firmly in charge, but you don't force your will on anyone."

"What's the point of that?" she asked. "I already know what I think. I'm looking for their ideas."

"Not everyone thinks that way."

She didn't know what to say to that.

"You're still mad at me," he said, making it a statement not a question, so she had no reason to deny it.

"I don't understand why you're determined to think the worst of Helen. From what I can tell, you barely know the woman. If you'd spent time with her and she'd been horrible, I would understand your less-than-flattering opinion. But you're basing it all on a few casual meetings and the mythology that stepmothers are inherently evil."

One corner of his mouth twitched. "It's not about her being my stepmother."

"Then what is it?"

He hesitated. "She's much younger than my father," he began. "My father was not a kind man."

Samantha stood. "Oh, I see. You're saying she married him for his money? Is that it?" Anger filled her. "I've known Helen for years. In fact, she used to be my babysitter. We've stayed close. She's like family to me. She loved your father. Maybe you and he didn't get along so you're having trouble with that concept, but it's true. She considers him the love of her life. I can't help defending her. It's like you're attacking my sister."

Jack rose. "You seem very sincere."

"I am."

They stared at each other. His dark gaze never wavered. At last he shrugged. "Then you must be right."

She nearly collapsed back in her chair. "What?"

"You've never lied to me, Samantha. I knew you pretty well back in grad school. You were never dishonest and you weren't stupid about people. So I'll respect your opinion on Helen."

Okay, she heard the words, but they didn't make sense to her. "What does that mean, exactly?"

"That you believe she's a good person. You're right, I haven't spent much time with her. I don't know the woman at all. Maybe she's nothing I've imagined."

Just like that? She studied him, looking for some hint that he was toying with her, but she couldn't find it. And to use his own words, she'd known *him* pretty well back in grad school and he hadn't been a liar, either. A little rigid maybe, but that was hardly a crime. Not that he'd done anything to admit *he* might be wrong in this case.

"Okay, then," she said. "That's good."

"So we're not fighting anymore?" he asked.

"I guess not."

"You sound disappointed."

"I have a lot of energy floating around inside of me," she admitted. "I'm not sure how to burn it off."

The second she said the words, his body stiffened. Tension filled the room and it had nothing to do with them not getting along. Every inch of her became aware of every inch of him and some of those inches were especially appealing.

Her mind screamed for her to run as far and as fast as she could. Her body begged her to stay and take advantage of the situation.

He broke the spell by glancing at his watch. "I have to prepare for the board meeting tomorrow."

"Is everyone flying in for it?" she asked.

"Most. A couple will tap in by phone. It's not going to be pretty."

She couldn't begin to imagine how that conversation would go. "I checked the papers this morning. There wasn't a leak."

He shrugged. "I didn't expect there to be. As of eight last night, only you and I knew."

"Oh." She'd assumed there were more people in the loop. "I didn't say anything to anyone."

"I knew you wouldn't."

With that, he excused himself and left. Samantha sank back in her chair and waited for the ache inside to fade.

What was it about Jack that got to her? He was everything she didn't like in a man—well-off, controlling, powerful. And yet he'd just said he was wrong about Helen. In all the years they'd been married, Vance had never once made a mistake—at least in his mind. Certainly not one he would admit to. So in that respect the two men were different.

But it wasn't enough, she thought. And she couldn't

take a chance on making another mistake like the last one. If she did, the next one could kill her.

Three of the board members lived in the Chicago area. Two flew in and two would be on speakerphone. Mrs. Wycliff arranged for coffee and sandwiches, but Jack doubted anyone would be in the mood to eat. Not when the news was this bad.

He waited until exactly eleven-thirty, then walked into the boardroom. The five people standing there turned to look at him.

He knew a couple by sight, having met them at various functions. The other three introduced themselves, then introduced the two who hadn't been able to make the meeting. The chairman, a craggy man in his late sixties named Baynes, motioned for everyone to take a seat. Jack found himself sitting at one end of the long conference table, while Baynes took the other. Jack had filled each of them in by phone so now they could get right to it.

"Sorry business," the older man said. "How did it happen?"

Everyone looked at Jack. "I have no idea," he said. "Until you asked me to step in for my late father, I'd been busy with my law practice."

"He never talked about the business with you? Never mentioned how things were going?"

"No." Jack didn't see any point in explaining he and his father had never spoken much at all, about the company or anything. He set the second set of books on the conference table. "I found these when I was cleaning out his credenza. There was a false bottom on one of the shelves. He didn't want anyone to find them."

He pushed the books to the center of the table. No

one seemed to want to be the first to touch them. Finally Baynes motioned for them and the lone woman on the board pushed them in his general direction.

"The chief financial officer has made copies of everything," Jack said. "She's already running the numbers to find out where we really are. We should have some accurate information by the end of the week."

"The auditors are going to have hell to pay," Baynes said absently.

Jack nodded. Every publicly traded company was required by law to be audited by an independent accounting firm. Somehow George's double books had gotten past them.

But their problems were the least of Jack's concerns. "I've prepared a statement," he said. "We'll issue it after the board meeting."

Several of the board members looked at each other, but no one suggested not going public. Just as well, Jack thought. He didn't want to have to remind them of their legal or fiduciary responsibilities.

"You asked me if I knew about this," he said. "What about all of you?"

Baynes looked at him. "What are you suggesting?"

"That you were his board. Many of you had known my father for years. He would have talked to you."

Baynes shook his head. "George didn't confide in anyone. This was his company. He made that clear before he went public. Things would be done his way."

"So you just let him run the company into the ground?"

The woman, Mrs. Keen, leaned forward. "George presented us with financial reports. We had no reason to doubt their validity or his. Your father wasn't a bad man, Jack, but clearly he was in over his head."

That seemed to be the consensus, he thought. "Shouldn't you, as his board, have noticed that? Shouldn't you have made sure the man running Hanson Media Group knew what he was doing?"

"Attacking us isn't going to solve the problem," Baynes said firmly.

Right. Because they were all more concerned about covering their collective asses, Jack thought grimly.

"We need to present a united front," Mrs. Keen said. "Perhaps the board should issue a statement as well."

"Do what you'd like," Jack told her.

"Things would go better if we could announce that you would be taking on your father's job permanently," Baynes said.

Jack narrowed his gaze. "I agreed to three months and that's all. I'm not changing my mind."

"Be reasonable," the older man said. "This is a crisis. The company is in real danger. We have employees, stockholders. We have a responsibility to them."

"No, *you* have one."

"You're George Hanson's oldest son," Mrs. Keen said. "People will look to you for leadership."

"I'm not his only son," he pointed out. "I have two brothers."

Baynes dismissed them with a wave of his hand. "Who are where? They don't have the experience, the education or the temperament for this kind of work."

Jack did his best not to lash out at them. Losing his temper would accomplish nothing. "Three months," he said. "That's all. In the meantime, I suggest you start looking for an interim president. Hire someone who knows what he or she is doing."

"But—"

Jack stood. "There's no point in having a conversation about me staying or going. I'm not changing my mind. Besides, we don't even know who owns the majority of the company. My father's shares are in limbo until the reading of the will. Who knows—maybe he'll want them sold on the open market."

The board members paled at the thought. While they were still taking that in, he made his escape. As he walked down the hall, he loosened his tie. But that wasn't enough to wipe away the sense of being trapped.

"Come on, come on," Samantha called as she stared at the basket and willed the ball to slide cleanly through the hoop. There was a moment of silence, followed by a *swish* of net.

"Woo hoo." She held up her hand to Patti, one of her directors. "Two more for our team. We're up by six."

Patti gave her a high five, then went back into position. Perhaps playing basketball in the corridor right outside her office wasn't standard corporate procedure, but Samantha found it really helped her people clear their heads after a long day of brainstorming.

"Lucky shot," Phil said as he dribbled the ball. He jogged in to take his shot. Samantha moved in front of him. When he stretched up to shoot, she batted the ball away and it bounced off the wall before rolling down the hall.

The game went quiet as Jack rounded the corner and picked up the ball. Samantha could feel her staff looking at her. She knew Jack had endured the meeting from hell with the board and braced herself for him to take that out on her.

He raised his eyebrows. "Who's winning?"

"My team," she said quickly. "We've been brain-storming all day and we're—"

"No need to explain," he said, then bounced the ball. "Got room for one more?"

She glanced at Phil, who shrugged. "Sure," she said.

Jack tossed the ball back, then took off his jacket. After pulling off his tie, he went to work on rolling up his sleeves.

"Who's on the other team?" he asked.

"I am," Phil said, then he quickly introduced every-one else. "Any good at this?"

Jack grinned. "Just get me the ball."

Ten minutes later, Samantha knew they'd been had. Jack wasn't just good—he was terrific. He could shoot from any angle and he rarely missed. His team pulled ahead and then beat hers by six points.

"You're a ringer," she said, trying to catch her breath.

"I've had some practice."

"Where'd you play?" Phil asked, after slapping him on the back.

"Law school. We all did, to unwind. Grad school, too, but not so much."

Samantha remembered that Jack had attended law school before going to Wharton. She also vaguely re-called him hanging out with friends on the basketball courts, but she'd never paid much attention.

Now she knew she'd made the right decision. Being close to Jack while he ran, dodged, threw and scored bordered on dangerous. She liked the way his body moved and the energy he put in the game. She liked how he worked with his team and how, when his shirt came unbuttoned, she got a glimpse of some very impressive abs.

Bad idea, she reminded herself. Lusting after the boss could only lead to trouble. Okay, so she wasn't ready for a real relationship—maybe it was time to find rebound guy.

"Thanks for letting me play," Jack told Phil.

"Any time."

"There's that pub on the corner," Jack continued. "Why don't I buy you all drinks." He glanced at his watch. "Say half an hour?"

"Great." Phil grinned. "Thanks."

"No problem."

Samantha waited until everyone else had disappeared into their respective offices. "You didn't have to do that."

"Buy them drinks?" He shrugged. "I wanted to. They let me play. I needed the break."

"The board meeting?"

"Yeah." He shrugged into his jacket. "You're coming, aren't you?"

She shouldn't. It wasn't smart. It wasn't a lot of things. "Sure. I'll be there."

"Good."

He smiled and her toes curled. She walked into her office. Rebound guy—absolutely. She would have to get right on that.

Jack didn't just order drinks, he ordered platters of appetizers, then proceeded to talk to each member of her team individually. Samantha watched him work the crowd and did her best not to react when he smiled at one of her female staffers.

Finally he settled in the stool next to hers. "You've done well," he said in a low voice. "You have good people working for you."

"Thanks."

Despite the easy conversation around them, she was aware of being watched. Some of her team were mildly interested while a few—the single women—were trying to figure out the score.

"How did it go?" she asked.

"About as expected. They're more interested in protecting themselves than what really happened. We're making an announcement first thing in the morning. I have two phone calls scheduled with investors. The first is to tell them what happened, the second will come later when I announce our specific plan to rectify the situation."

"Do you have a plan?"

He sipped his drink. "Not yet, but I'm hopeful." He glanced around. "They're all working their butts off. I want to make sure it's not for nothing."

"It won't be. There will be some bad press, but we'll get through it."

"Until the next crisis."

"The company is in transition," she said. "There are always adjustments."

"I know. What I don't understand is why my father never had a successor picked out. He had to know he wasn't going to live forever."

"Maybe he was waiting for one of his sons to get interested in the company."

Jack took another drink. "Probably. I don't see Evan and Andrew making a beeline to Chicago and, honestly, I can't see either of them being willing to take things over."

She touched his arm. "You don't have to do this if you don't want to."

"I'm aware I can walk away at any point."

But he wouldn't. Jack had a sense of responsibility. She respected that about him.

Once again her body reminded her that he was nothing like Vance, but her head wasn't so sure. On the surface her ex had been a great guy, too. Successful, a caring father. He'd said and done all the right things—right up until the wedding. Then overnight he'd changed.

Her father had done the same thing. In a matter of weeks, he'd gone from a loving, supportive man to someone who'd walked out and had done his best not to have to support his only child.

Powerful men often hid dark, guilty secrets. As much as she was attracted to Jack, she was determined to keep their relationship strictly professional. She couldn't afford to take another emotional hit right now.

"I should go," she said, collecting her purse.

"I'm heading out, too," he told her. "Want a ride home?"

Ah, the close confines of a car. So tempting and so dangerous.

"No, thanks. I have a few errands to run on my way home. I'll walk."

"Are you sure? I don't mind."

She smiled. "I appreciate the offer, but I'll be fine on my own."

She'd learned it was the only safe way to be.

Chapter Five

Roger Arnet was a tall, thin blond man in his mid-fifties. He shook Jack's hand, then sat in the visitor's chair on the other side of the desk.

"How are you settling in?" Roger asked pleasantly. "Your father was a great man. A great man. You won't find filling his shoes easy."

Jack didn't know how to answer the question. News of the second set of books had been released to the public. The response in the press had been relatively mild since Hanson Media Group wasn't a major player in the city, but there had been plenty of uproar in the office. He wondered if Roger had any way of reconciling his insistence that George had been a great man with the reality of a company president who lied to his entire staff.

"I'm finding my way," he said, going for a neutral response.

"Good. Good." Roger smiled. "I understand you're a lawyer."

"Yes. I attended law school, then went on to business school. It was my deal with my father. I would study both and then pick."

"You chose the law. George was very disappointed."

Had his father spoken about him with everyone in the firm? "I'm here now," Jack said. "Which is why I wanted to talk with you. We're making some changes."

"I heard about them," Roger said. "I've been on vacation and when I got back, everyone was buzzing. Internet expansion, eh? Are you sure about that?"

"Very sure."

Roger took off his glasses and pulled out a handkerchief. "Arnie's been filling me in on your plans. Very ambitious. Very ambitious. A bit too much, if you ask me."

Jack leaned back in his chair. "Are you saying we're not capable of expanding our websites?"

"Expansion is one thing, but what you're proposing is something else. But then it's not you, is it? It's that new girl. Samantha something."

"Edwards. And she has my full support."

"Of course. She's very energetic, but in my experience, it's better if we take things slowly. Sort of feel our way. Digital is all fine and good, but this company was founded on print media."

"Magazines are expensive and change slowly," Jack said. "We don't have any publication that has circulation over a million. We're barely breaking even on thirty percent of our magazines and we're losing money on the rest. The Internet is a significant part of our culture and increasingly where people are spending time and money. ."

Roger nodded. Jack felt as if he'd just stepped into an alternative universe. If Roger was the head of IT in the company, shouldn't he be pushing for *more* technology, not less?

"Arnie mentioned all of this to me," Roger admitted. "But he's young and he tends to get ahead of himself. I hope he wasn't filling your head with a lot of nonsense."

Jack was willing to respect those older than him and he was certainly willing to listen to qualified opinions; however, he wasn't willing to be treated like an idiot.

He straightened and stared directly at Roger. "Let me be as clear as possible," he said. "This company is on the brink of financial ruin. I'm sure you've read about our recent problems. The announcement that my father kept a second set of books wasn't happy news. Doing business the old way isn't going to keep this company going. We need change and we need it quickly. I believe that digital expansion is our best solution. Now you can get onboard with that program or you can find another company that is more to your liking."

Roger blinked. "That's very blunt."

"Yes, it is. I've heard good things about you and I hope you'll decide to stay, but if you do, be aware that we have a new direction and I expect everyone to be excited about it."

"All right. I'll consider what you said. As far as the Internet expansion, I'm concerned about the safeguards. Your target market is children and there are many predators out there."

Jack wasn't sure how to read him. Still, the truth would come out quickly enough. Either Roger was with him or Roger was gone.

"Protecting the children using our site is our first priority," Jack told the other man. "Samantha's first presentation was on Internet safeguards. She and Arnie are working very closely on that project. I appreciate your concern as well and I would ask you to oversee their work. Feel free to report back to me on any weak areas."

Roger seemed surprised. "Why should you trust me?"

"I believe you're genuinely concerned about the children," Jack said. "You're also slightly mistrustful of the changes. That will make you a good custodian of the security programs. You won't let anyone cut corners."

"Thank you for that. Let me think about all that you've said and get back to you."

"Of course. Thanks for coming in."

Roger shook hands with him, then walked to the door. Once there, he turned back. "I wish you could have seen your father at work here, Jack. He was brilliant. Simply brilliant."

"So I've heard."

Restless after his meeting with Roger, Jack headed to Samantha's office.

"Got a minute?" he asked as she hung up the phone.

"Sure. Have a seat."

He glanced at the light wood furniture, the bright prints on the walls and the purple sofa by the corner. In a matter of a week or two, Samantha had taken the space and made it her own.

"Interesting decorating," he said as he settled in a chair.

She grinned. "You hate it."

"Hate is strong."

"There's a lot of really cool stuff in the company storage facility."

"Some of it dating back to the sixties," Jack murmured.

"You're right. I didn't want to get too wild, but I like having color to inspire me."

Which, apparently, applied to her clothes, he thought as he took in the orange-and-gold top she'd pulled on over black slacks. Her hair was loose, in a riot of red curls that tangled in her beaded earrings.

By contrast, his suit that day was gray, his shirt white and his tie a traditional burgundy. They couldn't be more different. Which is what had always made their relationship interesting, he reminded himself.

"What's up?" she asked.

"Have you met Roger Arnet?"

She wrinkled her nose. "Arnie's boss, right? I shook hands with him in passing, but we haven't spoken."

"Be prepared. He's not one to move with the times. He's opposed to the Internet expansion on many levels. He thinks the plans are too ambitious."

"Great. Just what I need. The person in charge of a critical department for me not getting onboard."

"I know he's going to be a problem. I told him he could get with the program or get out."

Her eyes widened. "That's not subtle."

"It's my style. I think he's a little more willing to compromise now. He does have one legitimate concern and that's to keep the site secure. Children are vulnerable."

"I agree and I've been working with the IT guys on different ideas for that. We're going cutting edge. No stalkers allowed."

"Roger felt very passionately about it, as well. You might want to put him on the team."

Samantha recoiled physically. "Do I have to?"

She sounded more like a twelve-year-old than a responsible adult.

"No, you don't," he said, holding in a smile. "It's your show. You can do what you like. I'm simply pointing out that sometimes it's better to find a way to work with those who don't agree with us. If you make Roger feel important and really use him on the project, you're more likely to win him over. I'll fire him if I have to, but I would prefer not to. He knows the company and he knows his job. All my reports about him are excellent."

"Good point," she murmured. "I'll do the mature thing and work with him. But I won't like it."

"No one is asking you to."

"Good to know."

She stood up and walked to a coffeepot on a low table by the window. When she held it out to him, he nodded. She poured two cups.

He took the one she offered and watched her walk back to her seat. He liked the way she moved and the way her clothes swayed with each step. When she sat back down, she sniffed her coffee before sipping, as if making sure no one had accidentally changed her drink for something else.

She'd been doing that for as long as he could remember. He used to tease her about it, which always sparked a furious argument during which she denied the action. Then he would hand her coffee and she would sniff and they would both laugh.

But this time he didn't say anything. A couple of nights ago, at the pub, she'd shut him down good. She'd been doing it in various ways ever since they'd first met. At some point he was going to have to accept the truth. Samantha simply didn't want him.

In his world, chemistry usually went both ways, but she was the exception to the rule. No matter how powerful the need inside of him, she didn't feel it. It was time to accept that and move on.

"Nothing about this job is boring," she said. "You have to admit that."

"Right now I'd be happy with a few days of boring. That would mean no new crisis."

She sighed. "You've been going from one to the other. That can't be easy."

He shrugged. "It is what it is. I'll deal with it. Are you still enjoying your condo?"

"Very much. You were right—the location is fabulous. Have you had pizza from that place across the street?"

"I'm a regular."

She sipped her coffee, then sighed. "I ordered it the other night. It's amazing. It was so good, I actually had some for breakfast. I've never done that in my life— not even in college. Until I tasted their pizza, I never really understood the whole deep-dish thing. But now I get it. Heaven. Pure heaven."

"Wait until you order their pasta."

"Really? I might do that tonight. I'm hoping to get out this weekend and explore a little more of the neighborhood. So far all I've seen is work and my building."

He consciously had to keep from offering to be her guide. He generally spent Saturday mornings with Charlie in the park, but a walking tour would give his dog plenty of exercise. They could—

No, he told himself. Samantha had made her position incredibly clear. He wasn't going to push anymore.

"The city's website has lots of information about points of interest, planned walks, that sort of thing."

"Thanks," she said, sounding a little puzzled. "I'll check it out. But if you're not busy we could—"

Mrs. Wycliff knocked on the open door. "Mr. Hanson, you have a call from Mr. Baynes."

He rose. "I need to take that," he told her, aware she'd been about to suggest something for the weekend. While he wanted to accept and spend more time with her, he knew it would be a mistake. He'd spent too much time wanting what he couldn't have where Samantha was concerned. He needed to move on.

Saturday, Samantha dressed for the cool, clear weather, then collected what she would need for a morning spent exploring. As she stepped out of her condo, she thought about going up to Jack's place and asking him to join her. Except she had a feeling he would say no.

Not that she could blame him. She'd been so careful to shut him down time and time again, shouldn't she be happy that he finally got the message? It was better for both of them if they were simply work colleagues.

She walked to the elevator and hit the down button. It was better, she told herself. Sure Jack was a great guy, but he was also the type of man to push all of her buttons and not in a good way. As much as she liked him, she was also wary of him. He was too much like her father and Vance. Too much in charge. She'd been fooled already—she wasn't willing to go there again.

Not that she was even looking for a serious relationship, she reminded herself. The best thing would be to find rebound guy and make that work. If only Jack weren't so sexy and smart and fun to be with.

She stepped out into the crisp morning and drew in a deep breath. Enough, she thought. For the rest of the day, she refused to think about Jack. She would simply enjoy herself and—

Something bumped into the back of her legs. She turned and saw Charlie. The border collie gave her a doggy grin, then barked. Jack smiled.

"Morning," he said, looking delicious in worn jeans and a sweatshirt.

"Hi."

"Out to see the sights?"

She tugged on the strap of her purse/backpack. "I have everything I need right here. I downloaded some maps and packed water and money for a cab in case I get lost."

"You picked a good day. It won't get too hot."

Was it just her, or had things taken a turn for the awkward? "So you and Charlie are headed for the park?"

He nodded. "Every Saturday, regardless of the weather."

She rubbed the dog's ears. The smart choice was simply to walk away. But she was lonely, she liked Jack and she wanted them to be friends.

"Can a non-dog owner come along?" she asked.

He hesitated, but before she could retract the question, he smiled. "Sure. When I get tired of throwing Charlie the Frisbee, you can take over."

"I'd like that." She fell into step beside him. "So how did you get Charlie? Did you grow up with dogs in the house?"

"No. I wasn't actually looking for a pet. Then a buddy from my law firm invited me over for dinner. I learned later it was with an ulterior motive. His dog had six-week-old puppies he was looking to sell to un-suspecting friends. Charlie and I bonded over a game of tag."

She laughed. "I wouldn't have thought a hotshot-attorney type could be influenced so easily."

"Don't tell anyone. He moved in a couple of weeks later and I quickly found out that puppies are a ton of work. For a year he chewed everything he could get his teeth on. Then I took him to obedience training and now we understand each other better."

They stopped at the red light on the corner. Charlie waited patiently until the light changed, then led them along the crosswalk.

"Have you been reading the papers?" Jack asked.

She had a feeling he didn't mean the fashion reports. "I've noticed there was some local coverage on Hanson Media Group, but I could only find a couple of stories in the national media. You're right—there wasn't all that much press."

"Sometimes it's good to be small, relatively speaking. Now if we were one of the networks, it would be a different story."

"I'm surprised no one ever made any offer to buy the company out," she said. "So much of entertainment is now controlled by conglomerates."

"For all I know my father's been fighting off offers for years. He wouldn't sell and risk losing his name on the letterhead."

He sounded bitter as he spoke. "You don't agree?" she asked.

"It's not my thing. I don't need to be the center of the universe, at least as my father defined it."

They'd reached the park.

"The dog zone is on the other side," he said. "Hope you don't mind the hike."

"Exercise is my friend," she said with a grin. "At least that's what I tell myself."

"There's a gym in the building."

"They showed it to me on my tour. Very impressive." There had been several treadmills and ellipticals, along with weight machines and three sets of free weights.

"I work out every morning," Jack said. "It's pretty quiet at five."

"In the morning?" She shuddered. "That's because more normal people are sleeping. I can't believe you get up that early."

"I'm lucky. I don't need a lot of sleep."

"Apparently not. Most of the year, it's dark at that time."

"They have lights in the gym."

They'd need more than that to get her there. Coffee, for starters. And bagels.

"I'm not really into the whole sweat thing," Samantha told him. "I've been lucky. I don't seem to gain weight."

It sort of went with what was kindly referred to as a boyish figure. She decided it was a trade-off. Sure she didn't have anything to fill out her bras and padding was required to hint at anything resembling cleavage, but she'd never counted calories or given up carbs. She could eat what she wanted and still have the world's boniest butt.

"Exercise isn't just about weight loss. It keeps you healthy."

"So does getting enough sleep. Besides, I'm a big walker. I can go for miles." As long as there was plenty of food along the way. One of the things she missed about New York. All the street vendors and little delis where a pretzel or ice-cream craving could be instantly satisfied.

They walked through a grove of trees and came out in a huge open area. There were already a half-dozen dog owners and their pets running around. Jack found a spot in the sun and set down his backpack.

"Equipment," she said. "So what exactly is involved in your Saturday-morning ritual?"

He pulled out a blanket. "For me," he said. Then a ball. "For Charlie. We start with this and work up to the Frisbee."

He unclipped Charlie from the leash, then threw the red rubber ball what seemed like at least a quarter mile.

Charlie took off after it, grabbed it and raced toward him.

"Impressive," she said. "The dogs don't get crabby with each other?"

"Not usually. Most people know if their dogs are social or not. There have been the occasional fights, but it's rare."

Charlie bounded toward them and dropped the ball at her feet. She winced.

"I throw like a girl," she told the dog. "You won't be impressed."

Jack laughed. "Come on. He's not going to be critical."

"Uh-huh. You say that now, but neither of you has seen me throw."

She picked up the slightly slobbery ball, braced herself and threw as hard as she could. It made it, oh, maybe a third of the way it had before. Charlie shot her a look that clearly asked if that was the best she could do before running after the ball. This time when he returned, he dropped it at Jack's feet.

"So much for not being critical," she said.

Jack laughed and tossed the ball again.

They settled on the blanket. The sun felt good in the cool morning. She could hear laughter and dogs barking. Families with children in strollers walked on the paved path that went around the dog park. There was the occasional canine tussle, but as Jack had said, no real trouble.

After about fifteen minutes of catch, Charlie came back and flopped down next to them.

"He's just resting," Jack told her. "Soon he'll be ready for the Frisbee. Then watch out. He can catch just about anything."

She rubbed the dog's belly. "I can't wait to see him in action."

"He'll show off for you."

"I hope so."

Charlie licked her arm, then closed his eyes and wiggled in the sun.

"What a life," she said. "I used to see dogs in New York all the time. I wondered what it was like for them to be in a city, but Charlie is hardly suffering."

Jack narrowed his gaze. "Is that a crack about the doggy day care?"

"No. Of course not. Why would I say anything about that?" She was careful not to smile as she spoke.

"Somehow I don't believe you, so I'm going to change the subject. Do you miss New York?"

She crossed her legs and shrugged out of her jacket. "Sure. It's a great city. But I can already see the potential here. The feeling is different, but in a good way. In

New York I always felt I had to be going or doing or I'd miss something. I don't feel so frantic here."

"I like it. And the people. Are you missing your ex?"

A subtle way to ask about her divorce, she thought. It was a fair question. "No. The marriage was over long before I left. Unfortunately, I didn't notice."

"Did he agree with that?"

"No. Vance wasn't happy about me leaving." She ignored the memories of fights and screaming. "I just couldn't trust him anymore and once trust is destroyed, it's over."

"He cheated?"

The question surprised her until she realized it was a logical assumption, based on what she'd said. "Nothing that simple. I met Vance through my work—a fund-raiser I worked on. He's a cardiologist. He has an excellent reputation and everyone who knew us both thought we'd make a great couple. So did I. He was divorced, but was still really close with his kids. I thought that meant something."

Jack frowned. "You wanted kids."

She laughed. "Right, we used to talk about it. You thought two was plenty. I wanted four. You were uncomfortable with three because an odd number would make travel difficult. Ever practical."

"It's true. Try finding a hotel room that sleeps five."

"Okay. Good point. Anyway Vance knew I wanted children. We discussed it at length." That's what got her, she thought. That he'd agreed. "We even discussed names."

"He changed his mind?"

"More than that. He lied." She shook her head. "I was such a fool. We decided to wait a little, get settled in our marriage. Then, when I was ready to start trying, he kept putting it off. I never suspected anything. Finally I pressured him into agreeing it was time."

She paused as she mentally edited her past. There were so many other reasons she'd left Vance, but this was the easiest to explain.

"Nothing happened," she said. "Months went by. Finally, I spoke to my doctor, who agreed to do some tests. It made sense for me to go in first. After all, Vance had already fathered children. I came through fine and then it was time for Vance to make an appointment. Only he wouldn't. He finally came clean. He'd had a vasectomy after his youngest was born. He'd been lying the whole time."

Jack hadn't known where the story was going, but he sure as hell hadn't guessed the ending. "Samantha, I'm sorry."

"Me, too." She ducked her head and rubbed Charlie's chest. "I was so angry, but more than that, I was hurt. I couldn't understand why he hadn't told me the truth when we'd first started dating. It would have been so easy. He lied. Worse than that, he let me believe there was something wrong with me. He even hinted at it by telling me his first wife hadn't had any trouble getting pregnant."

He heard the betrayal in her voice and didn't know what to say. The man's actions made no sense. Why lie about something that was going to come out eventually? Why marry Samantha knowing she wanted kids and he didn't?

"What did he say?" he asked.

"Not much. That's what got me. He never took responsibility for his actions. He never thought he was wrong." She pulled her knees to her chest and wrapped her arms around her legs. "I can't tell you how much it hurt to find out the truth. It was as if I'd never known him. I thought he was different. I thought he was special, but I was wrong."

There was still pain in her eyes. Jack didn't know how long it would take to get over something like that. He knew a little of her past—that her father had walked out with no warning and had abandoned her and her mother. No wonder she was wary around men.

"Okay, this is boring," she said, a smile trembling on her lips. "Let's talk about something a little more perky. Like you. A lawyer, huh? Who would have thought."

"That's me—a man interested in the law."

"Really? But it's so stodgy."

He grinned. "Not to me."

"I don't know. All those thick books you have to read. Case law. So not my thing."

"Not to mention the clothes."

"Yeah. The dark suits would really depress me. So what's the game plan? You work your way up to senior partner, then torture new associates for sport?"

"That's one possibility."

"And the other?"

He didn't usually talk about his future plans with many people. Not that he didn't trust Samantha. "I want to be a judge."

She stretched her legs out in front of her. "Wow—that's pretty cool." She tilted her head and studied him. "I think you'd be good at it. You're very calm and you reason things through. If only the robe weren't black."

He chuckled. "Every career has drawbacks."

"True, and that's not a big one. Judge Hanson. I like it. All the more reason to get back to your law firm."

"Exactly."

"Which means every disaster is something you can

almost take personally," she murmured. "That's got to be hard on you."

He wasn't surprised that she understood. He and Samantha had never had a communication problem. Their friendship had been based on long nights spent talking, arguing and seeking common ground.

"I've agreed to stay for three months," he said. "When that time is up, I'm going back to my real job."

"The company won't be the same without you," she told him. "But I understand why you want to leave."

Charlie stretched, then stood and looked meaningfully at the backpack. Jack pulled out the Frisbee and threw it. Charlie raced after it and caught it in midair. Samantha scrambled to her feet.

"Did you see that? He's incredible. Does he always catch it?"

"Most of the time. Border collies are athletic dogs."

"I guess."

Charlie trotted the Frisbee back and put it at Jack's feet. Jack threw it farther this time.

"Amazing," Samantha said. "What a fun way to spend your Saturday morning. Do you always come to this park?"

"Mostly. There are a few other dog parks around the city. Sometimes we jog along the lake. You'll have fun exploring."

"I know," she said absently, watching his dog. "Although my travels will be limited by my lack of driving."

"What? You don't drive?"

She crossed her arms over her chest. "No, I don't. I never learned before I went to college and once there, I didn't have the opportunity. Since then I've been living in Manhattan. I did fine with public transportation or walking."

"You don't drive?" He couldn't imagine it. How could someone not know how to drive?

"No matter how many times you repeat the question, the answer's going to stay the same," she said. "It's not that big a deal."

"It's a little scary," he said. "Want me to teach you?"

The invitation came out before he could stop it. Instantly he braced himself for her standard refusal. What was wrong with him? Why couldn't he accept the fact that Samantha just wasn't into him that way?

"I've seen your fancy car," she said. "Too much pressure."

Was that a yes? Did he want it to be? Wasn't he done trying to make points with her?

"I can get my hands on an old clunker."

"Really? I'm tempted. I've always felt, I don't know, weird about the whole driving thing." She studied him. "You wouldn't yell, would you?"

"Not my style."

Charlie barked, urging the Frisbee game to continue. Jack ignored him.

"Then thank you for asking," she said. "I'd be delighted to take you up on your offer. But if you change your mind, you have to tell me. I don't want you doing something you don't want to do."

"Again, not my style."

She laughed. "Jack, you're currently doing a job you hate because it's the right thing to do."

He chuckled, realizing she had a point. "Not counting that."

Charlie barked again. Then he picked up the Frisbee he'd dropped and brought it to them. Jack reached for it, as did Samantha. Their arms bumped, their shoulders crashed and the two of them tumbled onto the blanket.

Jack twisted and put out his hands to pull her against him, so he could take the weight of the fall. They landed with a thud that pushed out most of his air.

Her hands were on the blanket, her body pressed intimately against his. His legs had fallen apart and she lay nestled between his thighs. He could feel her breasts pressing against his chest.

Their eyes locked. Something darkened hers and all he could think about was kissing her.

There were a lot of reasons not to and only one reason he should.

Because he wanted to.

Chapter Six

Samantha felt the light brush of his mouth on hers. She knew she could easily stop him by saying something or simply rolling off him. It was the sensible thing to do. And yet she found herself not wanting to move. Her recollection of her previous kisses with Jack, from that one extraordinary night they'd shared, were still vivid in her mind. She was confident that she'd inflated their impressiveness over time. A kiss now would allow for comparison.

When she didn't move, he cupped her face with his hands and angled his head. Then he kissed her again, this time moving his lips back and forth. She felt heat and soft pressure. Blood surged in her body, making her want to squirm closer. She was already right on top of him, their bodies touching in so many inter-esting places, but suddenly that wasn't enough. She needed more.

He moved his hands, easing them past her ears so he could bury his fingers in her hair. Then he parted his mouth and bit down on her bottom lip.

The unexpected assault made her breath catch. He took advantage of her parted lips and slipped his tongue inside.

It was like drowning in warm, liquid desire. Wanting crashed over her, filling every cell until it was all she could think of. His fingers still tangled in her hair, which made her impatient. She wanted him touching her…everywhere.

Even as he circled her tongue with his, teasing, tasting, arousing, her body melted. She felt herself softening, yielding, kissing him back with a desperation that made her the aggressor.

She took control of the kiss, following him back into his mouth, claiming him with quick thrusts of her tongue. At last he moved his hands to her back, where he stroked the length of her spine. Her hips arched in an involuntary invitation, which brought her stomach in contact with something hard, thick and very masculine.

Memories crashed in on her. She remembered how he'd touched her and tasted her everywhere. She recalled the sight of him naked, of how many times he'd claimed her. She'd been sore for nearly two days, but the soreness had only reminded her of the incredible pleasure they'd shared and had made her want to do it again. But she'd resisted—because of who he was and what he could do to her heart.

She hated the logic filling her brain, the voice that asked what was different now. She wasn't interested in danger or reality or anything but the way their bodies fit together. If she—

But an insistent barking distracted her and at last

she lifted her head only to find Charlie's nose inches from her face.

Below her, Jack groaned. "I'm going to have to have a talk with that dog."

She became aware of their intimate position and the very public location. Without saying anything, she slid off him, then scrambled to her feet.

"We're in the park," she said more to herself than him. "In public."

Jack rose more slowly. He reached down for the Frisbee and tossed it, all without looking away from her.

"I doubt anyone noticed," he told her.

"Still." She pressed her hands to her heated face. Talk about acting out of character. She had always been a strictly-in-bed, lights-off kind of date. The only exception to that rule…was standing right next to her.

Of course. She was fine as long as she resisted Jack's particular brand of temptation, but if she gave in, even for a second, she completely lost her head.

"I, ah…" She glanced around, then returned her attention to him. "I'm, um, going to let you get back to your morning."

His dark eyes glowed with passion. "You don't have to."

"It's for the best."

His mouth straightened. "Let me guess. This was a mistake."

His tone of resignation caught her more than his words. He expected her to pull back because that's what she always did. There were several good reasons, but he didn't know them. If she had her way, he never would.

"Thanks for everything," she said, trying to smile. "I'll see you Monday."

She hesitated, then walked away when he didn't

speak. A slight feeling of hurt surprised her. What did she expect? That he would come after her? Not likely after all the times she'd turned him down.

Jack watched her go. Once again Samantha was the queen of mixed signals. She had been from the beginning. Is that what made him want her? He never knew where he stood?

"Not exactly the basis of a great relationship," he murmured, throwing the Frisbee again.

The good news was Samantha wanted him sexually. The truth had been there in her response. For some reason, she couldn't handle the idea of it, but at least she didn't find him repulsive.

Was it him in particular or would she have run from anyone?

But she still liked to run and a guy with a brain in his head would let her go. Funny how he'd always been smart, everywhere in his life but with her. What was it about her that made him want to keep trying? It wasn't that he thought that they were soul mates. He didn't believe in that sort of thing and he sure as hell wasn't interested in a serious relationship. What was the point?

He was in it for the sex. Not a one-night stand. That wasn't fun anymore. He liked to take a lover for a few months, make sure they were both completely satisfied, then move on when one or both of them got restless.

Somehow he doubted Samantha would be up for anything like that.

Which left him where? Wanting a woman who didn't want him? There was a way to start the weekend. Okay, he was back to his original plan—forgetting about her as anything other than an employee.

Easier said than done, he thought as he remembered the feel of her body on his. But not impossible.

* * *

Jack reached for his coffee and cursed whoever had invented speakerphones and teleconferences. Spending an hour explaining to stock analysts and trade journalists how he had found a second set of books was not his idea of a good time.

"You're sure the investigation into how this happened has already begun?" a disembodied voice asked.

"Of course. It started less than twelve hours after I found the books. It would have started sooner, but I couldn't get an independent accounting team in here until morning."

"You're not using your regular accountants, are you?"

"No. No one who has ever been associated with Hanson Media Group is involved. As soon as we have a preliminary report, I'll make it public. Until then, I don't have any answers."

"Do you think more people were involved than your father?"

Jack hesitated. "I don't have any specifics on that, but my personal opinion in that my father acted alone."

"Has his death been investigated? Are the company's troubles the reason he died?"

The not-so-subtle implication that George Hanson had killed himself infuriated Jack. He spoke through gritted teeth. "My father died of natural causes. There was an autopsy. He didn't kill himself." And he would sue any bastard who reported otherwise, Jack thought. He might not have been close to the old man, but he wouldn't let any member of his family be dragged through the press that way.

"Is the company going to make it?" someone asked.

Jack stared at the phone. In truth, he didn't have a

clue. He continued to ride the bad-news train, with a
new crisis every day. From where he sat, he couldn't
imagine how this could be pulled off. In his opinion,
it would take a miracle or a buyout for Hanson Media
Group to survive, but he wasn't about to tell them that.

"We're going to come through this just fine," he
said, wondering if saying it would make it reality.

Samantha had spent much of the weekend giving
herself a stern talking-to. Being afraid was one thing,
but acting like an idiot was another. She had to pick a
side—any side. Either she was interested in Jack romantically or she wasn't.

She hated the mixed messages she sent every time
they hung out together. She didn't like that she had become that sort of woman. In truth, she found him sexy
and funny and smart and pretty much everything any
reasonable single female would want in a man. But he
was also rich, powerful, determined and used to getting his way, which terrified her.

There were actually two different problems. First,
that however much she told herself she *wasn't* interested, that she only wanted a platonic relationship with
him, her body had other plans. No matter how much
her head held back, the rest of her was eager to plunge
in the deep end and just go for it. The attraction was
powerful and ten years after she'd first felt it, it didn't
seem to be going away.

The second problem was also a head-body issue.
However much her head could intellectualize that Jack
was nothing like Vance or her father, her heart didn't
believe. So she got close, he made a move, she reacted,
then the fear kicked in and she bolted. It was a horrible

pattern and short of never seeing him again in any capacity, she didn't know how to break it.

Whoever said acknowledging the problem was half the battle had obviously never lived in the real world. Understanding what was wrong didn't seem to move her any closer to solving it.

But solution or not, she owed Jack an apology and she was going to deliver it right now. Or in the next few minutes, she thought as she paced in front of his office. Mrs. Wycliff glanced at her curiously, but didn't say anything. Finally Samantha gathered her courage and walked purposefully toward the door. She knocked once and entered, careful to close the door behind herself. She didn't need any witnesses for her potential humiliation.

"Hi, Jack," she began, before starting her prepared speech. "I wanted to stop by and—"

She came to a stop in the center of the room and stared at him.

He sat at the conference table, the speakerphone in front of him, notes spread out. He looked as if he'd received horrible news.

She hurried to the table. "What happened? Are you all right?"

He shrugged. "I'm fine. I had the phone call with several investors and some people from the street. It didn't go well."

Of course. The problems with Hanson Media Group. As if he weren't dealing with enough from that, she was torturing him on weekends. How spiffy.

"I'm sorry," she said, sinking into the chair across from his. "I'm guessing they had a lot of questions."

"Oh, yeah. Plenty of suggestions, too. None of them

especially helpful. But this is why they pay me the big bucks, right? So I can take the heat."

Maybe. But Jack wasn't interested in the money or the job. "Talk about a nightmare," she murmured.

"One I can't wake up from. But that's not why you stopped by. What's up?"

"I wanted to tell you I'm sorry about what happened on—"

"Stop," he said. "No apologizes required."

"But I want to explain. It's not what you think."

He raised his eyebrows.

She sighed. "Okay. Maybe it is what you think. I'm having some trouble making up my mind about what I want. I'm working on that. The thing is, I don't want you to think it's about you. It's not. It's about me, and well, who you are. Which isn't the same as it being about you."

He smiled. "None of that made sense, but it's okay. Let's just forget it and move on. You didn't like what happened and I'm okay with that."

She started to tell him that she *had* liked him kissing her, but stopped herself. That wasn't the point…at least she didn't think it was.

"You push my buttons," she admitted instead. "You have some qualities in common with my ex-husband."

Jack winced. "Not the good ones, right?"

"Sorry, no."

"Just my luck." He glanced out the window at the view of the city. Rain darkened the horizon and made the lights sparkle. "Life would be a lot less complicated without relationships."

"Not possible. Then we'd be nothing but robots."

"Or just very sensible people. Like Vulcans."

She smiled. "I'm not sure we should aspire to pointed ears."

"But their philosophy—no emotion. I understand the appeal."

"Too much pressure?" she asked, already knowing the answer.

"Too much everything. I remember when I was a lot younger. My brothers and I really got along. My father was busy with work, so there was just us and whatever nanny worked for him that month."

"I'm guessing the three of you were a handful."

He grinned. "Full of energy and imagination. It was an interesting combination. What I can't figure out is when we stopped being a family. That's David's big complaint and he's right. We don't pull together. I want to blame my father, but that only works so long. The three of us are grown-ups. We need a new excuse."

"Or maybe a way to change things. Would you like to be close to your brothers now?"

He nodded slowly. "Maybe together we could figure out how to fix this mess. But I can't get Evan and Andrew to return my calls. When it's time to read the will, I'll have to drag them back here. It's crazy."

"But they will come back," she said. "You could talk to them."

"I don't know what to say anymore. How sad is that?"

She had to agree it was pretty awful. If she had a brother or sister, she wouldn't ever want to lose touch.

"Maybe if you talk to Helen," she said without thinking. "She might have some ideas."

Jack looked at her. "No, thanks."

Samantha felt herself bristle. "What is it with you?" she asked. "Why won't you even give the woman a chance? Name me one thing she's done that you don't approve of. Give me one example of where she screwed up big time."

"I don't have any specific events," he said.

"Then what's the problem? You said you trusted my opinion of her and were going to stop assuming the worst." He made her crazy. Jack could be so reasonable about other things, but when it came to Helen, he refused to be the least bit logical.

"I don't think the worst," he said.

"You certainly don't think anything nice. She's pretty smart. Why don't you talk to her about the business?"

"My father wouldn't have told her anything."

"How do you know?"

"He didn't talk to anyone about the company."

"To the best of your knowledge. Did it ever occur to you that he might have married her *because* she's smart and capable? That maybe when things went bad, he talked to her." She held up both hands. "I'm not saying I know anything. But neither do you. You treat Helen like she's a twenty-one-year-old bimbo your father married because she had big breasts. It's crazy. You have an asset there you're not using."

He looked at her. "You're a very loyal friend."

"Helen makes it easy to be. Will you at least think about what I've said?"

He nodded. "Promise."

She was fairly sure she believed him. Jack had never lied to her. But why was this an issue in the first place? Why didn't he already know his stepmother's good points? Every family had secrets, but this one seemed to have more than most.

"It was just my mom and me," she said. "I can't relate to problems inherent in a large family."

"Want to trade?" he asked, then grimaced. "I'm sorry. I know you and your mom were close. You must still miss her."

She nodded, thinking she'd missed her most during the last few months of her marriage. When she'd wondered if Vance was really what she'd thought or if she'd been overreacting.

"We'd always had a special relationship," she said, "but we got even closer after my dad left. There was something about worrying about our next meal that put things in perspective."

"The man was a first-class bastard," Jack told her. "You haven't talked to him since?"

"He never wanted to talk to me. When I got older, I tried a few times, but eventually I gave up. He just wasn't interested. I heard he passed away a couple of years after my mom."

"I won't say I'm sorry. Not about him."

"I always think that things could have been different. I wasn't interested in him for what I could get. I just wanted a relationship with my father. But he never understood that. Why do relationships have to be so complicated?"

"Not a clue."

She stood. "Okay, I've taken up enough of your time. I just wanted to tell you that I'm sorry."

"Don't be."

"Thanks, Jack."

She left, not sure if she'd made things better or worse between them. She had a feeling that the only way to really solve the problem was to make a decision one way or the other and stick to it. If she was going to keep things business only, then she should not go to his office to chat. If she was interested in something else, then she should do that.

Complications, she thought. Questions and no answers. At least her life was never boring.

Jack returned from his working lunch meeting with the vice president of finance to find his stepmother waiting for him in his office.

Helen smiled when she saw him. "I was in the neighborhood," she said.

Under normal circumstances, he would have been polite and done his best to get her gone as quickly as possible. Since his last conversation with Samantha, he was curious to find out what Helen wanted.

He motioned to the leather sofa in the corner. Helen crossed the room and took a seat. He followed and settled in a club chair, then tried to figure out what was different about her today.

She was still pretty, blond and only a few years older than him. Not exactly a bimbo, as Samantha had pointed out, but still very much a trophy wife.

While she wasn't dressed in widow's black—did anyone still do that today?—she'd replaced her normally bright clothes with a navy tailored pantsuit. She'd pulled her hair back and, except for simple earrings and her wedding band, she seemed to have abandoned the heavy jewelry she usually favored.

"How are you doing?" he asked. "Is everything all right at the house?"

She frowned slightly. "I don't understand."

"You're alone in the house. I know it's large and I wondered if you were coping all right."

Eyebrows rose slowly. "You can't possibly be concerned about me."

He shrugged. "I'm asking."

"Hmm. All right. I'm doing fine. Yes, the house is big and empty, but your father worked long hours, so I'm used to being there alone."

Jack shifted in his seat and wished he'd never started the damn conversation in the first place. But he was already into it. "Are you, ah, sleeping?"

She sighed. "Not really. I still expect George to walk in and apologize for working late again. But he doesn't." She smiled. "Enough of my concerns. They're not why I stopped by. I wanted to check on you. It's been a difficult couple of weeks."

"You've been reading the paper."

"Several. There wasn't a lot of mention in the national press, which is something, but we're getting plenty of local coverage. I feel just horrible, Jack. I wish I could make this all better."

So did he. "Did you know about the second set of books?"

He watched her as she spoke to see if she got uncomfortable, but her cool gaze never flickered.

"I didn't. George didn't talk about the business very much with me. I wanted him to. I was interested. But he just wasn't one to do that. I do know that for the last year or so before he died that he was under a lot of stress. I had an idea there were problems with the company, but I had no idea they were this bad."

He wanted to believe her. Right now he had enough bad news without thinking there was someone making trouble from the inside. Not that Helen worked for the company, but until the will was read, she controlled his father's stock. Speaking of which...

"Do you know what's in his will?" he asked bluntly.

"No. He never discussed that with me, either."

"So what did you talk about?"

"Everyday things." She crossed her legs. "Jack, I'm not the enemy here. I always thought things would be better if you, your father and your brothers could reconcile."

"How magnanimous of you."

She drew in a breath. "So you still don't like me."

"I don't know you. Why is that?"

"I don't know," she said, surprising him. "I wanted to get to know you and Evan and Andrew. I invited you all over several times. You were the only one to come."

Jack remembered the lone uncomfortable dinner he'd attended. His father had spent the entire time telling him that his decision to go into the law instead of joining Hanson Media Group was foolish at best. That no good would come of it. Jack recalled walking out sometime between the salad and main course.

"He wasn't an easy man," he said.

"I know, but for what it's worth, I don't think he meant to be so difficult. He tended to see things one way."

"His."

"He wanted you to be happy."

Jack grimaced. "He wanted me to run his company, regardless of what I wanted."

"Here you are," she said softly.

"Lucky me."

"I wish things were different," she said. "I wish he weren't dead. Not just for me, but for you. I wish you didn't have to do this."

"There isn't anyone else," he reminded her. "I'm stuck."

"You're the best choice. I'm sorry this is taking you away from what you love but the company is important, too. We all have to make sacrifices."

"Not from where I'm sitting. So far it's a sacrifice committee of one. I wish I knew what was in the will. Maybe he left everything to you and I can screw up enough that you'll fire me."

She shook her head. "Don't hold your breath on that one. George was always interested in surprising people. I doubt he wrote a boring will."

He believed that. "If he left the company to me, I'm selling."

She stiffened. "Just like that? Your father gave his life to this company."

"I know that better than anyone, except maybe you."

"I loved him, which means I can forgive his flaws."

The implication being Jack should do the same.

He wanted to ask her how that was possible. How could she give her heart to a man who made sure she always came in second. But he didn't. There wasn't any point. People who were supposed to love you left, one way or the other. Some disappeared into work or circumstances. Some walked away and some died. But at the end of the day, everyone was alone. He'd learned that a long time ago and he didn't plan to forget it.

Chapter Seven

Samantha was reasonably confident that driving lessons were a bad idea all around. For one thing, Jack should be really mad at her. For another, the situation had the potential to turn into a disaster.

"Second thoughts?" he asked from the passenger seat of the old import parked in an empty parking lot.

"Oh, I'm way past them. I'm on to deep regret and remorse."

"You'll be fine," he said. "It's easy. Think of all the crazy people you know who can drive."

"Telling me I'm likely to encounter the insane isn't a way to make me feel better," she told him. "Really. Let's talk about all the safe drivers instead."

"There are a lot of them. You'll be one of them. All you have to do is relax."

Oh, sure. Because that was going to happen. She peered out the windshield and was dismayed to note there wasn't a single cloud in the sky. Not even a hint of rain or bad weather or impending anything that would give her a good excuse to call off the session.

"You don't have to do this," she said. "I could hire someone."

"I don't mind. It will be fun."

Maybe for him. She curled her fingers around the steering wheel and sighed. "I don't think I'm up to it."

"Of course you are. You're afraid, which makes sense, but once you let go of the fear, you'll be fine. Think of the end goal. You'll be driving. You can go anywhere you want. You won't be dependent on bus schedules or trains. You're free. Close your eyes."

She looked at him. "I may not know much about driving but even I know that's a bad way to start."

He laughed. "You'll open them before we go anywhere. Close your eyes."

She did as he asked.

"Now imagine yourself driving on a big highway. The lanes are wide and it's divided so you don't have to worry about oncoming traffic. There are only a few cars and none of them are near you. It's a pretty day. You're going north, to Wisconsin. Can you imagine it?"

She did her best to see the road and not the flashing telephone poles or trees beckoning her to crash into them. She imagined herself driving easily, changing lanes, even passing someone.

"Now see yourself getting off the highway. At the top of the exit, you stop, then turn into a diner. You're completely comfortable. You're driving and it's easy."

She drew in a deep breath, then opened her eyes. "Okay. I'm ready."

"Good. We've been over the basics. Tell me what you remember."

She talked her way through starting the car, putting it in gear and checking her mirrors. Long before she wanted him to, he told her it was time to replace visualization with actual doing.

She started the engine. Of course it sprang to life. She carefully shifted into D and then checked her mirrors. They were blissfully alone in the parking lot.

"Here I go," she murmured as she took her foot off the brake and lightly pressed on the gas.

The car moved forward. It wasn't so bad. She'd had a couple of driving lessons back in college and she'd enjoyed those. These weren't all that different.

"Signal and turn right," Jack said.

Signal? She flipped on the indicator then turned. Unfortunately, she pulled the wheel too far and they went in a circle. Instantly she slammed on the brakes.

"Sorry."

"It's fine," he told her. "Don't worry about it. We're here to practice. If you could get it right the first time, why would you need to practice?"

He was being so logical and nice, she thought. Vance would have been screaming at her the whole time.

"Let's try that turn again," Jack said.

"Okay." She drove straight, put on her signal, then eased the car into a turn. It did as she asked.

"Wow. That was pretty easy."

"Told you," he said with a smile. "We'll make a couple more laps of the parking lot, then go onto the street."

"The street?" she asked, her voice a screech. From the backseat Charlie raised his head as if asking what was wrong.

"You can't stay in this parking lot forever," Jack said.

"Of course I can. It's a great parking lot. I like it. I could live here."

"You'll be fine. Come on. More driving. That way."

He pointed in front of them. She drove for another five minutes, making turns and coming to a stop when he told her. Despite her protests, he managed to convince her to head out onto the actual street.

"This is an industrial park," he said. "It's Saturday. There aren't going to be a lot of cars. Deep breaths."

She held in a small scream then took the plunge. Or, in this case, the driveway onto the street. Up ahead was an on-ramp to the highway and all the open road she could want. Like a cat let out of a carrier, she traded freedom for safety and took a side street. The highway would still be there tomorrow.

"And?" he asked as they cruised the produce section of the local market.

"You were great," she said. "Just terrific. Patient, calm and happy to explain everything fifty times."

He shook his head. "While I appreciate the compliments, they weren't the point. Admit it. The driving wasn't so bad."

It hadn't been. After nearly an hour in the industrial park, she'd actually driven back into the city. There had been a single harrowing experience at an intersection when some jerk had jumped the light and nearly hit her, but aside from that it had been…easy.

"You're a good teacher," she said.

"You're a good driver."

She sighed. "I am, aren't I? Soon I'll be really good. Then I'll have my license."

"Then you can buy a car."

"Oh. Wow." She'd never thought in actual terms

of getting a car. "I like it. There are so many kinds. I could get a little convertible."

"Not a great choice in winter."

"Hmm. You're right. But maybe something sporty. Or an SUV. Then I could haul stuff on weekends."

"Do you have anything to haul?"

"I don't think so. Is it required?"

"The dealer isn't going to ask."

"Okay. Or maybe I could get a hybrid. That's more environmentally friendly and I always recycle."

He looked at her as if she'd suddenly grown horns.

"What?" she asked.

"Nothing. You about ready?"

She eyed the strawberries, then nodded. "I'm always tempted by out-of-season fruit. It's a thing with me."

He pointed to her overflowing basket. "You know, this store delivers."

"I heard, but I like to buy my own groceries. Check stuff out. What if I change my mind about what I want for dinner?"

"What? You don't carefully plan a menu for the entire week and then stick with it?" he asked.

She felt her eyes widen a split second before she realized he was teasing her. "No, I don't. But you rigid types plan everything."

"I've had a few surprises lately."

She was sure he was talking about the company, but she suddenly wished he were talking about the kiss they'd shared. That had been...nice.

She'd enjoyed knowing that her nerve endings hadn't died in the divorce and that, yes, eventually she would want to be with another man. Although she had a feeling that her powerful sexual reaction had specifically been about Jack, there was still hope for her future. Eventually she would find someone else to be interested in.

They went through the checkout, then Jack helped her load her bags of groceries into the trunk.

"Let's go," he said, opening the passenger door.

She stood on the sidewalk. "Wait. I can't drive back to our building."

"Why not? It's just around the corner."

"Yes, but once there, I'd have to park. I might even have to back up." She wasn't ready for backing up. Not on her first day.

"You can do it," he said and closed the door.

She glared at him for a full minute, but he didn't budge. That forced her to get behind the wheel and consider her options.

"I could just walk home," she said.

"What about your groceries?"

"You could carry some."

"But I won't."

He might not have screamed during their lessons, but he was very stubborn.

"Fine. I'll drive back, but if anything bad happens, you have to take over. And I'm seriously reconsidering the dinner I promised as a thank you."

"You don't have to do that. I was happy to help."

She looked at him. His eyes were dark and she couldn't tell what he was thinking. Maybe he didn't want to have dinner with her. After the way she'd overreacted to his kiss, who could blame him.

"I'd like to cook you dinner," she said. "But I'll understand if you don't want to come over."

"We're friends, right?"

She nodded.

"Then sure. I'll be there."

Friends. The way he said the word made her wonder if the statement had been to help him remember their relationship, or if it had been about telling her. Maybe he was making it clear that where she was concerned, he'd made his last move.

Jack arrived at Samantha's apartment exactly at seven. He'd brought Charlie, even though the dog was tired from his day and would only sleep. Still, if conversation got slow, they could always talk about the dog.

Pathetic, he told himself. He was completely pathetic. Yeah, he wanted to do the right thing where Samantha was concerned. Be a friend, a boss and let the rest of it go. But no matter what he told himself or how many times she rejected him, he couldn't seem to stop wanting her. Even now, standing outside of her door, he felt his body tighten in anticipation.

He knocked and promised himself that when he got home, he was going to figure out a way to get over her for good. But until then, a man could dream.

"You're here," she said as she opened the door and smiled at him.

"Was there any doubt?" he asked.

"I hoped there wasn't. Come on in."

He let Charlie lead the way, using the microsecond before he entered to brace himself to withstand the assault of color, gauzy fabric and perfume.

She'd changed out of her jeans and sweatshirt—both covered in sewn-on flowers—and into a loose top and flowing skirt that nearly touched the top of her bare feet. She was a kaleidoscope of color, causing him not to know where to look first.

There was her hair, long and flowing and curly,

but pinned up on one side. Her blouse that fell off one shoulder, exposing pale, creamy skin. Her feet with painted toes and at least two toe rings. Her arms, bare except for jingling bracelets.

"So you're back," he said.

She closed the door behind him. "What do you mean?"

"You've been a little conservative since you moved here. Oh sure, you've been playing basketball in the halls and wearing bright colors, but not in the way I remember. This is the first time you're exactly like you were."

She smiled. "That's about the nicest thing you've ever said to me. Thank you."

"You're welcome."

"Come on," she said, grabbing him by the arm and tugging him toward the kitchen. "I have wine and I'm going to let you be all macho and open it."

"It's what I live for."

They settled in the dining room with a bottle of wine and some appetizers. Charlie retreated to an ottoman, where he curled up on the cushy surface and quickly went to sleep.

"I can get him down if you want," Jack said, jerking his head toward the dog. "He's great, but he sheds."

"No problem. A few dog hairs will make the condo seem more lived in. Right now it's still too perfect."

"And we wouldn't want that."

She dipped a chicken wing into spicy sauce. "Life's beauty is found in the irregular and unexpected. Ever see a perfect waterfall? A symmetrical sunset?"

"Technically the sun goes down in the same way every—" He broke off and grinned when she swatted him with the back of her hand.

"You know what I mean," she said. "I'm talking about the clouds, the colors—and you know it."

"Maybe."

"My point is, dog hair is fine."

"Great. Maybe you'd like to take over grooming him, too."

"I wouldn't mind it. He's a great dog."

"I agree."

She sipped her wine. "I've noticed a bit more positive press in the past couple of days," she said. "There were at least two mentions of the upcoming advertisers' party. How Hanson Media Group is getting some things right."

"I saw them, too. David is doing a hell of a job trying to counteract the negative stories."

"You really like him."

"In some ways he's more like my father than George ever was. Or maybe a big brother. He's not that much older than me. He was always there, making time in ways my father wouldn't. Even though he traveled a lot, he kept in touch. He took the time. Sometimes that's all that's required."

"I know." She grabbed for a piece of celery. "After my father walked out, I missed him terribly. Sure there was the whole trauma of going from the rich princess to the kid in castoffs, but it was more than that. Given the choice between getting the money back and getting my father back, I would have gladly picked him. But either he didn't get that or he didn't care."

"I know he walked out on your mom, but didn't he see you at all?"

She shook her head. "One day he was just gone. That played with my head. How was I supposed to believe my father had ever loved me when he walked away and never looked back?"

She sipped her wine. "Mom was great. She really fought him. Some of it was about the child support. It's crazy that a guy that wealthy paid almost nothing. But he could afford excellent lawyers and they knew all the tricks. As for seeing me, he would make promises and then not show up. There was always a good reason. Eventually my mom stopped pushing. She saw that it was hurting me more to hope."

Jack couldn't imagine what kind of man simply walked away from a child. His own father—no poster child for perfect parenting—had at least gone through the motions. He'd shown up to graduations and big events.

"It was his loss," he said.

"Thanks. I used to tell myself that, too. Most of the time I even believed it. I grew up determined not to repeat my mother's mistakes. I didn't care if the guy had money, as long as I was important to him and we wanted the same things."

Her words hit him hard. Ten years ago, he'd been that guy, but she hadn't been willing to see that, or maybe she'd just never thought of him as more than a friend.

"Vance?" he asked.

"I thought so. He'd been married before, so he was cautious. I liked that wariness. It made sense to me. I could tell he liked me a lot, but he wanted to take things slowly and I respected that, too. In hindsight, I was an idiot."

"In hindsight, we all are."

"Maybe. But I was a bigger idiot. He talked about how his first wife had been obsessed with how much money he made. She wanted the best, the biggest, the newest. I decided not to be like her, so I didn't ask for anything. It took me a while to figure out that had been his plan all along."

Jack didn't like the sound of that. "He set you up?"

"I think so." She sighed. "Yes, he did. It's hard for me to say that because it makes my choice even more crazy. He's a cardiologist in a big, successful practice. When we talked about getting married, he was concerned about losing that. I wanted to reassure him."

Jack grimaced. "Prenuptial?"

"Oh, yeah. I was sensible. I read the whole thing. But I didn't bother to get a lawyer. Why spend the money? Later, I realized he'd played me. He'd made a joke that his first wife was so stupid that she wouldn't have been able to get past the first page. But that I was really smart and would understand it all."

She shook her head. "I don't know if it was ego or my need to prove I wasn't her. Either way, I did read it, but I didn't get a lawyer to and I missed all the subtleties."

Jack practiced criminal law, but he'd heard enough horror stories from co-workers practicing family law that he could guess the outcome.

"It wasn't what you thought."

"Not even close. Not only couldn't I touch his practice or any income from it, but everything of mine was community property. I got nothing of his and he got half of mine. The only bright spot is I didn't have a whole lot to take half of."

He reached across the table and covered her hand with his. "I'm sorry."

"Don't be. I learned an important lesson. My mother used to tell me the trick was to marry a rich man and keep him. I think the real trick is to not need a man at all."

"Speaking on behalf of my gender, we're not all jerks."

"I know." She squeezed his fingers. "I blame myself as much as Vance. There were warning signs. I didn't pay much attention to them."

While he knew intellectually that she was right—that she did have to take some responsibility—his gut reaction was to hunt down Vance and beat the crap out of him. Talk about a low-life bastard.

"Want me to have someone look over the settlement and see if anything was missed?" he asked, suspecting she wouldn't appreciate the offer of physical violence.

"Thanks, but I'm okay. I'm doing my best to put my past behind me. It's been hard. Not because I'm so crazy about Vance, but because I tried to be so careful and he made a fool out of me in so many ways."

"Which makes you naturally wary," he said.

"Oh, yeah. Between him and my father, I'm now convinced any man I meet is out to screw me, and not in a sexual way." She grabbed another chicken wing.

"Ah, isn't this where you say present company excluded?" he asked.

She looked at him. "I want to. You're a great guy, Jack. I know that."

"But?"

"You're still a rich, powerful man. I'm having a little trouble letting go of that fact."

"I see your point. Here we sit, you thinking if you trust a guy he'll take off and dump on you in the process. I'm convinced anyone I care about will leave. We're not exactly a normal couple."

She grinned. "I like to think there is no normal."

"Do you believe that?"

"Sometimes. I know that I can't be afraid forever. I'm trying to get myself back." She tugged on the front of her blouse. "Dressing like this, for example. Vance hated my bohemian ways. He kept telling me I had to grow up."

Jack frowned. "Your free spirit is one of your best qualities. I'm sorry he didn't see that."

"Me, too. But there it is. He liked me to dress a certain way, that sort of thing."

"Controlling?"

She shrugged. "He was a cardiologist. He had an image."

"I know lawyers like that. It gets bad for their wives after they make partner. Suddenly what was great before isn't good enough anymore. I don't get it."

"That's because you're reasonable. Not everyone is." She released his hand and leaned back in her chair. "Now that you know the basic story of my pathetic divorce, I hope you'll understand why I'm becoming the queen of mixed messages where you're concerned. I know my past doesn't excuse my actions. I don't expect it to. I just hope you'll understand and accept my apology."

He stared at her. Until that second he'd never considered there was a reason for her behavior that had nothing to do with him.

"What?" she asked. "You have the strangest look on your face."

He shook his head. "I was just thinking that you being cautious around me was about you, not me. On the heels of that I realized I can't separate myself from who I am. I come from a wealthy family, I have a challenging, professional career. I am, on the surface, a walking, breathing manifestation of everything you're not looking for."

"Exactly."

At least she was being honest, he thought grimly. "A lot for us to overcome," he said, going for a light tone of voice. "I guess I should stop trying so hard."

She winced. "I feel really horrible. You've been nothing but nice to me. And before, in grad school, I loved us being close. You were terrific. I know in my head that you'd never hurt me."

"It's the rest of you that can't be convinced," he said.

"Yeah. But I've also decided it would be a good thing for me to face my fears."

While he liked the sound of that, he wasn't sure why she should bother. "You don't have to."

"It's the mature thing to do and I like to think of myself as mature. I want us to be friends."

Great. So much for making progress. "We *are* friends."

"I'm glad. I really love my job and I don't want to blow this opportunity."

"You won't," he told her.

"I hope not. It's just that…" She pressed her lips together and looked at him.

In any other woman, he would swear he was being given an invitation. But with Samantha? He wasn't sure. Better to stay on the safe side of the road.

"Remember that time we were studying in the park and that woman's dog got away from her?" he asked. "She was running around calling for him and you said we had to help."

She grinned. "Yes. And you told me that a dog would never come to strangers so I said we had to tempt it with food. So we went to that butcher and bought bones."

He'd felt like an idiot, he thought, but he'd been with Samantha so he hadn't cared.

"There we were, running around, calling for a dog and throwing bones around. Every stray in a three-mile radius started following us."

"It was sad," she said. "I felt so badly for those dogs."

"You felt badly? You're the one who insisted we find a rescue place for them. Then it was my car we crammed them into. Of course you hadn't realized that dogs like to mark what they think of as new territory."

She winced. "I felt really horrible about the smell, but the dogs got adopted. So that's something."

"Unfortunately none of the new owners was willing to buy my smelly car."

He'd been forced to get rid of it for practically nothing. Still, it had been worth it, he thought, remembering how happy she'd been about the dogs.

She leaned close. "Doesn't taking the moral high ground ease some of the financial sting?"

"Not as much as you'd think," he said, finding his gaze riveted on her mouth.

Dumb idea, he told himself. On a scale of one to ten, ten being somewhere between stupid and idiotic, this was a twelve.

But there was something about the way she smiled and the light in her eyes. Something that spoke of promise and desire.

Hadn't he always been an idiot where she was concerned?

He shifted toward her and lightly touched her cheek with his fingers. He thought that if he gave her plenty of warning, she would have time to bolt before he kissed her.

But she didn't. Instead she parted her lips slightly and drew in a quick breath.

He took that as a yes and kissed her.

He moved slowly, only touching her mouth with the lightest of brushes. He kept his hands to himself, or at least didn't do more than rest one on her shoulder and the other on her arm. He waited for her to kiss back.

And waited. One heartbeat. Two. Then slowly, almost tentatively, her lips moved on his. She pressed a little harder, then touched his bottom lip with the very tip of her tongue.

It was as if she'd just taken a blowtorch to his bloodstream. Heat and need exploded and he was instantly hard. He'd heard that it took longer for a man to get aroused as he got older. Apparently he hadn't crossed that threshold yet.

But as much as he wanted to pull her close, to rub his hands all over her until she was wet and weak and begging him to take her, as much as he wanted to take off her clothes and run his tongue over every inch of her, he did nothing. He sat there letting her take control of their kiss. Let her set the pace.

When she touched the tip of her tongue to his lip again, he tilted his head and parted for her. She slipped into his mouth and traced the inside of his lower lip.

Everything got hotter, harder and more intense. The need to take control, to claim her, threatened to overwhelm him, but he was determined not to screw up again. She'd made it clear that he pushed all her buttons, so it made sense to go slowly.

But when she circled his tongue with hers and sighed, it took every bit of self-control he had not to reach for her. Instead he mentally ground his teeth in frustration. He kissed her back, but slowly, without letting her know how deep the passion flowed. And when she withdrew slightly, he straightened, as if he were unaffected by what they'd just done.

She ducked her head and smiled. "That was nice."

"Yes, it was."

She glanced at him from under her lashes. "I'm a complete adult and I accept responsibility for what just happened."

Was that her way of saying she wasn't going to back off and run this time?

"And?" he asked, knowing there had to be a punch line.

"No *and.* Just that. And me saying thanks for being patient."

"My pleasure." Although pleasure didn't exactly describe his painful state of arousal. He reached for another chicken wing and bit into it. In time, the need would fade to a manageable level. His erection would cease to throb with each beat of his heart and the temperature in his body would slowly cool. But until then, life was hell.

"You're going to have to go to a few Cubs games when the season starts," he said.

She laughed. "You're deliberately changing the subject."

"You noticed."

She smiled. "This is in an effort to erase the tension here and keep me from feeling awkward."

"Something like that." Some of his motivation was selfish. Thinking about baseball was a time-honored way to keep from thinking about sex.

Her smiled widened. "Okay. Then tell me everything you know about the Cubs."

"At least the news isn't getting worse," David said.

"Not exactly the sign of forward progress I would like," Jack said. "But it beats the hell out of our string of bad news. You've been working hard to get us favorable play in the press."

"It's my job."

Jack leaned back on the sofa in his uncle's office. "Helen came to see me last week. She wanted to talk about how I was doing. It was almost as if…"

David raised his eyebrows but didn't speak.

Jack shook his head. "It was almost as if she was worried about me."

"Is that impossible to believe?"

"Yes. Why would she care?"

"Why wouldn't she? You don't know anything about Helen."

"Do you?"

"Not really. George and I haven't been exactly tight these past few years. But I've spoken with her, spent a few dinners with her. She seems reasonable and intelligent. You might want to take the time to get to know her."

"That's what Samantha says. She's a serious advocate."

David smiled.

Jack narrowed his gaze. "What?"

His uncle's smile turned into a grin. "There's something about the way you say her name. So things are progressing."

"No and no. We're getting along. She works for me. That's it."

"Like I believe that."

"It's true. She is just getting over a divorce. I'm not interested in getting involved in that process."

"Have you considered the fact that you already are?"

Was he? Jack thought about the weekend, when he and Samantha had spent so much time together. Hearing about her past and her marriage made a lot of things more clear to him. But that didn't mean he was interested in her. Not in any way but sexually.

"I'm not involved," he told David.

His uncle nodded. "Keep telling yourself that. Eventually it will be true."

Chapter Eight

The company had gone all out for the advertisers' party. As this was the first one Samantha had attended, she didn't know if the stunning decorations, incredible view and fabulous food were normal or if this party was a little bit extra-special in an effort to soothe their accounts.

Either way, she was excited to be there and felt just like Cinderella at the ball. For once, she'd left her loose and comfy clothes behind and had instead worn a form-fitting strapless gown in dark apple-green.

The shimmering fabric very nearly matched the color of her eyes. She'd gone simple in the jewelry department, wearing vintage paste earrings that looked like amazing diamonds. The antique settings made them look like the genuine article. Last, she'd spent nearly two hours on her hair, curling it on big rollers and then drying it. But the effort had been worth it. Her normally tight, natural curls were now loose and sexy. She'd pinned up the sides and left the back to cascade over her shoulder blades.

She felt good and knew she looked her best. The question was had she done enough to dazzle Jack?

"Not that I care," she murmured as she made her way to the bar for the glass of white wine she would hold on to for most of the evening. She refused to define herself by a man.

Not that she was. Wanting to knock Jack's socks off had nothing to do with definition and everything to do with the fire she'd seen in his eyes last weekend when they'd kissed.

She saw David and moved toward him. It was early and most of the guests hadn't arrived.

"You look beautiful," he said with a smile.

"Thank you. Great place. I love the view."

From one set of floor-to-ceiling windows was the lake and from the other were the lights of the city.

"We have a lot on the line," David told her. "Are you rethinking your decision to take this job? This isn't Hanson Media Group's most shining moment."

"Jack asked me that as well. I meant what I said then. I'm excited about the opportunity to create something wonderful."

"I've seen the preliminary designs on the website. They're great. And I've been over the security you want to put in place. It could be called obsessive."

She laughed. "I'm sure I'll hear worse before the launch. The point is to make this a safe destination for children. I'm willing to do everything possible to make that happen. Even if it means driving the IT guys a little crazy."

David grinned. "Good for you. Next week let's set

up a meeting to talk about publicity for the launch. I've already reserved some space in a couple of kid magazines and there will be a few Saturday morning cartoon spots."

Samantha stared at him. "Television advertising?" She knew how much it cost.

"Jack said you were going to be the one to save the company. So he told me to think big."

She doubted Jack had ever said she would save the company but she knew the website expansion could go a long way to boosting the bottom line. Still, she was surprised and pleased to find out how much he was supporting her.

"I'll call you," she said. "I have a lot of ideas for the advertising."

"Why am I not surprised?"

She laughed. "I have ideas for pretty much everything."

"That's what Jack said."

There was something in David's voice that made her wonder what else Jack had been saying about her. Not that she would ask.

Several clients walked into the ballroom. David excused himself and went over to greet them. Samantha followed more slowly, wanting to give him a moment to talk before she moved close and introduced herself.

She'd done plenty of industry parties. They had a simple formula for success. She had to make sure she spoke with everyone, was charming and friendly and remembered their names. Then, during the second half of the evening, she needed to circulate, chatting about anything and finding subtle ways to talk up the company. She'd also learned to pay attention to anyone who seemed to be on his or her own. Being lonely at a party was never a good idea. Taking a little time to be a friend and then introduce the shy person to others went a long way to making the evening a success.

David spoke with the group of eight men and women. She waited for a lull in the conversation then moved in closer.

David smiled at her. "This is Samantha Edwards, one of our newest and brightest additions to Hanson Media Group. Samantha is working on an incredible expansion of our Internet site for kids."

One of the women raised her eyebrows. "Do I want my children spending more time looking at a screen?"

Samantha smiled. "Isn't technology so much a part of our kids' lives now?"

The woman nodded.

"It's a real problem," Samantha told her. "One I've been working on. My goal isn't to trap them inside for more hours, but to make their computer time more efficient, fun and safe, all the while making sure their homework gets done and their parents are happy."

"That's a big order," one of the men said. "Can you do it?"

She nodded. "Absolutely. Let me tell you how in two minutes or less."

She launched into the pitch she'd spent the last week perfecting, then stayed long enough to answer a few questions. When the group had moved away to sample the buffet, David took her by the elbow.

"Well done," he said.

"I believe in being prepared."

"Good. Let's go over here. I have some more people I want you to meet."

* * *

About an hour later, Samantha felt a distinct tingling on the back of her neck. Careful to continue to pay attention to the conversation, she casually looked around to find the source of her hyperawareness.

It didn't take her long to locate Jack standing by the window with two older men.

At the sight of him, she felt her blood surge a little faster. Her skin seemed to heat as her toes curled.

He looked pretty amazing in his tailored tux, but then he had the James Bond sort of good looks that were made for formal wear. The stark white of his shirt contrasted with his black tie.

Yummy, she thought, instantly recalling the kiss they'd shared and how her body had reacted to his nearness. Despite the fears left over from her previous marriage and her general wariness of men like Jack, she found herself wanting a repeat of their make-out session along with the time and privacy to take things further.

She forced her attention back on the conversation and away from Jack. After a few minutes, the tingle increased, then she felt a warm hand on the small of her back.

"Having a good time?" he asked everyone, even as he continued to touch her.

"Great party," Melinda Myers, the president of the largest string of car dealerships in the Midwest said. "Your father would be very proud, Jack."

Samantha guessed she was the only one who felt him stiffen slightly.

"Thank you," he said graciously. "Despite everything that has happened recently, I wanted to keep the family tradition going. Your business has been very important to us."

Melinda smiled. "Hanson Media Group has been a good partner for me. I don't want that to change."

"Nor do I," he told her.

Melinda nodded at Samantha. "I've been hearing great things about the new site for kids. Impressive. Samantha was just telling me about her plans and some innovative ways for my company to be a part of it."

"I hope you take her up on her offer," Jack said.

Melinda smiled coyly. "Of course I will. I know a good deal when I hear one. That's how I got to where I am now."

Samantha did her best to pay attention to the banter but it was difficult with Jack's fingers pressing against her skin. Heat radiated out from him, feeling hot enough to burn.

Warmth spread out in all directions, making her breasts swell and her thighs melt. She wanted to blame her reaction on the liquor, but she'd yet to take more than a sip of her wine. Her next best excuse was that she hadn't had much to eat that day.

A tall older man approached and asked Melinda to dance. Several other people excused themselves, leaving Samantha and Jack standing together beside the dance floor.

"So what do you think?" he asked, his dark eyes locking with hers.

She assumed he meant about the party and not her awareness of him. "The night is a hit," she said. "I had wondered how our advertisers would react to all the recent bad news, but they're taking it in stride. A lot of that is you." She grimaced. "I'm sorry. I know you don't want to hear that, but it's true. They see you as a capable replacement for your father."

"Nice to know they think I can do as well as a man who defrauded investors."

She touched his arm. "They don't mean it that way."

"I know." He set down his glass on a nearby tray. "Want to dance?"

She would never have thought he was the type to be comfortable on the dance floor and, to be honest, the thought of being that close to him was two parts thrilling and one part pure torture. Still, she'd never been able to resist things that were bad for her.

She set down her wine. "Absolutely."

He took her hand and led her to the edge of the parquet dance floor, then drew her into his arms. She went easily, finding the sense of being against him and swaying to music almost familiar. Had they done this before? In grad school? She didn't remember a specific time when they'd—

"You're frowning," he said. "I'll admit my moves are pretty basic, but I didn't think they were frown-inducing."

"What? Oh. Sorry. I was trying to remember if we'd ever danced together before."

"We haven't."

"You sound so sure of yourself."

"I am. I would have remembered."

Which meant what? But rather than pursue the question, she drew in a deep breath and consciously relaxed into the rhythm of the music.

The slow song allowed them to sway together, touching from shoulder to thigh. He clasped one of her hands while her other rested on his shoulder.

"Did I mention you look stunning?" he asked, his voice a low murmur in her ear.

"No, and because of that, I think you should have to say it at least twice."

"You look stunning. The dress is nearly as beautiful as the woman wearing it."

Ooh, talk about smooth. He certainly was a man who knew his way around a compliment. "I don't get much chance to dress up these days. It's fun for a change."

"And worth the wait."

The song ended, leaving her feeling as if she wanted more. A lot more. But this was a work-related party and she still had rounds to make, as did Jack.

"I'm off to dazzle," she said. "Thanks for the dance."

"You're welcome."

He held her gaze a second longer than necessary, and in that heartbeat of time, she felt her body flush with need. All the tingles and whispers and little touches combined into an unexpected wave of sexual desire.

Then Jack turned and disappeared into the crowd.

She stared after him, trying to remember the last time she'd felt safe enough to want a man. She'd spent the last two years of her marriage simply going through the motions of intimacy because it had been expected, but she hadn't enjoyed herself. She'd been too hurt and broken to let herself feel anything.

Had time begun to heal her wounds or was her reaction specifically about Jack? She knew what it was like to make love with him. The memory of their single night together had been burned into her brain. She remembered everything from the way he'd kissed her to the feel of him inside of her. He'd coaxed more orgasms from her that night than she'd had in the previous year.

Funny how a month ago she would have sworn she would never be interested in getting physical with a guy again in her life. But suddenly there were possibilities. Maybe not with anyone else, but certainly with Jack.

Jack didn't bother counting the number of times he was compared with his father and told he was nearly as great as the old man had been. He couldn't believe so many people could know about his father's mismanaging of the company and still call him a good man.

By eleven, he was tired and ready to be done with the party. But there were more advertisers to schmooze and more hands to shake. It came with the job.

Helen walked over and offered him a glass of scotch. "How are you holding up?" she asked.

She looked beautiful in a fitted gown that showed off perfect curves. Her blond hair had been piled on her head, giving her a regal air. He didn't doubt there were plenty of men willing to take her home for the night, or as long as they could get.

Had she done that? She was substantially younger than his father. Had she taken lovers to keep herself satisfied?

Then he pushed the thought away. Why was he once again assuming the worst about her? He'd lived in the city and traveled in similar social circles as his father and Helen. There'd never been a whisper of gossip about either of them.

"Not my idea of a good time," he said. "What about you?"

She glanced around the crowd and shrugged. "Last year I came with George. I can't stop thinking about that and I keep expecting to turn around and see him. It's difficult."

She took a sip of her drink. As she shifted and the light spilled across her face, he could've sworn he saw tears in her eyes.

He did swear, silently, calling himself several choice names for his earlier thoughts. "You really loved him."

"Stop sounding so surprised when you say that," she told him. "Of course I loved him. I'm very intelligent and very capable. I didn't need to marry someone to get what I wanted from life. I could have done that on my own."

He wanted to ask why his father. What qualities had the old man shown her that he'd managed to keep from his sons?

"They're saying good things about you," she said. "They're happy you're in charge."

"So that sharp clanging sound I hear is the door closing on my freedom?"

"I don't know," she told him. "No one wants you to keep a job you hate."

"Except the board of directors."

"It's not their job to be compassionate. I suspect, over time, they would come to see that an unhappy president wouldn't be best for Hanson Media Group."

"I don't think I have that much time."

"You could be right." She took another sip from her drink. "I saw you dancing with Samantha. You make a very attractive couple."

"She's a beautiful woman."

"And a friend. You're a great guy, Jack, but I know how you are. Serial monogamy is great in theory, but sometimes someone gets hurt."

She wasn't being subtle. "You don't want that person to be Samantha."

"She's just been through a difficult time."

"I know about her divorce."

Helen smiled. "I wonder if you really do."

"What do you mean?"

"Be kind to my friend."

"I'll do my best." He shook his head. "You put her name on the short list. I'd wondered how it got there."

"I knew she would do a good job and I thought she was someone you could trust."

There was something in her voice that implied she knew more than she was saying. How much had Samantha told her about their previous relationship?

"Good call on your part," he said.

"Thanks. I have my moments." She looked around at the large gathering. "Ready to plunge back into the hordes?"

"No, but there's not much choice."

She glanced back at him. "I know you don't care or even want to hear this, but your father would have been very proud of you."

He didn't say anything because he was starting to like and respect Helen, but as she walked away he acknowledged she was right. He didn't care about what his father thought.

Samantha knew she was babbling. It was late, she was tired and hungry and she couldn't seem to stop talking.

"I think the party had a real positive impact on our relationships with our advertisers," she said as Jack stopped at a light. "There was so much good feedback and I have some great ideas to bring to the next creative meeting for the website."

He drove through the quiet, empty streets, nodding every now and then. She knew neither of them was really interested in business and that he already knew everything she was saying.

"The band was good, too," she added with a bright smile. "A lot of people were dancing. That doesn't usually happen at parties like this. But everyone seemed really relaxed. Didn't you think so? Weren't you relaxed?"

He stopped for another light and turned to glance at her. "You don't have to entertain me on the drive home," he said. "It's okay if we don't talk."

Great. So she'd bored him.

She firmly pressed her lips together and vowed not to say another word between here and the parking garage at their building. From there it was a short elevator ride to her condo.

Silence, she told herself. She could do silence.

"I like your car," she said before she could stop herself. "Is it new?"

"About two years old. Why are you so nervous?"

"Me? I'm not. I'm fine. I had a good time tonight."

"You sure didn't drink. As far as I could tell you didn't eat. So what's going on?"

"Nothing. I'm fine. Perfectly. See? This is me being fine."

He pulled into the parking garage and drove to his space. When he turned off the engine, he shifted so that he faced her.

"Are you worried I'm going to make a pass at you?" he asked.

The blunt question shocked her into silence. If she looked at things from the right perspective, life sure had a sense of humor. For the past few weeks she'd been hoping Jack wouldn't notice her as anything but a co-worker. Now she wanted him to see her as a desirable woman and he was worried she thought he was going to come on to her. Which meant he wasn't.

She'd spent the entire evening in shoes that made her feet hurt for nothing.

"Why would I worry about that?" she asked, not able to meet his gaze.

"Because of what happened the last time we were alone together."

Ah, yes. That magical kiss. "It was nice," she whispered.

"I thought so, too. Still do." He leaned across her and opened her door. "Come on. I'll walk you home."

He came around and helped her out of the car, then took her hand as they walked to the elevator. Seconds later the doors opened and they stepped inside.

She wanted to say something. Maybe invite him inside or at least come off as cool and sophisticated. But she couldn't think of anything good and she didn't know how to tell him she wasn't exactly ready for the evening to be over. Maybe in her next life she would understand men and deal with them better. In this one, she was batting a big, fat zero.

The elevator stopped on her floor. She turned to say good-night, only he was stepping off the elevator and leading her to her door.

She dug for her key in her tiny evening bag and clutched it in her hand.

Her place was at the end of the hall. Jack took the key from her, opened the door then cupped her face and smiled at her.

"You've told me no plenty of times," he said quietly. "Tonight your eyes are saying something different. Which should I believe? Your words or your eyes?"

Her stomach flipped over, her throat went dry and it was all she could do to keep hanging on to her purse.

It all came down to this. What did she want from Jack?

"Talk has always been overrated," she whispered.

"I agree," he said as he eased her into the condo and closed the door behind them.

She heard the lock turn just before he bent down and kissed her.

She instinctively leaned into him, wanting to feel his mouth on hers. When his lips brushed against her mouth, she wrapped her arms around his neck to hold him in place.

They surged together, need growing until her mind overflowed with images of them together, naked, craving. Even as she tilted her head and parted her lips, she dropped her purse on the floor and stepped out of her shoes.

He took advantage of her invitation with a quickness that heated her blood. He nipped at her lower lip, then swept his tongue into her mouth, where he claimed her with an eagerness that made her thighs tremble.

His hands were everywhere. Her shoulders, her bare arms, her back. She touched him, as well, stroking the breadth of his shoulders, before starting to tug on his jacket.

He quickly shrugged out of it, letting it fall, then he pulled off his tie. He broke the kiss, then turned her so her back was to him.

"Cuffs," he murmured as he pushed her hair over her right shoulder, then held out his hands in front of her.

But removing the gold-and-diamond cuff links was more difficult than it should have been. Even as she reached for the fastening, he nibbled on her bare shoulder, then licked the same spot.

Goose bumps erupted on her arms. Her nipples got hard and she felt the first telltale wetness on her panties.

At last she managed to free the cuff links. She started to turn, but he stayed behind her, put his hands on her hips and drew her back against him.

He was already hard. She felt the thickness of his need as he rubbed back and forth. Wanting filled her, turning her body liquid. He moved his hands up her body until he cupped her breasts.

Her curves were modest at best, but exquisitely sensitive. Even through the fabric, she felt his thumbs brush over her nipples in a way designed to make her his slave.

"I've wanted to do this all evening," he breathed before biting down on her earlobe. "That damn dress. You were driving me crazy. I couldn't decide which would be more erotic—coming up behind you and touching you like this or just saying, 'The hell with it,' and shoving my hand down the front of your dress."

Either would have taken her breath away.

"I want you naked," he murmured as he kissed her neck. "I want to touch you all over until we're both exhausted and then I want to do it all again."

He'd talked to her before, she remembered, her brain turning mushy from too many hormones and too little sex. She hadn't been with a lot of men, but except for Jack, they'd all been silent.

She loved his words. They not only turned her on, but they left no doubt that she did the same to him.

She turned in his arms and pressed her mouth to his. He kissed her with an intensity that shook her to the core. When she felt his fingers on her zipper, she trembled in anticipation of being naked with him.

Her dress fell in a whisper of silk. Underneath she wore tiny panties and nothing else. He continued to kiss her even as he brought his hands around to cup her breasts.

While she'd always wanted to be voluptuous, she had a theory that her small breasts had the same number of nerve endings as big ones, so hers were more sensitive. Apparently Jack remembered, because he touched her gently as he stroked her hot skin.

Fiery sensation shot through her, making it hard to keep breathing. Every part of her being focused on his touch as he moved closer and closer to her nipples. At last he touched them, first with just his fingertips. He lightly rubbed the very tips before squeezing them oh so gently.

She gasped with pleasure. He groaned, then broke the kiss and pushed her back. Seconds later three books, her mail and a plastic container of fake flowers crashed to the floor. Before she could figure out what he was doing, he lifted her onto the top of the wood console in her foyer, bent his head and sucked on one of her nipples.

Suddenly the mess didn't matter at all. She closed her eyes and arched her chest toward him. Her fingers tangled in his hair.

"More," she breathed as he circled her tight, quivery flesh. "Don't stop."

He didn't. He sucked and licked and circled and then moved to her other breast. He replaced tongue with fingers, arousing her with everything he did.

He put one of his hands on her thigh and moved it steadily toward her center. She parted her legs, then cursed the panties still in place as he rubbed her through the silk.

"Off," she begged, shifting on the console. "I need them off."

He grabbed them and pulled them down. When she was fully naked, he reached for her and slid his fingers into her swollen, waiting heat.

Heaven, she thought, barely able to breathe. Heaven and then some. He explored her, quickly finding her favorite spot, then teasing it. He shifted so that his thumb rubbed there and his first two fingers could slip inside of her.

Passion grew as her body tensed. She clung to him, barely able to absorb all the sensations. It was too fast, too soon. And yet…

"Jack," she breathed as she felt herself spinning higher and higher.

His only response was to suck harder on her breasts. The combination of pleasures was too much, she thought as she felt the first shuddering release of her climax. It overtook her body, leaving her unable to do anything but hold on for the ride.

She felt herself tighten around his fingers. He moved in and out, imitating the act of love. Toward the end, he raised his head and kissed her on the mouth. She kissed him back, then sighed as her contractions slowed.

She opened her eyes and smiled at him. "Wow," she breathed, both pleased and a little embarrassed at the speed of her response.

He grinned and then picked her up in his arms. She shrieked and wrapped her arms around his neck.

"What are you doing?" she asked.

"Taking a naked woman to bed. What does it look like?"

"A plan I can get into," she said, then lightly bit his earlobe. "Once we're there, you can get into me."

"I will," he promised. "In a second."

"What do you... Oh!"

He dropped her onto the bed, then quickly stripped out of his clothes. She gave herself over to the show, remembering how good he'd looked before.

Time had been kind. He still had a hard, sculpted body and his arousal was very impressive. She reached for him as he joined her on the bed, but he shook his head.

"Protection?" he asked.

She pointed at the nightstand and held back the need to explain that they were, in fact, very new. She'd bought them the day after he'd kissed her. More than a little wishful thinking on her part.

He pulled out the box of condoms and removed one. But instead of putting it on, he slipped between her legs and knelt over her.

"I want you," he said.

She saw the desire in his eyes and felt her body quicken with an answering need.

"Me, too. Despite my recent thrill ride."

"Good."

He bent down and kissed her belly. As he moved south, she knew what he was going to do. Politeness dictated that she at least offer him his own release before taking another of her own, but as she tried to speak, she remembered what it had been like that one night they'd spent together. How he'd kissed her so intimately, with an understanding of her body that had taken her to paradise so quickly.

"Just for a couple of minutes," she told him as he pressed his mouth against her. "Three at most."

He chuckled. She felt the movement and the puff of warm air. Then his tongue swept against her with the exact amount of pressure. He circled her most sensitive spot once, twice, before brushing it with the flat part of his tongue.

She was lost. Rude or not, she couldn't stand the thought of stopping him. Not when he made her feel so good. She pulled her knees up and spread her legs apart, then she dug her heels into the bed.

He moved faster, pressing a tiny bit harder. It was the most intimate act she knew and she'd trusted no one but him to do this to her. She might have trusted Vance, but he'd claimed it was disgusting, although he'd been plenty willing for her to do it to him.

Without warning, her body shuddered into orgasm. She lost control in a way she never had before. He kissed and licked and moved his fingers back and forth as she screamed her release into the night.

She lost track of time and reality. There was only the waves and waves of pleasure filling her. At last her body slowed. She felt him pull back. She reached toward him, not wanting to lose the connection, but then he was there, between her legs, pushing, filling her.

She opened her eyes as he slowly thrust himself inside of her. He was much bigger than his fingers and she felt herself stretching. The delicious pressure made her shudder again and again. She came with each thrust, milking him.

He braced himself on the bed and made love to her. Their eyes locked and she watched him get closer and closer. She wrapped her legs around his hips, holding him inside, feeling him climax and contracting around him as he did.

Chapter Nine

Jack opened the drapes and returned to the bed to watch the growing light creep across the room. He gently shifted the lock of hair curling across Samantha's cheek so that he could see the pale skin and the curve of her mouth.

She was beautiful, which wasn't news, but still struck him this morning. She lay across rumpled sheets, with the blanket tangled in her legs. Her bare arm stretched toward him and he could see her naked right breast.

Just looking at the tight nipple sent blood surging to his groin. He wanted her again, but after last night, he didn't think he should indulge himself. Three times was impressive, four was greedy. Besides, he didn't want to make her sore.

He touched her curls again, rubbing his fingers against the soft texture of her hair. He didn't even have to close his eyes to remember what it had been like the second time, when she'd straddled him, claiming him, moving faster and faster as her body gave itself over to pleasure.

He'd watched her as she'd arched her back, her breasts thrusting toward him, her hair spilling down, swaying with each thrust of her hips.

They were good together, at least in bed. But would she see that? Or would she revert to type—second-guessing what had happened and telling them both that this was all a mistake?

She stirred slightly, then rolled onto her back and opened her eyes. The sheet pooled around her waist, leaving her breasts bare and even after she'd seen him, she didn't try to cover herself.

"Good morning," she whispered. "Did you sleep?"

He nodded.

Her mouth curved into a smile. "You're looking so serious. What's wrong?"

"I'm fine."

She rolled toward him and touched his bare chest. "Then what?" she asked, her smile fading. "Are you sorry about last night?"

"That's your line."

"Oh."

He saw the hurt flash in her eyes and groaned. "Samantha, no. I didn't mean it like that."

She sat up and pulled the sheet so she was covered to her shoulders. Her messy hair tumbled across her bare shoulders and her mouth twisted.

"You did mean it like that and you have every right to expect me to bolt," she said firmly. "Based on how I've been acting, what else could you think? I'm sorry I was a total change-o girl."

He stared at her. "A what?"

"You know what I mean. I've been the queen of sending mixed messages. I hated that I was doing it and I didn't know how to stop. I've since given myself a stern talking to. I'm working on being in the moment and letting the future take care of itself. You've been nothing but terrific since I moved to Chicago. You're a great guy and I have no regrets about last night." She shook her head. "I take that back. I have one regret. That it took me so long to get you into bed."

He'd braced himself to hear a lot of things, but that wasn't one of them. "You're not sorry."

"Nope. Are you?"

He grinned. "Are you kidding? Last night was incredible."

"I do have a special talent," she said modestly, then smiled. "Okay, what happens now? What are your usual rules of play?"

"You assume I have rules."

"All guys do. Tell me what they are and I'll tell you if I agree."

Dangerous territory, he thought. Although maybe not. Samantha was coming off a rough divorce. He doubted she was looking for anything serious any more than he was.

"Serial monogamy," he said. "We stay together as long as it's good. No forever, no hurt feelings when it's over."

She batted her eyes. "So you'd be, like, my boyfriend."

He chuckled. "If that's what you want to call it."

"Would we get matching tattoos?"

"Never."

"Would we make love?"

"Almost constantly."

She flopped back on the bed. "What makes you think I want you?"

"Last night you were screaming."

Her cheeks darkened with color. "I don't remember that."

"Trust me. You screamed."

Her humor faded. "You've been really patient with me, Jack. I've been so scared about messing up and being taken. I thought it was best to just avoid any kind of relationship. But that's no way to live. Complicating the situation was my reaction to you."

He took her hand in his and rubbed her fingers with his thumb. "What reaction?"

"You know, mine."

"You have to be a little more specific."

She sighed. "Look at the situation logically. If I didn't want to get involved, why didn't I just stay away from you? Why did I keep coming back for more?" She shrugged. "You've always been something of a temptation."

He liked the sound of that. "Since when?"

"Since before. When we were in grad school."

What? "You blew me off. You said it was a mistake."

"I was scared."

"Not of me. What did I ever do wrong?"

"Nothing. That's my point. My fears were about me. But even they weren't enough to keep me away. I was so torn. You were a lot like my father in that whole rich, powerful way and I didn't know how to handle it."

Which meant he was also like her ex-husband. How did he convince her that he wasn't the enemy? That he wasn't interested in hurting her?

"I never forgot that night we shared," she said, not quite meeting his gaze. "After a while I convinced myself that I'd made it better than it was in my mind. That no one was that good. After last night, I know I was wrong."

He wanted to tell her that their incredible time in bed together had a whole lot more to do with chemistry than with him, but it was kind of nice having her think he was special.

"At least half of last night was about you," he said. "You're very responsive."

"Not all the time. Pretty much only here. So is this okay? Is this what you want?"

He nodded. "I'll be your boyfriend."

She laughed. "That sounds nice. I could use a little normal in my life right now."

"Normal?" He moved in close and pressed his lips against her ear. "Not normal. I have some very kinky fantasies in mind."

"Really? Like what?"

Samantha finished her speech to nods and smiles. She collected her materials and returned to her seat at the side of the room.

This had been her first ever presentation to a board of directors and it had been pretty high up on the nightmare scale.

"Sort of like facing down seven stern principals in school?" David asked in a low voice.

"Worse," she whispered. "Do they all have to look so disapproving?"

"It comes with being on the board. They're supposed to take things very seriously."

"Obviously. I'm just glad I wasn't trying to do stand-up."

She reached for her cup of coffee and swallowed the tepid liquid. When this was all over, she owed Jack a big apology. He'd insisted everyone practice their presentations several times before the board meeting. They had all endured long evenings, perfecting their pitches.

At the time, she'd thought his anal obsession was foolish. Wouldn't spontaneity be more interesting? But having just endured the stern expressions and pointed questions, she realized the importance of being prepared.

"I'm up next," David said as he was called.

Samantha leaned back in her chair and did her best to relax. She'd heard all the talks so many times, she knew what to expect and could tune out the words. So she found herself with a little time on her hands.

She used it to good advantage, turning her head so she caught sight of Jack sitting at the end of the long conference table.

He looked good—all buttoned up and formal in his black suit. If she didn't know him, he could have seriously intimidated her. But she did know him—every inch of him. And there were some mighty fine inches.

She watched the way he listened intently—as if he hadn't heard every sentence at least a dozen times—and took notes.

He was a great guy, she thought happily. Smart, caring, funny. The man owned a dog. How was she supposed to resist that? If she hadn't known about—

Samantha stiffened in her seat as a single thought flashed through her brain, on and off, over and over again. She wasn't able to think about anything else, and as she considered the truth of the statement, she wondered what on earth she was supposed to do about it.

Jack wasn't just some guy she'd hooked up with. He wasn't just an old friend or a new boss or a terrific lover. He was all that and much more.

He was the one who got away.

The board meeting was endless and three kinds of torture, Jack thought when the presentations finally finished. The board excused everyone but Helen and him. He thanked his team as they left and braced himself for the inevitable confrontation. He'd put it off as long as he could, but there was no going back now.

Baynes, the chairman, waited until the door closed before looking at Jack. "You've pulled the team together. I'm impressed."

Jack nodded, but didn't speak.

"Obviously our goal is to keep Hanson Media Group alive. Between the bad stories in the press and troubles internally, that's a challenge. You're well on your way here. The new programs are very exciting. But we need to do more. We need to provide stability over the long haul."

Several of the board members nodded in agreement. Helen shook her head.

"We don't have to do anything right now," she said. "I know where you're going and it's too soon. If we simply announce Jack as the new president, it will be seen as a knee-jerk reaction. Let's think this through."

Samantha might sing her friend's praises, but obviously Helen, like the board, was ready to sell him out if that's what was best for Hanson Media Group.

"Helen, it's necessary. Do you want to see George's legacy bankrupt, or worse, lost in some mega-conglomerate takeover?" Baynes shrugged. "I don't. The only way to keep Hanson Media Group going is to announce a permanent president. Jack, I know you're anxious to get back to your law practice, but we all have to make sacrifices. It's time for you to make one. I'm asking you to accept the job."

Jack looked at the older man. "What sacrifices are being made aside from mine?" he asked calmly.

"You know what I mean," Baynes told him.

"Actually, I don't. I'm not interested in running Hanson Media Group any longer than the three months I've already agreed to."

Several of the board members started speaking at once.

"This is a family company. Always has been. You owe it to your father."

Not an argument designed to get his vote, Jack thought grimly.

"Think of the stockholders. What about them?"

"You're the best man for the job. The only man."

Baynes quieted them. "Jack, your family owns the largest percentage of stock, but we still have an obligation to the financial community."

"I find it hard to believe you can't come up with a single qualified person to take over this company," Jack said. "Have you even been looking?"

"You're the one we want."

"Has it occurred to any of you that forcing Jack to stay when he doesn't want to is incredibly foolish?" Helen asked. "Someone unhappy in the position isn't to anyone's advantage. Now if he wanted to be here…"

"I don't," Jack said flatly.

Baynes narrowed his gaze. "I would think you, Helen, of all people would want a family member in charge of the company."

She leaned forward. "I agree that Jack is very qualified and I trust him implicitly. But I see no advantage in guilting him into staying on. It's a short-term solution and I don't want that. We're doing fine for the moment. Let's not make a change before we have to. Leave Jack alone to do his job. In the meantime, we can be looking for a suitable replacement. If there isn't one, then Jack gets my vote."

"I don't like it," Baynes said.

"Just so we're all clear," Helen continued, "until George's will is read, I control his voting stock, which means I get the final say." She looked at Jack. "I still believe you owe your father but I'm reluctant to put his legacy in the hands of someone who doesn't respect his vision."

Not respecting his father's vision was the least of it, Jack thought. But before he could protest, Baynes cut in.

"What do you know about the will?" he asked Helen.

"Nothing," she said. "I'll find out when everyone else does. That's not my point. We have time to think this through and make the right decision for Hanson Media Group. As long as the company is moving in the right direction, then I say let it be."

Samantha paced the length of Jack's office, then turned around and walked back the other way. He'd already been in with the board for nearly twenty minutes. What on earth did they have to talk about for that long?

Finally he walked in. She hurried over to him.

"All you all right? Did they pressure you to stay?" she asked.

He pulled her close and kissed her forehead. "You're worried about me."

"Well, duh. What did you think? Now tell me everything. You didn't accept the job permanently, did you?"

"What makes you think they asked?"

"It's just a matter of time until they start pressuring you. You're doing a great job. Why wouldn't they want to keep you?"

He led her over to the sofa, then pulled her down next to him. "You're right. That's what they wanted. Helen held them off, saying they should make sure they had the right candidate. While I'm not interested in staying, at least she bought me some time." He took her hand. "She's not on my side in this. She cares about the company."

She leaned back into the leather sofa and sighed. "You don't know that."

"Actually, I do. I respect her position. If I were her, I'd do the same thing."

"But you're not her. You still want to leave."

"I *will* leave."

She looked at him. "Were they all upset?"

"They weren't happy but until the will is read, Helen controls the majority of the stock. That puts her in power." He pulled her close. "Don't kid yourself, though. If she decides she needs me to stay, she'll be the first one holding out the employment contract."

"I don't want to argue about Helen," she told him.

"Me, either." He stood and crossed to a glass cabinet by the window. After opening one of the doors, he held up an empty glass. "Want a drink?"

"No, thanks."

He poured one for himself and took a sip. "I don't know where everything went wrong with my dad and his sons."

"You probably never will. Sometimes families have trouble connecting."

"If Mom hadn't died…" He shrugged and took another sip.

She stood. There was something different about Jack. He was hurting and that pain made him vulnerable. She'd never seen him as anything but strong and powerful, so this side of him surprised her.

She crossed to him and put her arms around him. "You did the best you could."

"Maybe. Can we change the subject?"

"Sure." She gazed up into his eyes. "You were right about making us practice. It made a big difference."

He smiled and put down his drink. "I'm right about a lot of things."

"Yes, you are."

He put his arms around her and drew closer. "I was right about you and the job."

She laughed. "So we're going to make a list of all your perfections?"

"I have the time."

She glanced at the closed door. "Or we could do something else."

He raised his eyebrows. "Ms. Edwards, it's the middle of a workday."

"Yes, it is."

"Are you making advances at me?"

"Actually, I was just sort of noticing how very big your desk is. I like a big desk."

Chapter Ten

"You've sent them e-mails?" Jack asked, frustrated because he already knew the answer to the question.

"Repeatedly," Mrs. Wycliff said. "I also sent letters using overnight delivery. I know the letters were received—Evan and Andrew had to sign for them."

His brothers were ignoring his attempts to get in touch with them. He suspected they were following the financial news and knew about the trouble with the company. He had a feeling neither of them would resurface until things were better or it was time for the reading of the will—whichever came first.

Someone knocked on his open door. He glanced up and saw David standing in the doorway.

Jack excused his assistant and waved in his uncle.

"Did you hear?" he asked.

"Most of it," David said. "Evan and Andrew are still refusing to get in touch with you?"

Jack nodded. "I don't suppose either of them has contacted you and asked you not to say anything about it."

"Sorry, no."

"We haven't spoken in years," Jack said. "How the hell did that happen? When did this family get so screwed up?"

"Your mother's death didn't help."

"I was just thinking that a few days ago. If she'd been alive, so much would have been different, but with her gone it was easy to go our separate ways."

"George didn't help," David admitted. "He was more interested in the business than in his family."

Jack nodded slowly. "I remember when I was young, people would tell me I was just like him. That always scared me. I knew I loved my father, but I wasn't sure I liked him. I wanted more than that from my kids."

"You don't have any kids," his uncle reminded him.

"I noticed that, too. After Shelby..." He shook his head. No reason to go there. "I think one of the reasons may be it's the only way to make sure I don't repeat his mistakes."

"Kind of like cutting off your arm to make sure you don't get a hangnail."

"You're saying I'm taking things to the extreme."

David shrugged. "You know what your father did that you didn't like. So don't do that."

Sounded simple enough. "When I was a kid, I didn't know what I was doing that made people think I was like him, so I didn't know how to stop doing it."

"You're not a kid anymore."

"None of us are," Jack said. "I haven't talked to Evan and Andrew in years and ever since I've been working at this damn company, I miss them. Oh, sure, I want them home to do what they need to be doing. I want them to help out. But I also want to talk to them. Hang out. Like we used to. We were a family once."

"Maybe it's time to make that happen again," David said. "Maybe it's time to start pulling together instead of pulling apart."

"I'm willing. What I don't know is how to do it. I can't even get my brothers to return my e-mails. I'm ready to resort to threats."

"Might not be a bad idea. Get them back for any reason, even if it's just to protect their personal interest."

"I agree," Jack said, "but I don't like it. They're my brothers. I shouldn't have to use threats to get them to communicate with me. There has to be another way."

"I'm out of ideas," David told him.

Jack was, too, but he knew someone who might not be.

"How do I get my brothers back?" Jack asked.

Helen raised her eyebrows. "Why do you think I would know the answer to that?"

"Because I've finally figured out you know us a whole lot better than we know you. I need them here and I'll do anything to get them in Chicago."

"Even ask for my help." She smiled. "Evil stepmothers are often invisible. It can come in handy."

"I never thought you were evil."

"I know. You simply didn't think of me at all. I wasn't trying to be your mother. I just wanted to be a friend."

"I couldn't think of you as anything but my father's wife."

"His *second* wife," she said. "We all know what that means."

Had she wanted more? Had she wanted it all?

She didn't have children, he thought. And at her age, she was unlikely to have any. Had his father been the reason there weren't any little Helens running around? Maybe George would have had better luck with a second family.

She held up both her hands. "Okay, this conversation is getting out of hand. Since your dad died, I've been living on the emotional edge and if we continue like this any longer, I'm going to find myself sobbing uncontrollably. I think we'd both find that uncomfortable. So let's talk about your brothers. Who do you want to start with?"

"I'll let you pick."

She considered for a moment. "Andrew will come home for money. You're going to have to be blunt. Either he shows up or you cut him off. Cruel but effective. You might want to start by cutting off one of his credit cards so he gets the message."

"Done," Jack said. "And Evan?"

Helen sighed. "He'll come home for the reading of the will. He always wanted to be close to George and he'll be looking for closure."

"Then if Dad left him anything, it would prove Evan mattered to him?"

"Something like that."

"I hope he's not disappointed," Jack muttered.

"Me, too."

"I know you loved the old man, but he wasn't exactly father of the year."

Helen nodded slowly. "He tried, in his own flawed way. He loved you all."

"He loved the business more."

"No. He loved it differently. It was safe to let everyone know how he felt about the business. It never went away and did something he didn't approve of."

"Like his sons," Jack said.

"Some parents have trouble understanding that when a child makes a decision that the parent doesn't approve of, it's not personal. Children are their own people—they have to make their own lives."

"My father wanted me to live his life."

She smiled. "He couldn't understand that what you chose to do for your career had nothing to do with him. He's the one who gave you choices, and then he was angry with what you picked."

"So was I," Jack admitted. "It was as if he'd changed the rules partway through the game."

"He had, but he still loved you."

Jack studied the woman who had married his father. She looked different since the funeral. She'd become elegant in her sorrow.

He could see why his father had been drawn to her. The combination of brains and beauty.

"You were good to him," he said.

She smiled. "You don't actually know that."

"Yes, I do. It's there in the way you talk about him. You were more than he deserved. He got lucky when he picked you."

"Maybe I was the lucky one."

She was consistent. He would give her that.

He narrowed his gaze. "You're good at this, at listening and offering just the right amount of advice and encouragement. You should have had children of your own."

Helen stiffened slightly, which answered the question he hadn't asked.

"I, ah—"

"It was him, wasn't it? He said he didn't want to start another family."

She sighed. "It seemed like the right decision at the time."

"And now?" he asked.

"There's no going back."

He had the feeling that she hadn't asked for much in her marriage, but his father had refused her the one thing she'd really wanted.

"He was a selfish bastard."

"Don't say that. I made my choices and I loved your father. Knowing what I know now, I wouldn't change anything. He was a great man." She held up her hand. "You don't have to agree with me on that, but I know it to be true. I loved him. I will never love that way again."

There was a certainty and a power in the way she spoke. For the first time in his life, he envied his father. Not because he had any romantic feelings for Helen, but because the old man had been loved completely. Helen saw his faults and accepted them. She believed he was the great love of her life.

At one time Jack had wanted that for himself. He'd believed he'd found it with Shelby, but he'd been wrong.

"Back up," Jack said.

Samantha held in a low moan. "See, I was thinking I could go through life in Drive rather than Reverse. Sort of like letting go of the past. Don't you think that's important? To always move forward? It's a Zen thing. Or if not Zen, then something else Zen-like." She smiled brightly.

Jack looked at her. "We're talking about driving, not your life, and one isn't a metaphor for the other. You're going to have to learn to back up the car at some point, so why not now?"

She'd been afraid he was going to get all logical on her. "The Zen thing didn't move you even a little?"

"No."

"But you have to admit it was clever."

"Very clever. Now back into the parking space."

Had he always been this imperious? she thought as she carefully checked the empty parking lot.

There weren't any other cars to be seen, just ominous white lines marking parking spaces. Very small parking spaces.

"Go slowly," Jack told her. "Think about where you want the car to go, not where it is. Check for anything in the way, then back up slowly."

She wasn't sure when this had become the advanced class, but she was determined not to balk, despite nearly blinding fear.

She drew in a deep breath and looked at where she wanted the car to go. There was a tree there, spindly and gray. She briefly imagined the car's rear bumper only a foot or so from the tree, then she put the car in Reverse and slowly began to back up.

"Keep your eyes on where you want to be, not where you are," he said.

"Hey, don't try to out-Zen the Zen master," she muttered, still watching the tree. She got closer and closer, then put on the brake and slipped the car into Park.

Jack grinned. "Pretty good," he said and opened his car door. "Check it out."

She jumped out and ran to the front of the car. "It's perfect," she yelled, ignoring the slight angle of her car. "Perfect. I'm in between the lines and in the middle of the space." She tilted her head. "Almost."

Jack walked over and studied the car. She bit her lower lip. Not that she cared what he thought, except she did.

He put an arm around her. "Great job. Let's do it again."

Later that evening, Samantha showed up at his condo with salad fixings and two large slices of choc-olate-chip cheesecake. As she shifted the bakery bag to her other hand so she could ring the bell, she realized she'd never been to his place before. All their rendez-vous had taken place at her apartment.

"Why is that?" she asked as he opened the front door and waved her in.

"Why is what?"

She waited for his kiss before asking, "Why haven't I been here before? Are you keeping secrets?"

"Have a look around and see for yourself," he said as he took her packages from her. "I'll open the wine."

An invitation to snoop. How often did that happen? But before she could take him up on it, Charlie came racing toward her.

She dropped down and hugged him. "How's my handsome guy?" she asked as she rubbed his ears. "Did you have fun this morning at the park?"

Charlie yipped his response, then led her into the condo.

The foyer opened onto a large living room with a to-die-for view of the lake and shoreline. To the left was a U-shaped kitchen with a high granite bar and three stools. Beyond that was a dining alcove that also looked out on the water.

"This place must be terrific during thunderstorms," she said.

"It is. Most weather looks pretty good if you're up high enough."

She took the glass of wine he offered and sipped. The color palette was typical guy—cream walls, beige furniture, black accent tables and cabinets for way too many electronics. Except for the fact that everything was new and expensive, the room reminded her a lot of what he'd had in grad school.

"Despite your fear of it," she said with a grin, "color doesn't kill. Imagine what this place would be with a red accent pillow or a bowl of green apples."

"Imagine."

Even his artwork was subdued—the two seascapes were muted and dark. There was an impressive abstract in the dining room that was mostly reds and oranges.

"This looks out of place," she said. "I'm guessing you didn't buy it."

He stared at the painting for a long time. Samantha got a twisted feeling in her stomach. There were memories in that painting. Good or bad? she wondered, knowing there was danger in both.

"Helen gave me that when I made partner," he said quietly. "It was her way of reaching out to me. I should have seen that before, but I didn't."

Samantha studied the painting again and felt the relief sift through her. "Helen always had great taste."

He waved toward the entrance to the hallway. "Have at it."

"If you insist."

The first door on the right opened to a small powder room with a pedestal sink. Next was a home office with a television on the wall and more law books than she'd ever seen in her life. There was also a very large and squishy-looking bed for Charlie. She found a linen closet—mostly empty and painfully neat, and, last but not least, the master bedroom.

Once again beige ruled the day. A beige-and-cream bedspread covered the dark wood sleigh bed. There weren't any throw pillows, nothing decorating the nightstands. Just lamps, a clock and a TV remote.

An armoire stood opposite the bed. She would bet money that inside there was a television, because God forbid he should miss a single play of whatever sports game he was watching. More massive windows offered an incredible view, while the master bath had a steam shower and a tub big enough for two.

Gorgeous, she thought, but impersonal. There weren't any family pictures, no little items picked up on travels, no magazines lying around. No memories.

"What do you think?" he asked as he walked into the room and leaned against the door frame.

"Beautiful, but a little too beige for my taste."

"Sorry. I tried to get out and buy a throw for the bed, but time got away from me."

She laughed. "Do you even know what a throw is?"

"Sure. It's something that you, ah, throw."

"What does it look like?"

"It's brown."

She grinned. "You're hopeless."

"You should even be impressed that I could use *throw* in a sentence."

"I am."

He walked toward her and took her hand. "Come on," he said. "I'll build us a fire. We'll get wild back here later."

"I like that idea."

She curled up on the sofa while he put in kindling,

then actual wood logs. Minutes later, when the fire had taken hold, he joined her on the sofa.

"Comfy?" he asked.

She nodded as she angled toward him. Then, thinking about the lack of personal touches, said, "You know all about my past, but you never talk about your own."

Nothing about his expression changed, still she sensed him pulling back a little.

"Too sensitive a topic?" she asked.

"Not for me. What do you want to know?"

"What you've been doing for the past ten years," she said, speaking honestly. "Romantically, I mean. I know all about your checkered career path."

"Checkered? I was a lawyer."

She smiled. "Exactly. Environmental law I could have understood."

"Because you have an inherent love of tree huggers."

"Absolutely. But criminal law. That's a little scary."

"Everyone deserves the chance to be defended."

She sipped her wine. "I don't actually agree with that. Some people don't deserve anything but punishment."

"How can you know they're not innocent?"

He was being logical, one of his more annoying features. "Sometimes you just know." She sighed. "Okay, perhaps it's best I'm not in charge of our criminal justice system. Which is why you'll be a much better judge than me. But this isn't what I wanted to talk about."

"You want to know about my love life."

"Pretty much."

He shrugged. "Shelby's the most significant relationship and you know about her."

That she'd died. "That must have been so horrible."

"It wasn't fun. After her, I didn't date for a long time."

"Because you were still in love with her?"

His mouth straightened, which didn't tell her all that much about what he was thinking. She tried to read the emotions in his eyes, but they flashed by too quickly.

"I'm not sure it was love as much as I didn't want to answer questions. I never knew when to tell someone I was dating that my fiancée had been killed shortly before the wedding. Too soon and it looked like I was fishing for sympathy. Too late and I was accused of keeping secrets. It was easier not to get involved at all."

Which all sounded reasonable, she thought, but she didn't buy into it. He didn't date because it was too hard to explain his past? Maybe for someone else, but not Jack. He was used to thinking on his feet. As for making a convincing argument, it was what he did for a living.

"So you avoided relationships?" she asked.

"Serious ones. I've fallen into a pattern of serial monogamy and it's working for me."

"Don't you get lonely and want more?" She held up her free hand. "I'm asking intellectually. I'm not fishing."

"You mean love and happily-ever-after." He shook his head. "I'm not a big believer in that. Are you?"

"I shouldn't be," she said slowly. "What with my divorce and all. But I know love exists. I loved Vance, at least at first. Helen loved George."

"Maybe it's something women are good at," Jack said.

"Meaning men aren't? There's an abdication of responsibility."

"I don't know a whole lot of guys who are in happy

relationships. Did my father really love Helen? I hope so, for her sake. But from what I saw about the old man, it seems unlikely. My brothers have sure stayed away from anything serious. Even David, who is the most normal, centered guy I know, has managed to avoid marriage."

"Are you saying it's a bad deal for men?"

"No. I'm not advocating that guys need to screw around. I don't know how anyone gives with his or her whole heart. How do you take that step of faith? In my world, people you love leave."

"Including Shelby?"

"Especially Shelby."

But his fiancée had died, Samantha thought. Was it fair to blame her for something that wasn't her fault?

"Is that why there aren't any pictures of her around?" she asked. "Because you're angry with her?"

"I stopped being angry a long time ago. It's not about anger. It's about letting go."

She took another sip of her wine and sighed. "It's funny—I'm fighting you on your theory about giving it all and truly falling in love when I know Vance didn't love me. Not the way I loved him. I don't know what he felt. If you were to ask him, he would swear he loved me. He would talk about all the ways he proved it. But that wasn't love."

"What was it?"

She didn't mean to say anything. The word just sort of slipped out. "Control."

Jack raised his eyebrows, but didn't speak. She found herself filling the silence.

"He wasn't like that before we got married. At least not so much. He might make a suggestion about something I was wearing, or what I planned to cook for dinner. I thought he was interested. I thought it was a good thing."

"It wasn't?"

"No. He began to monitor my life. How much time I spent at work, how long it took me to get home. He wouldn't let me wear certain things. He said they were too sexy. He accused me of being interested in a couple of guys at work, which was crazy. I wasn't interested in anyone. Then he started telling me it didn't matter because no one…"

She swallowed. Okay, how had she gotten into *this* conversation. Big mistake.

"Because no one what?" Jack asked.

She stared at her lap. "Because no one else would want me. He said I was lucky he wanted me."

"He abused you." Jack's words were flat.

She looked at him. "He didn't hit me." She made a harsh sound that was supposed to be close to a laugh. "Isn't that horrible? I told myself that for more than two years. He wasn't hitting me so it couldn't be abuse. He was just tired, or I'd made him angry. But he would scream at me and make me feel useless and small. I told myself I was letting it happen, because no one can make you feel anything if you don't let them, right? So there was something wrong with me. But I didn't know how to fix it and Vance was always there, in my face, speaking my worst fears."

She felt the tension in Jack and didn't want to know what he was thinking. Just talking about her past made her feel small and ashamed.

"I was a fool," she said quietly. "I equated attention with love. Vance was attentive. Too attentive. He separated me from my friends, my mom, he didn't like me spending long hours at work. I saw what I had become and I hated it. But I didn't know how to make it better."

"You left," he said.

She nodded. "I can't even tell you what happened. One day I came home and he was complaining about my clothes and my body and telling me I was stupid and I just snapped. I threw a vase at him. It hit him in the chest, then dropped to the floor. He screamed louder, saying I was in trouble now. It was like he was my father and I was his child. I suddenly realized I didn't have to be there. So I left."

Jack didn't say anything, but she could hear him thinking.

"You're judging me," she said, feeling defensive and vulnerable.

"No. You got out. That takes courage."

All the right words, but why was he staring at her as if she were a bug? "But?" she asked.

"I'm surprised it happened at all. You're strong and powerful. I wouldn't have thought a guy like that could mess with you."

"You're saying I should have seen it coming."

"No. Why would you? You trusted this guy. Any signs would have been…"

"Signs?"

He shifted uncomfortably. "No one changes overnight."

"I see. So you think I missed big clues. That I'm as much to blame?"

"No. Not to blame. If you'd never been in the situation before, you couldn't have known. You got out. You fought."

She stood. She hated this. Hated what had happened,

hated telling him. She felt exposed and flawed. Unworthy.

"We can't all make perfect decisions," she said, trying not to get angry, knowing her temper was a defense mechanism. "I screwed up with Vance. While it was happening, I kept wondering what I'd done wrong. Was I listening to my mother? Subconsciously trying to keep a rich powerful guy around so I would be safe? Only I wasn't safe. And if I knew that, why was leaving so hard? That's what I hate. How hard it was to go. How long it took me. I'm sure this is all too confusing for you. Your world is simply black and white. You don't get involved. You don't risk anything. That does make things simpler, doesn't it?"

"Samantha." He stood and moved toward her.

She flinched, then put her wine on the coffee table. "This wasn't a good idea. I need to go."

"Wait. We should talk."

Suddenly, she couldn't. The past was there, pressing down on her. He was wrong—Vance *had* changed so completely. There had been no warning. Vance had been so much like Jack.

She hurried out of the condo and ran for the elevator. Jack followed. The doors opened and she slipped inside.

"Samantha, wait."

But she didn't and when she got back to her apartment, he didn't bother to come after her.

Chapter Eleven

Jack had no idea what had gone wrong with Samantha. He mentally went over their conversation several times and still wasn't sure where they'd derailed. What had he said to upset her? Did she think he wasn't impressed she'd gotten away? A lot of women didn't. There were several cases in his law office, abusive husbands who had murdered their wives. Those women hadn't been able to get away, but Samantha had.

He clicked on another computer file, hoping work would distract him. Unfortunately, it didn't. He kept seeing the hurt in Samantha's eyes, the pain as she ran from him, as if he were just like Vance.

Vance. Is that where he'd gone wrong, saying that there had to be signs? He believed that was true. Maybe Samantha hadn't seen them, but he, Jack, was willing to bet that there had been clues.

Not that he would say that to Samantha now. He

doubted she wanted to speak with him about anything personal. He hadn't heard from her in a couple of days and he sure as hell didn't know how to open the lines of communication.

Under normal circumstances, he would simply accept that the relationship had unworkable flaws and move on. He'd told himself to do that just this morning. The only problem was he didn't want to move on. He wanted to know that Samantha was okay. He wanted to explain that he'd never meant to hurt her, and then he wanted to find a way to make it all right between them.

Yeah, right—because he had so much success in his personal relationships. Based on his track record, Samantha should stay as far away from him as possible.

He glanced at his watch and groaned. The last full staff meeting before Samantha's website launch was due to start in ten minutes. So he was going to have his desired chance to speak with Samantha. Unfortunately, it would be in front of her entire team and the IT guys.

He collected his notes and walked to the main conference room. Samantha and her people were already there, setting up their video presentation. Jack nodded and took a seat at the conference table, doing his best not to notice how feminine and sexy she looked in her loose, flowing blouse and long skirt.

"Morning," Samantha said, her smile bright, but still not reaching her eyes. "We're on schedule with everything. If you'll just give us a minute to fix a few last minute glitches, we'll be good to go."

"Take your time," Jack told her.

Arnie burst into the room and hurried to her side. After an intense, whispered conversation, Arnie handed over a memory stick, then grinned and took the seat next to Jack's.

"Hey," the younger man said. "Pretty exciting stuff, huh? We've been working day and night to get the website ready to launch. Some of the interactive stuff is going to blow everyone away."

"That's what we're looking for," Jack said as Roger walked into the room.

Arnie's boss sat across from Jack.

"Morning," Jack said.

Roger nodded, not looking happy. "This has all been rushed through," Roger said. "I hope we can meet the deadline."

Jack looked at Arnie, who shifted uncomfortably in his seat. "We'll get there, boss. You'll see."

Jack knew that the website wasn't Roger's idea of a good time. What he didn't understand was how someone could get to be the head of the IT department and not be interested in innovation.

Samantha stepped in front of the conference table. "All right, we're ready. Welcome to the new and improved Hanson Media Group interactive website for children. Today I'm going to give you a detailed look at the website—what's available, what's new, what we can expect to launch over the next six months. If you'll please direct your attention to the large screen on the wall, I'll begin."

Over the next ninety minutes, she outlined the website. Jack took a few notes, but mostly he divided his attention between the screen and Samantha.

She spoke with the confidence of someone who knew her material and believed in what she was doing. She fielded questions and offered opinions. When the discussion got too technical, she handed control over to Arnie, who explained things to the point where Jack was lost in a sea of computer terms.

When they'd finished, Samantha invited them all to the launch party Wednesday afternoon, when the site went live.

Everyone rose. Jack lingered until he and Samantha were the last two in the room.

"Good job," he said. "Arnie's worked out well for you."

She nodded. "He's been great. He's not only good at the technical stuff, but he understands the creative process. He's a big fan of yours and your dad's. He talks about George all the time. How George was really there for him."

"Good to know," Jack said. "Think he would be interested in running the department?"

She frowned. "Why do you want my opinion?"

"You've worked with him. You know how he thinks, what he's like. Could he do the job?"

"I think so. You're going to fire Roger?"

Jack sighed. "I don't know. I'm going to talk to him about his attitude. If he can't get onboard with what we're doing, then yes. It's never my first choice, but sometimes it has to be done. Given that, I would prefer to promote from within."

"Arnie's really popular with the IT team. That can be both good and bad. He might not enjoy the transition from one of the guys to being in charge."

"Once I decide what I'm doing with Roger, I'll talk with Arnie," Jack said. "I appreciate your candor."

She smiled. "No problem. As you know, I have opinions on nearly everything. Anything else you want to know about?"

What went wrong between the two of them, he thought, but before he could ask, she collected her files and tablet.

"Never mind," she said quickly. "I have another meeting."

And then she was gone.

She'd always done that, he reminded himself. Disappeared when the going got tough. Ten years ago, when he'd pushed for more, she'd resisted and then she'd retreated. She proved his point about people leaving.

So he should just forget about her. It was the intelligent thing to do. And he would. Just as soon as he figured out how to get her out of his head...and his heart.

"So what exactly is the problem?" Helen asked.

Samantha writhed on the cream-colored sofa and covered her face with her hands. "Nothing."

"Of course I believe you, what with how calmly you're acting."

"It's crazy. It's dumb."

Her friend curled up in the club chair opposite and tucked her feet under herself. "You screwed up."

Samantha looked at her. "Do you have to be so blunt?"

"It seems called for. What's the problem? Did you blow it with Jack? I know it's not work related. I've only been hearing good things about you in that respect."

"Really? What kind of things?"

"They would not be the point of this conversation. What happened?"

Samantha flopped down on the sofa and groaned. "I blew it. Seriously. I'm going to be a cautionary tale."

Helen waited expectantly but didn't speak.

Samantha groaned. "Fine, I'll tell you, but it's not pretty."

She detailed the conversation she'd had with Jack at his place a few days ago.

"I freaked," she admitted after she'd shared the specifics. "He didn't really say anything that bad, it was all me. I felt guilty and embarrassed and stupid. As if I'd disappointed him somehow. As if it were my fault. I didn't like feeling that way. I didn't know how to deal with it so I overreacted. Worse, I blamed him."

"Actually, I think the worse part is that you walked out without explaining."

Samantha raised her head and glared at her friend. "You're not being helpful."

"Of course I am. I'm telling you the truth. The problem isn't that Jack couldn't handle the past, it's that you still can't. You don't want to believe you were that stupid." Helen smiled. "I'm saying this with love. You know that, right?"

"Yes. I feel the love. Sort of. It's me. It's all me. I'm ashamed and I feel like an idiot. I'm strong and tough, just like Jack said. How did I let some guy abuse me? How did I let him cut me off from my support system? Why couldn't I see the signs?"

"Because you weren't looking for them. You took Vance at his word. That's not exactly a crime."

"Maybe not, but it turned out to be poor judgment on my part. I feel horrible."

"I'm not the one you should be sharing your feelings with."

Samantha rolled onto her side. "You're saying I need to go talk to Jack."

"I can't think of another way to fix the situation."

"But what if he hates me?"

"Gee, what if you stopped being so dramatic?"

Samantha grinned. "Okay. Hate is strong. What

if…" She sat up. "What if he doesn't respect me anymore?"

"What if he does? There's only one way to find out what he's thinking and that's to ask him."

Samantha knew her friend was telling the truth. "So when do I get to be the mature one in the relationship?"

"Next time."

"Ha. Like I believe that. You're so good at this. I guess it's because you had a great marriage. I want that. I want someone to love me and care about me, all the while seeing me as an equal."

"If you really want it, it will happen."

"Sort of like if you build it, they will come?"

"Yes, but this time in a romantic sense. If you know what you want, it's within your grasp."

Meaning Jack. Did she want him? Them? "We're doing the serial monogamy thing," she said. "Nothing long term."

"Okay, then after Jack."

After. Right. Because what were the odds of finding someone better than him? Someone more honest and funny and charming and better in bed?

"He doesn't want more," Samantha said. "He told me so."

"Do you know why?"

"Sort of. He doesn't believe people stay."

"A lot of people have left him, including you."

"I don't want to think about that."

"Maybe it's time you should," Helen said. "Why did you go?"

"Because I thought he'd hurt me. I thought he was too much like my father. But he's not. Although Vance was. This is confusing."

"What do you know for sure?"

"That I have to tell Jack I'm sorry."

Helen smiled. "Want me to show you out?"

Jack was home and he answered the door right away. Samantha had been hoping for a bit more time to figure out what she was going to say to him.

"Hi," he said and stepped back. "Want to come in?"

Just like that. No recriminations, no questions as to whether or not she was going to bite off his head.

"Thanks. Is this a good time?" she asked as she moved into the foyer and looked around for Charlie. Dogs were always a good distraction.

"Sure. What did you have in mind?"

He looked so good that she wanted to skip the conversation and suggest they move into the bedroom. He'd pulled on a sweater over worn jeans and pushed up the sleeves. He wore socks, but no shoes and had that weary end-of-the-day stubble that made her want to rub her hands against his jaw.

"I have a couple of things I'd like to say," she told him instead, not because it was the mature thing, and therefore the most Helen-like, but because she had a bad feeling he wouldn't be interested in sleeping with her right now.

Charlie came strolling down the hall, his yawn betraying his most recent activity.

"Did you just get up?" she asked the dog as she bent over and rubbed his ears.

"He had a tough day at doggy day care," Jack told her. "Apparently he played until he dropped from exhaustion."

That's right. Big tough ol' Jack took his dog to day care. How was she supposed to resist that?

"Come on," he said, leading the way into the living room. "Have a seat."

"Okay." She followed him, then perched on the edge of the seat cushion. "I just wanted to apologize for what happened the last time I was here. I kind of lost it."

He sat at the other end of the sofa and faced her. "You seemed upset."

"I was. And hurt and embarrassed. I sort of took all that out on you." Wait. There was no *sort of.* "I *did* take that out on you. I thought you were judging me."

"Samantha, I wasn't," he told her. "Never that."

"I figured that part out later. By then I was home and giving myself a stern talking-to. The thing is, I'm not proud of what happened with Vance. I still don't know how I let him take control of me, of the situation. I've tried to learn from what happened. The control thing started so small. With little tiny suggestions. They grew and before I knew it…"

She shrugged. "My point is, it was my problem. Your comment about seeing clues was valid."

"Maybe, but it was poorly timed," he admitted. "It's a guy thing—wanting to fix. I know better."

"You didn't do anything wrong. I just hated believing you think badly of me."

"Not that." He moved close and took her hands in his. "Never that. I admire what you did. You found yourself in a hellish situation and you got out. You fought. Shelby didn't."

What? "What does your late fiancée have to do with my poor judgment with men?"

He released her hands and stood. "I told you Shelby died shortly before our wedding, but there's more to it than that. She'd been depressed for a while. Looking back, I suspect she'd been depressed all her life.

We met during one of the times when she was feeling good. It didn't last." He walked to the window and stared out at the city.

"I didn't understand what was happening," he admitted. "She would get so sad and withdrawn. It was almost as if she disappeared from life. I thought it was me. I thought I was doing something wrong. But then the depression would ease and we'd be fine. She started seeing a therapist and she put her on medication. It helped. For a while. That's when I proposed. I figured this was just a manageable disease, like diabetes. I was wrong."

Samantha didn't know what to think. Jack was so vibrant and full of life. She couldn't imagine him with someone who was too depressed to deal with the world.

"Planning the wedding was too much," he said, his back to her. "I figured that out too late to do anything. Her mother tried to help. Helen offered, but I wasn't willing to deal with her. We had a bad storm and Shelby went driving in it. She lost control. At least that's what the police said. It was an accident."

Samantha couldn't breathe. Her heart ached for him. "It wasn't, was it?" she asked with a gasp.

He shook his head. "She left me a note. I burned it as soon as I read it. I knew the truth would only hurt her parents. They thought she was doing better, that she was finally happy. They actually thanked me for that at the funeral."

He turned to look at her. "I knew it was better to let them think what they wanted. Why hurt them after she was gone? Why tell them she would rather be dead than married to me?"

Samantha sprang to her feet and hurried to him. "Is that what you think? It's not true, Jack. Don't you see?

She was sick. You were right to call what she had a disease. Blaming yourself for her depression is as crazy as blaming me for Vance's abuse. You were there for her. You tried to help. In the end, she couldn't handle life and that has nothing to do with you."

She touched his arms, his back, trying to make him see. "You have to believe me," she whispered.

"I want to. You don't know how much. It's been a long time and I've let it go. But every now and then I wonder what I could have done differently. How I could have saved her."

"You can't save someone who won't save herself."

He turned then, and looked at her. "You saved yourself. That's what I was thinking the other night. You saved yourself."

They stared at each other. All their polite pretenses and shields were down. There was only the moment and the raw pain swirling around them, taking them to a level of emotional intimacy that was so real, so deep, it hurt.

Her first instinct was to run. If she stayed, if she let him in and they dealt with this together, there might not be an escape. She might start to care too much. She might get lost inside of him.

But there was no denying the truth. That they'd each shared their most intimate secret. They knew the worst about each other. So where did they go from here?

He must have read the question in her eyes, because he answered it by grabbing her, pulling her in close and kissing her. She responded by surging toward him, silently begging for more.

He wrapped his arms around her as if he would never let her go. She welcomed the heat and power of his embrace. He was not a tentative lover—he claimed with a forceful need that took her breath away. Right now she had to know he wanted her, she had to know this mattered, and he told her over and over again as his mouth claimed hers in a kiss that touched her soul.

Wanting grew as she tasted him and felt her body sigh and swell and dampen. She ran her hands up and down his back, then across his broad shoulders. His strength excited her. She loved the feel of his muscles bunching and releasing. When he dropped his hands to her hips and urged her closer, she arched toward him and felt the satisfying hardness of his desire.

"More," she breathed.

He took her at her word and raised his hands to her breasts. He cupped her slight curves, teasing the sensitive skin before lightly brushing her hard nipples. Pleasure shot through her. She gasped, then let her head drop back as she lost herself in the tingling, burning, arousing sensation of his gentle touch.

Over and over he teased her, rubbing her breasts, stroking her. Even through the layers of her blouse and her bra, the feelings were exquisite. He leaned in and kissed the side of her neck, then gently bit down on her bare skin.

She shuddered in anticipation of them making love. Her brain filled with images of them naked, reaching, surging, claiming. Suddenly she needed him naked and inside of her. She stepped back and reached for his clothes.

"Now," she commanded.

Either he wanted the same thing, or he understood exactly what she needed. He reached for her blouse as she reached for his sweater. Their arms bumped and it probably would have made more sense for them to each undress themselves, but she didn't want that. She wanted to be the one to reveal his warm, naked flesh. She wanted to undo his belt, push down his jeans and briefs and reach for him, even as he jerked her skirt and panties to her ankles.

She stepped out of both, along with her shoes. Then they were naked and reaching and they were touching everywhere. Even as he kissed her deeply, thrusting his tongue into her mouth, he reached for her bare breasts. She ran her hands down his back, pausing when she reached his butt. Once there, she caressed the high, tight curve, then squeezed.

His arousal flexed against her stomach. So hard, she thought, loving how much he wanted her. She was already wet—she ached with readiness.

Once again, he seemed to read her mind. He pushed her back until she felt the sofa behind her. They dropped onto the cool, soft surface, a tangle of arms and legs and need. He shifted her until she sprawled across the cushions, her legs parted, her body exposed. He slid onto the floor, then bent forward, bringing his mouth into contact with her most intimate spot.

Samantha surrendered to the magic of his tongue and lips as he explored every sensitive inch of her. He licked her thoroughly before focusing his attention on that single spot of pleasure. Even as she felt herself both melting and tensing as she strained toward her completion, he slipped a finger inside of her.

The combination was too much for her to stand. Her breath quickened as her muscles clenched. Her climax became a certainty so all she had to do was simply brace herself for the explosion.

When it crashed into her, she gasped her pleasure. Her body contracted and stiffened, only to become boneless. Still he moved in and out, while kissing and licking and circling. As long as he touched her, she came—again and again. The orgasm stretched out until every cell in her body sighed in delight.

At last he slowed and her contractions eased. When he raised his head and looked at her, she found herself feeling more exposed than she ever had. Raw emotion made her uncomfortable. But she was trapped and naked and there was no escape.

Then Jack smiled. "You're so incredible," he murmured. "So beautiful. I could do that for hours."

With a few simple words, he made her feel special and at ease. She opened her arms and welcomed him. He moved close, shifting so that he could slide his arousal into her waiting warmth. Her body tensed slightly and he groaned.

He put his hands on her hips and drew her closer, then he shifted one hand so he could touch her breast. She wrapped her legs around his hips, urging him deeper and deeper, wanting to get lost in him, as he was lost in her.

She felt him harden, stiffen, then still. His release claimed him. She kept her eyes open and watched his face tighten. At the last possible moment, he opened his eyes as well and they stared at each other.

It was a perfect moment of connection, she thought in wonder. She was truly one with this man. And in love with him.

The revelation stunned her but, once admitted, the truth wouldn't go away.

She loved Jack.

She didn't know if the feeling was new or if it had been in hiding for the past ten years, but she loved him and she didn't have a clue as to what she was going to do about it.

Chapter Twelve

"We have plans, Jack," Harold Morrison said as he handed a glass of scotch to Jack's boss.

Jack held his drink until everyone was served, then waited for the toast.

"To men who have the potential to go places," Morrison said.

Everyone glanced at Jack. He nodded, rather than smiled. "I appreciate the support and encouragement," he said before taking a drink.

"We think you can make it all the way," Morrison told him. "We've been talking about you."

Jack glanced around at the ten other people in the room. There were the four senior partners from his law firm, two congressmen, the junior senator and three officials from the state party office. Six men and four women, all of whom had the power to influence his future.

Morrison patted Jack on the back. "You need to get

things squared away at Hanson Media Group. You're doing a good job. We're getting excellent reports. Sure, you're not practicing law, but you're being a leader, making decisions. That bodes well. Just don't screw up there."

Everyone laughed but Jack.

"You'll be back at the law firm in another couple of months," Morrison continued. "Once that happens, you'll be put on the short list for an appointment to the circuit court as an associate judge. The law firms like to send good people into the judicial system. It makes us look good."

More laughter.

"I'll do my best," Jack said, knowing there was little he could do to move the process along. The launch of the website was only days away. Once that was up and running and adding to the cash flow, he could focus his attention on the many other problems. Two months, Morrison had said. Was it enough time?

Jack knew that legally he could walk away any time he wanted. Without signing a permanent contract with the board, they couldn't stop him from leaving. But legal obligations were different than moral ones. Hanson Media Group was the family company. Could he turn his back on it and let it fail so he'd be free to pursue his own dreams?

It was a question he had yet to answer.

Sarah Johnson, one of the firm's senior partners, leaned her hip on the conference-room table. "After working as an appointed judge, you'll run as an elected one. We'll have an organization in place to help with that. We've seen how you think and we like what we see. You're fair without being sentimental and you consider all your options. That's good for everyone. If you do as well as we expect, it won't be long until you're appointed to the federal bench." She raised her glass. "I like the sound of that."

"Agreed," Jack said, then took a sip of his drink. Big plans. Why did it have to come down to a choice between doing what he wanted and doing what was right for a family business he didn't care about?

"Was it wonderful?" Samantha asked as she walked into Jack's office for their quick lunch together.

"It's the first time I've had liquor before noon." He frowned as he thought about college. "At least in a lot of years."

"Oooh, you were drinking. That's good, right?"

"I'm not sure the drinking mattered, but there was a spirit of celebration."

She moved toward him and smiled. "I like the sound of that," she said as she raised herself on tiptoes and lightly brushed his mouth with hers. "They're impressed with you—just like me."

As always, her closeness made him aware of his ever-present need for her. It didn't seem to matter how many times they made love, the wanting wouldn't go away.

She set a tote bag on the coffee table and sank onto the sofa. After pulling out two wrapped sandwiches, she held one in each hand.

"Turkey or ham?" she asked.

"Either."

She passed him the ham, then dug around for take-out cartons of salad, two bags of chips and napkins. He took two sodas out of the small refrigerator in the corner and settled next to her on the sofa.

"There's a plan in place," he said as he unwrapped

his sandwich. "I have the support of the senior partners, along with a couple of guys from Congress and our junior senator."

"That's great," she said. "Did you get to meet them?"

He nodded. "They said they like the way I think. Plus having a former member of a law firm moving up the judicial food chain is always good for getting clients."

She frowned. "Because they think they'll get a break in cases?"

He smiled for the first time that morning. "No. Because it means they can pick and groom talent. Any sign that I was favoring one side over another in a case would mean getting thrown off the bench. I haven't busted my butt to get this far only to screw up over something that stupid."

"Okay. That makes sense. So if you look good, they look good."

"Yeah. There's only one thing standing in the way of all that."

She tilted her head. "I don't even have to guess. What are you going to do?"

"I haven't decided. Part of me wants to call a board meeting and resign. What do I care about this company?"

She touched his hand. "Except you do care. You don't want all the employees to be out of a job and there's a tiny part of you that can't face losing the company your father loved so much."

He stiffened. "I don't give a damn about my father." Why would he?

But instead of backing off, Samantha stayed exactly where she was and took a bite of her sandwich. The silence lengthened. Finally he exhaled sharply.

"Fine. I might not care about the old man, but you're right. I can't let this all be destroyed. It would be wrong."

She swallowed, then smiled. "Why was I afraid of you back in grad school? I kept seeing you as exactly like my father, but you couldn't be more different."

"Why were you afraid of me?"

"Because I thought you'd hurt me, then leave me."

Instead she'd been the one to walk out, he thought. "I'm not like him or Vance," he said.

"I know that now."

Better late than never, or was it? In the ten years they'd been apart, they'd both learned lessons. Unfortunately, his had been to be wary of trusting anyone to stay.

"I want to talk to Helen," she said. "About getting you back to your law firm. She can take on the board, she's good at that kind of stuff. There has to be someone else who can run things around here."

He leaned close and lightly touched her face. "Not your concern."

"I want you to have your heart's desire. Why wouldn't I?"

Very few people bothered to look out for him these days, he thought. David had when he'd been younger. Now Samantha was stepping into his life and doing her best to make his dreams come true.

"Why does it matter?" he asked, when what he really meant was "Why do *I* matter?"

She smiled. "It just does." She pushed his sandwich toward him. "You'd better eat. Mrs. Wycliff said you had a full afternoon."

He unwrapped the paper and took a bite, but his mind was busy elsewhere. Her words, her actions, all spoke of caring about him. He'd wanted that for a long, long time. Was it finally happening? Could he trust her not to bolt? And if she was willing to stick around this time, was he willing to open himself up or had he been burned one too many times?

"I'm going to throw up," Samantha muttered, doing her best to stay calm and keep breathing.

Arnie hovered at her side. "You'll be fine. We're all fine."

She laughed. "You look like you're going to pass out. That's hardly fine." Her humor faded. "Jeez, I hate this. Why can't it be tomorrow? Why can't the launch be behind us?"

"Because it's now."

And it was. She stood in the corner of an after-school center in the middle of the city. The large computer lab was filled with excited kids, members of the media and most of her team and the IT staff.

Dozens of conversations competed with laughter and loud music. There were bright balloons, plush toys licensed from animation on the website and a cake big enough to feed a hometown Bears crowd.

They had been live for all of eighteen minutes and she was still scared to go see how it was going.

"It's my job," she muttered to herself and took a step toward the computers.

"What do you think?" she asked the boy sitting closest to her.

He was maybe eleven, with bright red hair and freckles. "It's fun. I can do my math homework and get help when I need it. And it's like a game."

He clicked on several icons faster than she could follow and ended up in a math-based jungle where three different paths offered three different games.

Samantha made a few notes and then moved on to another child. About a half hour later, David Hanson strolled up and said, "You can't hide from the media forever," he said. "They have questions."

"I'm nervous," she admitted.

"It doesn't show. Come on. It won't be so bad."

Samantha followed him to the row of reporters and newspeople. David introduced her.

"We'll start with general questions," he said, "then we can schedule individual interviews and tape segments for the local news."

A pretty woman in a tailored navy suit jacket grinned. "I'm actually the network feed. This is going national."

"That's great," Samantha said, knowing it was amazing publicity and ignoring the sudden aerial formation of butterflies in her stomach. "Ask away."

She fielded several questions about how the new website worked.

"What about security?" one of the reporters asked. "How are you protecting our children?"

"In every way possible," Samantha told her. "We have all the usual safeguards in place, along with specific security triggers to flag potential stalkers. There's a special section for parents on the website. They can set up parameters, determining how much access each child in the family has. Older kids can do more, younger kids less. We're interested in feedback on the issue as well." She smiled. "I have the time logs in my office. On this project, we've spent as many hours on security as we have on content and we're very proud of that."

The next few questions were for the director of the after-school program. Samantha took the time away from the spotlight to look around and enjoy the success. She'd had the idea of making this a reality and now it was.

"We also owe a specific debt of gratitude to Hanson Media Group," the director was saying. "Not just for the wonderful website, but also for the new computers and Internet access they've donated to our center."

Samantha joined in the applause, but she didn't know what the woman was talking about. As soon as the media interviews were over, she found David.

"The company donated computers to the center?" she asked.

David nodded. "It was Jack's idea. He didn't think it was right to use them to get publicity without giving something back. Their computers were pretty old."

She glanced at the man in question and saw him sitting in front of a monitor with a little girl on his lap. Two more girls leaned against him, all raptly intent on the screen.

"The donation isn't mentioned in the PR material," she said. "I reviewed it last night."

David shrugged. "Jack didn't want to exploit the moment. I told him he was crazy, but he didn't listen. He's stubborn that way."

She knew he hadn't done it for her. In fact, she was confident she'd never crossed his mind. He'd quietly given thousands of dollars worth of computers because it was the right thing to do. That was simply the kind of man he was.

She'd let him walk out of her life once because she'd been afraid.

But not of him, she suddenly realized. Her fears

had never been about him. They'd been about herself. About how she would react. About how her world would change. She'd been afraid of depending on someone who would let her down and that she wouldn't be able to handle it.

Ten years ago she'd let Jack go, not because of who he was, but because of who *she* was.

She walked toward him and as she got closer, her chest tightened. There he sat with those girls, typing in what they told him to, patiently exploring the site with them. One of the girls pointed at a colorful animated parrot and laughed. Jack smiled at the child and nodded.

Samantha got it then—she saw it all. The acceptance, the caring, the goodness of the man inside.

She'd always wanted children. She'd put her dreams on hold because of her marriage to Vance. She'd lost so much time, but she'd been given a second chance. Was she going to blow it again? Or was she going to reach for the happiness waiting there, well within her grasp?

Friday night the website flashed with bright colors. The man at the keyboard typed furiously. This was wrong. All wrong. George wouldn't have wanted this. George would have wanted things to stay the same. He never approved of all this new technology.

It was the wrong direction for the company. How many times had George said Hanson Media Group was about magazines? Not this. Never this.

It was all going so well, too. Jack would get the credit. Jack who had never cared about his father. Jack who had broken his father's heart by refusing to go into the family business. The board and everyone else would say Jack was the hero.

He typed more quickly, working redirects into the software programming, putting them in places no one would think to look. Because they *would* look. The IT people always wanted to fix the problem themselves.

What they would forget was that he was better than all of them. The more they dug, the farther away they would get from the actual problem.

He tested the virus, then smiled. All done. Now all he had to do was crash the system. The techs on duty would work frantically to get it up and running again. When they did, they would see everything working fine. What they wouldn't see was that the website automatically linked to a porn site. They wouldn't know there was even another problem to deal with until it was too late.

That should punish Jack. That should punish all of them.

A fire crackled behind the grate. Jack felt the warmth on his legs, but only barely. He was far more interested in getting Samantha's bra off. But she wasn't cooperating.

"I want you naked," he murmured against her mouth.

She laughed and kissed him. "Do you see me protesting?"

"You're trying to get my shirt off. Bra first, shirt second."

"But I want to see you," she said. "You look good naked."

"See later. I want to touch now."

She smiled. "Touching is good. I would support touching."

He stared into her eyes and found himself wanting

to get lost there. This is how it was supposed to be, he thought. This is what mattered. Being with someone he cared about. Someone he could trust.

A voice in his head warned him that Samantha had run before and she would probably run again, but he didn't want to listen. He didn't want to think about her leaving. Not now.

But what to say to convince her to stay? After all, he wasn't one who truly believed in relationships working out. They certainly never had for him. Was this time different?

Maybe the difference was this time he wanted it to, he thought as he bent down and kissed her.

She parted for him and he stroked her tongue with his. He tilted his head so he could deepen the kiss, then claimed her with a passion that seared him to his soul.

"Samantha," he breathed as he rolled onto his back and pulled her with him.

She draped across his chest, her body warm and yielding. Her hands were everywhere, touching, pulling at clothes, teasing and exciting. She shifted so she could rub herself against his arousal.

The sharp sound of the phone cut through the night.

He swore and considered not answering it. It was after eleven on Saturday night—what could be that important? Only an emergency, he thought grimly as Samantha sat up and handed him the phone.

"Hello?"

"Jack? Is that you? Are you watching the news?"

"What? Who is this?" Then he recognized the frantic voice. "Mrs. Wycliff?"

"Turn on the news. Any channel. It's on all of them. Oh, Jack, it's horrible. This is the end. I don't see how the company can survive now."

He grabbed the remote and turned on the television. The local late-night news anchor appeared and behind her was a screen showing a raunchy porn site. Certain body parts were blacked out, but it was easy to see what the people on the screen were doing.

Jack swore and increased the volume.

"No one from Hanson Media Group was immediately available for comment," the news anchor said. "From our best guess, the new website for children has been linking to this porn site for the better part of the afternoon. Parents across the country are furious and no one knows exactly how many children were exposed to this sort of smut."

Chapter Thirteen

"It's been twelve hours," Jack said, more than ready to yell at the people assembled in his office.

Most of Samantha's team was in place, as were the IT guys, along with David and Mrs. Wycliff. Although he hadn't told his assistant to come in, she'd been waiting when he'd arrived.

"Twelve goddamn hours since the site crashed and no one—*no one*—thought to call me?"

His words echoed in the large room, followed by an uncomfortable silence. Right now he didn't care about anyone being uncomfortable. He wanted answers.

"Everyone has my home number," he continued. "I've told you all to get in touch if there's a problem and the only reason I know now is because Mrs. Wycliff watched the late news. How long would this have gone on otherwise? When exactly did you plan on letting me know?"

He directed the last question at the IT staff. Roger stepped forward.

"The site crashed yesterday morning. We're not sure why. I have a team investigating. They had the site up and running in about two hours."

"At a porn site?" Jack asked sarcastically. "Wouldn't it have been better to wait until our content was available?"

Roger swallowed. "Our content is available. But when the URL is typed in, users are redirected to the porn site you heard about. Our website is fine."

Jack narrowed his gaze. "I don't think I'd use that word to describe things right now." He turned to Arnie. "Did you pull the plug?"

The smaller man nodded quickly. "Yes. As soon as I heard, I came right in. When you type in the address, the user gets a message saying we're updating the site."

That was something, Jack thought grimly. At least no more children would be sent to view raunchy sex.

"Do we know what happened?" Jack asked in a quiet voice. "Do we know what went wrong?"

No one answered.

He leaned against the edge of his desk. "How bad?" he asked David.

"It's too soon to tell. We have to figure out how many hits we had this afternoon. With the publicity blitz all week, we were expecting a couple million."

Jack swore. A couple million? Was that possible? Was this company really responsible for exposing two million children to that kind of horror?

"We were supposed to be helping them," he said. "We were supposed to be providing a safe environment for children. A place where they could learn and have fun, away from everything bad. Instead we sent them right into the heart of the worst of it."

"Our stock might take a hit, but it will recover," someone said.

Jack stared at the man, not sure what department he belonged in and knowing it would be unreasonable to fire him for expressing an opinion.

"You think I care about the stock price?" he asked. "Do you think it matters to me if this company goes out of business tomorrow? We have done the one thing we vowed we would never do—we have hurt our kids. Nothing makes that right. And there's nothing we can do to make it right."

But people would try. He looked at David again. "Has the legal team been notified? Come Monday morning, people are going to be lining up at courts across the country."

"I have calls in."

"Good. I'm guessing most of the board members have heard, but in case some of them are out of town, I'll call them in the morning." He glanced at his watch. "Later this morning."

Arnie stepped forward. "Jack, I know it's not worth much, but I think this was done intentionally by a hacker. Oh, sure, the site crashed, but when we got it back up, it was working fine. The, ah, techs monitoring the site never saw the porn site because it wasn't there. I think there was an override in our server."

Jack stared at him. "You're saying the redirect was external to our system?"

Arnie shrugged. "It's a place to start looking."

The meeting broke up an hour later. After telling everyone to be in by six on Monday morning, Jack sent them home. Samantha stayed on the sofa, not only because she'd come with Jack but because she felt too sick to move.

He collapsed in a club chair and rubbed his temples. "This is completely and totally screwed."

"I feel so horrible," she whispered. "I can't believe this happened. We checked so many times. The security was all there. That's what gets me. The site wasn't compromised. It was the server."

"Regardless of the technicalities, Hanson Media Group is still responsible," he said.

"I know. No one is going to care how it happened, only that it did." She crossed her arms in front of her midsection. "All those children. Who would have done it and why?"

"Not a clue," he admitted. "But I'm going to find out and then that person is going to be prosecuted if I have to do it myself."

Her eyes burned, but she blinked the tears away. Crying wouldn't help anyone. Still, it was hard not to give in to the pain. So many people had worked so hard, only to have everything ruined by someone bent on destroying the company.

"This is revenge," she said. "Or an act of rage. It feels personal."

"To me, too. So who hates me that much and why?"

"Does it have to be someone hating you?" she asked. "Can it be someone who hates the company? A recently fired employee? Someone with a personal grudge against George, or one of your brothers. Who has enemies?"

"Who doesn't?" he asked.

She stared at him. "I'm so sorry, Jack. I thought the

new website was the answer to all the company's problems. Now I find I've just made things worse."

"You filled all the holes you saw."

"And missed a really big one."

She'd also gotten in the way of his future, she thought as her stomach clenched tighter. Jack wanted to do his job and get back to his dreams. What were the odds of that happening now? The board was going to be furious and they would blame Jack.

So not fair, she thought frantically. But how could she keep it from happening?

"Jack, I—"

A knock on the door cut her off.

"Come in," he called.

Mrs. Wycliff stepped inside. "The police are here."

Samantha's breath caught. "The police?"

Jack shrugged. "What did you expect?"

Not that. Some of her shock must have shown on her face. He stood and walked toward her.

"It's all right," he said gently. "David is waiting in his office. He'll take you home."

"I don't want you to have to deal with the police by yourself."

He touched her cheek. "Don't worry. You'll get your chance to answer their questions later today or Monday. Try to get some sleep."

Before she could try to convince him to let her stay, Mrs. Wycliff had ushered her out of the office and into the hallway. There she saw several police officers. They nodded politely.

She walked past them toward David's office. A part of her couldn't believe this was really happening. It was all wrong and there didn't seem to be anything she could do to stop it.

* * *

Jack grabbed a couple of hours of sleep Sunday night and was at the office before five on Monday morning. He had multiple crises to deal with.

While it all hit the fan over the website disaster, there was still a company to be run. The emergency board meeting started at nine, followed by an afternoon with in-house legal counsel. At last count, there were over a hundred lawsuits ready to be filed as soon as the courts opened. If this didn't kill the company, it would be sheer luck. Best case scenario, Hanson Media Group survived as a smaller, less proud organization, which meant cutbacks and massive layoffs.

He was surprised to find Roger waiting outside his office when he arrived.

"Here to confess?" he said, then regretted the words as soon as they were out.

Roger looked at him. "I didn't do it. I'll take a lie detector test if that will help."

Jack looked at the lines of exhaustion on the other man's face, then waved him into the office. "Sorry. I shouldn't have said that. I have no reason to suspect you."

"No more than anyone else with the technical expertise," Roger said bluntly, then handed over a tall cup of Starbucks.

Jack was as startled by the coffee as by Roger's statement. "I was under the impression that you were more a manager than a techie."

Roger sipped his own coffee, then shrugged. "I've worked in the business all my life. I might be older and not as fast, but I can code with the best of my team."

News to Jack, as he tried to remember where he'd

gotten the idea that Roger didn't know what he was doing on the technical front.

"We've continued to investigate over the weekend," Roger said. "As I suspected from the first, it's not our website. The content there never changed and the address wasn't hacked. Instead, someone got inside the server and messed with it. When the server started to route the user to our site, it made a quick left turn to porn central."

Jack didn't know if the information made a difference or not. "Who did it?"

"I'm still working on that. My guess is someone from this end rather than the server, but the police will be investigating them. I'm in touch with the detective in charge of the case."

"Why do you think it's someone from this company?" Jack asked.

"The attack feels personal. That's just my opinion."

"I appreciate hearing it," Jack told him. "Anything else?"

Roger nodded. "The detective thinks there's a good chance the feds will get involved."

More trouble, Jack thought. No one wanted that. "It's all out of our control," he said. "What are you doing this morning?"

"Continuing the investigation."

"Stay available. I have an emergency board meeting. They may want to ask you more questions."

Roger nodded, then left. Jack stared after him. He'd never liked the man, but suddenly Roger was stepping up to take charge during a crisis. Did he need something like this to show his true nature, or was he the guilty party looking to be close to the action?

Several hours later Jack sat with the board and

wished to hell he'd never left his law practice. They were angry and out for blood and right now they didn't particularly care whose.

Baynes, the chairman, led the discussion.

"This has to be fixed, Jack, and the sooner the better."

Jack sat forward and braced his forearms on the table. "I agree, and I'm working on the problem. The in-house IT people are doing what they can to find out who's responsible. I've also hired an outside team to work backward from the server problem."

"Hired guns?" Baynes asked.

"Independent agents. They don't evaluate what they find, they simply report it. Someone told me this morning that the website crash feels personal and I agree with him on that. Someone somewhere wants Hanson Media Group to crash and burn. I want to find out who and I want to know why."

Baynes looked surprised by the information. "A personal attack? Against the company?"

"Until I know who did it, I can't answer that," Jack told him.

"You're working with the police?"

"Yes."

Baynes looked at the papers in front of him. "Samantha Edwards was in charge of the new website."

"That's correct. She handled content while coordinating with the IT team on technical aspects."

"According to previous reports, she came up with the whole idea."

Jack saw where they were going and didn't like it. "She had nothing to do with the crash and subsequent rerouting."

"You don't know that for sure," Baynes said.

"Actually, I do. Samantha simply isn't that kind of person and even if she were, she doesn't have the technical expertise."

"She could be working with someone."

"She's not. I know Samantha personally and I'm telling you she's not the one. You're wasting your time with her. She is as devastated as anyone by what happened."

Baynes didn't look convinced, but he changed the subject.

The board broke at noon. Jack barely had an hour until he met with the company's legal counsel. As he hurried into his office, he yelled for Mrs. Wycliff to get Samantha in to see him right away.

He didn't have time for any of this, he thought as he poured coffee and ignored the sandwich his secretary had thoughtfully left on his desk.

Samantha arrived less than five minutes later.

"What's up?" she asked as she walked toward him. "Is it awful? They all have to be furious, but they have to know none of this is your fault."

"They don't know what to think," he told her. "Right now they're looking for information. They want to talk to everyone involved in the project, including you."

She nodded. "Especially me. I was in charge and it was my idea. I thought this would happen. When do they want to see me?"

"After lunch."

"Okay. No problem. I'll clear my calendar."

She looked tired, but then they all did. It had been a long couple of days. Perhaps anticipating her presence before the board, she'd dressed conservatively—

at least for her. A simple blouse over a dark skirt. Her hair had been tamed by a clip at the base of her neck.

He led her to the sofa and urged her to sit. He settled next to her.

"They're going to ask a lot of questions," he said. "You don't have very long to prepare. Stay calm and answer as best you can. It would help if you had information to back up your plans."

She frowned. "What kind of information?"

"Your notes. How you came up with the idea of the website, the various forms it took. Logs of meetings with your team and the IT people. Transcriptions of discussions."

Samantha stared at him. "You have to be kidding," she said, knowing there was no need to panic, but wanting to all the same. "I don't keep records like that. I barely record the dates and times of our meetings in my date book. Jack, this was a very creative process. We would brainstorm together for a few hours, then go off to work individually. When we got back together, we compared what we had. No one took notes. Sometimes we worked over a game of basketball. You know that."

He nodded. "You'll need to go through the process as logically as you can. Our board members wouldn't be described as creative, so they're not going to understand what you're talking about. They'll want to see your e-mail assigning a task to someone."

"It doesn't exist."

He touched her hand. "It's okay. This is just a conversation. They're going to push you, but that doesn't mean you have to let them. Stand your ground."

She appreciated the advice, but wished she didn't need it. "Are you going to be at the meeting?" she asked.

"I wish I were, but I have to be with legal."

Which made sense, but didn't make her happy. Somehow all this would be easier with Jack in the room.

"I'll be fine," she told him, as much to convince herself. "I have nothing to hide, so what's the worst that can happen? They'll get crabby and I'll endure it. In the meantime I'll go through my notes and see if I can figure out a time line for putting the website together. I wonder if Arnie has any information."

"Don't check with him. It will look too much like collusion."

Until that moment, Samantha had only been nervous. Suddenly she was scared. "Jack, do they think it's me?"

"They think it's everyone. The only thing singling you out is that you were in charge. So you've come to their notice. That's all." He squeezed her fingers. "I mean that. I trust you completely."

She saw the sureness in his gaze and allowed herself to draw comfort from it. "You know I would never—"

He cut her off with a quick kiss. "Don't say it. You don't have to. I would suspect myself before you. This isn't about that. It's about an angry board looking for answers. Nothing more."

"Okay." She stood. "I'd better go get ready."

He rose and smiled. "Before you go…"

"What?"

He pulled her close and kissed her. Even as his mouth brushed against hers, his arms came around her. She leaned against him, savoring the heat and strength of his body.

This was where she belonged, she thought. This was home.

He licked her lower lip and when she parted for him, he slipped his tongue inside. They kissed deeply for a few minutes before they both drew back.

"That could get out of hand in a hot minute," he teased.

"You're right and neither of us have time."

He kissed her lightly. "Rain check."

"We don't even have to wait for bad weather."

"Good to know." He walked her to the door and opened it. "If it gets rough, if they start to get out of hand, excuse yourself and come get me. I mean it, Samantha. Don't let them get to you. They're just regular people."

"Crabby regular people," she told him.

"You'll do fine."

"I'll do my best."

"Ms. Edwards, what made you come up with the website expansion in the first place?"

The woman questioning Samantha was elegant, well-dressed and obviously furious.

"When I heard about the job at Hanson Media Group, I spent several days researching their positioning in the market. I knew cash flow was a problem and that while they needed to grow, another magazine wasn't the answer. The website offered a way to expand quickly and target a new demographic."

"You've done this sort of thing before? Launched a website?" a man asked.

Samantha wished they would all wear name tags, because except for Mr. Baynes, the chairman of the board, she had no clue who anyone was.

"I've been part of a launch," she said. "I've never been completely in charge."

The board members sat on one side of a long table, while she sat on the other. There was a vast expanse of space on either side of her, giving her the sensation of being very, very alone. She knew she could call Jack and he would come defend her, but she wasn't going to take him up on his offer. She would get through this on her own.

"How exactly did you come to work for Hanson Media Group?" Mr. Baynes asked. "You've been hired fairly recently."

"I heard about the job and applied."

"Heard about it how?"

"Helen Hanson told me. We're friends." Samantha clenched her teeth. Should she have admitted to the relationship? She didn't want Helen dragged into this.

"You've known Helen a long time?"

"Over twenty years."

The board members looked at each other.

"Were you jealous of Helen?" the woman asked. "Did you resent her successful marriage, her personal wealth?"

"What?" Samantha couldn't believe it. "Of course not. What does my relationship with Helen have to do with the website?"

"We're looking for a motive, Ms. Edwards."

"I didn't do it," Samantha told them firmly. "I love my job and I'm very supportive of what the company is doing. I would never endanger any child. The team and I worked very hard to make sure we had state-of-the-art security in place. While I do accept responsibility for this happening on my project, I would like to point out that the site itself wasn't compromised. It couldn't have been. Someone got into the server. As that is an outside company and beyond our scope of control, I don't see how we could have prevented that."

"Perhaps if you'd considered the threat," Mr. Baynes said sharply. "Perhaps if you'd looked past your quest for glory."

"My *what?*"

"You were very careful to take the spotlight in all the media interviews, weren't you?"

"No. This is crazy. I was in charge of the project, so it made sense for me to represent the company."

"Something that is normally David Hanson's job," Baynes continued.

Samantha shook her head. "David was with me. We coordinated our activities."

"So you say."

She got it then. She wasn't sure why it had taken so long for her to see the truth. Jack had been wrong— this wasn't an angry board. This was a board looking for a scapegoat. For reasons she couldn't understand, they'd decided that scapegoat was her.

She stood. "However much you search, you are not going to find a motive for me to have sabotaged Hanson Media Group. I wasn't involved in what happened in any way. I don't have a grudge against the company or anyone working for it. I was hired to do a job and I did it to the best of my abilities."

"Hardly a statement to reassure us," the woman said with a sniff.

Samantha ignored her. "I would never endanger any child. That was my mission from the first. To provide them with a safe environment to learn. Every memo, every e-mail, ever letter I've written on the subject supports that."

Baynes narrowed his gaze. "We've spoken with your

ex-husband, Ms. Edwards. He describes you as a very emotionally unstable person. After walking out on him for no good reason, you filed for divorce only to change your mind. You begged him to take you back. You threatened his children."

Samantha felt as if she'd been shot. There was a sharp pain in her chest and she couldn't seem to catch her breath. Damn Vance. He'd vowed he would get back at her for leaving him. He'd hated giving up control. By calling Vance, Baynes had handed him a perfect way to get revenge.

"My ex-husband is lying," she said, trying to stay calm. "However, it's very clear to me that you're not going to believe anything I say. What do you want from me?"

"Your resignation," Baynes said.

Right. Then they could issue a press statement and say the person responsible had been punished. The board didn't care about finding the person who had actually done this. They simply wanted to make the news cycle with good news. Something they could toss out in an attempt to salvage the company and the stock price.

"You want me to resign because you don't have any reason to fire me," she said.

"We'll get it soon enough," Baynes told her. "If you go quietly, we won't give the information from your husband to the press."

Talk about a low blow and a threat.

Indecision filled her. Her instinct was to stay and fight, but to what end? Wouldn't her leaving make things easier for Jack? With the board off her back, he could focus on getting the company back on its feet.

She could deal with lies and innuendo, but she didn't want to hurt Jack.

"I'll resign," she said.

Chapter Fourteen

Jack and the legal team took a break close to three. They had already developed a strategy of crisis control and cleanup. Jack did his best to remember his position as president of the company. He knew he was responsible for making sure Hanson Media Group survived. But every time he thought about what had happened, he wanted to throw a chair through the floor-to-ceiling windows.

He left the conference room and headed for his office to pick up his messages. David fell into step beside him.

"The board is still meeting," his uncle said. "But they've already found one victim."

"That's fast work." He hadn't expected them to act for several weeks. Investigations took time.

"It's Samantha."

Jack didn't break stride. He simply changed directions and headed for the stairs that would take him to the floor where the board met. David stayed with him.

"I know what you're thinking," the older man said.

"I doubt that." Worried, furious, frustrated didn't even come close. Dammit, he'd sent Samantha in there by herself. She'd had to face a firing squad alone and he hadn't been there to protect her.

"Jack, I know you care about her, but think before you act."

"Why? They didn't. How long did they question her? Fifteen minutes? We all know that Samantha isn't guilty of anything. She had great plans for the company. Someone deliberately screwed with that and I'm not going to let him, her or them get away with it."

"What are you going to do?" David asked as they climbed up to the next floor.

"Take control."

He walked into the conference room without knocking. The board was in the middle of questioning several of the IT guys. Jack jerked his head toward the now-open door and the three of them scuttled out.

Jack crossed to the long table, pushed the now-empty chairs aside and leaned toward the seven people who wanted to control his destiny.

"I understand you've had an admission of guilt," he said. "Why didn't you tell me someone had confessed?"

Baynes glared at him. "You're out of line, Jack."

"Not even a little. Come on, Baynes, how are you going to threaten me? Do you want to say you're going to fire me? That would only make my day. So how did you get the confession?"

"Ms. Edwards didn't confess. But as she was ultimately responsible for the program we all thought it was best if she—"

Jack slapped his hands on the table. "*I'm* ultimately responsible. While I'm in charge, then this is my company. You do not have the right to go behind my back and fire my employees for no reason."

"They had a reason," David said, his voice cold. "Tell him, Baynes."

The chairman of the board looked uncomfortable but didn't speak.

"They want to make the news," David said. "They want everyone to think they're making progress so the stock price doesn't tank."

"We care about this company," Baynes said. "Which is more than I can say about either of you."

Jack swore. "I've given everything I had to keep Hanson Media Group from going down. You were all happy about our new program."

"Until there were problems," Baynes said. "Obviously you have incompetent people running things around here. Ms. Edwards has a history of problems and I'm sure they—"

Jack leaned forward and glared at Baynes. "What the hell are you talking about? What problems?"

"We spoke with her ex-husband. He was very forthcoming."

"I'll bet he was."

Jack straightened and took a step back. If he didn't get out of here, he was going to beat the crap out of Baynes and anyone else who stuck around. Samantha must hate him right about now. To think the board had pried into her personal life. He had to find her. He had to know she was all right.

"You want someone to blame," he said. "Blame me. I quit."

Baynes stood. "You can't. We don't accept your resignation. We have a contract, Jack. You violate that and we'll haul you into court. We'll win, too. Then what will happen to your law career?"

Jack started for the old man. David grabbed his arm and pulled him out into the hallway.

"Think," his uncle told him. "Don't make things worse than they are. They're not going to let you go."

"You're right." Jack started for the elevators. "Where's Samantha? Has anyone seen her?"

"Here I am again," Samantha said as she reached for another tissue. "Curled up on your sofa and crying. Isn't this getting boring?"

"Not yet," Helen said with surprising cheer. "You always come for a new and exciting reason. That keeps it interesting."

"Thanks." Samantha knew her friend was trying to keep her from falling too far into the despair pit by using humor but it wasn't exactly working. "I never want to go through anything like that again."

"I don't blame you," Helen said. "I swear, if George leaves the majority shares to me, I'm going to consider firing the board."

Samantha wanted to take that as personal support, but she knew her friend well enough to know that Helen was making a business decision.

"I don't know what to do," she admitted. "I really wanted to stand up to the board, but I don't want to make things worse for Jack. I hate that this is happening to him. Taking over the business was his way of doing the right thing. I know he and his dad weren't close, but when it was important, Jack gave up the job he loved to help out. Now he's getting hit with this. I just wanted to make it better."

"Have you talked to him?" Helen asked.

"No. I sort of lost it and came right here. I guess I should put a call in to him."

Helen smiled. "I have a feeling he'll be looking for you."

"Why?"

"Gee, I don't know. The woman he's been involved with just got bullied by a board of directors he's already annoyed with. Don't you think that will make him react? I won't be surprised to hear he punched out Baynes."

Samantha sat up. "He wouldn't do that."

"Wouldn't he?"

She thought about all the ways Jack had been there for her. How he'd been patient and supportive and more than a little understanding.

"Oh, no," she breathed. "You're right. He's going to be furious." She felt her mouth drop open. "He really cares about me."

Helen rolled her eyes. "You think?"

Samantha grinned. "I care about him, too. I have since we first met."

"That would be the time when you were too scared to hang on to the fabulous guy who was crazy about you?"

"Pretty much." She stood. "What if he thinks this is me running again? What if he doesn't know I'm doing this to help him?"

Helen shrugged. "Have I mentioned how communicating would be a good thing?"

Samantha bent down and kissed her friend's cheek. "You're the best. You know that, right?"

"I've been told before."

Samantha laughed, then grabbed her purse. "I have

to go find Jack. If he calls here, would you tell him I'm looking for him?"

Helen reached for the phone. "Just go back to the office. I'll call Mrs. Wycliff so she can let him know you're on your way."

Jack paced in his office, not willing to believe the message until Samantha actually walked in.

"I wasn't leaving," she said as she rushed up to him. "Well, okay, I was leaving the company, but not you. I thought it would make it easier for you."

"Letting the board pin all this on you?" he asked gruffly, as he pulled her close and stared into her eyes. "Why would having you gone help?"

She smiled. "I had a momentary loss of brain function. It won't happen again."

"Good."

She felt right in his arms. Warm and soft and feminine. Also stubborn, difficult and outrageous and he didn't want her to change a thing.

"Oh, Jack," she said quietly. "This is a really big mess."

"Yeah, but we're going to fix it. For one thing, I've refused to accept your resignation, so don't think you can get out of working here."

"I don't want to try, but I did think of something that may be significant. While I was in the cab from Helen's I wrote out a time line." She pulled a small piece of paper from her purse. "There's something we've all overlooked. The website crashed."

He stared at her. "What?"

"Remember? The site went down. The tech guys got it up and running. From this end, the site was fine. But when the site came back online, something happened in the server, switching everyone who logged on to the porn site. I think the two incidents are related. I think the whole thing was rigged to be triggered by the rebooting of the website. Which means it could still be an inside job."

He grabbed her shoulders and swore. "It has to be. That's the only thing that makes sense. We've been talking about how this all feels personal. You haven't been around long enough for anyone to hate you—"

"Neither have you," she reminded him.

"I've been around my whole life. Even if I wasn't here, people knew who I was. They knew I wasn't involved. Then my father dies and I come in and take over."

"Or maybe someone was angry at your father and wanted to get back at him through the company."

A real possibility, he thought. He released her and lightly kissed her. "You're pretty smart."

She smiled. "One of my many good qualities. So we have this great theory. Now what?"

"We call in a friend." He walked to the phone and dialed a number. "Roger? It's Jack. Samantha and I have come up with a possible scenario. If I tell you what it is, can you tell me who is capable of doing it?"

He listened carefully, then thanked the man and hung up.

"Well?" Samantha asked. "Are there any names?"

"Two, and one of them is Arnie."

The two men arrived at Jack's office less than ten minutes later. Samantha took one look at them and knew Arnie was the culprit. The truth was there in the way he wouldn't meet her eyes.

Jack invited the two men to sit in the chairs by his

desk, but before he could start questioning, she walked up to Arnie.

"Why?" she asked softly. "I thought we were friends. We put in all those late nights together. You had great ideas and I listened. I trusted you. I don't know why you wanted to punish the company and I'll accept that you probably had a good reason, but you hurt children. Innocent children. What about them?"

Arnie stared at her and slowly blinked. "I have no idea what you're talking about."

The man with him, Matt, shifted in his seat. "Me, either. I didn't do it, if that's what you want to find out. The site went down and I worked on that, but I never touched the server." He swallowed. "I have kids of my own. Two. I wouldn't do this."

Samantha never took her gaze off Arnie. "But you would. I thought we were friends."

Jack moved up behind her and put his hand on her arm. "It's not about you, Samantha. It's about me. Am I right, Arnie? It's about me and my father and the company. Because I have it all now. The old man is gone and I have everything."

Arnie sprang to his feet. "You don't deserve it," he yelled. "You don't. You never cared about the business. You never respected your father. Did you think I didn't hear what you said about him? He was a great man. You'll never be like him. Never."

Samantha nearly forgot to breathe. "But you were so supportive of the website."

"He was playing you," Jack said tonelessly. "He played us all."

Arnie's lip curled. "You made it so easy. Both of you. I knew your father. We were friends. He liked me. Did you know he talked about you all the time? He missed you and wanted you in his life and you couldn't be bothered. George Hanson was a great man and now he's gone and you don't deserve to run his business. You don't deserve to even sweep the floors."

"So you wanted to take me down," Jack said. "You knew there was a good chance that I would be ruined by the scandal."

Arnie shrugged. "I had high hopes."

Samantha couldn't believe it. "This was your plan from the beginning?"

"Sure thing, babe. Did you really think you were all that?" His expression turned contemptuous. "I had you all fooled. I don't care about what happens to me because the company is ruined. You'll never recover from this. Face it, Jack. You're screwed. You'll stay on to save the sinking ship, but it can't be saved. I made sure of that. The lawsuits will bankrupt you and even before that, no one will ever want to do business with your company again. You're in charge of a worthless empire. And you have me to thank for it."

The door opened and Mrs. Wycliff led in the detective and several uniformed officers. They read Arnie his rights and took him away.

Matt excused himself, as did Mrs. Wycliff, leaving Samantha and Jack alone.

He led her over to the sofa and pulled her down next to him.

"I want to say that was easy," he told her, "but it's just beginning. Knowing Arnie did it and why doesn't clean up the mess any faster."

She snuggled up against him. "At least it gives us a place to start."

He kissed the top of her head. "Maybe I should just

give the board what they want. It's going to take years to get the company back on its feet."

She shifted so she could look at him. "Don't you dare. I mean it, Jack. Your dreams are too important to give up. You have a commitment here, so stay for now. But only on your terms. Don't walk away from everything you've ever wanted just because of this."

"What if what I want is you?" he asked.

Her heart flopped over in her chest. She felt the movement, along with a rush of gladness. Her mouth curved in a smile.

"I would say that's a good thing because I want you, too."

He stared into her eyes. "Seriously?"

"Yes. I've spent so much of my life running from the things that frightened me, but I never once stopped to think about what I might be missing out."

He took her hands in his. "Me, too," he murmured. "I haven't wanted to believe love lasts. For me, it didn't. Now I'm wondering if the reason I couldn't give my heart to someone else is because I'd already given it to you. I love you, Samantha."

Her breath caught. "I love you, too. I think I have from the first moment we met."

"So we wasted ten years?"

"No. We became the people we needed to be to find each other now."

"I like the sound of that."

He pulled her close. She went willingly into his arms. They kissed, their lips clinging.

"We can do this," she told him. "We'll fix Hanson Media Group, then we'll get you back to your law firm. You need to become a judge. You'll look good in black."

He laughed. "Hell of a reason."

She grinned. "Okay. You'll be great at it, too. How's that?"

"I like how you think." He kissed her again. "In fact, I like everything about you."

"I feel the same way about you."

"Want to get married?"

"Yes."

"Just like that? You don't have any questions."

She stared into his eyes. "I love you, Jack. I trust you and I want to spend my life with you. What questions could I have?"

"I'll do everything I can to make you happy," he told her. "I'll be there for you."

She knew he would. He always had been.

He put his arm around her. "I've been thinking about my brothers. I want to get them to come home. Not just because of the company but because we need to be a family again. You think I could get them back here for a wedding?"

She leaned against him and sighed. "Absolutely. And if they don't agree, we'll hunt them down and drag them back. That could be fun."

He chuckled. "This is why I love you. You always have a plan."

"It's one of my best features."

"And the others?"

"How much I love you."

"Right back at you, Samantha. For always."

* * * * *

Dear Reader,

I am beyond thrilled that Harlequin is reissuing *The Best Laid Plans*. I fell for both Ethan and Alex as I wrote this story, and the ending is still one of my favorites. I love how strong Alex is, and how hurt Ethan is—even though neither of them appears that way from the outside looking in.

It's only when they get to know each other as more than colleagues that they begin to peel away each other's layers and understand one another—and, of course, that's when they also fall in love.

One of the other things I really like about this story is that the hero and heroine are both "up there" in terms of age. Often romance is peopled by younger women and slightly older men, but I wanted to write about people who have seen a bit of life and have the scars and baggage to prove it.

I really hope you enjoy *The Best Laid Plans*. I love to hear from readers, so please drop me a line via my website, www.sarahmayberry.com, if you feel the urge.

Happy reading!

Sarah Mayberry

THE BEST LAID PLANS

Sarah Mayberry

This was a hard one. Big thanks and hugs and commiserations and air kisses to Chris and Wanda, my frontline pit crew who cheered me on from the sidelines and gave me the occasional kick when I needed it and listened to all my whining and gnashing of teeth.

Also thanks to the Libster for very generously sharing her knowledge of artificial insemination with me.

Chapter One

"Damn your eyes, where did you come from?"

Alexandra Knight plucked at the run climbing the right leg of her panty hose, sending it racing even farther up her leg. When she'd pulled on her hose ten minutes ago, they'd been perfect. And she knew for a fact that there wasn't another pair anywhere in her apartment since she'd already dragged these ones out of the laundry in desperation.

She checked her watch. She was already in the underground garage of her apartment building. If she went upstairs and changed into a pantsuit, she'd chew up ten minutes, minimum. But if she swung into the convenience store near her downtown Melbourne office, she might make her first meeting. If she hustled.

Decision made, she strode the final few feet to her car and beeped it open. She reversed out of her spot with a rev of the engine, then shot up the ramp and into the street.

The parking gods were smiling on her and she drove straight into a space in front of the minimart on St. Kilda Road. She was out of the car and heading for the door in no seconds flat.

She had three pairs of panty hose in hand when she hurried out the door two minutes later, only to find the sidewalk blocked by a tall blond man attempting to wrangle a complicated-looking stroller that had become entangled with one of the many bags hanging from its handle. She sidestepped, her thoughts on the day ahead. Her corporate client Jamieson was keen to have the contract of sale she was negotiating on their behalf signed off by the end of the week, which meant she had to redraft the contract by this afternoon so they could—

"Alex."

She turned instinctively.

"Jacob," she said, one foot on the curb, the other in the gutter, stunned by the unlikely coincidence of seeing her ex. Her gaze dropped to the small body strapped securely in the stroller he was pushing. There was no missing the resemblance between man and child.

He was a father.

Jacob, the man she'd lived with for seven years, the man who had refused to even discuss having a child with her, had had a child with someone else. Some other woman.

For a moment Alex could do nothing but blink.

She had begged him to reconsider his anti-child stance. They'd fought over it so many times she'd lost count. He'd always been so adamant. So certain, even when they were packing their things and going their separate ways.

And now…

She dragged her gaze from his baby to his face. He had the grace to look sheepish.

"I thought you might have heard through the grapevine," he said.

But she hadn't. If she'd known… She had no idea what she would have done.

"How old is he?" she asked. Amazing how calm her voice sounded when the rest of her was reeling.

"Four months."

She flinched. She and Jacob had broken up eighteen months ago. That meant he'd met someone and gotten her pregnant pretty damn quickly.

"Congratulations," she said, even though she wasn't feeling the least bit congratulatory. "What's his name?"

And her. What's her name, this mysterious, magical woman who got you to cough up your DNA when I couldn't even get you to discuss becoming a parent after seven years together?

"Theodore. Teddy for short."

"That was your grandfather's name, wasn't it?"

"That's right."

He was blushing. And she'd run out of things to say—except for the one burning question that her pride would never allow her to ask: *why not me?*

Hadn't he loved her enough? Had she been missing some vital, essential ingredient that had stopped him from fully committing to her?

Her hand curled into a fist. She wanted to hurt him. Punch him in the face. Grab him by the lapels and demand to know why, how, when. Instead, she forced her hand to relax and made a show of checking her watch.

"I really have to go if I'm going to make my first meeting. Good luck with everything, Jacob."

She stepped blindly into the street.

"Alex. Before you go… Just in case you thought—I mean, it was an accident," Jacob said.

"What?" Despite herself, she lingered and turned to face him when she should have gotten in her car and driven away.

"Mia didn't realize she'd missed a pill and then we found out she was pregnant. So, you know, all this was unplanned." His gesture took in his child, the stroller, the tangled diaper bag.

"Well. I guess that makes it all okay," she said.

She escaped to the sanctuary of her car. Except it wasn't really a sanctuary, since Jacob remained where he was, watching her, an expression on his face that was an equal mix of guilt and defensiveness. Alex concentrated on starting the engine so she could get the hell out of here.

She pulled over the moment she was around the corner and out of sight. She stared out the windshield, her hands gripped the steering wheel so tightly that her knuckles ached.

Jacob was a father. He had a beautiful baby boy. With someone else. A woman named Mia, who had "forgotten" to take a pill or two and forced Jacob into a position he had adamantly, passionately, avowedly claimed he wanted to avoid for the entire duration of his relationship with Alex.

He'd named his child Theodore, after his paternal grandfather. He was even on child-care duty, pushing one of the contraptions he'd once dubbed a "blight on civilization" because of the way they choked supermarket aisles and cafés.

She could hear her own breathing, fast and harsh as though she'd just run a race. She told herself that the past was the past and that what Jacob had done once they'd split was nothing to do with her. But not for a minute did she believe it.

The thing was—the thing that stung so bloody bitterly—was that he'd always been so *certain* about what he wanted. He'd informed her six months into their relationship that he wasn't interested in having children. By then she'd loved him so much, wanted to be a part of his life so badly, she'd convinced herself that he would change with time. Lots of men did, after all, and they'd both been only thirty. She'd told herself that once he saw his friends have kids, he'd understand the joy and challenges that children could bring. The love and hope and energy. All she'd have to do was wait him out.

And she had. She'd concentrated on achieving partnership at Wallingsworth & Kent and back-burnered her baby dreams until the issue had become a wedge between them.

And now Jacob was a father, and she was single and thirty-eight and still looking for the man she'd left Jacob to find. A man she loved who loved her and wanted to have the family that had always formed the cornerstone of her hopes and dreams.

For the second time that morning her hands curled into fists and she pounded them once, twice, three times against her steering wheel.

An electronic beep drew her attention back to the moment. She blinked, looking around to identify the source of the sound. Her gaze fell on her bag and her brain clicked into gear. Her phone. That's what the sound was. She pulled it from her handbag and touched the screen. It was her legal secretary, Franny, letting

Alexandra know her first client had arrived and was waiting in reception.

Alex laughed.

A client. Right. She had a meeting scheduled. Hell, she had a whole day scheduled. And here she was, thinking that the world had contracted to only her and the sick, angry feeling in the pit of her stomach.

She took a deep breath, then texted a quick reassurance that she was five minutes away.

Seeing Jacob pushing a stroller had dredged up a lot of the old feelings she thought she'd put to rest. But she didn't have time to sit in her car and gnash her teeth. People were relying on her.

She continued to talk herself down as she drove to the office.

She might feel justifiably angry and cheated by the way things had turned out, but it wasn't as though she was out of options. At thirty-eight, she had at least five good childbearing years ahead of her—Madonna had had her second child at forty-two, after all, and Geena Davis had had twins at forty-seven. Alex was fit and healthy and active. There was plenty of time for her to find Mr. Right and have the family she'd always wanted.

Plenty of time.

Ignoring the flutter of panic behind her breastbone, Alex reeled in her feelings and focused on the day ahead.

Plenty of time.

Eight hours later, Alex waited on the examination table as her doctor washed her hands after Alex's annual physical. As it had all day, her mind circled back to the encounter with Jacob. She made it a policy not to brood. It was a huge waste of energy, and it never changed anything. She had better things to do with her time and emotion. Still, she couldn't erase the image of Jacob and little Teddy. To be so close to everything she wanted and yet be so far removed…

Dr. Ramsay turned back from washing her hands. "Okay, we'll check your abdomen, then we're done. Hands by your sides, please. And a nice relaxed belly."

"Sure you don't want me to beg or fetch?" Alex asked.

"As if you'd listen to me anyway." Dr. Ramsay smiled, the lines around her eyes deepening.

She'd been Alex's doctor for ten years now and she always managed to fit Alex in, no matter how crazy her work schedule.

Dr. Ramsay's expression grew distant as she pressed down on Alex's lower belly.

"Let me know if you feel any pain or discomfort."

"Okay."

"How's that?" Dr. Ramsay asked, pressing near where Alex imagined her ovaries were located.

"All good."

"And here?"

Over her bladder this time.

"Fine."

A few more pokes, then her doctor was done.

"You can get dressed now. So unless there's anything else you were worried about, we're finished."

Alexandra sat up, swinging her legs over the side of the table.

"Nothing major. I have noticed my periods have been getting heavier over the past few months. More cramping, that sort of thing."

"Unfortunately, that's something that happens for

a lot of women as they age. You're, what, thirty-nine this year?"

"That's right."

"We'll keep an eye on it and if it becomes a problem we can look at your options. But given the average age of menopause is fifty-one, it might be an issue that will simply resolve itself."

Alex laughed nervously. "Menopause? I'm not even forty yet."

Dr. Ramsay shrugged. "But you are on the tail end of your fertility, and quite a few women go into menopause in their forties."

"But...I haven't had children yet."

Dr. Ramsay looked startled. "Oh. I didn't realize that was something you wanted. I always assumed you were a career woman."

"No. I mean, I am. I love my career. But I want a family, too."

There was concern in Dr. Ramsay's eyes now. "I see. Well, you probably don't need me to tell you that the clock is ticking."

"I've still got a few years up my sleeve yet, right?" Alex asked.

She hesitated a beat before speaking again. "Why don't you get dressed and we can discuss this further?"

The curtain hissed shut between them. Alex tried to push beyond the growing sense of dread as she reached for her clothes. It took her two attempts to button her skirt.

Dr. Ramsay was seated at her desk when Alex opened the curtain.

"Grab a seat," the doctor said, patting the chair she'd pulled up alongside her desk.

Alex sat and folded her hands into her lap. "Why

do I feel as though I've been called to the principal's office?"

Dr. Ramsay drew a diagonal line on the paper in front of her, sloping from the top left corner down to the right. Then she jotted some figures along the horizontal and vertical axes of her impromptu graph.

"Here's a crash course in female fertility," she said when she'd finished her sketch. "When it comes to having babies, the quality of the egg is what's important. The current understanding is that fertility as well as egg quality hit their peak at around twenty-seven. From then onward, it's a steady decline. After thirty-five—" Dr. Ramsay tapped the appropriate point on her downward-sloping graph "—fertility drops off dramatically. Statistically, the likelihood of a woman in her early forties having a successful pregnancy with her own ovum is only ten percent."

"Ten percent?" Alex repeated.

"Ten percent."

"But I'm only thirty-eight right now. Where does that place me on the graph?" Alex leaned forward urgently.

Dr. Ramsay tapped a spot scarily close to the bottom of her sloping line. "At about thirty-five percent. But remember, these figures are averages. There are always people who fall outside of the norm."

Alex stared at the tiny indentation the doctor's pen had made in the page. Thirty-five percent. She had a thirty-five percent chance of getting pregnant and successfully carrying a child to term. And next year that figure would drop again.

"I thought I had more time. I mean…Madonna. And Geena Davis. And I'm sure I read about a woman in her early fifties having triplets…."

"Unfortunately these high-profile late-in-life pregnancies give women a false sense that having a baby is as simple as deciding the time is right and going for it. Many, many older women have to resort to IVF to get pregnant in their late thirties and early forties. Many fail and are forced to look to donor eggs."

Alex's palms were damp with sweat. For so many years she'd dreamed of being a mother. She'd drawn up a list of names, she'd even bought her sensible, safe sedan with an eye to the future. She'd always assumed that she would be a mother, that when she was ready, her body would cooperate and she'd get pregnant…

"Are you telling me that it might already be impossible for me to have a child?" she asked. It was hard to get the words past the lump in her throat.

"Without invasive tests, without you having tried and failed to conceive for an extended period of time, it's impossible for us to know how fertile you are. What I'm trying to say and perhaps not doing a very good job of it is that if this is something you want, Alex, you need to move quickly. The sooner the better as far as your body is concerned."

Alex smoothed her hands down her skirt. She could feel how tense her thigh muscles were beneath the fine Italian wool. Her belly muscles were quivering and she was frowning so fiercely her forehead ached.

"I see," she said.

And she did. She saw Jacob's baby boy, his big blue eyes taking in the world, his fingers clutching the edge of his blanket.

So small and soft, so full of promise.

All the rage and resentment and bitterness that she'd suppressed this morning rolled over her.

She'd given Jacob *seven years*. Seven of her best

years, apparently. He'd said no to children again and again, and now he had what she'd always dreamed of and she was left to face the possibility that she would only ever be a godmother to her friends' children.

It was so unfair, so bloody cruel…

Alex realized Dr. Ramsay was watching her, an expectant expression on her face. She's missed something, obviously.

"I'm sorry, what did you say?"

"I said I'd be happy to jot down the names of some good books on the subject for you," her doctor said.

"Yes. That would be great. Thank you," Alex said.

She waited while Dr. Ramsay wrote down a couple of titles, then somehow found the strength to make polite small talk as the doctor saw her to the door.

She drove on autopilot to the gym to meet her coworker Ethan for their weekly racquetball game. It wasn't until she was pulling on her Lycra leggings and hooking the eyes on her sports bra that she registered where she was and what she was doing.

She sat on the bench that bisected the change room and put her head in her hands. She didn't want to run around a court and exchange smart-ass banter with Ethan between points. She wanted to go home and curl up in the corner with her thumb in her mouth.

She pressed her fingertips against her closed eyelids and sighed heavily. Then she straightened, pulled on her tank top, laced up her shoes and shoved her work clothes into her gym bag. As much as she wanted to go home, she couldn't leave Ethan hanging. Not when he was probably already standing on the court, waiting for her. She'd made a commitment to him and she always honored her commitments.

Shouldering her bag, she made her way to the wing

that housed the racquetball courts. As she'd guessed, Ethan was already there, warming up. She eyed him through the glass panel in the door, for once not feeling a thing as she looked at his long, strong legs, well-muscled arms and fallen-angel's face.

She smiled a little grimly. After months of telling herself that it was really, really inappropriate to have a low-level crush on her fellow partner and racquetball buddy, it seemed that all it took to neutralize his ridiculous good looks and rampant sex appeal was the news that she might have left it too late to have children.

She tucked her chin into her chest, squared her shoulders and fixed a smile on her face. Then she pushed open the door and entered the court.

"Hey. Thought you were going to chicken out on me," Ethan said as she threw her bag on top of his in the corner. A lock of dark hair fell over his forehead and he brushed it away with an impatient hand.

"Sorry. Got caught up," she said.

"No shame in admitting you're intimidated, slow-poke," Ethan said, his dark blue eyes glinting with amused challenge.

Most of the women in the office would turn into a puddle of feminine need if he gave them one of those looks, but Alex had been building up her immunity from day one. It was part of their shtick, the way he twinkled and glinted and flirted with her and the way she batted it all back at him, supremely unimpressed by his charmer's tricks.

According to their usual routine, she was supposed to rise to the bait of him using his much-disputed nickname for her but she didn't have it in her tonight. Instead, she concentrated on unzipping the cover on her racquet before turning to make brief eye contact with him.

"Let's play," she said. The sooner they started, the sooner this would be over.

He raised his eyebrows. "Don't want to warm up?"

"Nope."

She took her position on the court.

He frowned. "You okay?"

"I'm fine," she said. "You want to serve first…?"

Ethan's gaze narrowed as he studied her. She adjusted her grip on her racquet and tried to look normal. Whatever that was.

Finally he shrugged and moved to the other side of the court. After all, it wasn't as though they had the kind of friendship that went beyond the realm of the stuffy oak-paneled offices of Wallingsworth & Kent and the racquetball court. They might be the two youngest partners, and they might see eye to eye on most issues that came up during the weekly partners' meetings, but she had no idea what he did in his downtime—although she could take an educated guess, thanks to office scuttlebutt—and vice versa. Their friendship—if it could even be called that—was made up of nine-tenths banter and one-tenth professional respect. He was the last person she would confide her fears in.

Ethan bounced the ball a few times before sending it speeding toward the wall with his powerful serve. She lunged forward, racquet extended, and felt the satisfying thwack as she made contact. In a blur of stop-and-go motion they crisscrossed the court, slamming the ball into corners, trying to outmaneuver each other.

He was taller than her, and stronger, but she was faster and more flexible, as well as having four years on him agewise. The result was that they usually gave each other a good run for their money—although Ethan was slightly ahead on their running scoreboard, having beaten her last week.

Tonight she went after every point as though her life depended on it, pushing herself until she was gasping for breath and sweat was stinging her eyes.

After twenty minutes she'd won the first game and was ahead by three points on the second. Ethan shot her a grin as they swapped sides for her serve.

"You're on fire, slowpoke. But don't get too comfortable."

She didn't bother responding, bouncing the ball and sending it slamming toward him instead. Another frenetic few minutes passed as they fought for the point.

"I pity him or her, I really do," Ethan said after she'd won the battle with an overhead slam.

Alex tucked a stray strand of brown hair behind her ear. "Sorry?"

"Whoever pissed you off."

"I'm not angry," she said.

"If you say so."

She prepared to serve again but he walked to the corner and grabbed a bottle of water from his bag. She waited impatiently for him to drink, tapping her racquet against the side of her sneaker.

They'd just started their third game when she went long, lobbing a shot at the wall. It hit the high line and ricocheted toward Ethan but he let it fly past him to hit the rear wall without even attempting to take the shot.

"One, love," he said, his chest heaving, a big grin on his face. "Nice volley."

"Hang on, that was my point," she said. She wiped her forearm across her forehead.

"Sorry, it was out." His tone was final, utterly confident.

"It was in, Ethan. Right on the line, sure, but the line is in." She pointed toward the front wall with her racquet.

"Trust me, it was out."

"Oh, well, if you say so, it must be right. I mean, it's not like you'd ever lie to get your own way, is it? You're a man, and if it suits you, I'm sure anything goes—until it doesn't, right?"

Her words echoed off the hard surfaces of the court. There was a short silence as Ethan looked at her, his expression unreadable. Then she was looking at his back as he turned to collect the ball.

Heat burned its way up her chest and into her face. Talk about out of line.

"I'm sorry. That was really…I'm sorry," she said.

Ethan regarded her for a long beat. "Maybe we should take a break. Or call it quits until next week."

"No!" She heard the desperation in her own voice and tried to find the words to convince him to keep playing. It seemed vitally important that she be allowed to keep running around this small box, smashing the hell out of a rubber ball. She opened her mouth, but her throat seized and heat pressed at the back of her eyes. She spun away.

Don't cry, don't cry, don't you dare cry.

She stared fiercely at the floor, clenching and unclenching her hand on the grip of her racquet.

"Hey." Ethan's hand landed on her shoulder. "What's going on, Alex?"

"I'm fine," she managed to say.

"No, you're not."

"I'm fine." But her voice caught on the last word then tears were falling down her face.

"Shit," she said under her breath. Of all the people to break down in front of.

"It's okay," Ethan said from behind her. "Whatever it is, I'm sure you can work it out."

It was so far from the truth that she laughed harshly. "Sure I can. I can make myself younger. I can turn back time and make Jacob want to have a child with me. Hell, I can probably click my fingers and make myself pregnant."

The moment the words were out of her mouth she was acutely aware of how much she'd revealed, how exposed she was and how really inappropriate this conversation was. This was Ethan Stone, after all. Mr. Suave and Sophisticated, her fellow partner. Just because they shared lunch occasionally and played racquetball regularly didn't mean he wanted to know all the gory, messy details of her private life. And she didn't want him to know. Work was work, this was… very private.

"Who's Jacob?" Ethan asked.

"Nobody important. Forget I said anything."

She wiped her cheeks with her fingertips and sucked in a shaky breath. She had to get a grip. Had to put on her game face and convince him that she was good and to forget what she'd said.

"Alex…"

"I'm okay. A little stressed, that's all." But the damned tears wouldn't stop.

Warm, strong arms closed around her, pulling her toward a big, broad chest. Instinctively she resisted his embrace, trying to pull away.

"Don't be an idiot," he said, the sound vibrating

through his chest and into hers, his arms tightening around her.

Finally she gave in, although she couldn't bring herself to return the embrace—that would be admitting too much, asking for too much. Instead, she stood with her arms hanging uselessly by her sides, her body rigid with tension, waiting for this moment of pity or sympathy or whatever it was to be done with so she could make her excuses and get the hell out of here.

He didn't seem in any hurry to let her go, however. She could hear his heart beating steadily beneath her ear and she could smell his aftershave, something with sandalwood and musk notes. It had been a long time since she'd been held by a man—eighteen months.

She'd forgotten how good it felt.

Slowly, despite herself, some of the tension eased from her body.

"Nothing wrong with being upset, Alex," Ethan said.

She sniffed, in desperate need of a tissue. This time when she pushed Ethan away he let her go. She kept her face averted as she crossed to her gym bag. She squatted to rummage inside for her towel, then pressed the soft fabric against her face until she was sure she'd blotted away all evidence of her outburst. Then and only then did she push herself upright and face him again.

They eyed each other for a long beat. Finally Alex cleared her throat.

"I don't suppose you'd be prepared to pretend the last few minutes never happened?"

"Who's Jacob?" he asked again.

"I appreciate the concern, I really do, but you don't

want to hear the pathetic details of my personal life." She worked hard to keep her tone light and dry.

His gaze searched her face for a long moment. "Let me guess. Jacob's your ex, right? What happened? Is he getting married? Moving countries? Dying from an obscure disease?"

"I really don't want to talk about it."

"So he's getting married."

"He's not getting married. Can we just leave it?"

"How long ago did you break up?"

She threw her hands in the air. "He was pushing a baby stroller, okay? He's a father. Is that what you wanted to know?"

There was a short silence. She could see the surprise on Ethan's face, as though she'd presented him with a puzzle piece and he didn't know where it fit. Like Dr. Ramsay, he was probably shocked that she wanted to be a mother. She'd done such a good job of building the facade of Alexandra Knight, cool, efficient corporate lawyer, that no one had any idea what lay behind the power suits and overtime. Which was the way she liked it. Most of the time.

"How old are you?" Ethan asked.

"Excuse me?"

"Thirty-five? Thirty-six?"

"I'm thirty-nine this year."

"Thirty-nine's not old—"

She held up a hand. "Please don't tell me that I have plenty of time to meet someone else and have a child. I know it might be hard for someone who only has to click his fingers to have half a dozen women panting at his front door to understand, but men over thirty-five who want to get married and have kids are a little thin on the ground. And I have it on the good authority of my doctor that my chances of conceiving drop to ten percent once I hit my forties."

"I see," he said.

And she knew he did—too much.

She stood, shouldering her bag. "Look, I really have to go. I'm sorry about the game. And the blubbering. I'll make it up to you next week."

She didn't wait for him to respond, simply strode for the door. She should have stuck to her first instinct and canceled the game. Should have gone home and gotten all the anger and hurt and despair out of her system before she'd had to face the world again.

She didn't relax until she was behind the wheel of her car, cocooned by the dark outside and the instant warmth of her heater. Then and only then did her shoulders and stomach muscles relax. She sank against the seat and exhaled noisily. She felt so bloody weary and defeated. Overwhelmed. Filled with regret.

But she couldn't turn back time, could she? Couldn't go back eighteen months and be the one to "accidentally" forget a few vital pills so that she could be the mother of Jacob's child and force him into fatherhood against his will.

Not that she hadn't considered doing that toward the end. She'd been tempted, more than once. The bottom line was that she hadn't wanted to build their family on the foundation of a lie. She'd respected Jacob too much to take such an important decision out of his hands.

And now it was too late. Or close enough as made no difference. She'd missed the boat. Waited too long. And no amount of temper tantrums on the racquetball court was going to change that fact. She was simply going to have to suck it up and get on with playing the hand she'd been dealt. And if that hand meant no children…well, so be it.

Chapter Two

Alex's mood of grim resignation held sway until she stepped out of the shower later that evening. She'd made herself dinner when she arrived home from the gym and eaten it mechanically, then she'd settled on the couch and determinedly worked her way through the contracts she'd brought with her. She didn't let herself think. She was good at that—it was one of her most successful survival techniques. It wasn't until she'd showered and was toweling herself dry that she caught sight of her naked body in the bathroom mirror and stilled. She let the towel fall to the floor and pressed her hands against her belly, spreading her fingers wide, feeling the resilience of her own skin.

How many times had she imagined what it would be like to grow big with her child? To smooth her hands over her swollen belly? How many times had she tried to imagine what it would feel like to have a small, new life fluttering inside her?

Time to put that dream away.

She let her hands drop, but unlike earlier when she'd first confronted her brutal reality, a small voice piped up in the back of her mind.

A voice of defiance. A voice of hope.

You could still meet someone. You've got a few years. And it's not like you've been knocking yourself out trying to meet anyone. If you really put your mind to it, you could still have a chance.

For example, hadn't she flicked past three whole pages of singles ads in the back section of the daily newspaper this morning? She'd always turned her nose up at the idea of advertising for a partner, no matter that she'd heard plenty of first- and second-hand accounts of how people had met their husbands and wives via dating sites. She'd been convinced that someone would come along through the normal routes—friends, or work or some other social event. But maybe it was time to make things happen instead of waiting.

She shrugged into her dressing gown and headed for the kitchen, her mind teeming with plans. She'd join every dating website she could find. She'd place her own singles ad. She'd date her ass off, make it an absolute priority in her life until she met the right man. Surely, if she committed herself to the task of finding a partner, treated it like a project, she'd be successful. After all, when hadn't she achieved what she wanted once she put her mind to it?

She'd held the household together after her mother's accident through sheer grit. And after her mother's death she'd bulldozed her way through law school, then put her head down and bulldozed some more until she'd made partner in one of Melbourne's top law firms a mere seven years after graduating. When she wanted something in her professional life, she was formidable. So why couldn't she transfer that ethos to her personal life?

Her jaw was tense with purpose as she rescued this morning's paper from the top of the pile in the recycle bin. She crossed to the kitchen table and spread the paper wide, thumbing through until she found the classifieds section. She stared at the columns of small print, aware of her heart beating a determined tattoo against her rib cage. Then she ran her finger down the page until she found the Male Seeks Female section and began to read.

After a few minutes she grabbed a pen from the caddy on her kitchen counter and started to circle the likely suspects.

Male, mid-forties, good sense of humor, professional, seeks woman in mid- to late-thirties, attractive, good sense of humor. Enjoys movies, hiking, reading biographies…

Man, 30s, seeks woman for potential relationship. Should enjoy outdoor sports and overseas travel…

Successful professional male seeks mature, attractive woman no older than 40 with strong sense of self and independence. You should enjoy dining out, weekends away and the theater…

By the time she'd finished she had a list of eight possible prospects. Response was via email so she hauled out her laptop and fired it up. There was no reason she couldn't send the same response to all eight men. Coming up with that response, however, that might take some time.

She called up a document program on her computer and sat with her fingers hovering over the keyboard. How to best describe herself? She needed to sound appealing but not desperate. She'd never considered herself a great beauty—her jaw-length dark hair was thick and healthy but nothing spectacular, and her mouth was too wide and her eyes too large for conventional standards—but she was attractive enough and Jacob had always said that he loved her plush mouth and full breasts. But she could hardly put that in an ad. She typed a few lines, then immediately deleted them. How to get the essence of herself across in a few short paragraphs? How to cut through all the other responses these men might receive and stand out from the pack? Because the more men she met, the higher the chance of finding someone compatible and the sooner she could sound him out on the subject of children.

She jotted down some sums in the margin of the newspaper. Say it took her six months to find someone. Then another, say, four months before she felt comfortable broaching the subject of children with him. Or was four months too soon? It was hard to know.

Maybe she'd have to simply play it by ear, see what came up in conversation. But if the man was keen for a family, then they should probably wait another six months before attempting to get pregnant. Just to consolidate the relationship. In the meantime, she could talk to Dr. Ramsay about all the things she needed to do to be in tip-top condition to conceive—folate supplements and whatnot—so that she would be ready to go at the drop of a hat.

So adding the six-month search time to the four-month vetting period, then the six-month double-check time—

What are you doing? Can you hear yourself?

Alex stared at the figures. A formula for desperation—that was what she'd calculated. A formula for a woman who was terrified that she was going to miss out.

Was this what she really wanted? Did she really want a baby this much? Was motherhood so important to her that she was prepared to put it at the forefront of any potential connection she developed with a man?

She was no psychologist, but she didn't need to be to understand that embarking on a relationship with someone while her biological clock ticked loudly in the background wasn't exactly the ideal way to go.

But what choice did she have? It was this, or leave it to fate to throw the right man in her path before it was too late. And at the end of the day, she'd never believed in luck. She'd had to fight for every good thing that had ever come her way. Why should this be any different?

What she was planning wasn't particularly pretty or dignified, but if it helped her reach her end goal, then so be it. Life, as she well knew, was often not pretty or dignified.

She stood and grabbed the scissors from the kitchen drawer then cut the relevant pages from the paper. She'd start a folder to keep track of the ads she'd responded to, in case she doubled up.

She was about to close the paper and return it to the recycle bin when her gaze caught on a small, neat ad in the bottom right-hand corner.

Sperm Donor Wanted
Our client is an independent woman with her
own home and business. She has a wide support
network and wishes to become a mother. She is
seeking a donor with a clean bill of health and
no family history of major illness. If you are a
male between the ages of 18 and 45, you can help
her attain her dream of motherhood by contact-
ing Fertility Australasia at 02 9555 2801. Inter-
state donors welcome, travel payments available.

Alex stilled. For a moment there was not a single
thought in her mind. Then she reached for the newspaper and read the ad again, and again.

A sperm bank.

It simply hadn't occurred to her before.

She stared at the kitchen wall. Not five minutes ago
she'd decided that she didn't believe in luck and that
she was prepared to fight for what she wanted, even
if it smacked of desperation and meant loosening the
tight grip she'd always held on her pride.

A sperm donor was a dead cert. There would be no
equivocating or pussyfooting around worrying about
compatibility if she went the route of sourcing frozen sperm, bought from a suitably qualified clinic.
There would be no responding to want ads and waiting anxiously in coffee shops for her date to show up,
no awkward first, second, third dates. She'd never
have to judge when it was appropriate to sound out a
man on whether he wanted children. She'd never have
to worry about the relationship being based more on
a biological imperative than mutual attraction and
shared feeling.

It would be clean. Direct. Honest.

Best of all, it meant she was in control of her own destiny—as much as any person could be. Her body might not want to cooperate, of course, but at least she would have tried. Given it her best shot. Several best shots, depending on the costs.

She waited for her conscience to catch up with her, to sound a warning chime. But there was nothing.

This was not the way she'd wanted to have a child. She'd wanted to be one half of a couple, two people working together to bring new life into the world. A family.

But she was thirty-eight years old, staring down the barrel of her thirty-ninth birthday. She didn't have the luxury of waiting for Mr. Right anymore. Not if she wanted to be a mother.

How much do you want this? Enough to do it alone?

She didn't have to stretch her imagination to know what it would be like to have to cope with the pressures and stresses of raising a child on her own. She was all too familiar with the sense that there were not enough hours in the day, that she was utterly alone, with no help in sight, and that the only thing that stood between her mother and herself winding up on the street was her determination. She knew what it was like to live with the constant fear that there wouldn't be enough food for tomorrow or that her mother would do something that would bring the wrath of social services down upon them.

She'd survived eight years of loving, nursing, corralling and policing her brain-injured mother after the accident. She could be a single parent. Absolutely she could.

She had money—more than enough to ensure she and her child would never want for anything. Years of obsessive saving had seen to that. She could easily afford to take a year off work, two years, even. She was resourceful and determined. And she wanted this. She wanted this with every fiber of her being.

Picking up the scissors, she sliced the ad neatly from the page.

Ethan leaned on the doorbell of his brother's Blackburn home and waited. Sure enough, a small face appeared in the window beside the door, grinning like crazy.

"Uncle Ethan!"

"Hey, matey."

There was the sound of fumbling from behind the door, then it was open and his eldest nephew, Jamie, was sticking out his tongue and making fake fart noises.

Ethan waited patiently for Jamie to get it out of his system. He could only blame himself, after all, that the first thing his nephews did when they saw him was to break out the noisiest, wettest raspberry they could come up with. His sister-in-law, Kay, had warned Ethan when he'd started teasing the kids with raspberries.

"You're making a rod for your own back, Uncle Ethan," she'd said. "You know you're going to be Uncle Raspberry for the next ten years, don't you?"

She'd been spot on, but he figured there were worse things in the world.

Stepping over the threshold, he grabbed Jamie around the waist and tucked him under his arm.

"Now, where's your mom and dad?" he asked as Jamie bellowed a delighted protest.

He hefted his nephew up the hallway to the kitchen, where Kay was stacking dishes in the dishwasher. Her dark blond hair was pulled back in a tie and she was wearing her tailored work shirt over a pair of seen-better-days tracksuit pants.

"You just missed dinner. You should have called, I would have saved you some."

"I've got stuff at home for dinner, but thanks anyway. I thought I'd drop in and see if Derek had finished with that boxed set of *The Wire* yet."

"He's finishing up some end-of-quarter figures for one of his clients in the study." Kay wiped her hands on a tea towel and gave him an amused look. "Let me guess what's on the menu tonight—wagyu beef, fresh green beans, potato dauphin, maybe some red wine jus. For dessert, vanilla semi-freddo with poached seasonal fruit." She cocked her pinky finger in the air as though she was having high tea with the queen.

His love of good food and wine had always been a source of amusement for his family. He set Jamie on his feet.

"As a matter of fact, it's chicken stir-fry. What did you guys have? Fish fingers? Mac and cheese? Beans on toast?" Two could play at that game, after all.

Kay laughed and threw the towel at him. "Walking a fine line there, buddy."

"Uncle Ethan, come and see the new trick I can do on my bike," Jamie said, tugging on his hand to drag him toward the door to the patio.

"Hold on there, mister. Didn't I ask you to put on your jim-jams? It's too cold and dark out there for you to show Uncle Ethan anything," Kay said.

"But—"

Kay put her fingers in her ears. "Nope. Can't hear it. We don't have that word in this house."

Jamie's sigh was heavy with resignation. "All right. But you are one tough customer, lady."

Kay and Ethan exchanged amused glances as Jamie slouched off to his room.

"Apparently I'm a tough customer," Kay said. "And a lady."

"Who would have thunk it? Where's Tim?"

"In the bath. You can go wrangle him if you want."

It wasn't until he was helping his wriggling five-year-old nephew into his pajamas that Ethan understood why he'd come to his brother's house instead of going home after racquetball. It had shaken him, hearing the longing and yearning in Alex's voice tonight. Reminded him of his former life.

Because once, a long time ago, he'd wanted kids, too. He'd wanted to hold his sons or daughters in his arms. He'd wanted to dry them like this after the nightly bath. He'd wanted to teach them to read and kick a footy or ferry them to ballet classes. He'd wanted to guide them and help equip them with the skills they'd need to grapple with the challenges life would throw their way. He'd been so bloody certain that children would be a part of his life…

He smiled a little grimly. Alex would probably wet herself laughing if he told her that. She'd think he was being ironic or making fun of her. She didn't know about his marriage. She only knew him as a guy in a slick suit with a fast car and a reputation for churning through women.

But then he didn't know much about her, either, did he?

If anyone had told him that formidable, sharp, street-smart Alex Knight was even capable of breaking down the way she had tonight he'd have laughed. As for the surprising revelation that she wanted a child... He'd always thought of her as the consummate career lawyer, a woman who'd dedicated herself to the job and moving up the ladder.

Yet she'd cried tonight as though her heart was breaking because she was afraid that she'd missed the opportunity to have a family of her own. Again he felt the echo of old grief as he remembered the way she'd curled into herself, her shoulders hunched as she tried to contain her pain.

Tim's pajama buttons were misaligned and Ethan fixed them. He didn't let his newphew go immediately. Instead, he tightened his grip for a moment, hugging his nephew close, inhaling the good clean smell of him.

"Love you, little buddy, you know that, don't you?" he said quietly.

"I know," Tim said. Then he wriggled, a signal he was over the hug, and Ethan released him.

"What's wrong with you tonight?" Tim asked, his big eyes unflinching as they studied Ethan.

"Nothing." Ethan dredged up a smile and used a corner of the towel to flick his nephew on the leg. "Time to hit the sack, matey."

"Are you going to read me my bedtime story?"

"I thought I was doing that tonight," an aggrieved voice said from the doorway.

Ethan looked up to find his younger brother wearing a mock-hurt expression on his face. Shorter than Ethan, he had the same strong cheekbones and dark hair but a slightly bigger nose and paler blue eyes. *Just enough ugly to save me from being a pretty boy like you,* Derek always joked.

"You can do it any old time," Tim said airily.

"Nice to know I'm so easily replaced," Derek said drily.

"I'm not replacing you, stupid, you're my *daddy*," Tim said, as if that explained everything.

"What brings you to this neck of the woods?" Derek asked.

"Just in the neighborhood," Ethan said.

"What's with the Bjorn Borg outfit?"

Ethan glanced down at his black midthigh-length shorts and charcoal hoody and raised an eyebrow at his brother's derisive description. "Racquetball."

"Ah. Still playing with that guy from work? Adam or whatever?"

"Alex. And he's a she."

"Really?" Derek's expression turned speculative.

Ethan stood, shaking out the towel before arranging it over the rack. "You're like a hairy, much less attractive version of *Hello, Dolly,* you know that?"

"What's she like?"

Ethan rolled his eyes. "I'm not in the market. And even if I was, she's a partner. And a friend."

"So you're seeing someone else? When can we meet her?" Derek asked.

For a moment Ethan considered lying, simply to get his brother off his back. "The tap's leaking on the tub, by the way."

"No shit. We could do dinner, the four of us. It's been a while since Kay and I ate somewhere where they don't have cartoons on the menu."

"I'm not seeing anyone. I'm just not in the market."

"Still racking up the notches on the old bedpost. What a challenge." His brother's tone was flat, unimpressed.

"Not everyone can have the white-picket dream, mate."

Ethan had deliberately kept the uglier details of his divorce from his family, figuring there was no need for the world to know exactly how spectacularly his marriage had failed. The downside to that bit of self-preservation was these little pep talks his brother pushed on him periodically. Just as there was nothing worse than an ex-smoker, there was no one more pro-kids and pro-matrimony than a happily married man.

Even though he'd never admit it to his brother, Ethan's social life was a lot less hectic than anyone imagined. Sleeping around had gotten old quickly after the divorce. Like drinking till you passed out and bragging about your exploits, being a man-slut was apparently something that a guy grew out of. Go figure.

"You seen *The Girls Next Door* lately? Hugh's looking pretty tragic, shuffling around in that smoking jacket," Derek said.

"Will you let it go, Derek?" Ethan said, an edge in his voice.

Most of the time he didn't mind his brother's old-lady nagging, but tonight…tonight it was really getting up his nose.

"Just trying to save you from yourself."

"Yeah? Ever thought that maybe I don't need saving?"

"Nope."

Ethan turned his back on his brother and walked to the living room. If he stayed, they were going to wind up in an argument. Derek had good intentions, but he needed to let go of the idea that Ethan was going to meet a good woman and marry again. It was never going to happen. Ever.

Kay looked up from tidying the coffee table when he entered.

"Better get home to my wagyu," Ethan said. "What time's Jamie's party again?"

"Midday. It's on the invitation. You don't want a coffee?"

He forced a smile. "I'm good. Got to go home and poach that seasonal fruit, remember?"

He blew her a kiss as he headed for the door.

Alex woke with a thump of dread. Something terrible had happened…

Then it all came back to her. Jacob, the doctor, the singles pages, the fertility clinic ad.

She lay in bed for a moment, thinking about the decision she'd made last night, walking around it, examining it from all sides, prodding it, seeing if she still felt the same way in the cold, hard light of a new day.

The answer was yes. She still wanted a child. And her smartest, most guaranteed, no-muss, no-fuss way of getting one was through a sperm bank. Which meant she had some work to do.

Ever since she could remember she'd been a facts-and-figures person. It was one of the reasons she'd opted for corporate law rather than criminal or family. She liked detail, and research, and she excelled at pulling together all the relevant information to make rational, smart decisions then going over and over and over the fine print until she'd plugged every hole, taken advantage of every opportunity.

As she rolled out of bed and made her way to the bathroom, she started strategizing. First, she needed to find a reputable clinic. She needed to explore the ins and outs of sperm donation, the screening process and the success rate for artificial insemination. Then she needed to get her life in order. If she was going to be pregnant in the foreseeable future, there were a lot of things she needed to get sorted.

A nursery, for starters.

She squeezed her eyes tightly shut.

Dear God, I'm really going to do this.

Pointless to deny that there was a definite thread of sadness mixed in with the determination and excitement. She'd grown up without a father. She would have preferred for her child to have one. But there were hundreds of thousands of single-parent families in the world. She would do her best by her child, if she was blessed with one, the same as any other mother. That would have to be enough.

She dressed in one of her dark tailored skirt suits, matching it with her steel-gray suede pumps, then brushed her hair until it fell smoothly to her jawline. She never wore much makeup apart from a dusting of powder, mascara and lipstick. Five minutes later, she was on her way to work.

It wasn't until she was about to slide out of her car in Wallingsworth & Kent's underground garage that she spotted Ethan in her rearview mirror and remembered the other part of last night—the embarrassing, revealing part where she'd lost it and somehow wound up confiding in him. She'd been so caught up in her plans this morning, so determined not to waste another minute, that she'd forgotten how thoroughly she'd exposed herself.

Instinctively she slunk down in her seat, waiting for Ethan to reach the elevators before checking the rearview mirror again. Only when the doors had closed on him did she sit up straight, feeling absurd and foolish and relieved all at once.

Why, oh why, hadn't she gone home instead of giving in to obligation and playing that stupid racquetball game with him last night? She had an overdeveloped sense of responsibility, that was the problem. And look where it had gotten her.

There were plenty of women, she knew, who would line up around the block to take solace in Ethan Stone's arms. But he was Alex's colleague and fellow partner, and while she was prepared to privately acknowledge that he was an extremely attractive man, she had never, ever allowed herself to do more than that. She valued her hard-earned reputation as a professional who knew her stuff and who didn't let emotion get in the way, far too much to indulge in office flirtation. Especially with a man who went through as many women as Ethan did. As for blubbering all over him like a histrionic schoolgirl, moaning about her declining fertility…

Aware that she'd been hiding in her car too long, Alex made her way to the elevators. She told herself that when she saw Ethan this morning, she would simply pretend it was business as usual. He'd have to take his cue from her and follow suit. A few days from now, he'd have written off her confession as hormones and they'd be back to their old footing.

Except the moment she exited the elevator on the fifteenth floor she heard his voice and spotted him standing in the kitchenette, chatting with Franny while he poured himself a coffee.

Do it. Grab a coffee, talk about the weather. Show him that you're back to your mouthy, smart-ass self and normalize the situation.

She took a deep breath—then pivoted on her heel

and walked the long way to her office. Which made her an enormous chicken, she knew, but she was only human.

She ducked him twice more that morning, bowing out of a meeting she was supposed to attend with him and taking the stairs when she saw him heading for the elevator. She told herself she was merely buying herself time—for her to get over her self-consciousness and for him to forget the details from last night.

She had half an hour free before the partner lunch at midday and she spent the time checking out fertility clinics on the internet, one eye on her office door the whole time.

She found a number of information pages, complete with testimonials, and she followed the links to yet more sites. She bookmarked a few, then found a recent newspaper article reporting that there was a drastic shortage of sperm donors in Australia, particularly donors who were willing to offer their sperm to single women or same-sex partners. According to the article, for some time Australian women had been ordering sperm from banks based in the U.S. Curious, she clicked on a link and found herself staring at literally hundreds of profiles on a U.S. website. She scanned the first one with growing incredulity.

Donor 39 is five foot eleven inches, average build, blue-eyed, blond hair. His background is Russian, German and English. He is a professional, tertiary educated…

It was a little shocking to Alex that all this information was so readily available and that the ordering process was so easy. She'd assumed she'd have to jump through more hoops, but according to the website all she had to do was supply her credit-card number and she could purchase the specimen of her choice and have it shipped out to a clinic in Australia within the week.

Feeling a little dazed, she hit the print button so she could take the donor profiles home and read them in privacy. It wasn't until she closed the screen down that she jolted back to reality.

She was at work, for Pete's sake, and she shared her printer station with *her legal secretary* and *two other lawyers*. All of whom could be standing around the printer right now watching her profiles spit out of the machine.

Shit!

She was on her feet and rounding her desk in seconds. Her high heels dug into the carpet as she bolted for the door. She raced past Fran's desk to the printer alcove and sagged with relief when she found no one there.

Thank God. Thank. God.

The machine was spewing out pages and she collected them anxiously. She checked the first page—one of twenty! And it was only on page nine. She shot a look over her shoulder, then refocused on the machine.

Come on, come on!

She snatched each page as it appeared, adding it to the pile pressed to her chest. By the time she was down to pages nineteen and twenty her armpits were damp with nervous sweat.

"Hey. I've been looking for you. You missed our meeting earlier," a deep voice said behind her.

She started, almost dropping her armful of incriminating documents.

"Ethan, you startled me."

"No kidding. No more coffee for you today, tiger."

"Yeah." She smiled nervously, painfully aware that there was still one page outstanding from her tally. "So, um, how was the meeting? I had a scheduling conflict that I didn't see until the last minute."

Out of the corner of her eye she saw the last page emerge from the printer. She grabbed it as it hit the tray. Only when all twenty pages were pressed tightly to her chest did she give Ethan her full attention.

"Dull, as usual. Remind me again why we volunteered to head the billing-software review."

"Because we thought we could avoid making the same mistakes that were made last time?" she suggested.

"Right. How noble of us." He moved a little closer and lowered his voice. "How are you doing today?"

She'd known this was coming from the moment she heard his voice. She steeled herself to meet his deep blue gaze.

"I'm great," she said firmly. "Really great."

"Yeah?"

He was standing so close she could smell his aftershave again. Embarrassed heat rose up her face. She dropped her gaze to the lapel of his charcoal pinstripe suit.

"Absolutely."

She didn't need to be looking at Ethan to know he was studying her closely.

"Honestly," she said, forcing herself to make eye contact again. "I had a minor freak-out. I went home, got a solid night's sleep and now I'm all good."

He looked as though he wanted to say more and she made a big deal out of checking her watch.

"Wow. We're both going to be late for Sam's birthday lunch if we don't put our skates on," she said.

"I'm ready to go. I thought we could walk together."

"Oh. Great idea. Except I've still got one last call to make. And I don't want to make you late, too," she fibbed. "Why don't you go ahead and I'll see you at the restaurant?"

Again, she didn't give him a chance to object, brushing past him and walking toward her office. She didn't let her breath out until she was through the doorway and safely out of sight.

This was why it always paid to keep work and her private life separate. She lifted the sheaf of papers and smacked them against her forehead. From now on, anything to do with her personal life stayed at home and was handled after nine to five. No exceptions.

As for Ethan... He would get the message. He'd have to, because she wasn't exposing herself any more than she already had. The sooner they both forgot her breakdown last night, the better.

Ethan watched Alex disappear into her office, a frown on his face. In the two years he'd worked with her, she'd never once had trouble meeting his eye—except for today. Mind you, she'd also never let him as close as she had last night. Prior to that, the most personal topic they'd discussed had been her hatred of black cherries. To be fair, he hadn't volunteered the intimate details about his own life, either, but he'd always had the sense that even if he'd tried to get closer to Alex she would have kept him at arm's length. She was happy to joke and spar and compete with him, but anything deeper than that was out of bounds. It had never really bothered him before, but today he felt distinctly pissed that he'd been shut out.

He straightened his cuffs and buttoned his suit jacket and told himself to get over it. It wasn't as though he was in the market for a new bosom buddy—he had his brother and a handful of mates he could rely on to have his back. And it definitely wasn't that he was keen to play Dr. Phil and pass the tissues. It was no skin off his nose if Alex didn't want to share.

He was about to head for the elevator when a blinking red light caught his eye. The printer Alex had been hovering over so urgently was jammed.

He couldn't say what made him open the various flaps and trays to check for a paper jam. Perhaps it was because Alex had been so jumpy and furtive. Or maybe some other instinct guided him.

Whatever it was, it took him only seconds to find the culprit—a single page that had folded in on itself instead of exiting to the out tray. He pulled it free and straightened it, shaking toner dust off his fingers.

He scanned the first few lines but comprehension was a few moments in coming. His head came up and he turned to stare toward Alex's office.

What on earth…?

Surely she wasn't seriously thinking…?

He took a step, the incriminating evidence in hand, then stopped. What was he going to say to her? Hadn't he just established for himself that their friendship was limited to work and the racquetball court? That she didn't want to discuss her private life?

He slowly folded the sheet in half, then into quarters before slipping it into his jacket pocket. He went to join the rest of the partners for lunch.

He had it right the first time—this was nothing to do with him.

Chapter Three

Ethan kept an eye out for Alex as the rest of the partners arrived and seated themselves in the private dining room at Grossi Florentino, but she didn't slip through the door until a good ten minutes after everyone else was perusing the menu.

He watched as she made her excuses and took the last remaining chair between Keith Lancaster and Toby Kooperman at the other end of the table. She smiled at Keith when he said something, then leaned back to allow the waiter to place a napkin across her knees. He returned his attention to his menu, but the sound of her laughter drew his gaze.

She had one hand pressed to her chest and her eyes shone with amusement as she talked animatedly with Keith. Ethan watched the tilt of her head and the flush in her cheeks and the way she gestured with her hands and had to remind himself that it was none of his business that she was planning to buy frozen semen from some faceless donor in the U.S. because she was afraid she'd missed the boat. It was her life, her decision. Nothing to do with him.

And yet…

She was only thirty-eight years old and she was an attractive, sexy woman. Not conventionally beautiful, perhaps, but incredibly appealing with her rich brown eyes and chestnut hair. More than once when they'd been lunching together he'd found himself fixating on her mouth, with its lush, full lower lip. She was smart, too, and funny. If she hadn't been a fellow partner and if he hadn't instinctively known that she was not the kind of woman who did casual affairs, he would have asked her out long ago. There had to be a bunch of men out there who would give their eyeteeth to meet someone like her.

And yet she was planning on using a sperm donor to become pregnant. It simply didn't make sense to him that a woman with as much as she had to offer was taking such a compromised route to motherhood. He wanted to push back his chair, grab her arm and drag her somewhere private so he could point out that she was selling herself short, big-time.

He didn't. She'd made it more than clear that they didn't have the sort of friendship that invited that kind of straight talking. They were work buddies. Good for a little bitching about office politics, a joke at the water cooler and a weekly workout. That was it.

He dragged his gaze away, joining in the conversation around him. As with most partner lunches, the wine flowed freely and the room became noisier as the meal progressed. Ethan stuck to one glass since he had a heavy afternoon schedule and kept an eye on the time. Occasionally, against his will, he found himself watching Alex and his mind did a loop of the same circle of thoughts. He repeated his mantra—*nothing to do with you, nothing to do with you, nothing to do with you*—and returned his attention to his end of the table.

He decided to give it twenty more minutes before he made his apologies when Alex pushed back her chair and stood.

"Well, someone has to pay for this lunch," she said. "I'd better get to it."

Laughter greeted her announcement as he pushed back his own chair.

"Exactly what I was thinking."

She looked at him and he caught a flash of unease in her eyes. He crossed to the door and waited for her to join him.

"I don't think they'll be billing many hours this afternoon," he murmured as they made their way through the restaurant.

Her gaze flashed toward him before skittering away again.

"Probably just as well, given the way they're working their way through the wine list."

They both stopped when they reached the double front doors. Outside, the sky was a dark, leaden gray, and rain was pouring down.

"Good old Melbourne," Alex said, then she glanced ruefully at her shoes. "What are the odds of us finding a taxi that'll take us half a block up the road?"

He didn't bother responding, simply flipped up the collar on his suit jacket.

"Yeah, that's what I thought." She sighed and turned up the collar on her own jacket.

He was about to open the door when a waiter rushed to their side carrying a large golf umbrella.

"With our compliments," he said, offering the umbrella to Ethan.

"Thank you. We'll get it back to you this afternoon," he said.

Although given the amount of money the firm would drop on lunch, the restaurant could afford to give every partner an umbrella and still come out on top.

He held the door open and Alex stepped out under the restaurant's portico. He followed, breathing in the smell of wet cement and rain.

"Should have checked the weather report before we left the office," she said.

He unfurled the umbrella and lifted it.

"Ready?" He gestured toward the teeming, wet world that awaited them.

She joined him beneath the curve of the umbrella, her shoulder brushing his, and they both started walking, falling into step with one another after a few paces.

"How was your meal?" she asked after a short silence.

"Good. Yours?"

"Yeah, good."

He glanced at her, but her head was lowered. They'd never been reduced to small talk; even at the very beginning of their friendship they'd always found plenty to say to each other. He felt as though he was being punished somehow. Frozen out with the silent treatment because he'd witnessed her in a moment of weakness last night.

"Alex—"

The world flashed white and a huge roll of thunder cracked overhead as the heavens opened even further, sending rain pelting down out of the sky. He operated on instinct, wrapping an arm around her waist and hustling her beneath the scant shelter of a nearby shop portico.

She shot him a startled look when he finally let her go.

"Can't use an umbrella in a lightning storm," he explained as he furled the soaked umbrella.

"No. Of course not." Then, to his surprise, her mouth quirked as though she was suppressing a smile.

"What's so funny?"

"I don't think I've ever been rescued before," she said. "For a moment there I felt like I was in a Cary Grant movie."

"Are you suggesting that I manhandled you?" he asked.

"Absolutely."

"Lucky I didn't give in to my first urge to throw you over my shoulder, then."

She laughed, her eyes crinkling at the corners attractively. He looked into her face and it hit him again that what she was planning was just plain *wrong*.

"Don't do it, Alex," he said. "Don't sell yourself short."

She stilled, the smile fading from her lips. "Sorry?"

Rather than try to explain, he pulled the sheet of paper he'd rescued from the printer from his pocket and passed it over. She made a small distressed sound when she unfolded it and understood what it was.

"You're panicking right now, and the last thing you should be doing is making irrevocable decisions," he said.

Dark color flooded her face. "This is none of your business." She crumpled the paper in her hand and glanced over her shoulder as though she was afraid someone else might have seen it.

"Someone has to point out the obvious—this is a mistake."

Alex blinked, her brown eyes wide with shock at his bald pronouncement. "At the risk of repeating myself, this is *none of your business,*" she said.

Ethan knew she was right. She was a fellow partner, and he was stepping way over the line, but he couldn't help himself. She deserved a million times better than what she was considering.

"I'm not going to stand by while someone I like and respect makes a mess of her life. Look me in the eye and tell me this is the way you want to have a child."

She flinched, then her chin came up. "I'm not having this discussion with you, Ethan. Just because I had a moment of weakness while you happened to be around last night doesn't give you a free pass into my private life."

"Answer my question." He took a step closer. "Or are you afraid to?"

He knew that would get her—he might not know what school she went to, but he did know that Alex prided herself on never retreating from a challenge.

She lifted her chin and eyed him angrily. "What do you want me to say, Ethan? You want me to admit that I'm desperate? That this is my last resort? Okay, sure. I am and it is. You want me to tell you that when I was a little girl and I dreamed of having a family of my own, never in a million years did I imagine myself picking his or her father from an online catalog? Absolutely. And if there was any other option on the horizon, there is no way in the world I would consider doing this. But there isn't, and I refuse to sit on my hands while my last chance to have a family fades away."

"It's not fading away. You're thirty-eight, not forty-eight, and there are hundreds of men who'd break a leg to meet a woman as attractive and together as you."

She made a rude noise. "You think men are lining up to ask out a busy woman with a mind of her own who probably earns more than they do? Especially when there's some young blonde thing in her twenties hanging around at the bar who only wants to have a good time?"

"You think all men are a bunch of morons who'd rather go out with a centerfold than a woman with a brain in her head?" he countered.

"You tell me—when was the last time you bypassed the beauty and went for the brain?"

"This isn't about me. You're copping out, Alex, and you're going to regret it."

"Don't you dare judge me. You have no idea what it's like to know that in a few years' time your own body is going to take away your options. So don't stand there and lecture me about what I'm worth or what I deserve. Life isn't about what you deserve—it's about what you can get and what you can live with. And I will not be able to live with myself if I don't try to make this happen."

She turned on her heel and walked into the rain.

"Alex," he said, darting after her to pull her back beneath the shelter of the awning.

She jerked free of his grasp. "No, Ethan."

She kept walking, her head down, her shoulders rounded against the force of the rain.

He swore under his breath—but he didn't go after

her. He'd already stepped over the line and he didn't trust himself not to do it again.

She was making a mistake. But maybe he should have listened to his first instinct and walked away.

Maybe.

Alex was dripping wet when she returned to the office. Fran took one look at her and shot to her feet.

"I've got a towel in my gym bag."

"Thanks."

Alex had toed off her shoes and was peeling off her wet suit jacket when Fran returned.

"You're soaked to the skin," Fran said, sliding a mug of tea onto Alex's desk and draping a towel around Alex's shoulders. "I brought you something hot to drink."

"Thanks. If you wouldn't mind, there's some dry cleaning in my car...?" She shivered as a trickle of cold water ran down her spine.

"Give me your keys, I'll go and grab it for you."

Alex gave her assistant a grateful smile as she handed over her car keys. "You're the best, Franny."

"I know," the older woman said drily. "Won't be a tick."

She pulled the door shut behind her as she exited. Once she was alone, Alex let the smile fall from her face.

She still couldn't believe that conversation. The things Ethan had said... The fact that he *knew*...

Her hands were shaking as she tugged her wet shirt from her waistband. She gripped them together, willing the trembling to stop.

He'd shocked her, that was all. She hadn't planned to tell anyone that she was using a sperm bank, even her friend Helen, who lived in the apartment across the hall, or Samantha, whom she'd studied with. Once she was pregnant, she'd decided to simply claim the father was no longer on the scene. It happened every day, after all. Why not to her?

But now Ethan knew. And he didn't approve. Which was pretty rich coming from a guy who made George Clooney look like an advertisement for celibacy.

Ethan thought she was *selling herself short*. Remembering the way he'd said it made her angry all over again. Did he truly think this was her method of choice for having a child? That she hadn't considered all other options? That she was taking some kind of expedient shortcut to motherhood?

She started working on the buttons on her shirt.

Stupid, but she felt betrayed. She'd always respected him and valued his opinion. He was smart and funny and generous with his time and he never, ever patronized her or treated her as less than an equal the way some of the older partners did. Even on the racquetball court he never gave her quarter. And now—

A knock sounded at the door. "Alex."

She tensed. She could hear the determined note in Ethan's voice even through an inch of varnished wood.

"Go away."

The door swung open and she gave a squawk of outrage, clutching the gaping neckline of her shirt together to keep herself decent.

"Do you mind?"

His suit was dark at the shoulders and trouser cuffs and he dismissed her modesty with an impatient wave of his hand.

"I'm sorry, okay? What I said before…you have every right to be angry with me. I just…I don't want you to regret this."

There was so much sincerity and concern in his voice and his deep blue eyes that the angry words in her throat dissolved. She stared at him for a long moment, then turned away to rebutton her damp shirt.

"I want a child," she said, her voice very low. "Am I supposed to miss out because the music has stopped and all the chairs are full?"

"No."

She turned to face him again, arms crossed over her chest defensively. "Then you tell me what I'm supposed to do, Ethan. Join a dating site and trawl for a man who's looking for commitment and not just sex? How long do you think it's going to take to find one of those? And if I do, when do you suggest I bring up the subject of children with him? First date? Second? Sixteenth? And if he says yes, sure, I'd love kids, how long should we wait before we start trying? A week? A month? A year?" She could hear her voice becoming strident and she made an effort to remain calm. "Do you honestly think that's any less desperate and compromised than me going to a sperm bank? Really?"

He looked away, then ran a hand over his damp hair. "There's no easy answer."

"No, there isn't."

A line of water trickled down the side of his face and she passed him the towel. She couldn't help noticing that he looked as good wet as he did dry. She didn't need a mirror to tell her she looked like a drowned rat.

"Maybe you can't understand this because you're a man, but this is something I've wanted since I was a little girl," she said. "To be a mother. To love unconditionally. To watch a new person find their way in the world. Not very revolutionary or daring by today's standards, but it's what I want. And I think I'd be a decent mother."

Ethan loosened the knot on his tie and unbuttoned his top shirt button. "I'm not questioning your ability to be a mother, Alex. I think you'd make a great mom. But you spoke to your doctor last night and today I find you printing off information on sperm donors. It's a pretty big leap, you've got to admit."

"I'm researching, not placing an order."

"You're panicking. You ran into your ex and you're freaking out."

She seriously considered kicking him in the shin. Wasn't he listening to her? Hadn't he heard a thing she'd said?

"I'm facing facts. Time is running out for me. And yes, in a perfect world I would want my child to know his father. But this is what's on the table and I'm not too proud or precious to take it."

There was a rap on her office door before it opened and Fran entered.

"I had trouble finding your car. Thank God for these beepy door-open things," she said.

She stopped in her tracks when she saw Ethan, glancing between the two of them.

"Sorry. I didn't mean to interrupt."

"You didn't. Ethan was leaving." Alex gave him a meaningful look.

"I see you got caught in the rain, as well," Fran said, running a disapproving eye over Ethan's wet suit. "Do you want me to try to do something with that jacket?"

"Thanks, but I'm sure it will dry out okay."

"Well, don't let us keep you," Alex said pointedly. "Wouldn't want you to catch a chill or anything."

Ethan gave her a dry look. "I'll see you later, Alex."

He managed to make it sound like both a threat and a promise as he exited.

Fran closed the door after him. "I hope I didn't walk into the middle of something."

As fishing expeditions went, it was far from subtle. "You didn't. We were discussing something that came up over lunch."

"I see."

Alex could see the older woman didn't believe her. Great. That was all she needed—her assistant thinking there was something going on between her and Ethan, the office sex god. That would get the jungle drums pounding.

"Pity he wouldn't let me take care of his jacket. I was kind of hoping I could convince him to whip his shirt off in front of us," Fran said.

Despite everything, Alex laughed. Couldn't help herself. For a woman in her late fifties, Fran sometimes came out with the most outrageous things. "Careful, Fran, or you'll be up on a sexual-harassment charge."

"It would almost be worth it. I bet he's got an amazing chest. Don't tell me you haven't thought about it. And those thighs… What am I saying? You play racquetball with him. You must have seen him in all his glory."

Fran was looking at her expectantly and Alex concentrated on taking her clean shirt off the hanger.

"I really haven't noticed, to be honest," she lied.

"Then you need your head read and your eyes tested. A gorgeous man like him—I tell you, if I was a few years younger, I'd be more than happy for him to park his slippers under my bed."

"I think he's pretty busy parking his slippers around town already."

Fran sighed. "Well, who can blame him? At least he's spreading the joy." On that outrageous note she headed for the door. "Next appointment's in ten," she called over her shoulder before she disappeared.

"Thanks."

Alex tucked her shirt in and pulled out her compact to check her hair. She had no idea what to do about the fact that Ethan was privy to her most private plans. It had been bad to lose it in front of him last night, but for him to know her pregnancy plot…

She stilled when she recognized what she saw in her reflection: shame.

There had been many occasions in her life when she'd felt the sting of shame. When one of the kids at her high school had learned about her mother's brain damage and she'd arrived at school one morning to find everyone whispering and staring at her. When she'd had to wait for hours in the waiting room at social services, feeling the pitying eyes watching her and wondering. When she'd found herself rubbing elbows with some of Melbourne's most privileged sons and daughters at Melbourne Law School, her well-thumbed secondhand textbooks and thrift-shop clothes marking her as an outsider as obviously as if she'd been carrying a flare.

It was only with the hindsight of age and experience that she'd finally understood that those moments had not been cause for shame. Her mother had suffered a terrible injury, and as a consequence her whole life had changed. They had been poor, and they had struggled. There was no shame in any of those circumstances.

Alex straightened her shoulders. There was no shame in what she was doing now, either. She was single. She wanted a child. She wasn't breaking any laws or hurting anyone or acting immorally.

She made a promise to herself on the spot: from now on, she wasn't going to apologize or explain what she wanted to anyone. And she wasn't going to waste precious energy worrying about what Ethan thought or didn't think. If he was her friend…well, he would support her. And if he wasn't then she was well shot of him.

Either way, it wasn't going to stop her from pursuing her goal.

Ethan went home to an empty apartment. No surprises there, that was the way he liked it. He showered and changed into jeans and a sweater, then wandered aimlessly from room to room. He picked up the magazine he'd been reading, then put it down. Flicked on the TV, only to turn it off again.

For the second night in a row, Alex Knight was in his thoughts.

No two ways about it, he'd been an ass today, blundering into her business when he wasn't welcome. But it wasn't his own ham-fisted behavior that kept him moving restlessly. What kept rising to the surface of his mind was the memory of the unadulterated, unashamed yearning he'd heard in Alex's voice when she'd talked about wanting a child.

He understood what it was like to have life pull the rug out from beneath you and lay waste to all the plans you'd made. When he'd married Cassie, he'd had a vision in his head of how their life was going to be: the two of them working hard to complete their respective degrees, the house they would buy, the amount of time they'd wait to get their careers established before starting a family, the partnership he'd earn, the schools the kids would go to...

He'd been so certain about all of it, so confident it was his for the taking.

He crossed to the window and stared down at the cars moving along St. Kilda Road.

It had been five years since his divorce, five years since he'd understood that his plans for his life differed wildly from reality. He'd long since resigned himself to the fact that certain things were never going to happen for him.

Alex, however, wasn't even close to being content with the hand she'd been dealt and a part of him admired her for her refusal to simply accept that she'd missed out. He might not think her solution was the greatest, but she wasn't prepared to give up on her dream, and she was going to go to the mat fighting for it.

Hard not to be impressed by that kind of determination. But he'd always found her impressive, hadn't he? From his first days with the firm he'd noticed her— those direct, clear brown eyes, that mobile mouth, all that attitude and energy.

Heartily sick of his own circling thoughts, Ethan went into the kitchen and concentrated on dinner. Half an hour later he had the tagine steaming on the stove and the smell of Moroccan spices filled the room.

He opened a bottle of wine, steamed some couscous and sat down to chicken with green olives and almonds for one. Then he found a good documentary and poured himself another glass of wine. By eleven he was over TV and over himself and he went to bed.

He woke with a start several hours later, his heart racing, his body clammy with sweat. It took him a moment to orient himself to his bedroom, to understand why Cassie wasn't in the bed beside him and why he could hear the faint sound of traffic passing by outside instead of the hushed quiet of a suburban street.

He glanced at the alarm clock. Three in the morning. Great.

He rolled out of bed and walked naked to the bathroom. He sluiced water onto his face, then glanced at his shadowy reflection in the bathroom mirror. In the dim light, all he could see was the outline of his features and the glint of his eyes. He grabbed his robe and shrugged it on before making his way to the kitchen.

He couldn't recall what he'd been dreaming about before he woke. All he could conjure were vague shadows and a pervading sense of loss. Better than a teeth-falling-out or going-to-work-naked dream, but not by much.

He poured himself a couple of inches of cognac then took his drink to the living room. One of the advantages of living so close to the city was that there was always a sense of activity—life—happening nearby, no matter the time, day or night.

He drew up a chair near the window. If it was summer, he'd go out on the balcony, but it would be bitterly cold tonight so he settled for resting his forehead against the cool glass and watching the bright lights of the city.

He thought about the night Tim was born, how he'd felt when his brother had passed his brand-new son into Ethan's arms. Ethan had been moved at Jamie's birth, had even felt a little ambushed by the tug of connection and protection he'd felt toward his brother's child. But with Tim, it had been different. Cassie had walked out on him by then, and he'd looked into Tim's unblinking, bewildered, unfocused blue eyes and understood absolutely that this would be as close as he'd ever come to being a parent. It had been a watershed moment. A moment of resignation and acceptance and grief.

But maybe he wasn't as resigned as he'd thought he was. Maybe he wasn't quite ready to abandon the dream of being a father. Maybe, like Alex, he wasn't prepared to walk away without a fight.

He felt as though he was standing on the edge of a precipice, teetering on the brink of...something. A mistake? An opportunity? A second chance?

He lost track of how much time had passed. Slowly the sky lightened and brightened. Birds started to appear, swooping in and out of the treetops in the Alexandra Gardens opposite his apartment. He stood and stretched out his tight shoulders and back. Then he went into the bedroom and dressed.

He only had to wait for ten minutes before his brother emerged from his house and started doing his pre-run stretches on the front lawn. Derek glanced over his shoulder at the sound of the car door closing and stilled for a split second when he saw who it was. Then he straightened and crossed the road to join Ethan.

"What's going on?" he asked. His breath was visible in the cold morning air.

"Relax. It's not an emergency. I wanted to run something by you."

Derek scanned his face then obviously decided to take Ethan at his word. "Okay. Can you do it while we run?"

"If you think you can keep up."

Derek smiled. "Try me."

They ran in silence for a few minutes, neither of

them pushing the other. Finally Derek stopped, forcing Ethan to stop, too.

"You gonna spill or what? The suspense is killing
me."

Ethan eyed his brother. Then he stared down at the
toes of his sneakers. After a long beat he met his brother's eyes again.

"First up, I want you to understand something. I
know we joke about it a lot and I let you nag me, but
I'm never going to get married again. Period."

Derek frowned and Ethan could see he was about to
launch into the same-old "you don't know what might
happen in the future, don't close yourself off to possibility" speech.

"This isn't a stage I'm going through, it's not something that's going to change, and I need you to accept
that. Okay?"

Derek's focus shifted down the road, his hands on
his hips. Then he shrugged and looked at Ethan. "It's
your life."

"Yeah, it is. Which brings me to my next question."
He took a deep breath. He knew his brother was going
to have strong feelings about what he was about to suggest, but he needed a sounding board before he made
any irrevocable decisions or commitments.

"I'm thinking of offering to become a sperm donor
for a friend," he said.

Derek opened his mouth. Then he closed it again
without saying anything.

Fair enough. Ethan was aware that he was hitting
his brother with this out of the blue.

"She's a friend. She's worried she's running out
of time and she hasn't met anyone. She doesn't want
to miss out. She's considering using a bank. And I'm

thinking that I could step up instead. Offer to be the father. Have a kid."

"Jesus. I don't even know what to say," Derek said.

"Lots of people do it."

"Yeah. Gay people. Infertile people. Desperate women. You're forty-two, Ethan. Kay could name half a dozen of her friends who would lie down right now in the middle of the street and make a baby with you."

"I covered that. I'm not getting married again."

"Then don't. Live with someone, whatever. But don't become a parent by proxy."

"It wouldn't be by proxy. I mean, the conception would be, obviously. But I'd want to be a part of the kid's life. We'd raise him or her together, like any divorced couple. A custody agreement, child-support payments."

"You're really serious, aren't you?"

"Yeah, I am. I've always wanted kids. After everything with Cassie I thought I'd put it behind me. But now this opportunity has come up and maybe I don't have to miss out. Maybe there are other ways to do this."

Derek blew out his breath and shook his head. "Who is this woman, anyway? How close a friend is she?"

"I work with her. I respect her. She's smart, funny, attractive. I think she'd be a great mother and we could parent together really well."

"Wow. She sounds almost too good to be true. Why hasn't some other lucky sucker snapped her up?"

Ridiculously, Ethan felt himself bristle on Alex's behalf. He knew his brother was only trying to protect him, but this wasn't about Alex. She didn't deserve Derek's scorn.

"The guy she was with for seven years didn't want

kids. She thought she had more time, but the doctor says once she's over forty it's slim pickings."

"Right."

Ethan cocked his head and waited but Derek remained silent. Ethan made a beckoning motion with his fingers. "Come on. I know you've got more. Hit me with it."

"That's why you came here at five-thirty in the morning? For me to play devil's advocate?"

Ethan shrugged. "I knew you'd have an opinion. And there's no one I trust more."

"Damned right I have an opinion. For starters, what are you going to tell your son or daughter when they ask how mommy and Daddy met? 'Mommy and Daddy had a great date down at the lab'?"

"We'd tell them that we were friends, which is true. And when they were old enough to understand, we'd tell them the full truth."

"What about the fact that this kid is never going to know the security of having both his parents under the same roof? Right from the start he's born into a broken home."

"You want me to go over the stats for single-parent families in Australia? There are plenty of people raising kids on their own, right from day one. Then there are the divorces and the custody arrangements. For sure any arrangement Alex and I come up with has to be better than what a lot of divorced couples agree to—and I'm in a position to know. This would be all about the child, not us. We wouldn't be using the kid to punish each other, there'd be no issues with child support or access. No jealousy over new partners, no acrimony."

Derek's eyes narrowed. "Alex. That's the woman you play racquetball with, right?"

Ethan hesitated. Until he made his final decision, he hadn't planned on revealing Alex's identity. After all, it was her business—until it became his. But he'd already blown the gaffe.

"Yeah. That's right."

"You say there'd be no acrimony. You're kidding yourself if you think there aren't going to be moments when the two of you want to rip each other's heads off. It doesn't matter whether you're married or in a relationship or divorced or whatever, you're going to disagree about something. Raising kids is like that, and no neat little contract you guys draw up beforehand is going to make any difference to that."

"How do you and Kay work it out?"

"We fight. Then we have sex and make up. What are you and Alex going to do to get over the rough patches? Play a game of racquetball and exchange lawyer jokes?"

"We'd work it out." It had been a long time since he took anyone at face value or trusted his own instincts entirely where other people were concerned, but his gut told him Alex was a good and genuine person.

And if his gut was wrong…well, he'd be protected. He'd make sure their co-parenting agreement was watertight and rock solid.

"Doesn't it worry you that this child would be the product of a medical procedure and not the result of an act of love?"

"You trying to tell me that every kid who's born into the world is born of love?"

"All right, passion then. Something human and real. What you're talking about is so…calculated. Like a business transaction. Call me a traditionalist, but I can't help thinking that the creation of new life should at least be accompanied by *some* sentiment."

Ethan considered his brother's words. He understood where Derek was coming from—he'd had the same gut-level rejection of Alex's idea at first. He'd confronted her in the street, he'd been so determined that she hold out for the "real thing." But after talking to her, he understood her urgency. She didn't have the time to play the odds and hope. As a man, he had no such constraints, but given his vow to never again marry, it was unlikely he'd have a child any other way.

Like Alex, he recognized that right here, right now there was an opportunity for him to perhaps fulfill a long-held dream. It was an unconventional opportunity, possibly a calculated one, as Derek said. But it was there, up for grabs.

What had Alex said yesterday? *This is what's on the table and I'm not too proud or precious to take it.*

He focused on his brother. "I appreciate your honesty."

"But it's not going to change your mind, is it?"

"No."

"You always were a stubborn bastard."

They resumed running. Ethan glanced at his brother, aware Derek seemed troubled. No doubt Derek would go home and tell Kay what Ethan intended and the two of them would rant and rave to each other about how crazy it was.

Was he crazy for thinking about doing this? He had a good life—a lucrative career, the respect of his peers, the security and peace of mind of relying on no one but himself. Was he nuts to even think about throwing fatherhood into the mix?

I want a child.

He could still hear the longing in Alex's voice. He glanced up at the pale morning sky.

So do I.

And that was what it came down to in the end.

Chapter Four

Alex gave herself a stern talking-to when she arrived at work the next day. She would not be avoiding Ethan today, for any reason. True to her promise to herself, she was going to deal with this head-on. If he attempted to dissuade her again, she was going to let him know in no uncertain terms that while she appreciated his concern came from a sincere place, it was inappropriate. It was more than time for him to butt out and go polish his car or chat up a hot blonde. It was her life, her decision, and he didn't get a vote.

She was tense all morning, convinced he would ambush her in her office, but he never came. When she went out to grab a sandwich for lunch he wasn't waiting for her in the foyer, either, as she'd half suspected he might be.

It was possible he was in court, of course, or attending off-site meetings. But she saw him at the end of the corridor midafternoon and he caught her eye as he walked toward her. Adrenaline squeezed into her belly and her chin came up.

Be strong. Tell him to mind his own beeswax. No explanations or justifications.

She took a deep breath, ready to fire the opening salvo as he drew closer and closer. Then he nodded, murmured hello and passed her by.

She stared at the empty hallway for a full ten seconds after he'd gone before forcing her shoulders down from around her ears and returning to her office. She told herself he was biding his time, but by the end of the day he hadn't so much as sent her an email or left a phone message.

Perhaps he'd reconsidered his interference after a good night's sleep. Maybe, like her, he'd asked himself how her private life was any of his business.

She didn't fully relax until another day had passed and he still hadn't approached her. Apparently she was off the hook. She told herself she was relieved, that it was best for their friendship and their working relationship that he back off. And she *was* relieved—but she was also conscious of a sense of disappointment. Which was crazy. He'd barged his way into her business, forced his opinions and concerns down her throat, almost made her doubt herself… She should be grateful that he'd finally decided to leave her alone.

The truth was that she was embarking on a lonely journey. She'd be vetting fertility clinics on her own, selecting the donor on her own, waiting anxiously on her own. If she got pregnant, there would be no one to offer her crackers if she had morning sickness or rub her back or tell her to have an early night. And when the baby was born, she would be dealing with all the minor and major crises of raising a child on her own. Ethan's interest and concern had been unwanted and frustrating and inappropriate, but it had also been sincere and real, born of friendship and genuine goodwill. There was something to be said for having someone looking out for you.

She reminded herself that she'd been alone the bulk of her adult life and much of her childhood. She'd never needed anyone to watch her back or catch her if she fell. Why should now be any different?

She spent the weekend going over her financial records. She had a couple of investment properties as well as the apartment, along with a healthy stock portfolio, and she sent an email to her financial advisor to make an appointment for the following week to discuss the best way to structure her affairs during her maternity leave.

Once she was satisfied she had a good handle on things, she sat down in her living room with a cup of strong black coffee and read over the donor profiles. Once she'd exhausted the ones she'd accidentally printed at work, she accessed more via the internet. By midday Sunday she was awash with the details of over forty men and was feeling more than a little overwhelmed. A little depressed, too. As lovely as some of the donors sounded—if she could trust the profiles— she'd always imagined her heart would choose the father of her child, not her head. But it wasn't as though she had a choice, right?

She decided she needed a break. She turned off her computer, changed into her workout clothes and walked across busy Queens Road to Albert Park Lake. It was a clear, cold winter's day and there were plenty of people walking their dogs or jogging along the track that circled the lake. She warmed up before running two laps, the cool air making her eyes sting. Then she spent twenty minutes stretching on the grass, easing the accumulated tension of the week from her hips and legs and back.

Her head was much clearer when she returned to the apartment and she reviewed the profiles again until she had a short list of three donors.

One was a firefighter in California, then there was a Ph.D. candidate and lastly an engineering student. On paper, they were all good options. Healthy, intelligent, kind. All of them claimed they were donating sperm because they had close friends or family members with fertility issues and they wanted to help others in similar circumstances. She chose to believe them, even though she knew that American donors were paid, while it was illegal in Australia for donors to receive anything except reimbursement for travel expenses. Given what she'd read about the sperm shortage from Australian men and the limited number of them who were prepared to donate to single women, she was almost certain she would end up using an American donor.

Short list in hand, she was ready to put her plan in motion.

Alex arrived at work early on Monday morning, keen to clear her in-tray so she could close her office door and make a preliminary inquiry at the fertility clinic she'd researched. She also needed to make an appointment with Dr. Ramsay.

Her step was brisk as she crossed the underground garage, her briefcase in hand.

"Alexandra."

She glanced over her shoulder to see Ethan walking

toward her, his chocolate-brown overcoat flaring behind him. Something fluttered in the pit of her stomach and she reminded herself that he'd had plenty of opportunity to corner her last week.

"Hey," she said.

"I was going to drop by your office this morning," he said as he fell into step beside her. "You got anything on for lunch today?"

"Lunch?" she asked, instantly wary.

"Yes, lunch. You know, sandwiches, sushi, soup. Other foodstuffs."

She glanced at him. His hair looked very dark in the dim lighting.

"Is it only lunch?" she asked. "Or is there going to be a side order of your unsolicited opinion on the table?"

He held up a hand. "Don't shoot, I come in peace."

"Do you?"

"Alex… Can we just have lunch? My treat. And I promise not to give you any more grief." He drew a cross over his heart.

Despite her wariness, it was hard not to be charmed by the childish gesture. It was one of the things she liked about him the most—despite the five-thousand-dollar suits and handmade Italian shoes and his undeniable good looks, he wasn't afraid to be silly or humble or foolish.

"We can walk to Pellegrini's," he added. "Have some spaghetti Bolognese and garlic bread."

"Right, and scare off our clients for the rest of the afternoon."

He spread his hands wide. "Exactly. It's a win-win."

Her mouth curled at the corner and she made an effort to contain her smile. He really was a charming bastard when he put his mind to it—something he was no doubt well aware of.

She leveled a stern finger at him. "No lectures, no questions. We go, we eat, we bitch about Leo's latest cost-cutting memo, we come back."

"You're the boss," Ethan said.

She narrowed her eyes, trying to read him. What was this really about? Was it possible he was simply trying to restore their friendship to its usual level? Or was she setting herself up to be browbeaten again?

The sound of footsteps heralded the approach of one of the legal assistants. Ethan glanced over his shoulder, then back at her.

"I'll swing by your office at twelve," he said.

Then they were no longer alone and she was forced to swallow her uncertainty. She stood slightly behind him in the elevator as they traveled to the fifteenth floor, studying his profile covertly.

She wanted things to be okay between them. Their relationship might be only a work-based one, but she would miss the lunches and their racquetball games if this issue came between them.

She shook off her doubts as they left the elevator and went their separate ways. If he broke their agreement, she would leave the restaurant. It was that simple.

Despite being distracted, she managed to clear her desk by eleven and she told Fran to hold her calls for fifteen minutes while she "dealt with a few matters." She shut the door and called the fertility clinic.

Ten minutes later she had an information package on its way to her in the mail and a list of tests she needed to discuss with her doctor. Once her health check was clear and she'd mapped her ovulation cycle, she could make her first appointment with the clinic.

She opened the calendar on her computer. A month, maybe two months from now she might be peeing on a stick and holding her breath for the outcome. It was almost surreal.

Her intercom buzzed.

"Alex, I've got senior counsel for Brackman-Lewis on the phone, Alistair Hanlon. You said if he called to put him through."

"Sure. What line?"

"Three."

Alex took the call. The next time she looked up it was nearly midday and Ethan was standing in her doorway.

"You ready to go?"

"Um, sure. Just give me a sec to grab my bag."

She'd meant to check her hair and lipstick before he showed up, but he was going to have to take her the way he found her. Not that he'd probably notice.

"How was your morning?" he asked as they exited the foyer into busy Collins Street.

Her mind flashed to her phone call with the clinic. "Promising."

"Wish I could say the same."

They talked work for the whole of the brisk walk to Bourke Street, where Pellegrini's had been serving pasta to the working folk of Melbourne for over thirty years.

They both ordered a bowl of the restaurant's famous spaghetti Bolognese and café lattes before taking stools at the aged Formica counter running along the wall while they waited for their meals.

"I meant to ask—are we still on for racquetball tomorrow night?"

Alex shot Ethan a look. She hadn't thought about

their regular game. Not in the context of canceling it, anyway. She'd simply assumed that they would play together, as usual. Which was probably a little naive, given what had happened last week.

"The court's booked," she said. "But if you've got other plans...?"

"No, I'm good. Gotta keep moving or I can say goodbye to my toes." He patted his perfectly flat belly.

Normally if he made a comment like that she'd have felt honor bound to rag on him about his vanity, perhaps even crack a joke about how he couldn't afford to put on weight given how much money he'd invested in his wardrobe.

Today she slid the napkin dispenser an inch to the left and tried not to look too relieved. She enjoyed their weekly games. Looked forward to them. Although she'd always been careful not to focus on her enjoyment too much—Ethan was a fellow partner, after all. But there was no denying that their hour of sweat and smart-assery had long been a highlight in her week.

Ethan shifted to one side as the waitress set down their coffees. It was only when he reached for a sugar packet and almost knocked his coffee over that she registered how tense he was. She glanced at him out of the corner of her eyes.

She wasn't imagining it. The tendons in his neck were as taut as bowstrings and a muscle flickered in his jaw. Then Ethan reached for his coffee and she saw that there was a slight tremble in his hand.

It took her a moment to understand what she was seeing: Ethan was nervous. Really nervous, if that hand tremble was anything to go by.

She frowned. Why on earth would a man as inherently confident and cocky as Ethan Stone be nervous about having a bowl of pasta with her?

"What's going on, Ethan?" she asked. "Are you okay?"

He looked at her, then he glanced at his coffee for a long beat. Finally he met her eyes again.

"Last week, you said you'd prefer for your child to have a relationship with his or her father if it was at all possible."

Her stomach sank. He was going to lecture her again. Tell her she was wrong, that what she was planning was wrong. She'd really hoped that they could get past this, that he could accept her decision and they could remain friends. Hell, she'd even imagined that their friendship might deepen now that they had breached the invisible wall between their work and private lives.

But apparently Ethan wasn't going to let this go. Which meant she was going to have to leave. Then she was going to have to cancel their racquetball game and let their friendship fade to polite nods in the hall and the occasional discussion about the weather when they crossed paths in the kitchenette.

"We had an agreement. No more lectures." She pushed her coffee away and started to slide off her stool.

Ethan's hand curled around her forearm.

"Give me five minutes. I promise it's not a lecture," he said.

His hand felt very warm where it gripped her arm.

"What is it, then?" she asked.

Ethan's gaze searched her face. "I've been thinking about what you said last week. About always wanting to be a parent. About not wanting to miss out."

She frowned, trying to understand where this was going.

"I don't know if I ever told you, but I was married once. Cassie and I divorced five years ago. When we got married, we planned on having at least three kids. But it never happened."

If he was about to tell her that he'd resigned himself to missing out and that she should, too, she was going to dump her coffee over his head.

Ethan swallowed nervously. "I guess what I'm trying to ask in the least eloquent possible way is how would you feel about me offering to be your sperm donor?"

Alex stilled. For a moment the world seemed to go quiet. Or perhaps she was simply so stunned she'd blocked out everything except for him and her.

"I'm...sorry?"

"I'd like you to consider me as a potential father for your child," he said. "You should know up front that I'd want to be actively involved in his or her life. I'd want visitation rights and equal say on important issues like education and health. I'd expect to contribute financially. I'd want it to be a real partnership."

He reached into his coat pocket and pulled out a folded sheaf of papers. "I've had a complete medical checkup. My doctor says there are no issues there." He slid the folded sheets toward her.

Alex looked from him to the papers then back. She shook her head, utterly blindsided.

Ethan frowned. "Is that a no? You don't even want to discuss it?"

The intense disappointment in his face was enough to spur her past her shock.

"Ethan. This is—this is not what I was expecting," she said.

Understatement of the year.

"Right. Well, I've been thinking about it since last week but I didn't want to say anything until I had the go-ahead from my doctor." He gestured toward the printout. "I had my sperm tested, as well. Apparently it's good to go. Strong motility, the report said. Good count. It's all in there."

He shifted uncomfortably on his stool and she realized he was blushing. Would there be no end to today's revelations regarding Ethan Stone? If anyone had told her a week ago he was capable of blushing, she would have laughed in their face. As for him wanting to be a parent...

"I don't know what to say," she said. "I mean, obviously actually knowing the father of my child would be a huge bonus. Ideal, really. But I never even considered... I had no idea you were interested in children. Or that you'd want..." She lifted her hands in the air to indicate how helpless and blown away she felt.

At that moment she registered that the waitress hovered behind them impatiently, two plates of pasta in hand. They both leaned to the side to allow her to slide them onto the counter, then they were alone again.

Ethan shot her a rueful look. "Not the best venue. Sorry. I wasn't really thinking...."

She shook her head to indicate she wasn't worried about where he'd chosen to make his proposal. She was too busy trying to work out how she felt about what Ethan had suggested.

Shocked, obviously. She'd never had any inkling that he was interested in parenthood. Even if she'd considered approaching a friend for sperm—and she hadn't—he wouldn't have been on her list. Not in a million years. He was the office hottie. She simply couldn't picture him with baby puke on his shirt and bags under his eyes from sleepless nights.

Also, they didn't have that kind of relationship. She'd never let her imagination stray outside of the parameters of business. The moment he'd joined the firm she'd privately acknowledged that he was a very attractive, very dynamic man—and that only a very foolish woman would allow herself to fall under his spell. She valued her career far too much to jeopardize it for something as ephemeral as lust.

But now he was offering to become a whole lot more. He was offering to merge his DNA with hers to create a child that would bind them inextricably forever.

Not exactly small potatoes. Definitely not something she could get her head around in the matter of a few minutes. There were so many things to consider. So many potential problems—

"What if you meet someone and fall madly in love? You're going to want to have children with her and then you'll look back at this and wish you'd waited."

"It's never going to happen, Alex."

"You sound pretty sure about that."

Ethan hesitated a moment, then nodded toward her food. "We should eat before this gets cold."

She frowned.

"Eat *and* talk," he said with a slight smile.

He led by example, twirling strands of spaghetti around his fork. She followed suit.

Ethan waited until he'd swallowed before talking again. "I was married for eight years, Alex. I won't go into the details because there's no point, but I don't ever want to go there again."

"Not every marriage ends in divorce."

"Enough do. I'm not prepared to play the odds. The stakes are way too high."

His gaze was direct. She had no doubt that he utterly believed what he was saying. And yet...

"You say that, but what if you fall in love?" she asked quietly. "It happens every day, after all. Whether people plan it or not."

He smiled cynically. "It's been five years and I've never even come close. And, frankly, I'm not interested in the high drama and the headaches. Life is much simpler without all the bullshit."

"Wow. You've got a real romantic streak there."

He pointed his fork at her. "You loved Jacob, right? Can you honestly tell me that the fun bit at the start of the relationship was worth all the pain when things went bad at the other end?"

She thought for a minute. Absolutely it had been hard toward the end with Jacob. The tears, the fights, the almost constant ache in her chest as it became more and more apparent to her that their relationship was doomed. She'd been flat for months afterward, wondering if she'd made a mistake, missing him like crazy.

"It was hard, definitely. But that doesn't mean I'm not prepared to try again."

"Then let me ask you the same question. What if you meet someone and fall in love? How's he going to feel about your baby?"

It was probably very revealing of her psychology at present that she hadn't even considered how her decisions might affect any future spouse. She'd been too busy focusing on not missing out to even consider how some hypothetical spouse might feel about her unconventional path to motherhood.

"I guess if I meet someone, he'll simply have to accept that my child and the way I conceived my child are a part of the package," she said slowly.

"Exactly," Ethan said.

She forked up more spaghetti. Her brain worked furiously, going over and over what he offered, pulling it apart, trying to find the loopholes and bear traps. It took her a moment to notice that Ethan had finished his spaghetti and was now watching her with unnerving intensity. She pushed the remainder of her meal away and turned to face him.

He didn't say a word but she knew what he wanted: to know if she was prepared to consider his offer. If she wanted him to be the father of her child.

There were so many conflicting thoughts and feelings racing through her mind that she literally felt dizzy.

She slid off the stool. "I'm just going to... Give me a minute," she mumbled. Then she made haste for the restrooms in the rear of the restaurant.

She pushed her way through the swing door and went straight into the first cubicle. She closed the lid and sat on it, then she stared at the graffiti-covered door.

She needed to think. Ethan was offering her something incredibly valuable and generous, something that had the potential to be wonderful—or potentially disastrous.

She took a deep breath and cudgeled her brain into some semblance of rationality.

There was no issue with the genetic side of things, obviously. Ethan was every woman's fantasy in that department—tall, dark, handsome, intelligent, fit and healthy.

There wasn't a doubt in her mind that her child would benefit from the best of the best in terms of DNA. Those eyes. That body. That wicked, sharp mind of his.

And her child would also benefit from actually knowing his or her father. Ethan had said he wanted to be an involved parent, that he wanted visitation rights and to be a part of major decisions. She had no reason to doubt his sincerity; she knew him well enough to know that he would never have made the offer in the first place if he wasn't certain. Look at the medical tests he'd had done in advance, for example. He'd already shown that he was considerate and prepared and thorough.

If she said yes, she wouldn't be alone. She'd have someone to bounce ideas off. Someone to call in the middle of the night for solace or sympathy. Someone to pick up the ball if she fumbled it. A partner, in fact, in almost every way except the most obvious.

So many pros—and yet the cons were not insignificant. For starters, she worked with Ethan. Not only worked, they were both partners, which meant they were doubly invested in their jobs. If things turned sour between them, if something went wrong, there would be no separation between home and office.

There was also the fact that despite having worked with Ethan for two years, despite all the lunches and racquetball games, there was still a great deal about him she didn't know. She'd never seen him really angry, for example. She had no idea how he was situated financially, what his attitude about money was.

She knew nothing about his family, whether he was close to them or estranged.

Admittedly, she wouldn't know any of those things about an anonymous donor she selected from an online catalog, either, but she wouldn't be co-parenting with any of those men.

The bottom line was that what Ethan was proposing could be a dream come true—or it could lock them both into a relationship that neither of them were really prepared for.

The bathroom door swung open, bringing with it the noise of the restaurant and reminding her that Ethan was waiting for her. Waiting for her decision. She stood and smoothed her hands down her skirt. Then she flushed the loo, more for show than anything else, and exited the cubicle to wash her hands.

Ethan was studying the coffee grinds in the bottom of his cup when she slid onto her stool. He looked at her, his eyes full of uncertainty. Nerves twisted in her stomach as she took a deep breath.

"We would need to sit down and talk things through in a lot of detail before we made any final decision. If we're going to even consider sharing the parenting of a child, we need to be on the same page on so many things…"

A slow smile spread across Ethan's mouth.

"It's not a yes, Ethan," she felt compelled to point out.

"But it's not a no."

He was trying to temper his smile but she could see the relief in his eyes. The hope.

He wants this as much as I do.

She'd spent so many years trying to coax, cajole, beg and plead with Jacob to get him to even consider becoming a parent that she'd forgotten that there were men who craved children as much as women did.

"We need to talk more," she said. "A lot more."

"Absolutely. How about dinner at my place on Saturday night?"

"Okay. That sounds good."

"Then it's a date," he said.

Even though she knew there were so many things that could go wrong, she felt lighter than she had in weeks.

If this worked out—

She clamped down on the thought. There was no point in getting excited over something that hadn't happened. Yet.

Ethan returned to his office after lunch and stared at his blank computer screen.

If things worked out, if he and Alex were both satisfied that they were on the same page, he had a shot at becoming a father.

He propped his elbows on his desk and pinched the bridge of his nose as a wave of emotion threatened to overwhelm him.

He'd thought that dream was done. He really had. And now he had a chance. Thanks to Alex.

Get a grip, Stone. It hasn't happened yet.

The thing was, he hadn't realized how much he'd staked on this, how much he'd invested until she'd returned from the bathroom and told him she was willing to consider his offer.

It was probably just as well that he and Alex had agreed not to discuss the matter again until Saturday night. He'd need the rest of the week to get his head together.

He had a preliminary settlement meeting booked this afternoon so he gathered his files and went to collect his client from reception. Jolie King had been married a little under five years and had two children under four. Her soon-to-be ex, Adam King, came from money. She did not. Like most of his clients, Jolie was not a happy woman. She was grieving and angry, bitter and hurt.

It went without saying that divorce lawyers rarely saw the nobler aspects of humanity.

Jolie gave him a wan smile when he greeted her.

"How are you doing?" he asked.

"Oh, you know. Okay."

He took her to his office and waited until she was settled before saying the things that needed to be said.

"Tomorrow's going to be a tough day, Jolie. And I know it's going to be hard for you, but I need to reiterate that you need to let me handle the negotiation. Okay?"

Jolie shifted defensively. "Yeah. Of course. Why wouldn't I?"

Ethan was tempted to remind her about the constant string of angry text and phone messages that had passed between her and her ex since divorce proceedings had started. He'd asked her to limit conversations to day-to-day matters and issues surrounding their two children but had little faith that Jolie had listened to his suggestion. She had too much emotion invested in this situation to see past the here and now.

But tomorrow was important. Tomorrow could keep them out of court and save her thousands of dollars.

"Listen. I know you're pissed with Adam. I know you want to take him to the cleaners and punish him, but my job isn't to make Adam hurt. My job is to help set up you and your kids so that you can move on and start living your life again. Scoring points is meaningless at this stage. It's not going to change anything, and it's only going to make things uglier, more drawn out and more expensive. We have much more control if we settle out of court. If we leave this in the hands of the judge, anything could happen."

And usually did. He knew a number of family court judges who prided themselves on ensuring that no one walked away a winner from their courtroom. They considered their job well and fairly done if neither party were satisfied or happy at the end of the trial.

Jolie frowned. Then she began ranting about her ex. Adam was a cheat, a liar. He'd never been a good husband, she didn't know why she'd married him. He said he loved his kids but he was hardly around to spend time with them—and that was when they were married. Now they were separated, the kids could barely remember what he looked like....

Ethan sat back and waited. There'd be no talking to Jolie until she'd vented her spleen. He had plenty of clients who couldn't engage the rational part of their brain until they'd off-loaded their anger. Something about divorce seemed to short-circuit otherwise sensible human beings and turn them into muddled, emotional messes. And he was often the dumping ground for their rage and confusion. As much as he told himself it was part of the job, it took its toll. So much anger, so much disappointment and bitterness... Most of the time he tried to let it wash over him, but there were days when it got to him. Definitely.

It wasn't as though he hadn't been there himself. He knew what it was like to be so filled with hurt and injustice that he'd felt as though his skin would split with the force of it. He knew what it was like to want to punish the person who had once been the center of his world. And he absolutely knew what it was like to look back over the years together and wonder what it had all been worth and if it had ever meant anything.

When Jolie had finally run herself down, he offered her a cup of coffee and a cookie then began to outline what he hoped to gain from tomorrow's round table.

He sent her home with instructions to get a good night's sleep, then lost himself in the sea of emails and other paperwork on his desk. Then he went home and did more work.

Alex and the conversation they'd had over lunch was never far from his thoughts, always hovering in the background, ready to slip to the fore when his concentration lapsed.

If things went well, they might have a child together. He might have a chance to become a father, without the attendant risks of embarking on another doomed-to-failure relationship.

It was enough to keep him awake, staring at the ceiling for hours.

Chapter Five

Alex practiced her serve while she waited for Ethan to join her on the racquetball court after work the following day.

He was late and she was beginning to wonder if something had come up at the office. They hadn't spoken since yesterday's lunch and she'd been with a client all day. But surely if he couldn't make their game, he would have called or emailed or something. Unless, of course, he was regretting his offer and didn't know how to face her.

She dismissed the notion immediately. Ethan's offer hadn't been made impulsively. He'd gone to his doctor. He'd had his sperm checked out, for Pete's sake. And if he had changed his mind, he'd look her in the eye and tell her. She knew that much about him.

She felt a cool breeze on the back of her neck as the door to the court swung open behind her.

"Latecomers forfeit first serve," she said without turning around.

"Sorry. Road work near the Art Center," Ethan said.

"You used that excuse last time you were late."

She glanced over her shoulder, determined to treat this like any other Tuesday night despite the important question sitting between them. Then she saw Ethan's face and every other consideration went out the window.

"Ethan! My God, what happened?" She took an involuntary step toward him.

His left eye was bruised and painful looking, not quite black but heading that way. She fought the absurd, utterly inappropriate urge to touch him to reassure herself that he was okay.

"Don't worry, it's worse than it looks."

"Who did this to you?"

"It was an accident. Things got a little out of hand during my settlement conference this afternoon and I got in the way of the wrong person." He shrugged as if to say it was no big deal but she could see he was angry.

"This happened in a settlement conference? I hope you had the guy up on assault charges?"

"It was a woman, and I figured it might be difficult having her charged since she's my client. Not to mention what it would do to my reputation if it got out."

"Your *client* did this?"

"Great, huh? Nothing like a good settlement conference to bring out the love." He sounded bitter.

She'd often wondered how he handled all the acrimony and bad energy that came with divorce and custody cases. Apparently, sometimes, not so well.

He glanced at her and shook his head. "Sorry. I didn't mean to dump on you. It gets to me sometimes."

"It'd get to me, too. There's a reason I chose corporate law. All that conflict..." She shuddered theatrically. "Give me a nice, complicated contract any day."

"Yeah. There are days I wonder why I chose this specialty, too."

"Why did you?" She'd always wanted to know. Why volunteer for an area of the law that was so personal and painful?

"I thought I could help people, believe it or not. But sometimes I wonder. I really do...." He ran a hand over his head and gripped the nape of his neck, visibly making an effort to calm down.

He was silent for a long moment, then he shook his head.

"You know what I don't get? Why we even go through the pretense of getting married anymore. I get the historical reasons—primogeniture, keeping power within families, property acquisition, blah, blah. But none of that matters these days. The world has moved on. Yet we still cling to the completely unrealistic idea that men and women can make a bunch of pretty vows to one another and stand by them for the rest of their lives."

"I know you probably don't want to hear this right now, but there are some good marriages out there. What are the stats—one in three marriages end in divorce? That means two-thirds don't," she said. "Ever stop to think that you're seeing the worst of marriage because of your profession?"

"Just because two-thirds of marriages don't end up before the divorce courts doesn't mean they're happy marriages, Alex. Believe me."

Was he talking about his own marriage? Was that what this was about?

"I guess some people are prepared to make trade-offs," she said carefully.

"To gain what? Companionship? Security? Children? Is it really worth it? Lying in bed next to someone who is at best indifferent to you or at worst actively hates your guts?"

Wow. He was really feeling the pain today.

"Is that what happened for you and your wife? You didn't want to live with the compromise?"

He stared at her for a long beat and for a moment she thought she'd stepped over the line.

"Let's just say that there wasn't enough love to go around. Which is exactly my point. Once the hormones wear off, love's a thin foundation to build a lifetime on. Take this couple today—married four years, two kids under three, and this afternoon they couldn't even tolerate being in the same room as one another."

Alex looked away from the bleak cynicism in his eyes. She understood that something had happened to Ethan to make him lose faith in people, but she believed in love. She'd seen firsthand how strong it was. The doctors had claimed her mother should have died in the car accident that had damaged her brain irretrievably, but she hadn't. Rachel Knight had known that she was the only thing her daughter had and she'd hung on to life tenaciously because she refused to leave Alex to the tender mercies of social services.

"What about children?" she said. "If we have a child together, you'll love him or her, won't you?"

"That's different," Ethan said.

"Is it?"

"You don't choose to love your children. It just happens."

"You think people choose to love each other or not?

That you can choose to fall in or out of love with someone?"

"I think that human beings are unreliable and fickle and childish and selfish and ultimately unknowable," he said.

"And yet you want to make a baby with me?"

He looked blank for a moment, then he smiled self-mockingly. "Which only proves my point, right? People are unreliable."

She understood what he meant. Jacob had let her down, hadn't he? He'd proven to be all the things Ethan described. And yet her relationship with him hadn't turned her into a cynic. It hadn't destroyed her faith in love.

She looked at Ethan, wondering. What would it take to do that to a person? What had gone wrong between him and his wife?

She forced herself to swallow the questions crowding her throat. He didn't want to talk about it. That much was obvious.

She leaned down and picked up one of the balls she'd been practicing with. "Think you can play with a dodgy eye?"

He didn't immediately shift gears, but when he did he came out with all guns blazing. "Better still, I think I can beat you, slowpoke. Again."

"*Again?* I won the last two matches in a row."

"Are we counting last week? Because I believe I was up on points before we called it a night."

"No, we're not counting last week and you're full of it, you know that?"

He smiled, and it felt like an achievement. As though she'd given him a small moment of lightness in an otherwise dark day.

"It's been said before. Usually when I've got a game or two over you," he countered.

"Don't bank on that happening tonight."

"We'll see."

"And don't go thinking that I'm going to go easy on you because you smeared a little axle grease under your eye," she added.

Ethan laughed, the sound loud in the enclosed court. "Them's fighting words, Ms. Knight."

"And talk is cheap, Mr. Stone."

She watched him as he moved into position on the court. There was still a grim cast to his features but she could tell he was making an effort to shake off his mood. She felt as though she was seeing two people— the man she'd always thought Ethan was, and the man he truly was. The charming, slightly shallow, witty playboy, and the complex, damaged man.

He must have loved his wife a great deal once upon a time.

Because great disappointment was almost always preceded by great hope and great happiness, wasn't it?

"Haven't got all night, slowpoke. Clock's ticking."

He was watching her, one eyebrow cocked in challenge. She shook off her thoughts and bounced the ball.

"Buckle up, big guy. It's going to be a bumpy night."

The trash talking continued as they played the first game. Despite what she'd said about not giving him special treatment because of his injury, she kept a close watch on him and when he winced and rubbed his temple when he thought she wasn't looking she walked straight to the corner and grabbed her towel.

"Don't tell me you're admitting defeat after one game?" Ethan asked.

"You've got a headache. Time to go home, Rocky."

She started zipping the cover over her racquet.

"I don't suppose it would make any difference if I said I was fine?"

"Nope. Go home and take an aspirin."

Ethan joined her in the corner, crouching to collect his racquet cover.

"Worried about me, slowpoke?" He glanced at her, his head tilted to one side, a playful, warm light in his deep blue eyes.

They were close, a few feet apart, and for a moment she was flustered, unable to tear her gaze from his. Then she rallied.

"Of course I am. I've got a vested interest now, remember. Unless you've come to your senses and changed your mind?" She could hear the note of uncertainty in her voice and she winced inwardly. Hadn't she already decided that Ethan wasn't the kind of man to offer something so important on impulse?

He stood. "I'm not going anywhere, Alex."

"Then you'd better get home and rest that pretty head of yours." She knelt and fussed pointlessly with her gym bag, feeling ridiculously self-conscious.

Over the past week she'd revealed an enormous amount of herself to this man and it seemed she revealed more with every conversation. She didn't like feeling at a disadvantage.

Better get used to it. If you're going to make a baby with him, it's only going to get worse.

She saw him bend to collect his bag out of the corner of her eye.

"I'll see you tomorrow, okay?" he said.

"Sure thing."

She threw him a quick smile but her shoulders didn't relax until he'd left the court.

You're an idiot.

Despite having had a night and a day to process Ethan's offer, she was still trying to get her head around the concept that he wanted to be the father of her child. It was too, too surreal. In the space of a few days they'd leapfrogged about a gazillion intimacy levels and she simply couldn't get the idea to stick in her head.

Saturday night ought to go a long away to helping on that score. A whole evening of hashing out the details of their proposed arrangement would surely make this about as real as it could get.

She checked the time. There was still twenty minutes left of their hour on the court. She unzipped her racquet and stood.

Perhaps if she ran herself ragged she'd sleep tonight.

Alex woke early on Saturday morning and spent the bulk of the day fretting—double-thinking everything, conjuring all the many, many things that could go wrong with what Ethan was proposing. She exorcised her demons by dusting, then she broke out her mosaic-tile supplies and spent a messy but satisfying few hours on the balcony making progress on a decorative tabletop that would never see the light of day.

By the time she was finished she was feeling calmer and more settled within herself. She cleaned up, then sat at the kitchen table with a pad and pen and composed a list of questions for Ethan. She started with the basics—questions about his family, his parents, his siblings. Then she started thinking about the things she needed to know about the man who might be the father of her child. By the time she'd finished, she had two pages. She stared at all her questions, a little embarrassed by how many there were. How was she going to remember them all? She couldn't simply pull them out in front of Ethan and put him through his paces. Could she? Then she remembered what this was all about and decided that she owed it to herself and to him and to their potential child to be as nosy and intrusive as necessary to be comfortable with this arrangement.

She dressed carefully in a pair of tailored chocolate-brown pants and a soft beige silk blouse with a cowl-neck, brushed her hair until it behaved itself, then selected a bottle of wine and headed for the door.

He'd emailed her his address during the week and she'd learned he lived five minutes away from her Queens Road apartment. She smiled to herself as she pulled up in front of his building. Her own much more modest building had been built before the Second World War and would probably disappear inside the foyer of the sleek, stylish residential tower looming above her. But then she'd hardly expected Ethan to live in a hovel—the man spent thousands on his suits. It stood to reason that his residence would be equally stylish and exclusive.

She grabbed the wine, locked the car and approached the formidable front doors. It took her a moment to find his apartment number amongst the cluster on the door panel.

His voice sounded very deep when it came over the intercom. "Alex?"

"Hi," she said. "Want to beam me up, Scotty?"

"Up you come."

The door opened automatically—far classier than her own building, where the door made a loud buzzing noise and visitors had to push the door to enter—and she took the elevator to the tenth floor.

There were four doors leading off the hallway she

stepped out into but only one of them was open, light spilling onto the plush carpeted hall. She walked toward it as Ethan appeared in the doorway, wiping his hands on a tea towel.

"Hey. Come on in," he said with a smile.

He was wearing a pair of faded jeans and a V-neck long-sleeved T-shirt in gunmetal gray. His hair was ruffled and his feet were bare and she could see a few crisp, dark curls peeking over the neckline of his top.

She stared at his long, strong feet and wondered if they wouldn't have been better off doing this on more neutral territory. Then she gave herself a mental slap. They were here to talk about an incredibly intimate, incredibly private subject. Where better to do it than at his place or hers?

The problem was—and this was something she should have considered earlier—Ethan was a compelling, charismatic man. She'd deliberately treated him like a buddy and not a man for that very reason. It had helped that he dated a lot and was clearly not the kind of man she was looking for. But now they were about to talk about joining forces to create a new life. A child that would be half him and half her. Even if the act of conception itself occurred via a clinical procedure, she and Ethan would be connected, bound together for life. He would become a mainstay of her world.

She glanced at him as he gestured for her to precede him into his apartment. His bruised eye had faded to a mottled yellow and blue, yet he was easily the best-looking, sexiest man she knew.

You're going to have to be very careful if you do this.

She made an effort to pull herself together as Ethan led her through a small entrance hall and into a large, spacious living room with huge floor-to-ceiling windows. She stepped closer to the glass to admire the breathtaking view of the Alexandra Gardens and the Yarra River.

"This is pretty spectacular," she said.

"Yeah. It sold the apartment for me, actually."

"If I hang off the edge of my balcony, I've got a corner of Albert Park Lake." She held her fingers an inch apart to indicate how limited her view was. "Nothing like this."

He held out a hand. "Let me take care of that for you."

She glanced down and saw that she was strangling the neck of the wine bottle. "Sure. Thanks. I wasn't sure what we were having, so I brought a pinot noir...."

"Perfect. I'm making us slow-roasted lamb."

He moved toward a doorway that she assumed must lead to the kitchen. She spared a quick, assessing glance for his living space before following him. His decor was bold—two black leather Simone Peignoir couches, a pony-skin Le Corbusier chaise lounge, a deep, bloodred rug and three vibrant modern paintings in primary colors that made her think of thunderstorms and wild, tempestuous seas. A red-gum dining table with clean, graceful lines dominated the corner near the window.

He was pulling the cork from the bottle when she joined him in the kitchen.

"I like your paintings," she said.

"This is where I confess that I know nothing about art but I know what I like."

"Well, I really do know nothing about art. I suspect I'm a bit of a Philistine at heart."

She glanced at the array of ingredients and tools he had spread before him—little bowls of sliced-up herbs, halved lemons ready to be juiced, a fancy-looking whisk and an expensive copper-bottomed saucepan.

"You cook," she said. "I mean, you really cook."

"You sound surprised."

"I've never pictured you wearing an apron."

He gave her a dry look. "Just as well, since I don't own one. Cooking is my way of unwinding."

"I thought racquetball was your way of unwinding."

"Racquetball is my way of not turning into a fat bastard. What about you?"

"Are you asking if I'm worried about turning into a fat bitch?"

He smiled. "What do you do to unwind?"

"I do mosaics."

"As in tiles?"

"That's right. Tabletops, mirror frames, that kind of thing." She felt silly admitting it. It wasn't as though she was any good.

"See, I would never have guessed that about you. You'll have to show me your work sometime."

"Or not."

He laughed. "Not going coy on me, slowpoke?"

"Merely sparing you from having to be polite. I'm not very good. Most of my projects are never seen by human eyes once I'm done."

"You're exaggerating," he said as he poured the wine and handed her a glass.

"No, I'm not. Trust me. My last creation wound up looking like a dropped pizza."

She took a swallow of her wine. Alcohol coated her belly in soothing warmth and she took another big mouthful.

"Is there anything I can do to help?" she asked.

"You can set the table if you like—cutlery's in the

top left drawer under the counter there. Place mats in the one underneath."

She selected two settings and a couple of place mats and headed to the living room. She placed the knives and forks carefully on the polished table, marveling at all the little insights she was gaining into Ethan tonight, things she'd never even thought about—the fact that he cooked, that he came home to this view every night, that he liked modern art. That he owned place mats—several types!—of all things.

The kitchen was rich with the smell of fresh mint and lemons when she returned. A butterflied lamb roast was resting on the cutting board and Ethan was busy doing something with the juices in the pan.

"What's that you're doing?" she asked, elbows propped on the counter.

"Making the sauce. Have to skim off the surface fat first so we don't have coronaries before dessert."

"Ah."

"Let me guess—you thought sauce came in a packet from the supermarket, right?"

"No. I thought sauce came in a plastic tub from the take-out place."

His mouth quirked up at the corner. "Can't argue with that logic."

He sliced the meat next, then pulled a tray of beautifully roasted vegetables from the oven. She watched as he plated the meal, adding sugar snap peas and baby broccoli at the last minute. He made it all look so effortless, his long fingers working confidently. And perhaps it was, for him. All her culinary experiments ended with swearing and pot banging and the inevitable high-pitched chirrup of the smoke alarm when she burned something. She simply didn't have the patience.

No surprises there, given all the years she'd made dinner for two every night, week in, week out.

"Okay, we're ready to go."

He handed her a plate and they walked to the table.

"This looks great. Will I shame myself even more in your eyes if I confess that this is probably the best meal I've sat down to in months?"

"You couldn't possibly be more shamed in my eyes," Ethan said, absolutely deadpan.

"Well, I guess I asked for that," she murmured under her breath.

Ethan laughed quietly. She concentrated on her meal, slicing into the lamb. She could feel him watching her as she took her first bite.

"Oh, wow," she said, her eyes widening. "This is good. I mean, really, really good."

"Thanks. Enjoy," he said, raising his glass in a casual toast.

He was pleased that she liked it, she could see. He'd gone to a lot of trouble for her. For tonight. It gave her a funny tickle in the pit of her stomach to think of him planning a meal for her, wanting to impress her.

He wants you to have his baby, Alex. Didn't we cover not getting carried away with any of this?

She sat straighter in her chair. The bossy-britches in her head was right—they were here for a purpose. She needed to keep that top of mind.

In accordance with her resolution, she took a big gulp of wine then cleared her throat. "So, Ethan, are your parents still alive?"

It came out sounding much more officious than she'd intended, as though she was conducting a job interview.

"My father is. Mom died ten years ago. Emphysema. Smoked all her life, and eventually it killed her."

"I'm sorry."

"It was tough at the time, but Dad remarried last year and seems happier now." He shrugged. "What about you?"

"I don't know about my father. I never knew him. My mother died when I was twenty. Complications from surgery."

"Twenty's young to lose a parent."

"There's not really any good time, though, is there?"

"No."

"Do you have any brothers and sisters?" she asked.

"A brother, Derek. He's younger—thirty-nine—and married with two kids, Jamie and Tim. How about you?"

"No brothers and sisters."

"Ah. Spoiled only child."

She thought about how she'd helped her mother dress every morning, the loads of washing she'd done, the household chores, and smiled faintly. "Something like that."

She concentrated on her meal for a moment, trying to find a way to frame her next question. "So I take it there are no major health issues in the family...?"

Ethan put down his fork and regarded her with amused eyes. "Are you asking if there are any genetic skeletons in my family closet, Alex?"

"Yes, I guess I am."

"Then the answer is no, not that I know of. Any other questions?"

"A few."

"Well, hit me with them."

"You must have some of your own," she said.

"A few."

They eyed each other for a beat, then Alexandra

reached into her pocket and pulled out her list. Might as well be up front, since she'd already blundered her way into this conversation. Anyway, this was who she was. She'd never been the kind of woman who came at things sideways or indirectly.

She unfolded the pages, smoothing them flat before placing them on the table in front of Ethan. She waited for him to balk or laugh but he simply raised his eyebrows.

"Only two pages." He stood and crossed to the coffee table, bending to access the shelf underneath. When he returned to the table he was carrying a legal notepad. He slid it in front of Alexandra.

"I ran to three. But my handwriting is messier than yours."

Alexandra stared at his questions resting on the table beside her own, then glanced up at him. His eyes danced with amusement and they burst into laughter at the same time.

"This is like that old joke. How do porcupines mate?" she said.

"I don't think I know that one. How do porcupines mate?"

"Very carefully."

He laughed. "Not a bad analogy." He leaned forward to check her list. "I see we're being careful about some of the same things. That's a good sign."

"Do you think?" she asked, suddenly anxious all over again. She wanted this so badly.

"Yeah, I do. Hit me with your next question." He forked up a mouthful of food, watching her expectantly.

His calm acceptance and openness went a long way to easing the tension in her shoulders.

"Why don't we take turns?" she suggested.

"Good idea."

As he'd noted, there was a lot of crossover on their lists. They both wanted to discuss the custody arrangements, and they quickly agreed that it would be difficult for Ethan to have overnight visits until the baby stopped breast-feeding. But after that they would both like the visitation rights to be split fifty-fifty.

"I'd like to try to breast-feed for at least six months, twelve if possible," she said.

"This is an area I know next to nothing about," Ethan said.

"Well, me, too, to be honest. But my understanding is that breast-feeding is supposed to be better," she said.

She could feel her face becoming warm and hoped that Ethan would blame it on the wine. She'd never sat at a dining table and discussed her breasts before. Perhaps after a few months of nursing she would be as casual about them as some of the women she saw in restaurants and cafés, but she wasn't there yet.

Ethan raised the subject of education, and here, too, they readily found common ground.

"Private," she said firmly. "The best we can find."

Her years at an underfunded state school were still vivid in her memory. Even though she'd eyed the "rich kids" from the private schools with angry resentment on the bus, she'd always understood that they were getting a head start in life. She wanted her child to have every opportunity possible.

"Absolutely. I went to Scotch College, but I'd prefer a coed school," he said.

They talked about sharing the workload and making allowances for their mutually busy schedules and how they would handle differences of opinion. Over two glasses of wine and a bowl of the most sinfully rich chocolate mousse she'd ever tasted, Alex found herself relaxing more and more.

It seemed the rapport they'd always enjoyed on the court and during their lunches extended beyond the boundaries they'd set. She'd already known that Ethan was good at his job—he had a reputation for being a fair-minded litigator, a lawyer who always looked after the best interests of his clients even if it meant billing fewer hours—and she'd known that he was smart and that he listened well and had a good sense of humor. And now she knew that they saw eye to eye on many of the key issues around parenting.

She was sure other issues would crop up along the way, problems and situations they couldn't even conceive of in their childless state. But if tonight was anything to go by, they could handle them. The bottom line was that they were two intelligent adults with lots of common ground. Whatever came their way, they would deal with it.

They moved to the couches for coffee and chocolates. By mutual unspoken consent the conversation shifted to other subjects, as though they both needed some breathing space while they processed everything they'd learned about each other.

Alex told him about her recent holiday to France and Italy and they compared notes on Florence and Rome. Ethan pulled out a book he'd bought on the architecture of Venice and they pored over stunning photographs of basilicas and piazzas and palaces.

"Tell me about your childhood," he asked as she closed the book.

She leaned forward and returned the book to his coffee table. "What do you want to know?"

"The usual. Were you happy? Were you lonely, being an only child? What was your childhood like?"

She shifted on the couch. She didn't like talking about her childhood. People tended to become uncomfortable when she explained about her mother and the accident. They didn't know what to say or they tried to paint her as some kind of a long-suffering saint. But Ethan might be the father of her child, so she had to be prepared to offer up her truths.

"My childhood was pretty typical, really. Mom was on her own, so we weren't exactly rich. But we got by. She was always pretty creative with presents and making money go a long way."

She smiled, remembering how much she'd longed for something new—anything!—because her mother bought all her clothes from the thrift shop. By the time her mother was finished altering or embellishing them they were unique and special but Alex had always craved clothes that had never been worn by anyone, ever. When she'd gotten her first real job after graduating she'd saved up a nest egg, then spent it all in an uncharacteristic splurge, replacing everything in her wardrobe in one fell swoop. To this day she still had a weakness for the pristine freshness of new clothes.

"What did your mom do?"

"She worked at a dry cleaners. She did the repairs and alterations and managed the front desk. I used to go there after school and do my homework."

She couldn't smell dry-cleaning fluid without thinking of that milk crate in the corner, where she'd sat and read her books and puzzled over her homework. Her mom used to quiz her on her times tables between customers.

"She was a good mother. I hope I can be half as good as her," Alex said.

"So you didn't go through the mandatory stage of hating her when you were a teenager?"

Here we go.

"Not really." She took a deep breath. "My mom had a car accident when I was twelve. She was a passenger, but she wasn't wearing her seat belt and she went through the windshield. She fractured her skull and for a while there they thought she was going to die."

Ethan was watching her intently and she was grateful that he didn't interrupt.

"She pulled through, though." She reached for one of the cushions, resting it in her lap. Like the rest of Ethan's things it had clean, strong lines but the fabric had a pleasing nap and she ran her hand over it a few times before making eye contact with him. "She was different afterward. She couldn't remember things, she cried for no reason. She couldn't count past ten and sometimes she'd have trouble finding the right word for what she wanted to say. If I didn't keep an eye on her, she'd try to cook and put an empty pot on the stove. Or leave the fridge door open. Or go out and leave all the doors and windows open."

"So you wound up being the mother," Ethan guessed.

"Someone had to do it. And she was still very loving. She was still my mom." She smoothed her hand across the cushion again.

"Did you have any help?"

"Oh, yes," she said drily. "Social services were *awesome*. They wanted to put me in a home and institutionalize Mom. Fortunately I was nearly sixteen by the time they started getting really aggressive and I was able to prove I could look after both of us."

"You said she died in hospital?"

"Yes. She was having headaches and they found some scar tissue on her brain they wanted to remove. She had a heart attack coming out of the anesthetic."

"So you dusted yourself off and put yourself through law school?"

She nodded. "Not exactly the cheeriest tale, I know. But not the worst, either. Like I said, she was a great mom."

"Sounds like you were a pretty good mom, too."

She thought about it. "I was okay. I used to get angry with her sometimes. And resentful."

"Thank God. I was beginning to feel really inadequate."

She laughed.

"You want another coffee?" Ethan asked.

She looked at him. She'd expected him to probe more, perhaps mouth some platitudes about how hard it must have been. Instead, he was offering her more coffee.

He raised his eyebrows. "What?"

"Nothing. It's just you're the first person who didn't want to turn it into *Angela's Ashes*."

"Really? You have friends who are stupid enough to think you want their pity?"

She laughed. Apparently he knew her better than she thought he did.

"Believe it or not, yes."

"Obviously they've never been pounded by you on the racquetball court."

She laughed again.

"So was that a yes to coffee?"

"I'll be up all night if I do. But thanks," she said.

They both fell silent. She glanced at the time on his DVD player and blinked when she saw it was past one in the morning.

Wow. How had that happened?

"I should really get going," she said, unfolding her legs from the couch and searching for her shoes with her toes.

"Sure."

There was a new tension in the room as she pulled on her shoes and stood. Ethan stood, too.

"Thanks for tonight. And thanks for being so open to all my questions," she said.

For some reason she didn't know what to do with her hands. She settled for clasping them loosely at her waist.

"Ditto."

"Do you feel like there's anything else that we should cover? Anything else you need to know?" she asked.

"No. Do you?"

She looked at him, watching her so carefully. Did she need to know anything more?

Probably. But she felt she knew the important things. He was a nice man. Surprising, given the invitation to be not-so-nice that Mother Nature had handed him when she gave him that face and that body. She thought he would make a good and loving father. And that they would find a way to pull together, no matter what came their way.

"I think we should do this." Her voice sounded very firm, very sure, even though she was quivering inside.

The tight look left Ethan's face. "Yeah?"

"Yes. I think that between us we could be decent parents."

"Absolutely."

He was grinning and she couldn't help smiling in response. She'd made the right decision. She could feel it in her gut.

"So, what next?" he asked.

"I've got my first session with the clinic next week. There's a mandatory counseling session and some tests they need to do. Then it's simply a matter of waiting until I ovulate again."

"Right. Any idea when that might be?"

"Four weeks or so. Give or take."

"Four weeks. Okay. I'll make sure I've got some clear days in my diary."

Ethan followed her to the door. Now that the decision was made and they were about to embark on this crazy, wonderful journey together, she didn't know what to say to him.

"Thanks for the meal. I'd offer to return the favor but I'm guessing you're not a fan of charcoal. But maybe I could manage cheese on toast and some two-minute noodles. And I dial a mean takeout, too."

"I'm game," he said.

"Spoken like a true sucker." She palmed her car keys. "I'll see you on Monday."

She turned to go.

"Alex."

He waited until she'd turned back before reaching out and pulling her into his arms.

It was totally unexpected and for a second she didn't know what to do as his arms tightened around her and she felt the hard warmth of his chest against her breasts.

Then she lifted her arms and returned the embrace, her hands flattening against the firm planes of his back.

He smelled good—more of that sandalwood scent that she liked—and their knees knocked together briefly.

"Thank you," he said, his voice gravelly with emotion. "I think we're going to make a great team, slow-poke."

Then he released her, stepped back and it was over. She hoped like hell she didn't look as flustered as she felt. She told herself that she simply hadn't been expecting the close contact.

"Me, too," she said. Then she glanced over her shoulder toward the elevator. "I'd better go."

He nodded. "Sure."

She took a step backward. "I'll see you on Monday."

"Before you go…"

She stopped. "Yes?"

"It's my eldest nephew's birthday tomorrow. If we're going to do this, I'd really like you to meet my family."

"Oh." She hadn't thought that far ahead but she realized he was right. He'd referenced his brother and his sister-in-law a few times tonight. It was obvious they were close. "Well. I'm not doing anything apart from catching up on work. As always. What time is it?"

"Midday. I'll swing by and pick you up if you like."

"Okay." She frowned. "Do they know? About any of this, I mean?"

"I talked it over with my brother before I talked to you. I think it's safe to assume that Kay knows, since they're joined at the brain and various other body parts."

"Huh."

"Is that a problem?"

"No. No, it's fine. They're your family, right? And if we have a baby, then your nephews will be our baby's cousins." And not telling Ethan's relatives about their arrangement would mean they'd be sentenced to a lifetime of lies and half-truths.

"That was pretty much what I figured."

"I'll see you tomorrow, then."

She lifted her hand in a last goodbye and walked to the elevator. She waited until the doors closed before sagging against the wall and pressing her face into her hands.

She was going to try for a baby.

In four weeks' time.

With Ethan Stone.

It felt surreal and scary and wonderful and strange all at the same time. She pressed a hand to her flat belly, trying to imagine what it might be like to feel a baby moving inside her.

It was too big a stretch, too far outside her experience. But maybe one day soon it wouldn't be.

Chapter Six

Alex was waiting out in front of her building when Ethan arrived the following day. She was wearing jeans, sneakers and a black sweater with a jade-green duffle coat. Her hair whipped around her face in the breeze as he got out of the car to open the passenger door for her.

"I wasn't sure what to get, but I figured that anything that runs on batteries and makes lots of noise is good, right?" she asked, and he saw she was carrying a gift.

"You didn't have to do that."

"A kid only turns nine once."

She was much shorter without her heels and he found himself looking at the crown of her head as she slid into his car. Amazing that so much grit could be contained in such a small package.

He'd always known Alex was a strong person. But

hearing her story last night, he'd been quietly blown away by what she'd endured. She was a survivor, there was no doubt about it. A tough cookie.

It explained a lot, that childhood of hers. The way she'd fought to hold in her tears that night on the racquetball court. The way she was always so quick to assure him that she didn't need his help and so slow to confide. He bet tears had been a rarely indulged luxury when she was growing up. As for helping hands—in Alex's world, they'd probably been few and far between.

Was it any wonder she'd thrown herself at the problem of her ticking biological clock like a SWAT team going through the door on a drug bust? She'd probably never backed down from a challenge in her life.

And yet there'd been that soft, vulnerable expression in her eyes last night when she'd been talking about her mother. He wondered if she had any idea how expressive her face could be sometimes.

He circled the car and got in. She was busy inspecting the interior, opening and closing compartments and running her fingers over the burled walnut dash.

"I don't think I've been in your car before. It's pretty nice—but dick cars usually are."

He smiled. No way was he rising to such obvious bait. "Do I detect a little car envy, Dr. Freud?"

"Not at all. Not when I know how much it's going to hurt you to have to part with it."

"I'm not getting rid of the Aston Martin." He'd worked hard for this car. Lusted after it for many, many years.

"Can't put a baby seat in it," she said. "Just sayin'."

He turned and frowned at the tiny backseat. She

was right. There was no way a baby capsule would fit in his sleek, sexy car.

"Bummer," Alex said. "This upholstery is so soft. I guess it's Italian calfskin, yeah?"

She wasn't even trying to hide her schadenfreude.

"If you think I'm trading this in for a boxy Volvo like yours, you've got another think coming," he said. "I'll just buy a second car."

"Good plan. You got two parking spaces when you bought your apartment, right?"

He looked at her and knew that she knew he hadn't.

"Smugness suits you, slowpoke," he said as he started the engine. "Brings out the brown in your eyes."

She laughed outright then and they bantered during the trip to his brother's place. He'd phoned Derek this morning and warned him he'd be bringing Alex along. He'd be lying if he pretended he wasn't a little nervous about his brother and his opinionated sister-in-law meeting the woman he was planning on donating sperm to. Not exactly your everyday situation, and he could think of about a million things that could go wrong.

He glanced across at Alex. He was confident she could hold her own, but he still felt protective of her. He wanted his family to like her. He wanted her to like them.

"So give me the highlights of your sibling rivalry," she said as he trawled his brother's crowded street looking for a parking spot.

"Derek's two inches shorter. When we were on the same football team in our early twenties he outscored me two seasons in a row."

"Ouch. How'd you let that happen?"

"Thanks for the support."

She flashed him a broad grin.

"When he was the best man at my wedding, he lost the ring for a whole half hour before we 'found' it down the back of the seat in the limo."

"No way!"

"I made him wait for forty-five minutes until I coughed up his when he married Kay."

Alex hooted with laughter. "You guys play hard-ball."

"Yeah. You'll fit right in."

She gave him a dry look before opening the car door and getting out. He grabbed his gift for Jamie from the trunk and crossed the road. His brother's mailbox was decorated with a cluster of balloons to mark the birth-day house and even from the sidewalk they could hear the high-decibel screaming of kids having a good time.

"Don't worry. Your ears will stop ringing after a day or two," he told her as they walked up the stairs.

"Good to know."

She looked a little uncertain and he caught her free hand in his as they entered the house.

She glanced at him, startled, and he offered her a smile.

"Courage, corporal."

She pulled a face. "If that makes you my captain we're in big trouble."

But she didn't pull her hand away.

They walked into pandemonium. The kitchen and living room had been decorated with balloons and streamers and it looked as though every toy Tim and Jamie owned had been dragged out of storage and flung around the room. Screaming and laughing chil-dren chased each other around the furniture, their faces painted to resemble lions and tigers and other jungle animals. There was more chaos outside where a queue had formed around what Ethan guessed was the highlight of Jamie's birthday booty—a brand-new trampoline, complete with safety pads and netting.

He scanned for Derek or Kay but came up empty.

"Man. You weren't kidding about the noise," Alex said, wincing.

"Let's go outside. Fewer hard surfaces for the noise to bounce off."

He'd barely set foot in the yard when Tim appeared out of nowhere and wrapped his arms around his legs.

"Uncle Ethan. Wait until you see the tramp'line. It's awesome!"

"It looks pretty amazing. Has Jamie let you have a bounce on it yet?"

"He says I have to wait until he's drawn up a roster."

"A roster. Interesting." He glanced at Alex. "Tim, this is my friend, Alex. You want to say hello?"

"Hi, Alex. Why do you have a boy's name?" Tim said.

She laughed. "It's really Alexandra, but that's a bit of a mouthful, isn't it?"

Ethan caught his brother's eye across the lawn where he was manning the barbecue. Derek jerked his head toward Alex as if to ask *is this her?* Ethan rolled his eyes. *What do you think, idiot?*

Derek immediately handed the tongs over to someone else and made his way toward them.

Alex was talking to Tim but she looked up when Derek joined them.

"Derek, Alex, Alex, Derek," Ethan said.

Alex offered her hand and Derek shook it.

"Nice to meet you, Alex." His tone was a little on

the neutral side of friendly but Ethan could live with that. For now.

"Good to meet you, too. That's some family resemblance you guys have got going on."

"Nice of you to say so, but no one's got a patch on Pretty Boy here." Derek clapped Ethan on the shoulder.

"Pretty Boy?" Alex asked, eyebrows raised. A smile was lurking around her mouth. "Family nickname?"

"No," Ethan said.

"Yes," Derek said.

Ethan scowled at his brother.

Derek gave him his best innocent face. "What?"

"You'll keep."

Derek took Alex by the elbow. "Come and meet Kay."

Before Ethan could object, Derek had whisked Alex away. He was tempted to go after them, but Tim wanted to show him something in his room. Besides, Alex could take care of herself.

Still, he glanced over his shoulder as he followed Tim. He caught Alex glancing back at him. Their eyes locked and she smiled. He smiled back.

Yeah, she could hold her own.

Alex felt as though she'd run a marathon. Her fingers were sticky from eating fairy bread and chocolate crackles, she had a tomato-sauce stain on her jeans, and she was almost certain her butt was covered with grass stains but couldn't be bothered getting up to check.

Ethan had a nice family. His brother had been a little cool at the beginning, but Alex hadn't held it against him. After all, he didn't know her from a bar of soap and what she and Ethan were planning on doing was a little…unconventional to say the least. His wife, however, had welcomed Alex like a long-lost friend and after ten minutes of shooting the breeze with the two of them she'd felt Derek relax, which had in turn meant that she could let down her guard a little, too.

As for Ethan's nephews... They were adorable. She knew that she was probably hormonally charged to find any children adorable right now, but there was no denying that both Jamie and Tim were very engaging little guys. Their manners were terrific, and Tim in particular had a way with words that kept her in stitches. It didn't hurt that they both had blue eyes and dark hair like their dad and that when she looked at them she could almost see what Ethan's child might look like.

She glanced to where Ethan was playing with Jamie on the trampoline. Ethan had taken his shoes off and stripped off his sweater so that he was wearing only his jeans and a plain white T-shirt. He was holding Jamie's hands, double bouncing his nephew to send him flying high in the sky. She wasn't sure who was enjoying the exercise more—the nine-year-old birthday boy or the forty-two-year-old family lawyer with the huge goofy grin on his face.

Watching Ethan with his family had been a revelation. She'd seen him serious and intent in partner meetings. She'd seen him charm the admin staff in the kitchenette. She'd seen him determined and playful on the racquetball court. But she'd never seen him laugh so easily or wholeheartedly as when he was standing by the barbecue having a beer with his brother. She'd never seen his eyes take on so much gentle depth as when he was bending his head to listen to something one of his nephews was telling him. She'd never seen him so mischievous and, yes, naughty as when he was teasing his sister-in-law about her noodle salad.

"He's a good man."

Alex started as Kay dropped onto the lawn beside her, a big glass of water in hand.

"A lot of people don't see past that gorgeous face of his to the man underneath, but he's one of the best men I know." She took a mouthful of water. "Of course, it's possible I'm a little biased."

Alex smiled. "I think family's supposed to be biased. That's kind of the point."

They were both silent a moment as they watched Ethan bounce Jamie then lift him on the rebound. Jamie's squeals of delight rang across the yard.

"We were pretty worried about him for a while there after Cassie left," Kay said, not taking her gaze off the trampoline. "Her asking for a divorce really took him by surprise. She messed him up big-time."

Alex didn't know what to say. Part of her felt uncomfortable talking about Ethan behind his back. The rest of her was sucking up every bit of information Kay was throwing her way.

"He hasn't said much about his divorce," she said cautiously.

That wasn't too gossipy, right?

"He doesn't talk about it. Even to Derek. I know he likes to come off as a playboy, but Ethan is the kind of guy who loves really deeply, you know? Derek's the same. Once they invest, that's it for them. Ethan invested in Cassie and she burned him, bad. That's why I was so glad when I knew you were coming today. He's never brought a woman to meet us before."

Alex stirred uncomfortably. She'd been under the impression that Kay knew all about the sperm donation thing, but the way she was talking she seemed to think that Alex and Ethan were a couple.

"Ethan and I are just friends, really," she said awkwardly.

Kay raised her eyebrows and took another mouthful of water. "Of course."

What could Alex say to that? Kay flitted off to resolve a dispute over a video game a few minutes later and Ethan joined her instead. He had his shoes and socks in hand and was still grinning ear to ear as he stretched his long legs out beside her.

"Pretty hard to fit one of those things on your balcony," she said, deadpan.

"Yeah. I know. I was just thinking about that. Kind of dangerous if you got a little rogue double-bounce action going, too. It's a long drop from the tenth floor."

"Absolutely."

"Plus I think I'm technically over the weight limit for that thing."

"But it was good fun," she said.

"It was bloody good fun."

He glanced at her and she looked straight into his eyes and for a moment it was only the two of them, sitting in the late-afternoon sun with grass-stained backsides and sticky fingers.

"You've got grass in your hair," he said, and he leaned closer to pull it out.

His fingers brushed her cheek, then her neck as he plucked the grass from her hair. Suddenly she felt breathless. Her gaze skittered from his eyes to his mouth and got stuck there for a moment.

"Do you mind if we get going soon?" she said. "I've got some more work I need to get done tonight."

Ethan sat back and checked his watch. "We can head off in five minutes if you like. Just give me a chance to say goodbye."

He pulled on his shoes and socks and pushed himself to his feet. She watched as he entered the house in search of his brother.

He's a nice man. One of the nicest men I know.

Hard not to agree. But she had to remember that he wasn't *her* man. A small but very important fact.

"I like her. A whole lot more than I thought I would," Derek said the moment Ethan picked up the phone later that evening.

Ethan reached for the remote to turn down the volume on the television. He'd come home to watch football after dropping Alex off at her place and was lying with his feet up on the couch.

"Phew. Huge relief. Thank God." Ethan didn't bother hiding the sarcasm in his voice.

"I thought the whole idea of her coming to the party was so we could get to know her."

"So *she* could get to know *you* and run screaming for the hills before it was too late if she needed to," he corrected his brother.

"Anyway. She's nice. I was expecting some shoulder-pad-wearing corporate ball-breaker, but she was like you said. Smart, funny. Normal."

"I'm sure she'd be very flattered to hear that description."

"We should all do dinner one night. The four of us."

Ethan smiled. Couldn't help himself. His brother was about as subtle as a sledgehammer.

"We're not dating, buddy. And you and Kay need to get a life."

"Tell me you don't think she's hot. I dare you."

Ethan was not having this conversation with his brother. It would only create false expectations that were never going to be fulfilled. Even if there had been that moment on the grass when he'd looked into Alex's eyes and felt an almost overwhelming compulsion to press his lips against hers to see if she tasted as sweet and spicy as she looked. A moment of madness, obviously, and not something he was about to share with his brother.

He deliberately changed the subject, asking how Jamie was after the excitement of the day. After a short pause Derek took the cue and let the subject drop.

They talked for a few more minutes, then Kay roped Derek into service to help get the boys to bed and they ended the call.

Ethan turned up the sound on the television but found it hard to stay focused on the game.

He'd had a good day today. The kids had been great fun, as always, and as much as his brother's old-lady nagging ticked him off sometimes, he'd enjoyed his brother's company. And, yes, it had been nice to see Alex laughing with Kay or kneeling to talk to Tim or sitting watching the mayhem with a big smile on her face. It had been good to eat a sausage on a bun with her and to tease her about her well-concealed sweet tooth when he caught her going back for seconds on the trifle. He'd expected it to be a little awkward, had worried that maybe Derek's ambivalence about what they were doing would show through, but Alex had fit right in.

Which boded well for the future. If the procedure was successful and Alex got pregnant, there would be no problems with her mixing with his family at birthdays and Christmases. If she wanted to do so, of course. There was no guarantee of any of that, given the nature of their agreement. But the option was there if she wanted it.

Before he could double-think it, he picked up the phone again and dialed her number.

"Hello?" She sounded sleepy.

"It's me. I didn't wake you, did I?" He checked the time on his DVD player. It was a little past eight. Surely she hadn't gone to bed that early?

"I fell asleep on the couch. *Damn*."

"What's wrong?"

"My pen leaked on my T-shirt."

He laughed, a picture filling his mind: Alex stretched out on the huge amber-colored velvet sofa in her living room, fast asleep with paperwork and pen resting on her chest.

She'd invited him upstairs for a coffee when he dropped her off and he'd been surprised by her apartment. He wasn't sure what he'd been expecting but it certainly hadn't been the slightly cluttered, very eclectic home he'd walked into, decorated with antiques and floral cushions and colorful throw rugs.

She'd been a little sheepish, explaining that she needed to have a bit of a clear out as he'd inspected her novelty teapot collection and the cluster of mounted animation cells on her wall.

"What color pen?" he asked, reaching out to flick the TV off.

"Red. What else?"

"A sign from the gods that you're working too hard."

"Yeah, well." She sighed. "What's up?"

"I was thinking that we need to draw up that co-parenting contract we talked about."

"Yeah. I was thinking that, too."

"How about I draft something, then we can pass it back and forth until we get it right?"

"Sounds good. Don't forget to bill me for your time."

"I'm expensive, so brace yourself."

"I hope you're worth it."

"Oh, I'm worth it. Rumor has it I'm very good." He was grinning, balancing his ankle on his drawn-up knee.

"Is that a fact? How very…modest of you."

"Modesty is overrated."

"Says the egotist."

He laughed and knew she was smiling on the other end of the phone, proud of herself for puncturing his ego.

"Well. On that note. I'll see you tomorrow," he said.

"Retreating, Pretty Boy? That's not like you."

"No," he said, very firmly.

"I beg your pardon?"

"You are not appropriating my family nickname."

"Why not? I like it."

"Because it drives me nuts."

"Isn't that the point of family nicknames?"

"I'm forty-two. Derek came up with that name twenty-five years ago. It's time to move on."

"Ah. So it's the boy part you object to? You'd prefer Pretty Man? I can work with that."

He could hear the delight in her voice as she teased him.

"Enjoying yourself?" he asked.

"Oh, yes."

"Good night, Alex."

"Good night, Pretty Man."

He'd known she wouldn't be able to resist getting a final shot in. Typical Alex.

* * *

Ethan drafted a rough version of their agreement the following evening and he and Alex had pizza at her place after racquetball to fine-tune it.

They met again on Thursday for tweaks, and by the weekend had a document they were both satisfied with. It laid out their responsibilities and obligations as well as their expectations. Alex had wrangled with him a little over money, insisting that she didn't need or want his financial support, but he'd won the day by reminding her that the beneficiary of the arrangement would be their child. She could hardly argue with that.

He combined the formal handover of their signed agreement with a visit to the Ian Potter Gallery in the city. He'd noticed an ad for a current exhibition during the week and he led Alex into the gallery after they'd signed and dated their agreement in the adjacent coffee shop.

He watched her face as she walked into the gallery space, enjoying her pleasure and delight as she marveled at the latest efforts by Australia's foremost mosaic artists.

"This is amazing. Do you know how much time it takes to get this gradation of color? And the way she's cut the tiles. I wonder what she's using because there's a really nice bevel on the edges…" She hovered beside a large piece by well-known Melbourne artist Mirka Mora.

The following Tuesday she caught him going through the car section of the daily paper in his office, checking out what was available in the more family-friendly end of the market. Just out of curiosity. No solid plans yet. She didn't say anything, but the next day he found a small brown parcel sitting in the middle of his desk blotter when he arrived at work. He opened it to reveal a miniature version of his Aston Martin, accompanied by a handwritten note in Alex's neat print:

> So you'll always have an Aston Martin, if not *the* Aston Martin. And remember, size doesn't count.

To show her there were no hard feelings, he drove her to the fertility clinic on Friday for her mandatory counseling session. She was subdued afterward and he left her to her thoughts for the bulk of the drive home.

Alex had mapped her ovulation cycle by now and they had a firm date fixed for the first procedure—a Thursday, two weeks away.

He tried to put it out of his mind and concentrate on his current cases. Mostly he was successful—he'd become a master at burying himself in work after the divorce—but he knew Alex was becoming increasingly anxious as the date approached. They both had a lot riding on this. A lot of hope and expectation. He took her to a movie the Friday before the procedure to try to take her mind off it, and the following Tuesday he let her win the first game of their weekly match.

"I know what you're doing, Pretty Man," she said as she wiped sweat from her brow.

"Do you, slowpoke?"

"Don't pander to me. I will not be pandered."

"I don't know if you can stop it. I mean, the pandering is pretty much in the hands of the panderer, unless I'm mistaken. The panderee—that's you, by the way—has to grin and bear it."

"Really?"

She'd proceeded to play her worst game of racquetball ever, so bad that it was almost impossible for him to play worse. But he gave it his best shot.

She was laughing so hard by the time they'd battled it out to see who could lose the last point that she had to sit down on the court and wipe her streaming eyes.

Then she got back to her feet and proceeded to hammer him in the third and final game. A blow to his point average, but worth it to see the smile on her face.

And then, too quickly, it seemed as though time folded in on itself and it was Wednesday night and he was psyching himself up for the following day. D-day—or B-day as he and Alex had jokingly been calling it. He was picking her up at ten so they could drive to the clinic together.

If things went well, they would be making a baby. *They* being him and Alex and a team of doctors and nurses.

He laid out his clothes for the next day, then tried to settle himself in front of the TV. Nothing appealed, and he paced restlessly for a few minutes before grabbing his car keys and heading out the door.

The supermarket in nearby St. Kilda was lit with brutal fluorescent lighting and filled with tinkling canned music. He cruised the aisles, throwing unsalted butter, brown sugar, eggs and vanilla extract into his shopping basket. He'd go home and make Alex some fudge to feed that sweet tooth of hers.

He was heading for the liquor section in search of crème de cacao when he rounded a corner and stopped in his tracks. A young couple stood at the other end of the aisle. She was heavily pregnant, her hair pulled into a ponytail, her baby bump covered by a floral top. He was standing in front of her, both hands pressed to her belly, her hands resting over his. They were staring into each other's eyes as they concentrated on the movement of their unborn child. She was smiling and he had an expression made up of equal parts pride and awe.

It was a very private moment, a moment between lovers, and Ethan told himself to walk away. But he didn't.

He watched as she laughed and looked at her belly and said something to her partner. He moved his hand higher up her belly and his eyebrows shot toward his hairline. Then he laughed, too, and leaned forward to kiss her.

They registered Ethan watching then and he jerked his gaze away, feeling every bit the voyeur he was.

"Sorry, mate, first baby," the guy called after him cheerfully as Ethan turned way.

He lifted his hand to signal he hadn't been offended. Far from it.

He bought his groceries but when he got home he didn't make fudge.

Instead he went out onto the balcony. It was cold and he'd dumped his coat when he walked in the door, but he stood at the railing and looked at the city anyway.

He watched the cars race up and down. He watched the bats flying to their usual haunt in the Botanical Gardens. He watched a tram pull to a stop and release a flood of passengers.

So many people—old, young, middle-aged, rich, poor, gay, straight. Who were they going home to tonight? Husbands? Wives? Boyfriends? Girlfriends? Brothers? Sisters? Housemates?

He turned his back on the view and crossed his arms over his chest, staring into his apartment. He could see his couches and his artwork. The profile of his big-screen TV. All the stuff he'd surrounded himself with since the divorce. All the distractions, the consolations he'd bought to make up for the things he'd resigned himself to missing out on.

He closed his eyes and saw that moment in the supermarket again—her big belly, his hands spread wide, hers pressed on top of his. The delight and hope and excitement in their faces. The love. They were about to embark on a huge adventure together.

Together.

No matter what contract Ethan and Alex negotiated, they would never be able to capture that dynamic. There would be no moments of shared joy and love for them.

That's the way you want it. Remember?

His arms were covered with gooseflesh. He pushed away from the railing and entered the apartment. He was picking up Alex at seven the next morning.

He flicked off the living room light and went to bed.

Alex slept badly. She was too wired, her mind too full to tune out enough to let her drift off, even though she really, really wanted to sleep. She wanted to be fresh for tomorrow. Ready to face the doctors and nurses and all the hoopla of her first procedure.

She finally gave up on sleep and made herself breakfast while it was still dark out. Once she'd made it she didn't want it, and she pushed the toast around her plate for fifteen minutes before throwing it in the garbage. So, no sleep and no appetite—a great start to what might be the biggest day of her life.

She showered and dressed and made sure she had everything she needed—all her medical reports and paperwork, important phone numbers, a list of questions she'd thought of since her last visit...

She glanced uncertainly toward the pile of magazines and printouts she'd stacked neatly on her coffee table, ready for Ethan's arrival. Then she glanced away again and killed the remaining time until Ethan's arrival doing laundry and cleaning. The closer seven came, the more tense she became. Her stomach was churning and she could feel her heartbeat kicking against her breastbone.

It's only adrenaline. You're excited. It's perfectly natural.

It didn't feel like excitement, though.

She almost leaped out of her skin when the intercom buzzed. She took a deep breath, then crossed to the unit and pressed the button.

"Hi. Come on up."

She opened her front door. The elevator was slow, so it would take him a while to ascend to her level. She slipped her thumb into her mouth and tore at her thumbnail while she waited. She snatched her thumb from her mouth the moment she registered what she was doing and slid her hand into the pocket of her jeans. She hadn't bitten her nails since she was in law school. It was one of the things she'd left behind when she graduated. No one wanted to hire a lawyer with chewed-up hands.

She heard the mechanical groan of the elevator arriving at her floor, then the doors opened and Ethan stepped out into the hall.

He strode toward her, perfect as always in a soft-looking black V-neck sweater and dark denim jeans.

"Hi," she said.

"Hi. Did you sleep okay?"

She wrinkled her nose to indicate it hadn't been a great night, then stepped back to allow him to enter her apartment. He brushed past her, trailing the warm scent of sandalwood.

"This is new."

She joined him in her living room, where he was running his hand over the aged oak marquetry of her new French armoire. She'd bought it on the weekend, more for something to do than because she needed another piece of large furniture in her already full apartment.

"Genuine?" he asked.

"God, I hope so, after what I paid," she said. She smoothed her hands down the sides of her jeans. "Would you like a coffee? I thought we could go over the procedure again before we hit the road, so we're both familiar with everything...."

"Sure."

He followed her into the kitchen and leaned a hip against the counter while she ground beans and warmed up her coffee machine.

"And you say you can't cook."

She forced a smile. God, why was she so nervous? She felt sick with it. As though all her internal organs were vibrating with anxiety.

"Love my coffee. It's my one vice. No, that's not true, I have two vices—coffee and antiques. Which is pretty funny, really, because when I graduated from law school and got my first decent paycheck, all I wanted was new everything. Shiny, spanking-new stuff with the price tags still attached. As for the coffee thing, I can hardly boil an egg without close supervision, but for some reason I have all the patience and skill in the world for coffee."

She was talking too fast. She forced herself to concentrate on the small task of spooning coffee into the basket and tamping it firmly.

"Espresso? Latte? Cappuccino?" she asked without looking up.

"Espresso, thanks."

She nodded. Just as well he hadn't asked for a cappuccino—she didn't trust herself with the steaming wand right now.

"There we go," she said a minute later, sliding his coffee across the counter toward him.

"Smells fantastic."

"Yep. Nothing like the smell of fresh coffee." She took a deep breath. "So, shall we sit and have a last look at the stuff the clinic sent?"

He gestured for her to precede him into the living room and they sank onto a couch each, facing each other across her coffee table.

She slid the pile of papers and magazines toward herself and sorted through them until she'd found the two copies of the outline of the procedure the clinic had provided. She slid one across the table toward Ethan and started reviewing her own, even though she'd read it a dozen times already.

Once she got to the clinic, she would be taken into a treatment room and readied for the procedure. She'd be dressed in a hospital gown and placed in stirrups, and a soft plastic catheter would be introduced into her vagina to deliver the sperm directly to her uterus through her cervix. Ethan, meanwhile, would be handed a cup and left alone to produce a sample of semen. His semen would then be taken away and "washed" in the laboratory to remove any dead sperm and harmful chemicals that might interfere with the process of conception. Once the most active and motile sperm had been selected, they would be introduced to her uterus via the catheter. After a few minutes' rest, she and Ethan would then leave the clinic. In total, the whole thing would take under an hour, and in two weeks' time they could perform their first pregnancy test.

She glanced at Ethan and saw that he was frowning as he read.

"Is there something wrong?" she asked.

"No."

She wasn't sure if he was covering or not. "If there's a problem, we should probably talk about it."

"No problem. I guess it's just hit me that we're really doing this."

"Yes."

She dropped her gaze to the magazines stacked beneath her other paperwork. They'd seemed like a good idea last night. But maybe he'd already covered that end of things.

For Pete's sake, now is hardly the time to be squeamish. Offer him the magazines, and if he doesn't want them, it's no big deal.

"Listen. I didn't know what you wanted to do about... I thought the clinic might have some stuff, but I wasn't sure. Anyway, I bought these for you last night. I wasn't sure what you liked, so I got you a little bit of everything...."

She slid the magazines from beneath the other papers and pushed them across the table toward him. Ethan glanced at the cover of *Playboy,* his expression completely unreadable.

"There's a *Hustler* there, too, and another one with cars and women with big— Well, like I said. I wasn't sure what you were into."

There was a smile playing around Ethan's mouth

when she finally rallied the courage to look at him. "You're laughing at me, aren't you? I knew the magazines were a bad idea."

"They're a very thoughtful gift. But I think I can manage on my own."

She could feel herself blushing but she was determined to cover this issue. "You're not worried about... performing on demand?"

"I think I've had enough practice to get it right," he said, very dry.

"Right. Still, it's not exactly an ideal situation, is it?"

"For you, either. No wine and roses or soft music in the treatment room."

"No."

Instead, there would be a hospital gown that didn't close properly at the back and people with surgical masks on their faces and the smell of antiseptic and her legs in stirrups. The conception of her child would be a medical event, not the act of love and intimacy Alex had always imagined. There would be no lying in her lover's arms afterward, imagining the baby that might result. There would only be Ethan sitting in the waiting room. And while that was a hell of a lot more than she'd hoped for at the beginning of this process, it was still a far cry from how she'd dreamed of having her child.

She'd been shortchanged so many things in life. A father. A mother, in many respects. She felt as though she'd been fighting and making compromises from the moment she was born. And now there was this, the ultimate compromise. The making of a child without love or passion or even physical gratification.

So what? You're just going to have to suck it up.

The way you've always sucked it up. Do you want this or not? Do you?

She squeezed her eyes shut, fighting both the tears and the understanding rising inside her.

"Alex." The couch depressed beside her as Ethan joined her. "Talk to me. What's going on?"

She sucked in a breath but it was hard to get it past the words choking her throat. "I don't think I can do this."

The moment the words were out of her mouth she felt both enormous relief and terrible grief. How long had she been hiding this truth from herself? Weeks? Days? She'd been so determined to steamroller her way over everything, including her own qualms and concerns. So determined not to miss out, at any cost.

She'd allowed herself to be seduced into a false sense of intimacy and togetherness with Ethan. She'd shared her thoughts and feelings with him and made jokes about him having to get a new car and watched him with his nephews and allowed herself to believe that when she had her baby it wouldn't be *that* different from what she'd always wanted.

And she'd been wrong. So wrong and *stupid* and desperate.

She pressed a hand to her sternum and forced herself to look at Ethan. She'd started this journey. Offered him a chance he didn't think he'd ever have. He'd stepped up to help her. And now she was reneging on her end of the bargain. Copping out.

"I'm so sorry. I thought I was okay, that I'd reconciled myself to doing it this way. But I… It's so clinical. So…cold. If I'd tried to get pregnant the normal way and my partner and I wanted to exhaust all avenues this would feel like a godsend… But at the moment it feels like—"

"Giving up."

She glanced at Ethan through swimming eyes. "Yes. I want to be a mother so much—but not like this. Maybe that means I don't want it enough. I don't know. I just know that this feels wrong."

He reached for her tightly clasped hands. "It's okay," he said. He wrapped his hands around hers, the pressure warm and firm.

"No, it's not. You came to me with this incredibly generous offer and now I'm wimping out and leaving you high and dry—"

"Alex, it's okay. I was having second thoughts, too."

She dashed the tears from her cheek with a fisted hand.

"You don't have to say that to try to make me feel better. You're allowed to be angry and disappointed. You can even yell at me if you think it would make you feel better. Hell, you could probably even sue me for breach of contract."

"I'm not trying to make you feel better. I saw something last night that got me thinking, and reading over the procedure this morning… I don't know. Standing alone in a cubicle with an empty cup and a magazine isn't the way I've always imagined becoming a father."

Her gaze searched his face. "So it's not just me, then? This feels wrong?"

"It's not just you." He squeezed her hands then released his grip. "In theory, this seemed like a solution. But I guess we're both a little less hardheaded than we imagined."

He was being honest. He felt the same way—this

was one compromise too many. She could see it in his eyes, hear it in his voice.

"God."

She put her head in her hands. She was relieved that he wasn't angry, that she wasn't alone in balking at the last hurdle. It would have been terrible if he'd felt ripped-off or misled or cheated.

But none of that stopped her from feeling disappointed. There would be no baby. The past few weeks of planning and discussions and excitement had been for nothing. At the end of the day, neither of them were...what? Ruthless enough? Determined enough? Whatever. Neither of them was prepared to sacrifice a part of themselves for the dream of being a parent. Having a child wasn't an at-any-cost proposition, not for her or for him.

"I need to call the clinic," she said after a moment. "Cancel everything."

"I can do that, if you like."

"No, I'll do it. I started this thing." She pushed herself to her feet and looked down at him. "I'm so sorry you got caught up in my baby crisis, Ethan. If I'd stuck to my original plan and used a sperm bank, the only one feeling like crap right now would be me."

"We both went along for this ride. And you might have had second and third thoughts weeks ago if I hadn't been here, cheering you on from the sidelines."

He offered her the ghost of a smile. She leaned down impulsively and wrapped her arm around his neck, pressing her check against his in a one-armed but still fierce hug.

"You're a good man. A good friend," she said.

It was the first time she'd initiated contact between them. She was aware of the rasp of his beard against her face and the softness of his hair brushing against her fingers. His arms closed around her in response.

"You're a good woman. And don't worry—it'll happen for you, Alex. Some lucky bastard will come along and realize you're a woman in a million and it'll all fall into place."

She released him and after a second's hesitation he followed suit.

"I don't know if I should let myself believe in those kinds of happy-ever-afters. Maybe I should just start collecting cats," she said.

"Alex—"

She held up a hand. "Yes, I know, I'm an attractive woman, I've still got time left, yada yada. I guess I'll have to wait and see, won't I, since seizing the day hasn't really worked out for me."

She pushed her hair away her forehead.

"Now, before I get out my violin, I'll make that call."

She stared out her kitchen window while she waited for the call to connect. It occurred to her that they'd both taken the day off for nothing. She smiled grimly. Right now, wasted leave time was the least of her worries.

The receptionist at the clinic didn't sound surprised when Alex told her she wanted to cancel her appointment. Perhaps this happened all the time. Perhaps she was one of many desperate woman who found they didn't have the stomach to take the pragmatic route to motherhood when push came to shove.

Ethan was browsing her CD collection when she came back. She stood in the doorway watching him unnoticed for a few seconds. He was a good friend. A really decent man. Now that she'd gotten to know him—really know him—she could see past his beautiful face to the man underneath. He would have made a great father. She found it hard to believe that he planned to spend the rest of his life alone. She hoped that whatever it was that was holding him back resolved itself for him. He deserved better.

He glanced up. "All done?"

"All done."

There was a short silence, then he pulled a CD with a bright pink cover from her shelf.

"Cyndi Lauper. There's a guilty secret."

"Hands off Cyndi. She's very retro cool."

He raised his eyebrows. "That's drawing a long bow."

"Says the man with not one, not two, but *three* Barry White albums," she said.

"They were a gag gift from my brother."

"Sure they were."

"Don't get too high and mighty on me, lady-who-owns-Nana-Mouskouri's-greatest-hits."

He plucked the CD from her bookshelf with a got-cha flourish.

"Yeah, well. They were doing a retrospective on the radio. I got carried away—"

"At least you have the courage to admit your mistake," he said sagely.

She opened her mouth to say something sassy back, but suddenly her throat and chest were aching and she knew tears were not far away.

She cleared her throat. "Listen, I've got a few things I need to take care of. Loose ends and whatnot. You know."

"Right. I should go, then."

Yes, please go. Before I blubber all over you. Before I lose it completely.

"If you don't mind. I might as well make use of the day off to get something done."

His expression was unreadable as he replaced her CDs on the shelves then collected his coat from the back of her couch. She followed him to the front door. Ten more seconds and he would be gone and she would be alone and it wouldn't matter if she howled her eyes out.

"Listen. If you need to talk, call me, okay?" Ethan said as he reached the doorstep.

"Sure. But I'm fine, really," she lied.

His gaze searched her face, then he nodded. "Okay."

She waited until he'd reached the elevator before she shut the door. Then she walked into her living room and stared at all the fertility-clinic paperwork and those damned stupid mens' magazines she'd bought for Ethan.

The wanting-to-cry feeling hit her again and she closed her eyes.

All right, you big sook. Get it over and done with. Because this is the only chance you're going to get to wallow in this.

She waited for the tears to come. Her throat got tight. Her chest ached. She gripped the couch—but her eyes remained steadfastly dry.

Okay.

Okay.

Moving slowly and carefully, she did a circuit of her apartment, collecting anything and everything to do with the fertility clinic and pregnancy and babies. She dumped the paperwork in a carton, to be taken down to the Dumpster in the basement next time she left the apartment. She hesitated over throwing the pregnancy books in.

She was still only thirty-eight, after all.

Hope springs eternal.

She wavered for half a second more. Then she dropped the books into the carton. She didn't want anything hanging around to remind her of this debacle. It would be bad enough having to face Ethan at work every day with the memory of all of this sitting between them.

She pushed the carton close to the front door so she wouldn't forget it when she went out. The sooner it was gone, the better.

Then she returned to her living room, sat on her couch and burst into noisy, messy tears.

Chapter Seven

She'd kicked him out. Amazing that after everything that had gone down this morning, the thing he couldn't get past was that Alex hadn't wanted him around once they'd made the mutual decision not to go through with their plans. She'd been disappointed, on the verge of tears, and she hadn't wanted him to witness her moment of weakness. Because that was how Alex saw emotion and tears—as a weakness. A folly to be endured then brushed aside and ignored. He knew enough about her now to understand that.

If she'd let him stay, if she'd cried in front of him, he would have told her that tears didn't make her less strong or less capable. He would have held her and talked to her and together they might have made sense of the roller-coaster ride they'd taken over the past few weeks.

Instead, she'd kicked him out and he was making

bread at eleven in the morning, taking out his frustration and, yes, disappointment on the mass of dough under his hands.

Because he *was* disappointed, even though he knew they'd made the right decision. For a short while he'd convinced himself that he'd found a way to have what he wanted without the mess and entanglements and risk of a relationship. It had seemed like the perfect solution. Then reality had intruded.

He wanted more from parenthood. And so did Alex. When push came to shove, neither of them wanted to compromise.

Which left him…nowhere. His feelings hadn't changed regarding marriage. And he'd rejected the alternate route to parenthood. All of which meant that it really was over for him.

He was never going to be a father.

Might as well let the fact seep into his bones, permanently this time. He'd have to make do with his brother's children, be the best uncle he could be.

It wasn't the end of the world. Disheartening, yes, but he'd get over it. Accept it. Move on. After all, he had a pretty good life.

The dough had lost its elasticity. He'd over-kneaded it. He stared at it for a long, silent minute. Then he gathered the big, floury lump and dropped it in the rubbish bin.

His thoughts shifted to Alex again as he started cleaning the counter. Had she allowed herself to cry once he'd left? Had she allowed herself even a small moment of humanity and frailty?

He dried his hands and glanced around his kitchen. He should go for a drive. Or maybe call his brother, see whether he wanted to hook up for lunch. Anything other than haunt his apartment, fixating on Alex and what had almost been between them.

He pulled out his phone and dialed. His brother picked up after the second ring.

"It's me. You free for lunch?" Ethan said.

"I thought you had an appointment with a paper cup today."

Ethan gazed out across the park. "We canceled the appointment. You free or not?"

"Who canceled? You or Alex?"

"It was a mutual decision."

"What happened to wanting a kid?"

Ethan closed his eyes. What had he been thinking, calling his brother? He was only going to get the same grief he'd been getting for the past five years.

"You know what, forget I called." He started to hang up.

"Wait. I'm sorry. I wasn't having a go at you. I know how much you were banking on this."

"It was a crazy idea."

"Well, yeah. But it was a step in the right direction. You and Alex are closer now. You both know what each other wants—"

"Derek. I swear, you've got a one-track mind. Will you please give it a rest?"

"At least be honest with yourself. You have feelings for her, and all this stuff about a baby was your way of trying to smuggle them in under the radar."

Ethan didn't say anything for a long moment. "It doesn't matter how I feel about Alex."

Even if it had been a long time since he'd thought of her as simply a friend.

"So you're going to let her walk away?"

Ethan thought about what Alex wanted and what he wanted.

"Yeah, I am."

"Bullshit. You've never given up on anything you wanted in your life."

There was so much confidence in his brother's voice. He was so sure that all Ethan needed was to meet a good woman and he'd shrug off everything that had happened with Cassie and leap into the breach again.

Derek didn't understand. But how could he when he didn't know the full story? He knew only that Cassie had left, and that Ethan had not been interested in a reconciliation. They had never discussed the details because Ethan had never been able to reveal the full depth of his wife's betrayal and rejection. He literally hadn't been able to make himself form the words.

The day he'd come home from work and found Cassie waiting for him was etched like acid in his memory. She'd given him no reasons or explanations or warnings, she'd simply severed their marriage in the most brutal possible way. She'd sat there and told him she didn't love him anymore. Then she'd told him about the baby. And then she'd walked, leaving him to try to make sense of what remained of his life.

For a long time, there hadn't been a day that went by without him thinking about her, about what had gone wrong and how he hadn't seen it coming. He still didn't understand how he could have been so out of step with her. How he could have slept beside her every night and not known that she was quietly opening separate bank accounts and viewing apartments so that when she walked out the door she could step straight into her new life. Without him.

It hadn't been a perfect marriage, but what marriage was? They'd had their differences and their rough patches. But he'd believed in her, trusted her, loved her implicitly.

And she'd shed him like an old skin and never looked back.

"Maybe we should have lunch another day," Ethan said. "I'll call you on the weekend or something, okay?"

He ended the call before his brother could object. The phone rang immediately and he let it go through to voice mail.

He didn't need a pep talk or a lecture. He didn't need his brother spouting the joys of marital and family life. He was happy for Derek and he loved Kay. He would lay down his life for Jamie or Tim. But he could not and would not go there again himself. What was that old saying? *Fool me once, shame on you. Fool me twice, shame on me.*

He wasn't about to be fooled twice. No matter how much he was drawn to Alex. He may have toyed with the notion of intimacy over the past few weeks, but he didn't have it in him to go there again.

He just…didn't.

Alex flattened her fingers and stirred the tray of glass tiles in front of her. She needed another aqua tile—not bright blue or powder blue, but aqua blue. And if she'd used her last piece, she was going to seriously consider having a tantrum.

So much for mosaics as therapy. If anything, she was wound more tightly after an hour working on her latest project. She kept searching for an aqua tile, however, since the alternative was to wallow. And she'd done enough wallowing today. More even than when she and Jacob had finally gone their separate ways. More than at any other time in her adult life, in fact.

As always, it hadn't made her feel any better. Her eyes were still puffy and swollen from crying and she felt completely flat, interested in nothing. She knew herself well enough to know the feeling would pass, but the long hours of the evening stretched ahead seemingly endlessly.

Get through tonight. Then you'll have work tomorrow, and a week—okay, a month—from now you'll be over it. Mostly.

For a moment she was overwhelmed by the task ahead. She let her shoulders slump. She didn't want to play with mosaics. She didn't want to do anything. She felt hollow and empty. She felt defeated.

After a long moment she took a deep breath and forced herself to sit up straight. She edged one of the tiles a little to the left and was reaching for her tile nippers just as a knock sounded on the door.

She paused, glancing down at herself. She was wearing a baggy old pair of flannel pajama bottoms and a stretchy tank top. Her hair was still damp from her shower this afternoon and she wasn't wearing underwear or makeup.

She shrugged. There was only one person it could be, since the intercom hadn't buzzed to announce a visitor. It had been a month since she'd last caught up with Helen, her friend from the apartment across the hall. Having company tonight could only be a good thing— provided it was the right kind of company. By which she meant the kind that didn't know anything about her now-defunct baby plans and therefore wouldn't ask probing personal questions. Alex didn't want to be probed or questioned tonight. She simply wanted to process and grieve. And since she hadn't confided in anyone apart from Ethan, she figured she was safe.

She walked to the front door, rubbing her gummy fingertips together to try to remove some of the adhesive residue. She opened the front door—and discovered the wrong sort of company standing on her doorstep.

"Ethan."

For a moment she simply stood there, blinking stupidly. She should have known it would be him. Why hadn't she checked through the spy hole before opening the door?

"Hey. I brought you dinner," he said, hefting a heavy-looking recyclable shopping bag.

"Dinner...?"

He brushed past her and into her apartment. "Roast chicken, mashed potatoes, baby peas, homemade gravy. And a bottle of sémillon sauvignon. You want to eat out here or in the kitchen?"

He was already heading for the kitchen before she could respond. She chased after him, belatedly dragging the low-slung waistband of her pajama bottoms up to meet the hem of her tank top. She was very aware that she wasn't wearing panties or a bra and that it had been a long time since she'd considered herself fit for public consumption without either. But she could hardly race off to her bedroom to put underwear on while he made free with her apartment.

Then she remembered something else—her mosaic project was spread out across the kitchen table. No one ever saw her mosaics, for good reason.

She swore under her breath and lengthened her stride. She skidded to a halt in the kitchen doorway.

Ethan had left his shopping bag on the counter and was hovering over the table, examining her handiwork.

Too late. Damn.

"It's not finished yet," she said quickly.

"It's a tabletop, right?" he asked, glancing at her over his shoulder.

His gaze dipped briefly below her neck and she crossed her arms over her braless breasts.

"Yes. A side table. I found it at a secondhand shop."

"And this round thing at the top is a flower, right?"

"A daisy."

"And this is a rose. And that's a daffodil," he said.

They were pretty good guesses considering how un-rose-and un-daffodil-like her representations were. She was well aware that they looked more like clumps of ceramic confetti than anything else.

"That's right."

"It's good—"

"Don't. Don't lie and tell me it's good. It's terrible. I know it's terrible. That's why I don't show my mosaics to anyone. It doesn't matter if they're terrible or not when I'm the only one who sees them. So you don't need to butter me up by saying something nice when we both know it's not true."

Ethan's mouth curled up at the corner. "Are you finished?"

She let her breath out, aware she'd overreacted a little. "Yes."

"I was going to say it's good you put a cloth down because your glue's leaking."

"Oh. Right."

She joined him at the table and saw that the tube of tile adhesive was adrift in a sea of ooze.

"Damn."

"Where do you keep your paper towel?" he asked.

"Under the sink."

She shifted her tray of tiles and her tool kit to the floor, then lifted the half-finished tabletop and leaned it against the wall. When she turned around again Ethan was wiping the adhesive off her drop sheet with a wad of paper.

"Thanks," she said. "And sorry about the rant."

Ethan handed her the wad of paper towel. "It was a pretty good one, as rants go. And for the record, the tabletop isn't that bad."

She gave him a look. "It's not that good, either."

He grinned. "True. But it didn't make me want to poke out my eyes, so there's something to be said for that."

Sometimes she forgot how completely devastating he could be when he smiled. She swallowed, the sound audible.

"I'll get some plates. And I need to wash my hands…"

"Point me in the right direction and I'll serve while you go clean up."

She was quick to take him up on the offer, scuttling off to her bedroom at the speed of light. She degummed her hands in record time, then scrambled into underwear and a T-shirt and jeans.

She had no idea why Ethan was here, or why he'd brought her dinner, of all things. Their baby bargain was over. There was no reason for him to be here.

Unless he felt sorry for her?

She was brushing her hair when the thought occurred and she stilled with the brush midstroke.

Was that why he was here? Because he was worried poor childless Alex would lose it without close supervision? Had he imagined her huddled on the couch, elbow-deep in a bucket of ice cream and ridden to the rescue, the way he had so many times since this all started?

She threw her brush onto the bed. If that was the case, if she detected even a whiff of pity coming off of him, she was going to tell him in no uncertain terms what he could do with his chicken and all the trimmings.

And if it wasn't the case… She had no idea why he was here. Hadn't they said everything they needed to say to each other this morning? And weren't they going to see each other tomorrow at work?

There was one other reason he could be here, of course. But he'd made his feelings about settling down pretty clear—as had she. Only a very silly woman would allow herself to buy into the fantasy that he'd somehow had a change of heart since getting to know her.

He was pulling a plastic tub of gravy out of her microwave when she returned to the kitchen. His gaze raked her from head to toe but he didn't say anything about her quick-change routine.

"I couldn't find your bottle opener," he said.

She crossed to the fridge and pulled one of her own bottles from the built-in wine rack.

"Let's drink one of mine. It's the least I can do, since you've supplied the meal."

"Your call."

She busied herself with opening the bottle and getting out wineglasses. Then she joined him at the kitchen table. Her plate was heaped with food, all of which looked ridiculously good. She slid his wine across the table and watched as his long fingers wrapped around the stem of the glass.

"Thanks." He smiled faintly and it hit her that the last man who'd sat at this table and eaten a meal with her was Jacob.

"Why are you here?" She hadn't meant to blurt it out like that, but she needed to know.

Ethan was slicing his chicken but he put down his knife and fork and looked at her. "I felt like crap and I figured you might, too. So I thought I'd bribe my way through the door with chicken."

She frowned. "You didn't need to bribe your way in."

"Didn't I?" His blue eyes were searching.

"No. You're disappointed, aren't you?"

She'd let him down. Led him on a merry dance then left him gasping like a landed fish.

"Of course. Aren't you? If we were both a little more ruthless, we might have been shopping for a home pregnancy test in a few weeks' time."

"No, we wouldn't. I've already got one. A double pack, just to make sure."

"Exactly my point. We invested a lot of time and energy in this."

She looked down at her plate, away from the sadness in his face. He felt the same way she did. And he'd sought her out to both give and take comfort.

"You're a nice man, Ethan Stone," she said quietly, glancing up at him again.

"Let's not get too carried away."

Good advice, Alex. Listen to the man.

He deliberately changed the subject then and they talked about work and the day's political news. Maybe it was the wine, or maybe it was simply Ethan, with his easy charm and distracting wit, but by the time they were pushing aside their plates she was feeling decidedly more mellow.

She was glad he'd come. A dangerous admission to make, even to herself, but it was true.

They moved to the living room after she'd cleared the table and she raided her chocolate-cookie stash for dessert while Ethan opened the second bottle of wine. She found him examining her teapot collection when she returned to the living room with a plateful of Tim Tams and other indulgences.

"This is my favorite, I think. Although the one shaped like a cat is pretty damned cool," he said.

"The cabbage was a lucky find. But that cat... I nearly broke an old lady's arm to get that teapot."

"Excellent. Tell me everything." He rubbed his hands together with exaggerated anticipation.

So she told him how she'd spotted the teapot at the same time as a purple-haired old lady at a yard sale and how they'd both reached for it at the same time but she'd been a trifle faster off the mark and the old lady had lunged across the table at her and refused to let go until the woman running the sale had to step in to adjudicate.

Ethan was wiping tears from his eyes by the time she'd finished. She'd always loved making him laugh but tonight it felt like a special achievement.

"Alex. That's priceless. A million other women would have bowed to her brittle bones and handed the damned thing over but not you."

"Old people are just normal people with more wrinkles. Why should they be granted a get-out-of-jail-free cards on things like courtesy and finders keepers? Besides, it turned out she thought it was a dog, not a cat.

When she put her glasses on she was more than happy to let it go."

She had her feet curled up beside her on the couch and had been rubbing her arches absently throughout her story. Ethan slid his wineglass onto the coffee table in front of him, then stood and crossed to sit on the end of her couch.

"Come on. Give them here," he said.

It took her a moment to understand what he intended.

She shook her head. "I'm fine."

"I give a mean foot massage, Alex. It's about the only thing Cassie and I could ever agree on." He held up his thumbs and wiggled them in the air. "Magic thumbs."

She shook her head again. No way was she lying on her couch while Ethan rubbed her feet. It was way, way too intimate.

"I'm really ticklish. I'll only wind up giggling like an idiot."

"Clearly you've only had substandard massages in the past. Come on."

She started to object again but he simply circled her right ankle with one of his big hands and pulled her foot into his lap.

"Hey!"

"Shut up and take your medicine."

He started rubbing her foot then and it felt so good that even though she knew she should pull free and maybe even send him home before she forgot that tonight was about mutual sympathy and not…anything else, she subsided back onto the cushions and closed her eyes.

"Not ticklish?" he asked after a minute or so.

She cracked an eyelid. He was looking very pleased with himself.

"Strong thumbs, my backside," she muttered.

He laughed, the sound very low, and she closed her eyes again and didn't even try to suppress her own smile. And she didn't resist fifteen minutes later when he switched to her left foot, rubbing the tension from her arches and making her wish she had a third and even a fourth foot to offer him so she could prolong the experience.

Twenty minutes later it occurred to her that Ethan had stopped the massage a while ago and she opened her eyes to find him collecting his car keys from the coffee table.

"That was sneaky," she said drowsily. "I didn't even feel you move."

"I took origami lessons when I was a kid."

She was so out of it it took her a moment to understand he was joking. "Origami. Funny."

"I thought so."

She started to sit up.

"Stay where you are. I'll see myself out."

"I can't let you cook me dinner then rub my feet for hours on end and not see you out."

"Yes, you can. Stay where you are. That's an order."

He'd crossed to the couch to stand over her and she stared up at him mutinously.

"If I'm supposed to be intimidated by the looming-over-me thing, you can think again."

She stood, only realizing when she did so that it meant they were standing chest to chest, only a few inches between them.

"I won't ask if anyone has ever told you you're a

pain in the ass. You'll only take it as a compliment," Ethan said.

She tried to take a step backward, but the couch was against her heels and she lost her balance. His hand closed around her upper arm to stop her fall. He was smiling, clearly amused by her.

"Idiot," he said.

Then he lowered his head and kissed her once, very hard, on the mouth.

He looked as surprised as she was when he lifted his head. For a moment they stared at each other, then Ethan's gaze slid to her mouth again.

"Alex," he said, so quietly she almost didn't hear him.

He lowered his head again. This time his lips were gentle on hers, the pressure more a question than an expression of frustration. For a moment they stood locked together, neither of them moving, joined only by their mouths and his hand on her arm. Then she parted her lips the tiniest fraction. The merest hint of an invitation. He sighed and slid his hand to the nape of her neck and opened his mouth over hers.

He tasted of chocolate and wine, and she made an approving, needy sound as his tongue stroked hers. Her hands reached blindly for him, finding his broad shoulders, pulling him closer. And then, somehow, they were on the couch, Ethan's big body on top of hers, his hands gliding over her as their kiss became more and more intense. She whimpered as his hand cupped first one breast then the other, his thumb sliding over and over each nipple in turn until they were both hard and eager and she was quivering beneath him.

It had been eighteen months since she'd felt a man's weight on top of her and she'd spent the better part of

the past month living in the pocket of one of the sexiest men she'd ever known. So maybe it wasn't any
wonder that she was on fire for him now. She'd always
found him attractive. Always. She'd noticed his powerful body, she'd eyed his mouth and long fingers and
imagined... And now he was kissing her and his hand
was sliding beneath her top, pushing her bra out of the
way, and he was breaking their kiss to lower his head
to take her nipple into his mouth.

She clutched at his shoulders as the wet heat of his
mouth engulfed her. It felt so good. *He* felt so good.

She arched her back, offering him her other breast,
sliding her fingers into his hair when he turned his
head and pulled her nipple into his mouth.

Somewhere, in a very dark, distant corner of her
mind a warning knell sounded. This was Ethan. A fellow partner. And, more than that, her friend. A friend
who had made his feelings about relationships painfully clear.

She knew she should push him away and call a halt,
but she wasn't even close to being strong enough to
deny the need thrumming through her body. She'd
wanted him for so long.

She parted her legs and lifted her hips and Ethan
didn't need to be asked twice to take up her silent invitation. His hips pressed into the cradle of her thighs
and she wrapped her legs around his waist and rubbed
herself against the hard length of him.

"Alex," Ethan said again, pressing his erection
against her where she needed it the most.

She circled her hips, willing two layers of denim to
oblivion but unwilling to lose the delicious pressure of
his hips against hers for the short time it would take
to get undressed.

They kissed and caressed and rubbed against each other for long minutes. Alex was so turned on, so achingly ready for him that it almost hurt. She was the one who reached for the stud on his jeans, and she was the one who slid her hand beneath the soft cotton of his boxer briefs to find the hard, resilient shaft of his erection. He shuddered as she wrapped her hand around him and stroked her hand up and down his length. She felt him fumble at the stud on her jeans and she forgot to breathe as his palm slid over her belly and down, down, until his fingers were delving between her thighs.

He stroked her while she stroked him, their mouths locked in a searching, never-ending kiss. She was seconds away from her first heavy-petting-on-the-couch climax in years when Ethan broke their kiss and rested his forehead against hers.

"Alex. I need—"

"Yes," she said, already starting to peel her jeans down over her hips.

His weight left her for a brief moment as they both shed their jeans, then she heard the small, significant crackle of a foil pack before Ethan was on top of her again, his bare legs warm and slightly rough against her own as they tangled together on the couch. He ran his hand down the side of her hip, wrapped his fingers around the outside of her left thigh and lifted her leg up and to the side. She felt the firm probe of his erection at her entrance and she lifted her hips in welcome. Then he was inside her and there was nothing in the world except for the exquisite friction of his body moving within hers.

They rocked together, neither saying a word. Alex held her breath and squeezed her eyes tightly shut, chasing the licks of pleasure racing through her body. Ethan pressed his face into her neck and opened his mouth against her skin, sucking and licking as his thrusts became more and more urgent. One of his hands teased her breasts, the other gripped her hip, his fingers pressing into her flesh.

He shifted position. *So close. So close.*

She caught her breath, arched her back. And then she was there. Her hands clutched at his backside, holding him high and still inside her as she lost herself for a few precious seconds. Only when the waves of pleasure had passed and she'd relaxed her grip did he begin to move again, his thrusts deep and powerful. She felt the tension spike in him. Then he pressed his cheek against hers and shuddered out his own climax, the stubble of his whiskers a welcome roughness against her skin.

Neither of them said anything in the immediate aftermath. Ethan kept his face pressed into the curve of her neck. She stared at the ceiling over his shoulder. Where before there had been nothing but him and her and the maddening, crazy-making feel of his body against hers, she was suddenly aware of the fact that a couch button was jabbing into her backside and that they were both breathing hard and that her bra was pushed uncomfortably up around her armpits.

She was also hugely, painfully aware that what had happened between them had the potential to change everything. She didn't do casual sex—never had—and she had no plans to start now. But this was Ethan. Her friend and colleague—and the most commitment-shy man she knew.

Unless…

Don't. Don't go there. You know Ethan. You know what he wants—and it isn't this.

But it was too late. Hope was already unfolding inside her.

She was a smart woman. She knew Ethan was a bad bet. Whatever had gone on within his marriage had wounded him, badly. But she liked him. She liked him a lot. And right now they were lying skin to skin on her couch. He was still inside her. She knew he liked her. He'd cooked her dinner and brought it to her house and shown her in a hundred different ways over the course of their friendship that he admired and respected her.

Was it so crazy to imagine that maybe this could be the beginning of something and not just a really, really inappropriate outlet for weeks of tension and expectation?

Ethan lifted his head. They looked into each other's eyes. His expression was unreadable.

Which said something in and of itself, didn't it?

"I'm too heavy," Ethan said quietly, and she felt the loss as he withdrew from her and rolled to one side.

She watched silently as he stood, his body supremely sexy despite the fact that he was still wearing his shirt and socks. She glanced at his retreating backside—perfect, like the rest of him—as he went to the bathroom to dispose of the condom, then she sat up and pushed her hair from her forehead.

She stared blankly at the wall for a beat, her brain not quite up to speed yet, her body still warm and flushed from his touch. Then she heard the sound of his footfall in the hall and realized she should have used his absence to get dressed instead of sitting in a postcoital daze.

She pulled the jumbled tangle of her jeans into her lap in a belated attempt at modesty as he entered the living room. She didn't look at him for a moment as he sat beside her on the couch. Then, after a few long, tense seconds, she slid a glance his way out of the corners of her eyes.

He was watching her, a small smile on his mouth, concern in his eyes.

"You okay?" he asked quietly, reaching out to tuck a strand of her hair behind her ear.

She nodded. "Yes. You?"

"Yeah."

They were both silent for a long moment.

"That was probably a mistake, huh?" she said. It wasn't what she wanted to ask. But she wasn't stupid. She wasn't going to make this any more uncomfortable than it already was.

"Depends on your definition. I'd be lying if I said I didn't enjoy it. A lot. And that I hadn't thought about us being together like this."

She looked at him sharply. Was he saying that even before they'd been considering becoming parents together he'd been attracted to her?

"I thought you saw me as your work buddy."

"No."

"So why didn't you ever...?"

"Because I knew that it couldn't go anywhere. And I didn't want to hurt you."

It was exactly what she'd been telling herself—he'd been crystal clear about his determination to remain single, after all—but it still felt like a slap in the face.

Suddenly it seemed wrong to be sitting half naked in front of him. Way too vulnerable. She fished her tangled panties from the leg of her jeans and stood, pulling her panties on. Then she dragged her jeans up her legs. After a moment's hesitation, Ethan followed suit.

Only when they were both fully dressed, flies zipped and studs buttoned, did she look at him again.

"For the record, you haven't hurt me," she said. "I knew the score. But this wasn't exactly something I'd planned on happening."

"Me, either. But the past few weeks have been pretty full-on."

"Yes."

"Maybe it was inevitable. With all the donor stuff, all the time we've been spending together…"

"Yes."

She glanced around her apartment. She didn't know what else to say to him. There wasn't much more *to* say, when it came down to it. They'd both agreed that it had been a mistake to cross the line and sleep with each other.

She wanted him to go, she realized. They'd made their mistake, now she wanted to shower and go to bed and clear her head for tomorrow. She wanted to be alone.

"I'll help you clean up." He started gathering glasses and plates.

"Don't. I'll do it in the morning."

He ignored her, taking the plates into the kitchen. When she heard him clattering around in there she went after him.

"Leave it. Please," she said.

He was running water into the sink but he flicked the tap off. They stared at each other across her counter.

"I'm going to be really pissed with myself if this has messed things up between us, Alex. That's the last thing I want," Ethan said. "I'd hate to think we'd trashed a good friendship for the sake of one bout of crazy-monkey-couch-sex."

He was trying to make her laugh and she rewarded him with a small smile.

"It's been a big day. And this was kind of the cherry on top."

"Yeah. I know."

He ran a hand through his hair, then sighed deeply. "Okay, then, I'll bugger off."

She tried not to look too relieved but she suspected he knew she couldn't wait to close the door on him.

Well, tough. She was entitled to her reaction. Maybe this sort of thing happened to him all the time, but it was new territory for her.

"Thanks for dinner," she said at the front door.

Ethan looked down at her, his eyes very dark blue and very serious. "I meant what I said, Alex. Your friendship means a lot to me."

"Yours, too. To me, I mean."

He nodded. He hesitated, then he leaned forward and kissed her briefly on the lips.

"Good night."

"Good night."

She closed the door on him and stood very still for a long moment. It occurred to her that if they hadn't used a condom tonight, they might have become parents today after all. But they had. And she'd already decided she didn't want a child at any cost. She wanted a partner, and a child born of love. A fantasy, perhaps. But she thought it was worth holding out for.

She walked into the living room. The couch sat like a velvet reproach in the middle of the room. She flicked off the light.

She'd brooded enough today. She and Ethan had

taken a misstep tonight. That was all it was. She wasn't any better or worse off as a result of it, and neither was he. And even if things were awkward between them for a few weeks, there was no reason why they couldn't put this behind them. They were both intelligent adults, after all.

It would be so much better—so much easier—if she could believe her own spin. The truth, painful and embarrassing as it was to admit, was that she had always wanted Ethan as more than a friend. She'd known it was stupid and had pushed her desire and attraction and admiration into a corner and ignored it, but it had still been there and now she knew what it was like to be Ethan's lover…

He's not looking for a relationship, Alex. You know this. Don't set yourself up for a fall.

She'd always been sensible. All her life she'd relied on a strong streak of pragmatism to get her through. Ethan was a bad bet. As long as she kept that fact top of mind, she'd be okay.

She would.

Thoroughly sick of herself, she went to bed.

Chapter Eight

Alex had tasted like spiced wine and her skin had been warm and smooth and soft. Her breasts… Ethan had always wondered about her breasts. And now he knew. They were full, with small pale pink nipples that puckered up prettily in his mouth and beneath his hands.

Ethan rolled onto his back and punched his pillow into a new shape for the tenth time tonight. He'd been trying to get to sleep for over two hours. He'd come home full of regret, kicking himself for having stepped over the line with Alex, blaming himself for not having enough self-control to catch himself before he'd dropped that single, hard kiss onto her mouth and for not being able to resist the unspoken question in her eyes when she'd looked up at him.

And here he was, lying in bed, unable to banish the memories of those moments on the couch from his mind.

Guilt and desire. A great combo. A perfect antidote for sleep.

*Put it out of your mind. It was a one-off. You can't
go there again. There's no point thinking about it.*

Great advice. If only he could stop thinking about
the tight clench of her body around his. And the fierce-
ness of her kisses. And the way she'd gasped and held
him still inside herself as she'd come, her body bowing off the couch.

He'd denied himself where she was concerned for
so long. Kept her at arm's length. Made her his friend
instead of his lover because he'd always known she
wanted more from a man than he was prepared to give.

And still he'd slept with her.

He threw back the quilt and rolled out of bed. He
was driving himself nuts, going over and over the same
ground. He went into the bathroom and ransacked the
drawers and various storage baskets beneath the sink
until he found a blister pack of sleeping pills left over
from his last international trip. He swallowed one then
returned to bed to wait for it to kick in.

He should have stayed away from her. He should
never have gone over to her place. If he'd hurt her…

He'd make it up to her. He'd do whatever it took to
ensure Alex was happy. Because he wanted her to be
happy more than anything.

He arrived at work early the next morning. He
dumped his briefcase and coat and made his way to
her office. He didn't know what he was going to say
to her. He simply wanted to see her. For a few precious
minutes last night, they'd been as close as two people
could get. He wanted to see her.

She was frowning at a document on her desk when
he arrived in her doorway, kneading her brow with her

fingertips. She looked tired. As though she'd had as much trouble sleeping as he had.

You did that. You took what you wanted then bailed and you made it impossible for her to sleep.

But she'd wanted him to go. He'd offered to help clean up, but she'd practically ordered him out the door.

"Alex."

Her head came up. Her brown eyes were guarded as she looked at him. "Hi."

"You're in early."

"Usually am."

"Yeah." He'd run out of pleasantries, and all the things he wanted to say were impossible. The silence stretched.

"Um, did you want something?" she asked after a few taut seconds. "Because I've got a lot going on." She indicated the paperwork piled high in her in-tray.

"Just checking in," he said stupidly.

"Well, I'm fine. Don't worry, Ethan. I didn't spend the night embroidering your initials on a handkerchief or anything. I'm a big girl."

She gave him a smile that didn't come even close to her eyes. He'd never felt more distant from her.

You're an idiot. You've screwed everything up. You should have kept your freaking hands to yourself.

"Alex…I'm sorry."

She shook her head. "You don't need to apologize to me. It takes two to tango, remember? And I did my share of dancing last night."

He wasn't apologizing for the sex. He didn't know how to articulate his regret. She deserved more. He wanted her to have more, but he didn't have it in him to give.

He searched his mind for the one magical thing he

could say that would make everything all right between them again. But he couldn't turn back time. He
couldn't undo the moment when they'd crossed the line
irrevocably from friends to lovers.

"I'll leave you to it, then," he said.

"Thanks. I'll see you at the software meeting this
afternoon."

"Right."

He lifted his hand in farewell and returned to his
office. He stopped twice, wanting to go to Alex and
have a real conversation with her. Both times he forced
himself to keep walking.

He'd been playing house with her for the past few
weeks. Pretending to himself that he could have the
trappings of a relationship without the commitment and
the accompanying risks. Alex wasn't a game. She was
one of the finest women he knew. She deserved better. She certainly deserved better than his *friendship*.

Only when Alex was certain Ethan was gone did
Alex let out the breath she'd been holding.

She was proud of herself. She really was. The way
she'd held his eye and calmly told him she was a big
girl and that she'd done her share of dancing. No way
could Ethan have known that she'd barely had a wink
of sleep and that when she'd heard his voice this morning her whole body had tensed.

She'd thought she had it covered—that was the worst
thing about all of this. She'd thought that she, tough-
cookie, no-bull Alex Knight was immune to Ethan's
potent mix of good looks and charm. He might be gorgeous and smart and sexy and funny and kind and generous but she was a survivor. She was too smart to set
her sights on him.

Then he'd kissed her and all her lies to herself had been revealed for the tissue-thin excuses they were.

She liked Ethan. A lot. As more than a friend. She wanted him to like her, too. She wanted him to do more than like her. She wanted him to—

She pushed her chair away from her desk.

She'd already made a deal with herself not to dwell on it. She didn't have time to do the whole unrequited thing. If she was going to have a chance of having the family she wanted, she needed to throw herself into the dating scene, and she needed to do it wholeheartedly. *Whole*heartedly.

She was busy all morning, then she braced herself to spend the afternoon stuck in a small meeting room with Ethan and a handful of other people.

She told herself it wasn't as bad as she'd thought it might be, sitting opposite him for three hours, listening to his voice, meeting his gaze, laughing at his jokes. She kept her mind on the discussion—only once did it stray, and then only for a few seconds when Ethan raked his hand through his hair and she was reminded of how it had looked last night as he was lying on top of her, pressing her into the couch, stroking in and out of her...

She'd felt herself flushing, the heat rising up her body. She made an excuse to leave the meeting for a few minutes and didn't come back until she knew she could look him in the eye and not betray herself.

Later that night she made a very pragmatic, very ruthless decision. She needed to stop lying to herself and confront her own reality. If she wasn't very careful, she was going to slip all of the way into love with Ethan Stone. And that would be a bad, bad thing for a woman in her position. A woman who still held out hope of finding a man to love and have a family with.

Ethan was not that man. All her instincts told her that. He'd told her that, both covertly and overtly.

So. She needed to move on.

Which was why she took a deep breath after dinner and sat at the computer and composed a profile for herself to upload to three of the most popular online dating sites. She chose a picture of herself in a tank top and hiking shorts, looking fit and tanned and happy, and she described herself as smart and funny and looking for a committed relationship. She wrote off the top of her head, and once it was done she posted it straight away, no second-guessing herself.

Like she'd said, moving on.

She did some work she'd brought home, then she watched a couple of episodes of Jon Stewart's *The Daily Show* that she'd saved. Just before bedtime, she gave in to curiosity and checked her profiles.

It was early days yet, and she probably didn't have any responses. But if she did, it would be really good to be able to go to bed and think about something other than Ethan.

Ethan smiling. Ethan teasing. Ethan laughing with his nephews. Ethan whispering her name as he made love to her. Ethan standing in her office doorway this morning, his eyes full of questions.

One response would be fine. Just one to get the ball rolling.

To give her options.

She blinked when she saw the double digit next to her profile at the first site. Eleven. She'd had eleven hits in a couple of hours. Wow.

She checked the others. Four at the other site, six at the last one.

How about that. Clearly there were more single men in Melbourne than she thought.

She started working her way through the responses. The first guy looked to be in his fifties, although he gave his age as early forties. Stress could age people, she knew, and he claimed to own his own small business, but she was aware that many people doctored their ages and photos. Plus he had the overdeveloped neck and arms of a man who spent far too much time in the gym. She read his personal statement. He said he was looking for someone young and fun who wasn't afraid to "get adventurous."

Next.

Contender number two was wearing a three-piece suit and posing in front of his Ferrari. She ignored all the unkind penis-compensation jokes that popped into her mind and read his profile. HotKarMan was looking for someone who enjoyed the finer things in life. He'd been married three times and had five children. And he was only thirty-five.

Next.

By the time she got to contender number nine, she was slumped in her chair. It was undeniably depressing to realize that the vast majority of men believed that women were more focused on a man's bank balance and the size of his penis than they were on who he was and what he wanted in life and what he believed in— at least that was the only conclusion she could draw from the profiles she'd received. She'd never seen so many veiled references to *equipment* and *machinery* in her life.

There has to be one decent guy in amongst all these men. Please.

She clicked on profile number ten and read the introductory paragraph. SoloDoc was, not surprisingly, a doctor. He'd been married once, was in his late thirties and was looking for a woman to share his life. She sat a little straighter and leaned toward the screen.

He liked hiking, bike riding and reading biographies. Musically, he favored U2 and Coldplay. He liked to travel. And he'd ticked the box that said he had no problem with prospective matches having children.

She looked at his photograph. He had a slim build and a long face with slightly receding hair. His eyes were kind and intelligent. He was attractive, in a studious way.

She didn't give herself time to waver. She hit the respond button and typed in a quick greeting. Then she sent it and turned off her computer.

There. She'd done the smart thing. The practical, pragmatic, self-preserving thing.

And maybe one day soon she would be able to look back on the past few intense weeks with Ethan and think fondly of him as a good friend instead of feeling a heavy ache in her chest.

Because she was feeling low she ran herself a bath, even though she knew that the Green lobby would probably string her up if they could see her wasting so much water. She lowered herself into frangipani-scented bubbles and let out a deep sigh.

She felt as though she'd been to the moon and back. So many ups and down. So much hope and disappointment.

She slid deeper into the bath until she was completely submerged. She held her breath for as long as she could, listening to the thud of her heart.

If she could have just one wish…

But it would take more than one wish to right her world.

She pushed her feet against the end of the bath and broke the surface.

Wishes never came true, anyway.

"Ethan. Wait up."

Ethan had just exited the building but he stopped and pivoted on his heel, waiting for Alex to catch up. It had been a full week since they'd crossed the line. She was wearing her navy pinstripe suit and her red pumps. Her hair blew across her face and she tucked a strand behind her ear as she stopped in front of him. She looked good. She looked great. As always.

"Have you got a second?" she asked.

He'd been ducking out to pick up a book he'd ordered but he had fifteen minutes before his next client arrived.

"Sure. What's up?"

Pedestrians streamed around them on busy Collins Street. Alex started to speak but was jostled as two banker-types pushed their way past.

"Watch yourselves," Ethan called after them, grabbing Alex's elbow and steering her out of the main flow to where there was less competition per square foot of pavement.

She smiled faintly. "There you go with the manhandling thing again."

He let her elbow go. "Sorry."

A few weeks ago he'd have fired something in response, but the ease had gone out of their relationship since that night on Alex's couch. It had changed things, as he'd known it would.

Shouldn't have slept with her, moron.

"What's up?" he asked.

"I need to cancel our game next week," she said.

Maybe he should have been expecting it, but he wasn't. In over a year, he and Alex had only missed one Tuesday night, and that was because they'd both been attending a firm function.

"Sure. You want to reschedule for later in the week or skip it altogether?" he asked casually.

What he really wanted to ask was what she was doing, and who she was doing it with. But he didn't have the right to ask her those kind of things. Now more than ever.

"We could reschedule for Wednesday night, if that suits? Otherwise it'll have to be a skip—we've got the Heart Foundation fundraiser on Monday night, and the rest of the week is looking pretty solid for me, too."

"Wednesday it is, then." He'd have to reschedule the drink he'd organized with an old friend, but she didn't need to know that. "You out there painting the town red, slowpoke?"

He tried to make it sound as though he didn't give a damn what she did with her spare time.

"Not really. Anyway, I don't want to hold you up. You looked like you were going somewhere."

"Yeah."

She smiled her goodbye and he watched her walk away. He'd always admired the way she held herself, as though she was ready to take on all comers.

"Alex."

She turned, eyebrows raised.

"You got a hot date or something?" he asked. He hadn't meant to. But he needed to know.

She hesitated a second, then nodded. "Yeah. Although I'm not sure how hot it is."

She pulled a comic face, then gave him a little finger wave and turned away.

He hadn't expected her to say yes. He'd thought she'd tell him it was a client dinner or some other work obligation.

But she'd met someone.

And she was going on a date.

He turned blindly into the crowd and started walking, trying to ignore the *Lord-of-the-Flies* screaming in the back of his head.

He didn't want Alex dating other men. The knowledge was an acid-burn in the pit of his stomach. He didn't want her seeing anyone. He wanted… He didn't know what he wanted.

Liar.

He stepped out onto the road and a tram bell rang, jerking him to awareness. He returned to the sidewalk and waited for the light to change.

He had no claim on her. No claim on her at all. He had no right to any of the feelings churning in his gut right now.

So you're just going to let her walk away?

Yeah, I am.

He walked until he found himself in open space— the gardens beside Parliament House on Spring Street. He kicked at the grass and looked at the sky and paced.

Go to her. Tell her how you feel. Tell her…

What? That he found her compelling and beautiful and brave and that he wanted to sleep with her and spend time with her—but that he wanted to do it all with no strings, no commitment, no promises that either of them would one day feel compelled to break?

Oh, yeah. She'd really go for that.

It occurred to him that Derek would be delighted to see him pacing in the park like this, muttering to himself like a madman over a woman. Over Alex.

He sat on the steps to Parliament House and rested his head in his hands. He was going to lose Alex. If he sat back and said or did nothing, he was going to lose her. There was no doubt in his mind that it was going to happen, sooner or later. She was amazing, and the first guy who took the time to recognize that would snap her up.

Unless...

He knew what she wanted—a commitment. A relationship. Marriage. Children. The whole box and dice. If he offered that to her, if he took the plunge...

Something tight and hard squeezed his gut. What if he was wrong about her? What if he got it wrong again?

He shot to his feet and looked up and down the street. He couldn't do it. He simply couldn't do it.

His phone buzzed and he saw it was his assistant. He opened the message. She was texting to let him know his two o'clock meeting had arrived.

He headed back to the office.

So you're just going to let her walk away?

Yeah, I am.

Daniel Lowe—SoloDoc—had a good sense of humor. Alex knew this because he'd sent her a couple of very clever cartoons over the past week, both of which had appealed to her sense of the ridiculous. He'd also called her twice—the first to ask her if she felt ready to meet after their exchange of emails and phone conversations, the second to confirm his booking at one of Melbourne's most lauded restaurants.

He seemed like a nice man. His voice over the phone was a pleasing baritone, and he asked lots of questions and seemed genuinely interested in her and her work. He was a gastroenterologist, which meant he generally didn't have crazy on-call hours. He owned his home, had been divorced for four years and was completely frank about looking for another relationship.

"I know it'd probably get me kicked out of the boys' club if it got out, but I like being part of a couple," he'd said during their second phone call.

Returning to her desk after talking to Ethan in the street, Alex circled next Tuesday in her diary. Today was Thursday, so she had two nights and the weekend to find something new to wear on her date. More than enough time.

She frowned, tracing the circle she'd made over and over until the pen created a furrow in the paper and threatened to break through to the next page.

Ethan hadn't so much as blinked when she'd told him she was canceling their racquetball game. She wasn't sure what she'd been expecting from him. Annoyance, at the very least, at the inconvenience? Some reaction to the fact that she was throwing him over, abandoning their regular plans so she could go out with another man?

This, my friend, is exactly why you need to go out with Daniel Lowe on Tuesday night.

She threw her pen down. Her sensible self was right. She had to put Ethan out of her mind—really put him out of her mind, not just tell herself she was then secretly hope that he'd turn green and burst out of his clothes when he realized she was going out with someone else. Ethan had made his feelings about committed relationships—and her—painfully clear.

You don't have time for this, Alex.

She didn't. She was thirty-eight. In a few months she would be thirty-nine. She didn't have time to fall for the wrong man.

She went shopping that night, determined to find something that would knock Daniel Lowe's surgical slippers off. All part of the moving-on strategy—keep walking, never look back.

She returned home empty-handed. Ditto the following evening. Even though she had work that had flowed over into the weekend, as usual, she played hooky and went shopping again on Saturday afternoon.

She'd discarded half a dozen cocktail dresses and several mix-and-match options when she spotted an evening dress in a small designer boutique in one of the many bluestone cobbled laneways hidden in Melbourne's city center. It was nearly five o'clock and the shops were preparing to close for the day and she didn't have her perfect first-date outfit and should really keep moving....

She crossed to the dress and fingered the soft, sensuous silk knit and turned the price tag over to check if it was within her budget. She'd planned on wearing something tried and true from her wardrobe for the Heart Foundation fundraiser, but this dress was black and slinky, with a cowl neck and a low back decorated with tiny jet beads. The skirt was full-length and when she gave in and tried it on it swished around her feet when she walked back and forth in front of the mirror. She paired it mentally with her jet-bead necklace and earrings and black stiletto heels and reached for her credit card.

Most of the shutters were down on the shops by the time the saleswoman had wrapped her dress in tissue paper and slipped it into a glossy bag. Alex told herself she'd find time tomorrow to buy something for her date.

Sunday was a write-off, however. She woke to find rain slashing her windows and an urgent deal memo in her in-box for one of her clients. By the time she'd ironed out the creases it was past three. She did some mental math. By the time she'd showered and gotten herself to the shops it would be past four and she'd be racing from rack to rack in a panic.

She'd simply have to wear something from her wardrobe. Her black silk pants would look great with her red crossover top, or there was always her little black dress, a wardrobe staple that had saved her bacon on many an occasion.

She left work early the following day to have her hair cut and colored. She showered when she got home, careful to keep her hair out of the spray, then pulled on her new dress. It looked every bit as good as it had in the store and she twirled in front of the mirror. Wait until Ethan saw her in this.

She stilled and stared at her reflection.

Ethan. That was what this dress and the hairdresser and her careful underwear selection were all about? Ethan?

The answer was in her eyes. She turned her back on herself.

"You're a fool, Alex Knight."

So much for moving on.

The smart thing to do would be to drag the dress off and spend the night in front of the TV before she dug an even deeper hole for herself. But canceling was out of the question. Half the other partners would be at the fundraiser, along with a number of her clients. She had to go.

She rolled on black stay-up stockings with resigned determination, sprayed herself with her favorite Dolce & Gabbana scent and slipped some cash, her lipstick and powder and her house keys into her evening bag.

Only then did she check the mirror again. She looked good. But it didn't matter. The best dress in the world wasn't going to make Ethan the kind of man who believed in the same things she did. In a movie, maybe. Real life didn't work like that.

Her taxi dropped her outside the National Gallery on St. Kilda Road right on seven o'clock. She slid from the cab and took a moment to straighten her skirt before making her way into the building. A security guard checked her name off a list, then a waiter offered her a glass of champagne as she made her way along a red carpet toward the hall where the function was being held.

She took a mouthful of her champagne, savoring the dry, yeasty tang—then glanced up and locked eyes with Ethan.

Her hand tightened on the glass. He looked…incredible. He always showed to advantage in a suit, but in black tie he was devastating. Maybe it was the contrast of the white shirt against his olive-toned skin. Or perhaps it was the way the monochrome tones made his blue eyes seem even more vivid than usual.

She was aware of his gaze traveling from her face down her body to her feet then up again.

"Alex. You look amazing," he said.

She could see the admiration in his eyes. He wasn't

faking it. The dress had done the trick. On some level, he wanted her.

Never had a victory felt so hollow.

She forced a smile and reached up to dust some non-existent lint off his lapel.

"You look like a mess, as usual," she said.

It was the sort of thing she'd normally do. The sort of thing she'd normally say.

He smiled, the corners of his eyes crinkling. "Nice."

"How many marriage proposals have you had so far? Or proposals, full stop?" she asked.

She took a big swallow from her champagne. Her chest was aching. She let her gaze slide over his shoulder, as though she didn't care that he was standing so close. As though she wasn't aware of every single little thing about him.

"You're hilarious," he said.

"You realize that it's my duty to the rest of the women present to spill something on you at the first opportunity, don't you? Just to protect them from themselves."

"Stain my Armani and you'll suffer the consequences."

She'd run out of banter. For a moment she floundered, then she saw the wife of one of the partners standing with a group inside the hall.

"Look, there's Joan. I'd better go say hello." She didn't give him a chance to respond as she walked away from him.

She did her best to avoid him during the standing-around, drinks-and-canapés stage of the evening, keeping a watch out of the corners of her eyes and moving on whenever she saw him approaching. She couldn't do anything about the fact that they were seated at the same table at dinner, however, since the seating had been preordained by one of the senior partners' wives. Thank heaven for small mercies, Ethan was three people to her left and she didn't have to endure the torture of sitting next to him all evening, but she was nonetheless intensely aware of everything he did and said. She knew that he asked for a cabernet instead of a chardonnay to drink with his main. She heard him discussing a recent High Court finding with Keith Lancaster on his left. If she turned her head she could see his long, elegant hands, busy with cutlery and his wineglass and describing his words in the air.

She had no recall of what she said to either Gideon Lambert on her left or Sammy Master's wife on her right through the starter and main course, but neither of them seemed to notice anything amiss. She managed to choke down half her poached chicken with baby vegetables, and for once she allowed herself to break her one-drink-only rule for work functions. By the time dessert rolled around she was feeling numb around the edges. Not the worst way to be, considering the revelations of the evening.

The waiter had just delivered their desserts when Gideon leaned toward her.

"Would you mind swapping desserts?" he asked. "I have a bit of a thing for lemon meringue pie."

Gideon had scored the black forest gâteau. She hated cherries with a passion, but she didn't really want dessert anyway and Gideon was eyeing her lemon meringue pie as though it was made from solid gold.

"Of course," she said.

She was about to switch plates when Ethan leaned forward to address Gideon.

"You can have mine, Gideon," he said. "I was hoping for the gâteaux."

She looked at him directly for the first time since their brief conversation in the foyer. He winked at her and she recalled that she'd once told him that she hated cherries.

And he'd remembered.

She returned her gaze to her plate. Had he happened to tune in to what Gideon was saying at the opportune moment? Or was it possible he'd been as aware of her as she'd been of him all night?

It was such a willfully stupid, hopeful thing to wish for. She pushed back her chair abruptly. She needed some time out. And maybe a few glasses of water to counteract all the alcohol she'd been drinking.

She made her way into the foyer and retraced her steps along the red carpet until she found the ladies' room near the front entrance.

She pushed through the door. The space was blissfully quiet and empty after the noise of a thousand people eating and talking and laughing at once.

She stood in the open space between the cubicles and the sinks and closed her eyes and simply concentrated on breathing for a few minutes. In, out. In, out.

God, I want this night to be over.

She opened her eyes. She had a date with Daniel Lowe tomorrow night, and sometime before then she was going to have to decide whether to keep it now that she'd stopped lying to herself and acknowledged her own feelings.

She was in love with Ethan.

Not exactly a newsflash. She'd seen it coming, after all. Tried to avoid it. And yet here she was.

She eyed herself in the mirror. There was nothing

she could do about it. Not now, after the fact. She'd fallen for Ethan. It was done. Now she had to begin the slow and painful process of getting over him.

The woman in the mirror smiled, but it was not a happy smile.

How was she supposed to work with him, have lunch with him, play racquetball with him when she loved him? How was she supposed to not give her feelings away with every word and gesture and glance? How was she supposed to endure being so close and yet not close enough?

You've survived worse.

She had. Of course she had. And she'd survive this, because that was what she did.

But just once, it would have been nice—

She didn't let herself finish the thought. Life wasn't about What Ifs. As she'd once said to Ethan, life was about what you had, and what you could get, and what you could do with it. And she knew without asking that she couldn't have Ethan. He was the most un-have-able man she knew.

The door to the bathroom swung open and a trio of women entered, their high heels clicking on the tiled floor. Alex exchanged friendly smiles with them as she headed for the door.

Another hour or so and she could go home.

Thank. God.

Ethan had been a good boy. He'd kept his distance from Alex all week. Any time they'd run into each other in the kitchenette he'd talked about work and the weather and the economy. A couple of times they'd talked about something Jamie or Tim had said or done. Not once had Ethan asked about her upcoming date.

Even though the thought of her going out with some other guy was burning a hole in his gut.

Now, he watched as she returned to the table. She looked…amazing. Sleek and feminine and sexy. She'd worn her hair up and every time she moved her head the sway of her earrings drew his eye to the elegant line of her neck.

In the good old days, pre-couch, he'd have teased her about dressing so dangerously for a Heart Foundation event, of all things. He'd have told her she was a walking cardiac arrest waiting to happen, then he'd have spent half the night making her laugh and talking to her and simply enjoying her.

But they'd lost the ease in their relationship since they'd slept with each other.

He watched her out of the corners of his eyes as they drank coffee and the party finally began to break up for some post-dinner table-hopping and chat. She said something to Keith Lancaster, smiled, then stood. Then she collected her small evening bag and started weaving her way toward the exit.

He was on his feet before he could even think about it. Muttering a hasty excuse to his dinner companions, he followed Alex into the crowd.

He didn't know why he was following her, or what he was going to say to her when he caught up with her. All he knew was that he didn't want to go home tonight without having spent some time with her.

She lengthened her stride when she left the Great Hall. He ducked around a waiter and followed her onto the red carpet.

"Alex."

She glanced over her shoulder, then slowed her steps.

"Ethan."

"You're not going home?"

"Busted. My feet are killing me. And we've got work tomorrow."

"It's early days yet. Why don't we go find some place where they won't mind you being barefoot while we have a nightcap?"

The Southbank precinct was just around the corner. There were several good bars and restaurants there they could choose from.

"Thanks, but I was really hoping for an early night."

"Right. You've got your big date tomorrow night, haven't you?"

"That's the one. Candidate number one."

Don't say another word. Shut your mouth and back away.

"Where's he taking you?" he asked.

"Vue du Monde."

"Wow. Pulling out all the stops."

"I guess. Listen, I want to try to catch a cab before there's a queue." She gestured toward the foyer and took a step away from him.

"I'll walk you."

They resumed walking toward the entrance.

"So, what's this guy do again?" he asked.

"Um, he's a doctor. A gastroenterologist."

"A gut man."

"Yep."

They pushed through the doors into the cold night air. Alex glanced around for a taxi line, her arms crossed against the cold.

"So, let me guess. He drives a BMW, has a house in Kew, lunches at the Melbourne Club?" He knew he should stop, but he couldn't help himself. He needed to know.

"I don't know. I'll have to ask him tomorrow night. I thought there was a taxi stand around here somewhere?"

She was rubbing her arms now, her shoulders hunched.

"Here." He shrugged out of his jacket.

"Oh, no. I couldn't. Then you'll be cold."

"I'm tougher than you."

Before she could protest again he dropped his jacket around her shoulders. She ducked her head for a moment, then she pulled the edges of his jacket closer as she lifted her face and met his eyes.

"Thanks."

The streetlight struck red notes in her hair. She was wearing a different perfume from her usual, something heavier with more musk. His gaze followed the line of her neck, then her cheek. She was beautiful and fine— and she was going out with another man tomorrow night. A doctor. A guy who'd wooed her with phone calls and emails and would finish the job with a meal at Melbourne's most acclaimed restaurant.

"He's not good enough for you, you know."

Alex looked at him, confusion in her eyes. "Who?"

"The gut doctor."

"You haven't even met him yet."

"I don't need to meet him."

She stared at him for a beat. Then her gaze slid over his shoulder and she stepped out into the street and raised her hand. A taxi swerved to the curb. She turned to face him, shrugging his coat off.

"Keep it," he said when she offered it to him.

"I'm fine now," she said, arm still extended.

"Give it back to me at work tomorrow." He took a step backward. For some reason he really wanted her to go home in his jacket.

"All right. Thank you." She walked to the cab and slid into the backseat. She didn't put his coat back on, he noted. Instead, she draped it across her lap. And she didn't look back as the taxi pulled out into the traffic.

It was only when the taxi was long gone that he realized he was staring at nothing and that it was damned cold.

He shouldn't have said anything about her date. He shouldn't have asked anything, and he definitely shouldn't have said that thing about the guy not being good enough for her.

She wanted a family. She believed in happy-ever-after. Next time the subject of Mr. Perfect the Wonder Healer came up, he'd bite his tongue. If it killed him. He'd already made his decision. He simply had to stick to it.

Alex canceled her date with Daniel Lowe first thing the following morning. She told herself she should go, that he might be a lovely man and she'd be missing out, but she knew that going out with him would be tantamount to leading him on. She had no business going out with another man when she was in love with Ethan.

She had trouble focusing for the rest of the day. For the first time in many, many years, she felt overwhelmed by life. She'd always been a planner, a doer, but there was nothing to do when you loved someone who was out of reach.

Oh, she could probably seduce Ethan again if she wanted to. She was grown up enough and sophisticated enough to create a situation where she could tempt him and he'd allow himself to be tempted. She'd seen the admiration and desire in his eyes last night. If she played her cards right, she might even be able to negotiate some sort of relationship with him, the kind of thing that she assumed he enjoyed with his other women—no strings, sex, a bit of companionship.

No children. No love. No sense that he belonged to her and she belonged to him. None of the things that Alex wanted from a relationship.

She wouldn't do it to herself, even though a part of her was tempted. Even though a little voice in the back of her head whispered that maybe, if she bided her time, he might change.

She'd played that game before, for seven years. She'd waited and loved and hoped and yet here she was, nearly thirty-nine, on her own, childless.

Not again. I can't do it again. I can't live on hope anymore.

It was such a waste. Ethan was a good man. He had a lot of love to give—it was evident in every interaction he had with his brother and sister-in-law and nephews. And he'd been so attentive and thoughtful and generous with her. He would have made a great father, and, once upon a time, an incredible husband. But his marriage had broken something fundamental in him.

The incredibly sad thing was that she suspected he was lonely. He could surround himself with designer furniture and clothes and buy as many beautiful, sleek cars as he liked but none of it was going to make up for the fact that he would only ever experience family life secondhand through his brother. She'd seen him with those kids, and she'd seen the way he looked at Kay and Derek. He wanted the picket-fence dream. He simply didn't believe in it anymore.

She left work early but didn't go straight home. Instead, she went to Albert Park Lake and slipped off her pumps and put on her running shoes and walked around and around until the streetlights came on. Then she went home and poured herself a huge glass of wine and sat on her balcony, staring out at the world. It was cold out and after a while she went back inside and shrugged into Ethan's tuxedo jacket. She knew it was pathetic—the worst kind of teenage, maudlin droopiness—but she couldn't help herself. She sat on her balcony with her knees drawn to her chest, her heels resting on the front of the seat, the jacket wrapped around as much of her as it would cover.

She inhaled the smell of Ethan and looked out at the big, noisy city and drank her wine.

Maybe she'd take a leave of absence and go on a holiday, a good long one. She'd always wanted to return to France and explore Spain. Maybe she could fly to Paris and hire a car and drive around. It would be summer in the northern hemisphere. The wind would be warm instead of cold. She wouldn't have to wake up every day and know that she might see Ethan at work and that if she did, she'd have to smile and laugh and pretend nothing had changed between them and that if she didn't she would be miserable and wondering and her day would be that little bit less bright and less alive....

She rested her forehead on her knees and hugged herself tightly. She wanted...so much. She had so much longing inside her. And it was all pointless.

I love you, Ethan Stone. But I wish I didn't. I really, really wish I didn't.

Chapter Nine

Ethan checked the time again. It was nearly eleven. Was she home yet? Or was Doctor Smoothy taking her somewhere for a nightcap? Worse, was he taking her back to his place so he could—

Someone nudged his foot and he glanced up to find his brother standing over him.

"I need to go to bed. And you need to go home."

Ethan opened his mouth to complain that the movie wasn't finished yet then registered the blank TV screen and utter silence.

"When did the movie finish?" he asked.

"About half an hour ago. You were too busy brooding to notice."

"I wasn't brooding. I've got a big case on at the moment. I was going over some stuff in my head."

"You've been hunched over like the human question

mark all night. You've barely said a word to the kids. Do you know what Tim said before he went to bed?"

Ethan had a feeling he wasn't going to like it, whatever it was. Tim could be a keen observer of humanity when he wanted to be. Plus the kid had a pithy tongue. "What?"

"He said you reminded him of the sad orangutan we saw at the zoo last week. The one who looked like he shouldn't be allowed near loaded weapons."

"Tell Tim thanks from me." Ethan stood and reached for his coat. "I'll get out of your hair."

Derek growled in the back of his throat. "Or you could talk to me about whatever it is that's going on."

"Nothing's going on."

Kay stepped forward and stood on her tiptoes to kiss Ethan good-night.

"I'll leave you two big bulls to lock horns."

"We're not locking anything. I'm going home," Ethan said.

"Either way." Kay gave Derek's arm a squeeze as she walked past and disappeared through the door to the bedrooms.

Ethan dug in his pocket for his car keys. "Sorry for keeping you up. And I'll make it up to the kids next time."

"This is about Alex, right?"

"Derek, it's all right, you don't need to play Dr. Phil. I'll see you next week, okay?"

"Man, you drive me nuts when you brush me off like that. Did it ever occur to you that I might be worried about you?"

Ethan paused in the act of pulling on his jacket. Derek was serious, his face creased with concern and frustration.

Ethan straightened his collar. "You don't need to worry about me."

"Yeah? You know what this reminds me of? The time after Cassie left."

Ethan bristled, his pride stung. He'd been a mess when Cassie had dropped her bombshell. He was more than happy to acknowledge that. He'd hit rock bottom so hard he'd never thought he'd come up again.

Whatever was going on with Alex, it wasn't anything near the intensity of those dark days. They weren't married, for starters, and Alex hadn't made promises to him. He hadn't woven all his visions of the future around her and the idea of the two of them growing old together. He'd kept his distance, kept things nice and clean between them.

Except for that one night when he'd kissed her and she'd kissed him back.

But pretty soon even that would be a faded memory. As for the fact that he felt like ripping the head off someone every time he thought about Alex being out with another guy…that would pass, too.

"This is nothing like that."

"You can't give up on life because you fouled on the first ball, Ethan. You've got to keep slugging away."

"I haven't given up on anything." It pissed him off that his brother had reduced eight years of marriage—the intimate details of which he knew nothing about—down to a sporting analogy.

"What do you call dating a string of women who mean nothing to you and then almost getting into some stupid co-parenting arrangement with a woman you're clearly half-gone on because you haven't got the balls to step up to the plate again?"

Ethan stilled. For a moment he and his brother eyed each other silently.

There were things he could tell his brother, justifications, explanations. Instead, he turned away. "Thanks for the movie."

"Ethan."

He could hear the regret in his brother's voice but he kept walking. He pushed the speed limit all the way home, anger and unease dogging him.

It didn't help that his brother was right. Fear was what was holding him back where Alex was concerned. Fear and hard-earned caution. After what Cassie did, after the way his marriage had crumbled around his ears... How could he ever put so much faith in another human being again? How could he ever trust that what was said was real and true and sincere?

And if his own experiences weren't enough, there were the many small, sordid disappointments and betrayals he saw in his office on a daily basis to add weight to his argument.

He might be in love with Alex. He might want her and miss her and think about her all the time. But he simply wasn't up for the risk. He'd had to put himself together again piece by piece after Cassie had broken him.

So, yeah, his brother was right. He was a coward. Too afraid to reach out for what he wanted. So afraid— he hit his steering wheel with the heel of his hand and swore—so afraid that he'd sat on his brother's couch all night while she'd been out meeting another man. A man she might fall in love with and marry. A man who might be the one to make her happy and give her the babies and the life she deserved.

He pulled over to the side of the road with a screech

of tires. He barely got out of the car before what little he'd eaten for dinner burned its way up the back of his throat.

He stood with his arms braced on his legs for a long moment. Then he spat into the gutter. Feeling about a million years old, he climbed back into his car.

Alex almost canceled their racquetball game Wednesday night—it was her week for canceling things, after all—but she wanted to see Ethan. Which was on a par with wearing his tuxedo jacket for half the evening—pathetic and needy and destined to get her nowhere.

As she pulled on her workout gear in the change room at the gym she tried to remember if loving and losing Jacob had been this painful. Maybe time had faded her memories but she didn't think so. She'd done her level best and tried everything in her power to make things work. When they'd finally parted ways she'd at least had the satisfaction of knowing that she'd given it her best shot. With Ethan, there had been no shot. The gun had barely made it out of the holster. There had been the brief illusion of something—a fiction created by their agreement to try to co-parent a baby—then there had been that one night. After that, nothing but the painful realization that she had fallen in love with the wrong man yet again.

She shouldered her gym bag, grabbed her racquet and left the change rooms. Her heart pumped out a quick double-beat as she approached their regular court. She curled her fingers around the cool metal of the door handle, took a deep breath and entered the court.

He was stretching his legs out against the wall.

She'd only seen him once today in passing as they both grabbed coffees between clients. They'd barely had the time to exchange greetings before she'd had to race off. She stole a moment to admire the pull of his dark navy T-shirt across his broad shoulders and the snug fit of his shorts. Then she cleared her throat.

"Hey."

He glanced over his shoulder. "Hey."

She threw her bag beside his in the corner.

"How did your day go?" she asked.

"So-so. How about you?"

"Yeah, you know. The usual."

Normally they were knee-deep in mutual insults by now. She wracked her brain from something to say.

"Hope you're ready for me to wipe the floor with you, Pretty Man," she said.

He smiled faintly but didn't say anything.

She grabbed her racquet and took up position on the court. Ethan followed suit.

"Prepare to feel the pain," she said.

"You're perky today. Had a good night last night, did we?"

She glanced at him. His expression was unreadable. She pretended to examine the grip on her racquet. No way was she telling him she canceled her date. She manufactured a casual shrug.

"It was nice."

"*Nice.* What does that mean?" He bounced one of the balls and hit it at the wall so they could warm up with a few practice shots.

She returned the shot. "It means I had a good time," she lied.

Ethan caught the ball on the full and sent it back at her. "So are you going to see him again?"

She missed the shot and followed the ball into the corner to collect it. "You're full of questions tonight."

He shrugged. "Just being a friend. So are you going to see him again or not?"

"We haven't decided yet."

"So it didn't go that great then?"

She didn't know what to say to make him let it go. "Can we talk about something else? Head lice? Male-pattern baldness? Better yet, can we just play?"

"Sure."

He served and they raced around the court until she caught him with a short, sharp corner shot.

"So, was I right about the BMW and the house in Kew?" Ethan asked as she collected the ball and prepared to serve the next point.

"That's a pretty insulting question," she said, frowning.

"Why?"

"Because it implies I went home with him on the first date."

"Did you?"

Whoa. Where the hell had that come from?

If it was any other man she'd ascribe his questions and veiled hostility to jealousy. But this was Ethan and he'd already made his feelings where she was concerned more than clear.

She faced him, hands on her hips. "What's going on, Ethan?"

He was silent for a long beat. Finally he met her eyes, his gaze intense. "What if I asked you not to see him again?"

She stilled. Suddenly it felt as though all the oxygen had been sucked out of the room.

Was he saying what she thought he was saying?

All the hours she'd sat in his tuxedo jacket last night, breathing in his smell and telling herself she could never have him—had she been wrong? Had she let her experience with Jacob taint her judgment?

She took a step toward Ethan. "Why?" she asked, never taking her eyes from his face. It felt like the most important question of her life. "Why would you ask me to do that?"

"You know why."

"No, Ethan, I don't. I have no bloody idea about anything when it comes to you. I have no idea how you feel about me, or what you want or anything."

Her voice wavered on the final words but she swallowed the wash of emotion at the back of her throat.

"How about this? It nearly drove me nuts last night knowing you were out with another guy. I dream about you every night. I can't stop thinking about you. I spend half the day coming up with excuses to drop by your office. When I saw you at the fundraiser the other night I wanted to throw you over my shoulder and take you home. Does that clear anything up for you?" Ethan's face was anguished, his body rigid with tension.

She was so relieved, so overwhelmed she felt dizzy. Ethan cared for her. Maybe he even loved her. And he was declaring himself, which meant—

She bent her knees and sat on the floor before she fell down.

"Alex…" He was instantly at her side, crouching with his hand on her back. "Are you all right?"

She lifted her face to him. "I thought it was just sex. Or that maybe you cared but it wouldn't make a difference because of what happened with your divorce. I thought we didn't stand a chance."

There was a flicker of something behind his eyes

but she barely registered it as she reached out to grip his forearm, her fingers wrapping around the strong muscles.

"Ethan, I love you. And I didn't go on that date last night. I couldn't, not when my head is full of you."

He closed his eyes for a long moment. When he opened them again there was so much heat and need and want in them that she almost laughed out loud. He loved her. Ethan Stone loved her. She'd convinced herself that her love for him was a lost cause, that he would never, ever want the same things that she wanted, and yet he loved her.

She used her grip on his arm to pull him closer. They kissed, a hard, determined, fervent kiss, his hands gripping her shoulders to pull her closer, hers tightening around his forearm as she strained toward him.

He loved her. Ethan Stone, serial womanizer, Mr. Anti-Commitment, loved her. A bubble of relief and joy rose inside her and she broke their kiss to release it in the form of a laugh.

"My God, Ethan, if you only knew how pathetic I've been over you. Mooning around like a teenager…"

He kissed her again. It didn't take long for things to get heated between them. She wanted to touch his skin, to feel all of him against all of her. She needed the reassurance, the confirmation. Somehow she ended up in his lap, her legs straddling his waist, his hands up her T-shirt as he caressed her breasts.

She could feel his erection pressing against her. She broke their kiss and drew her head back a little so she could look him in the eyes.

"Let's go back to your place. Or my place. Hell, let's go out to the backseat of my car," she said, a big grin on her face. She felt as though she had champagne in her veins instead of blood, as though she would float to the ceiling if he let go of her.

Ethan loved her. He loved her.

She started to slide out of his lap but his hands tightened on her waist.

"Alex. Wait. There's something I need to say to you first."

He sounded very serious. She settled back into his lap.

"Okay."

She looked at him, waiting. His gaze searched her face, then he reached out to tuck a strand of hair behind her ear.

"Alex, I care for you enormously. I think you're a woman in a million. There's nothing I want more than to go home with you right now and get you naked. I want to have a relationship with you, but I need you to know that I don't ever want to marry again."

She blinked, the smile freezing on her face. "Okay. So…what, we live together? Is that what you're suggesting?"

Then she registered the other thing he'd said. Or, more accurately, the thing he hadn't said. *I care for you enormously.* Not *I love you.*

"I think we should play it by ear. You've got your place, I've got mine. We could see how things work out. But I'd be happy to try for a baby straight away. I know that's something you want and that we're on the clock. And we've already hammered out the basics of a co-parenting agreement, so if things didn't work out—"

She held up her hand. "Wait a minute. You're already thinking about the end of things before we've even started…?"

She was still sitting in his lap. It suddenly seemed

exactly the wrong place to be. She slid awkwardly out of his lap and moved so that she was sitting to one side of him, one knee drawn to her chest.

All the heat of passion and need and triumph had turned clammy on her skin.

"Let me get this straight," she said. Because it was becoming more and more clear to her that they were not on the same page. Not by a long shot. "You're happy to have a child with me, but you don't want to marry me or live with me. And you *care for me.* Am I getting this right?"

"Alex—" He sighed and lowered his head, pressing his fingers into his forehead for a beat. Then he lifted his head again. "This is really… I never thought I'd be in this place again. That I'd feel this way about another woman. I want to be with you, I do. But not marriage."

"Do you love me?" It hurt her somewhere inside to have to ask. Her pride, probably. Later she could lash herself for being so weak.

"Yes. Yes, I love you, Alex."

The words were hard for him to say.

She shook her head. "But you don't want to, do you? You don't want any of this." She pushed herself to her feet and strode for the corner.

"What are you doing?"

"What does it look like I'm doing? I'm going home. Alone. Because I'm an idiot. A willfully delusional idiot who apparently still believes in fairy tales." Her throat and chest were tight.

Ethan was standing behind her when she turned with her bag and racquet in hand.

"Alex. Let's talk about this," he said, stepping forward with his arms wide as though he was going to embrace her. There was pain in his eyes and a world of doubt but she was dealing with her own pain right now.

She warded him off with her racquet. "There's nothing to talk about. You know what I want, Ethan. I want a family. I want a man who loves me the way I love him. I want—" Her voice broke and she took a deep, fierce breath and forced herself to continue. "I want the whole loaf, Ethan, and you offered me half of one. And you know what the worst thing is? There's a part of me that wants to take it even though I know it would only make me miserable and sad and that I'd probably wind up hating you."

She dodged around him but he stepped in her path.

"Alex, I love you. I do. If you'll just listen to me—"

"No, I won't. I can't. I won't let you convince me. I deserve more, Ethan. I've put up with half a loaf all my life. And I deserve more from the man who loves me. I don't know the details of your marriage and your divorce because you've never trusted me with them, but I'm not Cassie, Ethan. I'm me, and I won't pay the price for her sins. *I deserve more.*"

He was very pale. "If I could give you what you wanted, I would, Alex, believe me."

The emptiness in his eyes…

"I know. And that's the saddest thing of all."

She left him standing on the court. The need to cry was like a giant's hand pressing down on her chest as she made her way through the gym and out to her car. She refused to give in. She needed to stay strong. She needed to cling to her resolve because she was terrified that if she let herself feel the pain and gave herself over to her grief she would be tempted to take the crumbs from Ethan's table.

So she kept her head high and her eyes dry as she got in her car and drove home. And inside, she died a little.

Ethan didn't know where to go so he went home. All he could think about was Alex. The look on her face when she told him she deserved more. The feel of her in his arms. The taste of her on his lips. The straight, sure line of her spine as she walked away from him.

He paced his apartment, agitated, his gut churning.

She was right. He knew she was right. What he'd offered her was a million times less than she deserved. It was selfish and self-serving and *it was all he had.*

He raked his hands through his hair and sat on the couch, his fingertips digging into his scalp as though the pressure could force his brain to forget the past and grab ahold of Alex and all that she represented. Love, hope, a chance to do it right the second time around.

His head felt as though it was going to explode. He wanted, and he was scared. The two warred within him, making his gut churn and his chest hurt.

He had no idea how long he'd been sitting on the couch when the intercom buzzed. His first instinct was to ignore it—he was hardly good company right now—then it occurred to him that it might be Alex. That maybe she'd reconsidered and was prepared to give him a chance to explain.

It was a flimsy hope and it died the second he heard his brother's voice.

"Ethan. I was on my way home. Buzz me up."

"I'm in the middle of something."

"It won't take long. I want to apologize for last night. I was way out of line—"

"You were right. But it doesn't matter. I'll call you later."

He walked away from the intercom, even though it buzzed three more times. He was in the kitchen pouring himself a hefty Scotch when there was a knock at his door.

No prizes for guessing who it was. Derek had obviously entered with one of the other tenants, the same trick he'd used at Alex's building.

He considered not answering but the knocking was already getting louder.

His brother started yelling as Ethan was approaching the door. "I'm not buggering off until I've spoken to you, so you might as well open the—"

Ethan swung the door open.

"—door."

His brother stared at him, then at the glass of Scotch in his hand.

"What happened?" Derek asked, pushing his way past Ethan and dropping his briefcase to the floor near the hall table.

"I don't want to talk about it."

"Wow. Where have I heard that before?" Derek strode into the living room, shrugging out of his suit jacket and loosening his tie.

Ethan found him in the kitchen, pouring himself a more conservative Scotch. He met his brother's eyes and took a deep breath.

"I appreciate the concern but I'm fine," he said.

Something warm and wet fell onto his hand. He looked down at it. It took him a moment to understand that he was crying. He put down his glass.

"Jesus," Derek said, and then his brother's arms were closing around him and he was being held tightly and he couldn't keep the rest of the tears from falling.

He fought them every step of the way until Derek gave him a shake.

"Cry, you big dickhead. It won't kill you."

Ethan turned his face into his brother's shoulder and gripped his shoulders hard. Five years of shame and anger and hurt soaked into his brother's Ralph Lauren shirt and still his brother didn't let him go. Only when Ethan sniffed mightily and tried to break away did his brother release his grip.

Ethan avoided his eyes, concentrating on grabbing some paper towel from beneath the sink.

"This is about Cassie," Derek guessed.

"And Alex." Ethan wiped his cheeks and blew his nose. Only then did he look directly at his brother again. "Sorry about your shirt."

"Screw the shirt. Talk to me."

Ethan crumpled the paper towel in his hand until it was a tight ball within his fist. He hated talking about this stuff. Small wonder, then, that he never had. That he'd never told anyone the full, ugly truth of his divorce. He tried to find a place to start, but there was so much shame and anger attached to the memories that he couldn't think past it.

"Something happened today. Tell me about that," Derek said.

"We were playing racquetball. I asked Alex about her date—"

"Alex is dating someone else? And you let that happen?"

Ethan rubbed the bridge of his nose. "Yeah, I did," he said heavily.

"So what happened?"

"I asked her what she would do if I asked her not to

see the guy again. And she wanted to know why. So I told her that I was crazy about her."

"About freaking time. What did she say?"

"She told me that she loves me." The memory made his stomach pinch. The look on her face when she'd said it. The way she'd laughed... For a few seconds he'd made her happy. Then he'd screwed it all up again because he didn't have the guts to follow through.

"That must have freaked you out."

Ethan looked up sharply. His brother shrugged.

"Pretty confronting, getting the thing you want when you're not sure you want it."

Ethan reached for his Scotch and swallowed a generous mouthful. "Yeah."

"So how did you screw it up?" Derek asked.

Ethan smiled thinly. "I told her I didn't want to get married again."

"Ouch."

"Then she asked if I meant we should just live together, and I told her we should see how it goes, keep our own places..."

Derek winced. "At which point she tore you a new one."

"At which point she told me that she wasn't Cassie and that she deserved better. And then she walked. And I let her go because I'm a freaking pussy."

He could hear the self-pity and contempt in his own voice but he was powerless to stop it.

There was a long pause before Derek responded. "I know a lot of guys who are divorced. Hell, me and Kay joke all the time about being each other's starter spouse. Most of those guys are pissed for a few months, maybe a year, then they get back on the wagon, and more than half of them are married again within two years. But not you."

"No."

"I know you see a lot of crappy marriages with your work, but it's not that, is it?" Derek said.

"No." Jesus, he wished it was. He took another swallow of his drink. Then he took a deep breath. "Those other guys, your friends. Some of them probably cheated on their wives. Or maybe they had money troubles and they fought about it too much, or maybe she met someone else or maybe they both realized they just didn't have what it took to go the distance. Cassie and I... We were together for four years before I proposed to her. I can still remember the day we met—I went to my first Ethics class and she was standing talking to someone. I took one look at her and fell for her on the spot. We moved in with each other after a month and we never looked back. I never had a doubt that we'd marry and have kids and the rest of it.

"That day when I came home from work and Cassie told me she wanted a divorce..." He stopped, shook his head. This was hard. Not only the telling of it, but the remembering. He'd done his damnedest to put it behind him. To move on. But it was all washing over him again.

The way she'd been sitting at the kitchen table when he came in, a crisp white business envelope on the table in front of her. The way she'd looked at him, as though he was a stranger. No, worse—as though he was one of her clients. Someone she had to deal with because it was her job. Then he'd noticed the overnight bag against the wall and he'd understood that something was very, very wrong.

"We need to talk," she'd said.

Then she'd slid the envelope across the table and told him that she wanted a divorce. She'd had papers drawn up. She didn't want anything of his but she wanted half of the house proceeds once it was sold and he was welcome to all their furniture. Once the mandatory year of separation was up they could file for the decree of dissolution and sign some papers and that would be it. Twelve years down the tubes.

"I don't understand," he'd said. They'd had some minor spats, but nothing that came close to being grounds for divorce. He loved her. She was his wife. They were in this thing together. "If you're unhappy, we'll get counseling. Whatever it takes. Tell me what's wrong and I'll fix it. We'll fix it."

"I don't love you anymore."

It had been like a fist in the face. And so out of the blue, so unheralded he couldn't believe it, couldn't make his mind grasp the words and accept them.

He'd sat beside her and taken her cold hands in his and told her that he loved her, that all marriages had ups and downs, that love ebbed and flowed and he was sure it would flow again.

Then she'd looked him in the eye and told him.

"She had an abortion," Ethan said, forcing the words past the lump in his throat.

"What?" Derek's expression was uncomprehending.

Ethan almost smiled. He remembered feeling that way. Being literally unable to believe what his ears were telling him. "She was pregnant, and she had an abortion without telling me."

Derek's face was pale. He swore. "Ethan…"

Suddenly Ethan wanted it all told, all of it out in the open.

"We weren't planning on trying for a baby until the

following year, but she got pregnant accidentally and when she found out she said she had a revelation. She didn't want the baby. Or, more specifically, she didn't want *my* baby. She didn't want our marriage anymore. She didn't want the life we'd made together. She didn't love me, and she wanted out. So she made arrangements to get rid of the baby and she got her shit together. Then she told me and walked."

Ethan swallowed strongly. Five years on and he still felt sick and angry and impotent.

"Mate." His brother was looking at him with a world of pity and compassion in his eyes.

This was why Ethan had never told anyone the truth behind his divorce. He didn't want his family to feel sorry for him. Then Derek pulled him into his arms again and Ethan decided that maybe a bit of compassion wasn't so bad after all. Maybe it was even exactly what he needed.

After a minute his brother released him, his eyes suspiciously bright. "I don't know what to say. If Kay had done that to me..." Derek shook his head. "But she'd never do that."

Ethan smiled grimly. "That's what I thought about Cassie."

"But Kay is—" Derek closed his mouth on whatever he'd been about to say and Ethan saw full understanding dawn on his brother's face.

Ethan had trusted his wife, just as Derek trusted Kay, and yet he'd had no idea that she was so unhappy that she'd choose to get rid of the child they'd made together rather than be bound to him for life.

"Jesus," Derek said quietly. "No wonder you're so messed up."

Ethan laughed. He had to, or he was going to disgrace himself by crying again. He'd always vowed he'd never tell anyone. He'd been so ashamed that something could be so wrong with his marriage and he'd not known about it. He'd been stupidly cruising along, living in a fantasy world where he and Cassie loving each other was more important than the lumps and bumps of everyday life, and all the time she'd been quietly dealing with her unwanted pregnancy and putting her affairs in order before she left him.

"Did you ever talk about it? Ask her why?" Derek wanted to know.

Ethan shook his head. He'd had questions, things he'd wanted to know, but the anger that had followed hard on the heels of her fait accompli had meant that he couldn't bear to be in the same room with her. Or, more accurately, he couldn't trust himself to be in the same room as her. He'd wanted to hurt her. Make her suffer for hurting him and making a decision about their child without consulting him. Most of all he'd wanted to punish her for not loving him even though he still loved her, even after what she'd done.

Then she'd taken up a job with a multinational insurance company and moved to Singapore and he hadn't heard from her until the divorce papers arrived a year later. She'd sent him a letter a month after their divorce was finalized, but he'd burned it without reading it.

"Maybe you should."

"What's to know? She changed her mind. She didn't want to be with me. Game over."

It was hard to say it out loud, but it was the truth. After twelve years together, the woman he'd loved had simply walked out of his life, leaving him gasping like a landed fish. He'd gone over and over and over it in his head, but that was what it boiled down to. She'd stopped loving him, and she'd left.

Derek started to say something then stopped when his stomach growled demandingly. "You got anything to eat? Some pretzels maybe?"

"Pretzels. No, I do not have pretzels. But I can make us some bruschetta if you like."

"I would like. I would like a lot."

Ethan started pulling ingredients from the fridge, glad to have something constructive to do. He could feel Derek watching him as he diced the onions and squeezed the seeds out of the tomatoes. When his brother finally spoke, his voice was low and careful.

"Falling for Alex must have been pretty freaking scary after all of that stuff with Cassie, huh?"

Ethan nodded shortly. He hadn't wanted to fall for Alex. Had done his damnedest for a long time to satisfy his need to be a part of her life without getting too close, too involved. Then she'd come to their racquetball game that night all churned up over seeing her ex and he hadn't been able to stop himself from comforting her.

"What she said is right, you know. She's not Cassie," Derek said.

"I know that." Ethan cut the remainder of a French stick into slices.

"But it doesn't make a difference?" Derek asked.

Ethan put down the knife and looked at his brother. "I don't believe in happy-ever-after. Not after everything I see in my job, and not after Cassie."

"But you want to."

Ethan let his breath out in a rush. "Yes."

More than anything he wanted to be able to let go of the past and take the hand Alex was offering him and step into the future alongside her. But he didn't know how to let go of the hard-won lessons of his past. He didn't know how to let down his guard and trust again.

"I'm not going to tell you that there's no way it could happen again and that Alex would never do that to you. Even though I think it's true, life doesn't come with guarantees and safety nets," Derek said.

"No shit."

"Do you love her?"

Ethan gave his brother a look. "Why do you think you've got a wet shoulder?"

"Then trust your gut."

If only it were that easy.

"I loved Cassie, too, and look where that got me. I thought I knew her inside and out. I slept next to her for twelve years and I had no idea how she was feeling, what she was thinking."

"I don't know what to say to you. I want you to be happy. I want you to have what I have. I see you with my kids and it kills me that you might never know what it feels like to be a part of something so amazing. But like I said, you've got every reason in the world to be gun-shy. The best I can do is tell you that Kay's my best friend. My day isn't right if I don't wake up and see her face on the pillow beside me. Pathetic but true, and if you ever tell her I said any of this I'll mess up those pretty-boy looks of yours for good. She's my rock, and I don't want to imagine my life without her in it. And yeah, there's a risk attached to all of that. But if the choice is between loving her or playing it safe… Well, I've made my choice."

Derek shrugged to indicate he'd run out of words but Ethan understood what his brother was saying: love was a leap of faith. After what had happened with his first marriage, Ethan appreciated that fact more than most, but at the end of the day it was the same for everybody. People were fickle, feelings changed, circumstances changed, and people grew together and grew apart. Love was a crapshoot. A risk. And the price of failure was high.

The question was, was a lifetime with Alex worth the risk?

A memory hit him: that night when he'd brought round his chicken dinner, she'd lain on the couch and he'd coaxed her into letting him rub her feet. She'd closed her eyes as he massaged first one foot then the other and he'd watched her face relax and a small smile curl her mouth. She'd been soft and vulnerable and content, and he'd helped make her that way and for a few precious moments he'd felt as though he was in exactly the right place with exactly the right person doing exactly the right thing. He'd felt as though he belonged, as though his cautious heart had found a home.

He reached for a tea towel and wiped his hands. Derek's gaze followed the action. A slow smile dawned on his face.

"Tell me you're going to find her."

"I'm going to find her."

"Good man."

His brother caught him in a one-armed hug and pounded an approving fist on his back. Ethan figured they'd used up their annual quota of physical affection in the space of a single hour, but he could live with that. His brother had been his lifeline tonight, the voice of reason he'd needed to help him navigate around the wreckage of the past.

"Thanks. I owe you."

"I figure we'll get it out of you in horsey rides and free babysitting."

"Done."

He strode for the door, scooping up his car keys from the hall table.

"I'm going to grab some of this bread to eat on the way home, if that's all right?" Derek said, trailing after him. "Since you don't have pretzels."

Ethan laughed. He'd forgotten all about the bruschetta in his rush to get to Alex.

"Help yourself." He opened the door.

"Call me," Derek said. "Let me know how you do."

Ethan gave him a look.

Derek shrugged. "I'm feeling a little invested here."

"Don't forget to lock up when you leave," Ethan said.

Then he headed for the elevator, praying every step of the way that Alex would be home.

Chapter Ten

Don't think about him. Don't think about him, don't think about him, don't think about him.

Alex kept up the mantra as she let herself into her apartment and searched for a distraction. There was no point dissecting what had happened between her and Ethan. It wouldn't change anything. She'd offered him her heart, and he'd offered her a time-share agreement. There was nothing left to explore.

If only she could exorcise the memory of his stricken face and the pain in his voice from her mind. If only there hadn't been those few seconds when she'd let her hope have wings and she'd believed for a small, precious moment that things were going to work out between them.

A memory hit her as she flicked on the light in her living room. The first time she'd ever seen Ethan had been in the foyer of Wallingsworth & Kent's offices.

He'd been arriving for a meeting with the senior partners, having been wooed away from one of the other big Melbourne firms. She hadn't known any of that at the time, of course—she'd simply seen him walking toward her across the polished marble floor, beautiful and dangerous and sexy, and she'd felt the low thud of instant attraction in her belly and thought to herself *Hello, heartbreaker.*

Prescient, indeed. She should have run a mile the first time he so much as smiled at her in the kitchenette. She should have taken out a restraining order against him when he suggested they play racquetball together, and she should have dug a moat around her office when he invited her to lunch.

Instead, she'd told herself she could handle him and she'd danced with the devil and fallen in love with a man who was so unavailable he could barely make himself say the words *I love you.*

And yet he had said them.

She wandered from the living room to her bedroom, thinking about those moments on the court despite her determination not to.

He'd said he loved her and that he wanted to try for a child with her. Amazing how something could be so close to a person's dreams and yet so far away. Amazing how little it took to tempt a woman.

But she'd drawn her line in the sand and she was going to stand by it. She might be sliding down that fertility graph her doctor had drawn, and she might be lonely and sad and frustrated, but she was not a masochist. There would be nothing worse than loving a man with all her heart and only receiving portions of his in return. No, she was wrong—there was something worse. She could have a child with that man, based on the misguided idea that it might draw them together, and never truly get over him.

So many pitfalls—and she'd cleverly avoided them all. She should be giving herself a pat on the back and mixing herself a cocktail to celebrate her street smarts instead of circling her flat like a madwoman.

She walked into the bathroom then left immediately when she caught sight of herself in the mirror. Best not to have confirmation of her own misery. Not while she was barely holding it together.

Do something. Do anything.

She went to the kitchen and looked around. It was sparkling clean, since she rarely made anything more messy than a tuna salad or egg on toast.

Dinner. She'd make dinner. Something elaborate, for her. Pasta. With a salad. That should keep her busy for half an hour or so. Whether she'd actually be able to choke it down or not was another question, but she'd cross that bridge when she came to it.

She crossed to the fridge and was about to open the fridge door when her gaze fell on the phrase someone had made using her fridge poetry magnets.

Banana people bend smiles and make monkeys laugh and love.

There was only one person who'd been in her apartment lately. She stared at the stupid, nonsensical poem Ethan had created and all the bullshit she'd been using to keep herself from feeling crumbled into dust.

She leaned forward and pressed her forehead against the fridge door. Her chest ached. Her eyes burned. She was all out of fight.

I love you, Ethan. I love you so much.

If only he weren't so damaged. And if only she didn't want so much more than he had to give.

* * *

Ethan turned into Queens Road and started looking for a parking spot near Alex's building. He had no idea what he was going to say to her, but he'd already decided to tell her everything. Cassie, the baby, all of it. He'd tell her that he was scared, even though it would be the most humbling, emasculating act of his life. She deserved the truth. To know what she was getting into.

He found a parking spot and reversed the Aston Martin into it. He was out of the car in seconds. He had to keep moving, mostly because he was terrified that if he stopped to think he'd chicken out.

I want this. I love her. She's not Cassie.

But he'd stored so much anger and fear and pain five years ago, packed it away so tightly within, that he was afraid he'd never get past it. That he'd never be able to trust. That he'd never be able to offer Alex the things she needed.

He had to try, though. He couldn't let her slip away without trying. He loved her too much to let that happen.

He approached the door to her building with a pounding heart.

Sack up, Stone. Where's your freaking dignity?

But he'd shed his dignity long ago. He was coming to Alex armed with nothing but hope and a desire to love her.

He pressed the buzzer for her apartment and waited, every muscle tense. After a few seconds he buzzed her again. Again, nothing.

She wasn't home—or she'd guessed it was him and was deliberately not answering him. He walked backward and craned his head to see if he could work out which balcony was hers. They all looked the same, and there was no dark-haired, dark-eyed woman on any of them.

He'd call her, then. And he'd keep calling and buzzing her until she let him in. He reached for his phone, then remembered he'd left it in the car. He was walking back to the Aston Martin to retrieve it when he glanced up the road and saw a slim woman in a hot-pink sweater walking briskly along Queens Road. Her back was to him, but he recognized both the straightness of her shoulders and the distinctive sweater.

Alex.

She was about a block away, heading east. He started after her. There were a number of other people out on the street, despite the fact that it was cold and dark—joggers coming home from their circuits of nearby Albert Park Lake, dog walkers, students heading out for a big night. He picked his way amongst them, lengthening his stride.

"Alex," he called, even though he was pretty certain she was too far away to hear him.

She didn't so much as falter or glance over her shoulder. He dodged around a guy blocking the footpath with a bike. Up ahead, Alex was approaching the corner intersection where a mini-mart was located and it occurred to him that the store was probably her goal—she was probably ducking out to get something, milk or bread or one of the disgusting frozen meals-for-one he knew she relied on.

The traffic lights changed at the intersection and Alex broke into a jog to catch the pedestrian light. The action unfolded in slow motion, the stuff of nightmares.

She'd barely set foot on the road when a low-slung red car raced past him, signal flashing to indicate a left turn into the street Alex was crossing. Ethan waited for the driver to see Alex, waited for the glow of brake lights to appear at the back of the car, but there was nothing. The driver hadn't seen her. *He hadn't seen her.*

"Alex!" he yelled, fear an icy rush through him as the red car whipped around the corner.

The world stopped. Then he heard the sound of impact, an explosion of glass and metal and the heavy, unmistakable thud of a body hitting a car. A passerby screamed. He broke into a sprint.

Alex. He had to get to Alex. And she had to be okay. A few scratches and bruises, sure, but she had to be okay.

His legs and arms pumped as he raced the final hundred or so feet to the intersection. It felt like a lifetime. It felt as though he was traversing the world.

A crowd had gathered. Someone was already on the phone, calling for an ambulance.

"Alex," he bellowed as he neared the crowd. "Alex!"

She had to be alive. She had to be. But the car had been going so fast, doing at least forty around the corner.

He reached the crowd, started shoving people out of the way to get to her.

If she was dead… *God,* if she was dead…

Then the crowd parted and he saw her lying on the road, blood gleaming in the streetlight beside her head—*and it wasn't Alex.* She was shorter than Alex, fuller-breasted, her hair slightly longer. She was wearing sandals instead of sneakers and a wedding ring gleamed on her left hand.

It wasn't Alex.

Relief hit him like a wall. She was alive. Alex was alive.

Shaken, his knees like rubber, he scrubbed his face with his hands.

He'd thought he'd lost her. For a few heart-stopping seconds he'd thought she was gone. The memory of it was enough to send bile burning up the back of his throat. All the things he'd never say to her, all the things they'd never experience together, the life they'd never have—all of it had flashed through him when he'd heard the terrible sound of impact.

But it wasn't Alex.

Ambulance sirens sounded in the distance. The woman on the ground was trying to sit up and someone was crouching beside her, advising her to remain prone until help got there. The driver was crying and pacing and explaining to anyone who would listen that he hadn't seen her, that the pedestrian light had been flashing red.

Ethan stood numbly in the crowd as the ambulance arrived and the paramedics got out to treat the woman. He watched as she spoke to them and gingerly allowed them to help her onto the stretcher. It wasn't until the unknown woman was in the ambulance, the doors closed behind her that he felt able to turn away.

"Ethan. What are you doing here?"

His head snapped around. Alex was standing at the edge of the already dissipating crowd, a bag of groceries in one hand, a perplexed frown on her face. He took a moment to simply soak in the sight of her, her hair tucked behind her ear on one side. Then he strode forward and swept her into his arms. She was warm and resilient and she smelled of lemons and fresh night air and he wanted to merge his body with hers, to become a part of her so that they could never be parted and he would never, ever have to stare down the barrel of almost losing her again.

"Ethan. What's going on?" she asked, her voice muffled against his shoulder.

"Don't ever, ever do that to me again," he said fiercely.

"Do what?"

He pulled back to look into her face. She lifted a hand to touch his cheek.

"You're crying," she said.

"Alex, I love you. I should have said it a long time ago but I've been too busy trying to cover my ass to understand that any risk is worth it if I get to have you in my life. I don't want half measures. I want everything you want and more. Kids, marriage, a mortgage, arguments over whose turn it is to put the dog out, I don't care what it is, I want it with you. I've wasted so much time, and I deserve for you to give me a hard time and make me jump through a million flaming hoops, but I love you and I want this and I'm not going anywhere until you say yes."

"Ethan," she said. Her eyes were wide, searching his face.

She didn't understand. She had no idea that he'd just had a glimpse of hell.

"Alex. I thought it was you," he said, his voice gravelly with emotion. "I saw the car turning, I thought you were dead…."

He pulled her close again, experiencing the wash of terror a second time. He pressed her face to his chest and cupped the back of her head in the palm of his hand. She felt ridiculously fragile, terrifyingly mortal in his arms.

He loved her so much. So much. And yet he'd almost let fear stop him from being a part of her life. It was only when he'd been facing the loss of everything that his world had become clear to him.

Cassie's abandonment and betrayal had been baffling and hurtful. She'd left him dangling and he'd made a fortress out of his bitterness and fear. But all the stuff he'd canvassed with Derek tonight, all his doubts and caution, none of it mattered when he'd been faced with the prospect of a world without Alex.

The ultimate wake-up call. Beside it, everything else assumed its rightful perspective. What counted was Alex. Being with Alex. Loving Alex. Building a future with Alex—if she would have him.

Her expression was grave when he finally felt able to let her go again.

He knew he should wait until they'd had a chance to talk properly. He knew that standing on a street corner a few feet from a traffic accident was probably the least romantic spot in the universe. He should take Alex home, tell her about Cassie and the divorce, make sure she understood what she'd be getting herself into if she took him on before he asked her to—

"Marry me," he blurted. "Save me from myself, and I'll do my best to save you when you need it, too. Marry me and have babies with me. Marry me and play racquetball with me until neither of us can bend to tie our sneakers on our own. Marry me, Alex, and make me the happiest, luckiest idiot in the world."

Her face crumpled. His gut clenched. He'd made her cry.

"Alex, I'm sorry—"

A fist landed in the middle of his chest. "How am I supposed to resist you when you say all the right things? Can you explain that to me? How am I supposed to be strong and do the right thing when you look at me like that and ask me to marry you?"

The dread clutching his gut receded a notch. "Doing the right thing would be marrying me."

She shook her head, her eyes swimming with tears. "You've just had a scare. You're not thinking clearly. Anything you say right now is under duress."

He smiled. Couldn't help himself. She was adorable, so earnest, so honest. So Alex.

She smacked him in the chest again. "Don't you dare laugh at me when I'm trying to save you from yourself."

"Maybe I don't need saving."

"You do. You don't want to be married. You've said so a million times. You're freaking out right now but once you calm down you'll regret this. And I don't want to be a regret in your life, Ethan. I love you too much for that."

"Alex, why do you think I came over here tonight? Why do you think I was following a woman I thought was you up the street so I could throw myself on your mercy and beg for a second chance?"

She gave him an arrested look. Had it really not occurred to her that his being here was about her and not simply a coincidence?

"Really? You really came looking for me?"

The hope in her face. The doubt.

"Baby, I've been looking for you all my life," he said.

Then he kissed her, because he needed to more than he needed air. She kissed him back, her arms around his neck, her hands clenched in his hair.

But a kiss wasn't nearly enough. He needed to feel

her skin against his. He needed to be inside her, part of her. He needed—

"Let's go back to my place," Alex gasped against his mouth.

"Yes."

They broke apart. He took the bag of groceries from her hand, then he drew her close and kissed her again. He didn't want to let her go. But they were standing on a street corner, and public nudity had been frowned upon for a while in the state of Victoria.

A tow truck had arrived, along with a police car. Ethan spared them both a glance as he and Alex turned toward her place.

"I was in the shop when I heard the smash. Must have been pretty scary," Alex said, following his glance.

He raised their joined hands and pressed a kiss to the back of her hand.

"Beyond scary. The worst moment of my life."

She squeezed his hand.

"You haven't answered my question," he said.

Her eyes were full of uncertainty when she looked at him. "Ethan…"

"A simple yes is more than enough."

"Since when have we ever been simple?" she said ruefully.

It was a good point.

She copied his earlier gesture and kissed the back of his hand. "Ask me again later."

It was almost a promise. Almost.

"All right," he said reluctantly.

He could wait, if he had to. In the meantime, there were things he needed to tell her.

They turned toward Alex's apartment and started

walking. He took a moment to assemble his thoughts, then he cleared his throat.

"I want to tell you about Cassie," he said.

Alex listened in silence as Ethan told her how he and Cassie had met, about their instant attraction and how quickly they'd moved in with each other. He described his ex variously as beautiful, fiery, smart, impulsive, and she imagined what it must have been like between the two of them, how in love Ethan must have been. Impossible not to feel a stab of jealousy.

He talked all the way back to her apartment, and when they arrived she led him to the couch and drew him down beside her and sat with her back against the arm so she could see his face and his eyes as he told her about the wedding and the tough few years afterward when he and Cassie had both been working so hard to carve out their careers.

He told her about the house they'd bought together in well-heeled Armadale and their big mortgage. He told her how they'd talked about trying for children once they'd both felt more solid in their jobs and managed to get the mortgage down a little. He told her that there had been problems, but that he'd always believed in the fundamental integrity of his marriage.

She knew he'd reached the tough part when he broke eye contact with her. He kept talking, though, and she reached for his hand and held it as he told her how he'd come home on what he'd thought was an ordinary work night to find Cassie waiting for him with her bags packed and the devastating news that she didn't love him anymore.

Then he told her about the abortion and she squeezed

his hand tight and shut her eyes and simply sat with him in silence, absorbing his truth and his pain.

She could not imagine how he must have felt. Could not imagine the hurt and the anger and the confusion and the self-doubt and the grief. He'd been devastated. Even though he hadn't said a word about his feelings or his reactions, simply delivering up the bare facts for her edification, she knew he must have been shattered because the man sitting on the couch before her still bore the scars from his marriage. He'd allowed them to dictate his life for the past five years while telling himself all the while that he was strong and tough and cynical and that he would never, ever be abandoned or betrayed or rejected again.

Because she didn't know what to say, she simply slid closer to him on the couch and put her arms around him. They sat holding each other for a long time. She felt his chest expand when he finally took a breath to speak.

"It was a long time ago." He said it apologetically. As though there was shame attached to the fact that he was still dealing with the fallout from his divorce five years later.

She lifted her head from his shoulder and caught his chin in her hand. Then she looked at him fiercely, very directly in the eye.

"Don't ever apologize to me for caring, Ethan Stone. For having a heart. For being able to be hurt. For being vulnerable. Okay?"

He nodded. She slid her hand up to cup his cheek. He was a beautiful man, a lady-killer. And yet he'd been betrayed, had his trust torn to shreds. He'd lost an opportunity to be a father. He'd lost his life as he knew it.

A terrible anger filled her as she processed the enormity of what had happened to him—what had been *done* to him. What kind of a person walked out on her partner of twelve years without trying to fix what was wrong? What kind of a woman told her husband that she had chosen to terminate her pregnancy because it was only when she was expecting his child that she understood she no longer loved him or wanted a life with him?

For a moment Alex was almost overcome with rage on Ethan's behalf. She wanted to hunt Cassie down and shake her until she begged for forgiveness. She wanted to scream at Ethan's ex-wife until the other woman understood how much pain she'd inflicted, how much she'd wounded him.

Then the wave passed and all she wanted was to do was comfort him.

She leaned forward and kissed him. She held his face in her hands and kissed his nose and the slope of his gorgeous cheekbones and his eyebrows and his forehead and his eyelids and his jaw and his chin. She pressed a long, lingering kiss to his mouth. She stared into his eyes as he looked back at her, vulnerable and stripped bare, offering himself up to her for understanding and forgiveness and succor.

She could offer him promises and guarantees, but they both knew that words were cheap and that there wasn't a pledge or vow in the world that could shape and mold the future. There was only who she was and who he was and their understanding of each other right now, right at this minute. It had always been enough for her, but she understood now why it might not have always been enough for Ethan.

"I love you, Ethan," she said.

There wasn't anything else to say, at the end of the day.

"I love you, too, Alex."

She took him into her bedroom then and took off his clothes, took off her clothes and showed him with her body all the things she couldn't say with words. She told him with her kisses that she was loyal. She told him with her arms that she adored him. She took him into her body and told him that she wanted to share her life with him.

As he moved inside her, she looked into his eyes, never once looking away.

He wasn't perfect. His trust issues were probably going to be a problem for both of them in the future. But she wasn't perfect, either. She'd never been great at letting people in and she found it hard to show her weaknesses, even to loved ones.

But they were going to make it work. They were going to be okay. They were going to get married and if Mother Nature was kind they were going to have babies and they were going to grow with their love.

"Yes," she said.

Ethan stilled, his body warm and heavy on hers.

"Yes?"

"Yes," she said.

And it was the easiest decision she'd ever made in her life.

Epilogue

"The thing about the Stone men is that they don't do anything by halves," Kay said.

"No kidding."

"It's not a bad thing, really. In most cases it's a good thing," Kay said.

"Sure it is."

"And anyway, it could be worse."

She and Alex both winced as a loud four-letter word floated across the yard to where the two of them were relaxing in sun loungers beneath the shade of a big old oak tree. The tree dominated the backyard of Ethan and Alex's new home, an Edwardian weatherboard house in Box Hill, a five-minute drive from where Derek and Kay lived. It was unclear whether Ethan or Derek was the perpetrator, since both men had their backs to the women as they hunched over the pile of furniture parts that might one day resemble a baby's crib if the two men glowering and swearing over them took the time to read the instruction booklet.

"How could it be worse?" Alex wanted to know, not taking her eyes from her husband's behind as he bent to sort through the pieces of wood spread across the patio.

"We could be living in Georgian times and Ethan could have you confined to your bedroom."

"Good Lord. Don't give him ideas. That's the last thing I need."

As though he could sense them talking about him, Ethan's head came up and he glanced over his shoulder. He was wearing sunglasses to combat the bright glare of the sun, but Alex knew he was looking straight at her. Could feel it in her bones.

Despite the fact that she thought he was being ridiculous right at this moment in time, she smiled. How could she not when she had so much to smile about?

Ethan stood and strode across the grass toward her. His jeans rode low on his waist and his white T-shirt had shrunk a little in the wash and she could see the muscles of his thighs flexing and contracting with each step. He was forty-four now, but he was a man in his prime.

Beside her, Kay fanned herself with her hand. Alex spared her a dry look.

"Pretty Boy strikes again."

"Hell, yeah," Kay said, and they both laughed.

Ethan's shadow loomed over them.

"What's wrong?" he asked. "Are you feeling okay? Do you need some crackers? Some milk?"

Alex looked up at her husband. "I was *smiling*, Ethan."

"It looked weird."

"Well, it wasn't."

"Are you sure? What about some cold water?"

Alex sighed. "Are you going to be like this all the way through my pregnancy?"

"I don't know. Ask me in six months' time."

He squatted beside her lounger and put his hand on her still-flat belly.

"I just want to make sure you're okay. I know how much this means to you."

And to him. This was their second pregnancy. Her first had ended in a miscarriage at nine weeks just over eight months ago and it had been a sad time for both of them. Now she was thirteen weeks and counting. The doctor had assured her their baby was doing well at her scan yesterday. With her fortieth birthday around the corner, Alex had her fingers crossed he was right. The moment the doctor had made his pronouncement, Ethan had disappeared to the shops and returned home with enough furniture to fill five nurseries.

"I'm fine. The baby's fine," she assured him.

She slid her hand over his where it rested on her stomach. Ethan was silent and she reached out with her other hand to push his glasses on top of his head. She didn't know what he was thinking when she couldn't see his eyes.

He looked back at her, love and worry and hope and excitement all intermingled in his gaze.

"I'm going to...you know," Kay said, waving her hand to indicate she was making herself scarce.

Alex hooked her finger into the neck of Ethan's T-shirt and pulled him toward her.

"Stop worrying. Whatever happens, we'll work it out."

She kissed him. He tasted like sunshine and beer and she made an approving noise. Ethan deepened the kiss and she felt his hand slide up her torso toward her breasts. She'd already seen Kay lead Derek inside to give them some privacy so she didn't do much more than shift restlessly as Ethan's hand closed over her breast.

She loved him so much. The past eighteen months of her life had been filled with so much joy and laughter with him by her side. He was her best friend, the most wonderful lover she'd ever had, the best husband she could imagine—even with his overprotectiveness and over-purchasing of nursery supplies.

He made an impatient noise and she scooted her leg out of the way as he dropped a knee onto the lounger and climbed aboard. She felt his weight settle over her and smiled against his mouth.

Then she let out a wild shriek as the legs on the sun lounger collapsed and they dropped half a foot onto the grass. She threw back her head and laughed, clutching Ethan's shoulders.

He was laughing, too, and she looked into his deep blue eyes and let the small perfection of the moment wash over her. Her life was full of moments like these now, and there would be even more of them to come, she knew.

After a moment they both sobered and Ethan reached up to tuck her hair behind her ear.

He didn't say anything, and neither did she.

Some happinesses were beyond words.

* * * * *

We hope you enjoyed reading

THE PRODIGAL SON

by *New York Times* bestselling author

SUSAN MALLERY and

THE BEST LAID PLANS

by *New York Times* bestselling author

SARAH MAYBERRY

Both were originally Harlequin® series stories!

Discover more compelling tales of family, friendship and love from the Harlequin® Superromance® series. Featuring contemporary themes and relatable, true-to-life characters, Harlequin Superromance stories are filled with powerful relationships that deliver a strong emotional punch and a guaranteed happily-ever-after.

⬥ HARLEQUIN®

super romance®

More Story…More Romance

Look for six new romances every month
from Harlequin Superromance!

Available wherever books are sold.

Find us at Harlequin.com

SPECIAL EXCERPT FROM

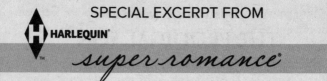

HARLEQUIN

super romance

This doesn't usually happen to Tess Ullo!
She's just met a great guy, Graham.
They're hitting it off as though they've known
each other for years. And now that the evening
is wrapping up...what's in store? Read on for an
exciting excerpt of the upcoming book

His Forever Girl

By Liz Talley

Tess paused to wonder if it was a good idea to extend thi
impromptu date with another drink. It was Monday and she
needed to be at work early. But even though Graham had ;
kid and felt not so much her normal type, she had this crazy
weird connection with him. She couldn't not stay.

And it had been a long time since she'd had no-strings
attached fun with a hot guy.

When their round of drinks arrived, Graham clinked hi
glass against hers. "I'm glad you stayed. Feels as though we'r
dancing around—"

"Hooking up?"

"Is that what the young kids call it?" he joked, his eye
lowering to her lips.

"Oh, please. Don't pretend you haven't been thinking abou
getting into my jeans."

"Into your jeans? I've been thinking about how to get you out of your jeans." Graham's eyes suddenly widened as if he might have gone too far. "I didn't mean to imply—"

Tess pressed one finger to his lips, effectively silencing him. "Please imply. I've been contemplating much the same thing."

He gave her a serious look. "Is this what we're doing? Hooking up?"

Heck, she still wasn't sure if this was a good idea. But this night with Graham felt right. It felt like something more than just fun. It felt like magic. Like Graham was her perfect match. "Maybe."

Moving slowly he lightly brushed her lips with his. Her pulse sped at the first touch, and she leaned in for more. She knew with absolute clarity that she didn't want just one night with Graham.

He drew back, his gaze locked on hers. "Is that a maybe? Or is that a yes?"

Will Tess get more than one night with Graham? Could there be more to this guy than she knows? Find out what's in store for these two in HIS FOREVER GIRL by Liz Talley, available February 2014 from Harlequin® Superromance®.

HARLEQUIN®

super romance®

More Story...More Romance

Save $1.00 on the purchase of

HIS FOREVER GIRL

by Liz Talley

available January 7, 2014,
or on any other Harlequin® Superromance® book.

Available wherever books are sold, including most bookstores,
supermarkets, drugstores and discount stores.

- -

Save $1.00

on the purchase of
HIS FOREVER GIRL
by Liz Talley
available January 7, 2014, or on any other
Harlequin® Superromance® book.

Coupon valid until April 7, 2014. Redeemable at participating retail outlets
in the U.S. and Canada only. Limit one coupon per customer.

52611272

Canadian Retailers: Harlequin Enterprises Limited will pay the face va
of this coupon plus 10.25¢ if submitted by customer for this product only. A
other use constitutes fraud. Coupon is nonassignable. Void if taxed, prohibi
or restricted by law. Consumer must pay any government taxes. Void if copie
Nielsen Clearing House ("NCH") customers submit coupons and proof of sales
Harlequin Enterprises Limited, P.O. Box 3000, Saint John, NB E2L 4L3, Cana
Non-NCH retailer—for reimbursement submit coupons and proof of sales dire
to Harlequin Enterprises Limited, Retail Marketing Department, 225 Duncan M
Rd., Don Mills, ON M3B 3K9, Canada.

5 65373 00076 2   (8100)0 11898

U.S. Retailers: Harlequin Enterpri
Limited will pay the face value of this coup
plus 8¢ if submitted by customer for
product only. Any other use constitutes fra
Coupon is nonassignable. Void if tax
prohibited or restricted by law. Consumer m
pay any government taxes. Void if copied.
reimbursement submit coupons and proo
sales directly to Harlequin Enterprises Limi
P.O. Box 880478, El Paso, TX 88588-04
U.S.A. Cash value 1/100 cents.

® and TM are trademarks owned and used by the trademark owner and/or its licensee.
© 2014 Harlequin Enterprises Limited